Nicola L. C

THE PRIVATE ENEMY

Dickimaw Books
SAXLINGHAM NETHERGATE

British Library Cataloguing in Publication Data
Talbot, Nicola Louise Cecilia
Private Enemy, The

ISBN 978-1-909440-05-0

A CIP catalogue record for this book is available from the British Library.

All Rights Reserved © Nicola L. C. Talbot 2014

The right of Nicola L. C. Talbot to be identified as author of this work has been asserted in accordance with Section 77 of the Copyright, Designs and Patents Act of 1988.

This novel is a work of fiction. Events and character names are the product of the author's imagination and any resemblance to events or to any persons fictional or real who are living or dead is purely coincidental.

Published by Dickimaw Books
Saxlingham Nethergate, Norfolk
United Kingdom
www.dickimaw-books.com

Typeset using Professor Donald Knuth's magnificent TeX engine with Dr Leslie Lamport's LaTeX format.

'Dickimaw Books' and the Dickimaw Books parrot logo are trademarks of Dickimaw Books.

Contents

1 Flight   1
2 A New Migrant   14
3 Adam   29
4 New Employment   53
5 Wanted   67
6 Medical Reports   91
7 A Trip to the Country   108
8 Interviews   140
9 A Change in Rental Terms   154
10 Sunday Lunch   182
11 Strangers   195

Contents

12	Colingham	210
13	On the Road	230
14	A Change of Circumstances	243
15	Family Matters	269
16	The Anti-Technology League	297
17	Sector House	325
18	The Aftermath	354
19	Investigating del Rosario	372
20	Murder	400
21	Night Time in Colingham	422
22	Unravelling	428
23	Evidence	452
24	Kidnap	458
25	Escalation	477
26	Settling Up	494
27	The Wynherne Estate	508
Acknowledgements		523
Norfolk Dialect		524

To my husband, Gavin,
and our son, Cameron,
with love.

Author's Note

The absences of the final 's' (or 'es') in the third person singular present tense of verbs in some of the dialogue are not typographical errors but are a peculiarity of the Broad Norfolk dialect. (For example, 'he like it' or 'she go there'.) See page 524 for further information about the Norfolk dialect.

— 1 —

Flight

The last Earl of Wynherne lay dead on the study floor. His daughter, Lady Coulgrane, sat at the desk reading a document, her fists against her temples. Her jaws were clenched. Tears could come later. There was no time for them now. The dull pain behind her eyes heightened the impenetrability of the legal phrasing on the paper in front of her. She reached for a jug and poured water into a tumbler. The spout chattered against the glass rim. Droplets splashed on to the oak desktop. The safety lid on a brown medicine bottle nearly defeated her trembling hands, but at last it clicked over the catch and spun free. She swallowed a couple of pills, checked her watch and glanced at the window while trying to refasten the lid.

There was a filing cabinet in the corner of the room, next to the window. One of the drawers was ajar, and they were all too stiff to slide open by accident. The medicine bottle slipped from her fingers, the lid tumbled off and pills spilled across the desk. She ran over, tugged open the drawer and clicked the folders across the rails, searching for anything missing or out of place amongst her well-ordered files. At last she found it: a crumpled letter poking up near the back as though it had been stuffed there in haste. She eased it out of the drawer and studied it, at first puzzled, but then she gave a cry of alarm.

A cattle grid rattled in the distance. For a moment she stared transfixed at the letter, then she snatched the legal document from the desk, darted into the hall, slammed the bolt across the front door, shot upstairs and tipped the contents of a cash box and jewellery case into a bag. A car came up the gravel drive, stones pinging on metal. She pressed herself against the wall next to the open window of her bedroom. Footsteps crunched over to the house. The latch jiggled downstairs, and someone hammered on the knocker. She glanced at a pair of scissors on the dresser.

Dr Carmichael stood in front of the mansion, clutching his medical bag, while Mr Allerton pounded the knocker.

'It's me, George Allerton. I've brought the doctor. Open the door.'

Allerton hurled himself against the oak door, but it held firm. Dr Carmichael gazed across the flat lawn and the heathland beyond that stretched off to the boundary wall. There was a small wood to one side of the mansion, but there wasn't a soul in sight. A train whistled in the distance. Did anyone work here on a Sunday? Even the cottage by the entrance gates had appeared empty. The faint sounds of farmyard animals — hens clucking, horses neighing — coming from the far side of the building were the only signs of life. He turned and looked up at the grey stone wall of the mansion. For a moment, he thought he detected a movement in an upstairs window but decided that it was just the breeze disturbing a curtain.

'Mr Allerton, that window up there is open,' he said. 'Maybe we could climb up?'
'Let's try downstairs before we risk our necks,' Allerton said. 'The kitchen door's that way. You try there. I'll give the French windows a go. You'd better prepare a sedative. She had a violent fit after the death of her uncle. Heaven knows how she'll react to seeing her father.'

With that, Allerton ran off to the right, so Dr Carmichael headed in the other direction, racing along the path that skirted the mansion. A climbing rose dislodged his hat as he rounded the corner, but he didn't stop to retrieve it. The kitchen door was locked, but a casement window was on its latch, so he poked his fingers through the gap, unhooked it, passed his bag in, scrambled over the sill, but slipped on the marble worktop and fell to the floor, his head smacking on the flagstones.

He lay there for a moment splayed out, his glasses tumbled down his nose, then he rolled on to his side, groaned, pushed his glasses back up his nose and propped himself up. A hundred tiny blacksmiths were hammering away at the back of his skull. His case was nearby. He blinked a couple of times, reached out, missed it, grabbed the handle on the second attempt and staggered to his feet. There were two internal doors. He tried one but found a narrow staircase behind it. The other led into a wood-panelled corridor that looked more promising. He stumbled along it, peering into every room he passed until he saw a man lying on the floor of what must be a study. He went over and felt for a pulse, but it was too late. That meant the hysterical daughter was now his priority. What had Allerton said? The shock had made her violent. He opened his case, fumbled in it and took out a hypodermic. Five millilitres of diazepam should do. He drew it, turned the syringe and tapped it to expel any air bubbles.

He heard the sound of a bolt being thrown back and feet crunching across the gravel drive. A yell ripped through the air. Dr Carmichael raced out of the room, still holding the syringe. The front door was wide open, and Allerton was sprawled out on the drive with a pair of scissors embedded in his thigh. A red stain was spreading out across his beige trousers. Carmichael glanced round and glimpsed a flash of yellow and white amongst the trees. He looked back at the fallen man, but Allerton waved him away.

'Go after her!'

The doctor ran over to the wood. The landscape seemed to be pitching about like a ship in a storm. A small voice at the back of his mind was trying to list the symptoms of concussion, like a medical student in a class, but there was no time for that now. Branches lashed against his face. The ground dipped beneath his feet. He slipped on the mud, stumbled and pitched down the bank into a stream. He fell on his face, the hypodermic needle jabbing into his left hand.

Detective Inspector Charles Hadley stepped out of the car on to the gravel drive and adjusted his homburg. He rested a foot on the running board and leant an elbow on the roof, his chin cupped in his hand. He had first stood here, in front of the Gothic mansion, thirty-two years ago — not as a detective inspector, just little Charlie Hadley from the nearby village. He, his parents and all the other villagers were weighed down with their baggage, trudging up the driveway to seek refuge from the raiders behind the thick, grey stone of Wynherne Hall. He could still see his dad smiling at him.

'Fare ye well, tergether. Dunt be afraid, Charlie. I'll be back soon. Jist you look arter yar mum.'

And then he had headed off with the other men to the armoury beyond the birch and alder coppice.

'Sar? Are you orl right?'

Hadley glanced up and saw Detective Sergeant Fenning on the other side of the car, tucking a dark curl under her slate-blue felt hat.

'I'm fine.'

He took out the voice recorder from his coat pocket and realised that he'd forgotten to charge the capacitor before setting out. He began to wind it up and looked around him as he did so. The mansion hadn't changed much since his childhood, but the intervening years had altered the landscape. The electricity pylons that had once straddled the countryside were no more than stubs of metal; in their place, generators hummed in outhouses. There was no trace of the old mobile phone mast, but the landlines had been restored — although the telegraph pole Hadley had passed near the entrance gate now had a branch tangled up in its cables. The wooden watch towers still ringed the estate just inside the high perimeter wall. Relics of the violent anarchy, they were now abandoned and, to the young, little more than landmarks.

The morning sun was just peering out above the chimney stacks. The front of the house was still in shadow. Rainwater left over from last night's storm dripped from the gargoyles gurning high up in the guttering. Mr Allerton was sitting on a stone step leading up to the heavy oak door, nursing a bandaged leg. Hadley leant towards D.S. Fenning and said in a low voice:

'Mr Allerton is apparently an eligible bachelor.'

Fenning, in her turn, leant towards him, resting her right arm on the car roof.

'You mean he hev munny and he look like a fillum star, but praps he hev a few mawthers listed in a little black book.'

'Fenning, that's most unprofessional.'

She smiled, and he turned away. Two men were approaching from the coppice. Hadley recognised the bent nose and scarred face of the older man. That was Amos, the Wynherne steward. The young sandy-haired man being supported by Amos was presumably the doctor. The orange light on the voice recorder went out, indicating that the capacitor was fully charged. Hadley tucked the crank away and moved over to Fenning's side.

'See if you can slip away at some point and do a quick look-over the house.'

'With no warrant? Do they see me snoutin' abowt, shall I say I'm looking for the bathroom?'

'I want to know what made Lady Coulgrane act like that,' Hadley said. 'Mr Allerton's solicitors won't be happy if we suggest he might've done something to provoke her, and the locals will go savage if we arrest the last of the Coulgranes. I don't want to start a war.'

'Is there still an armoury here?'

'That's technically a museum now, but I wouldn't be surprised if the exhibits are kept in good working order.'

Hadley and Fenning walked over to Allerton and waited for Amos and Carmichael. The doctor's worsted suit was covered in mud, his glasses splattered, and he seemed to have a twig behind his right ear. He looked as though he was about to throw up, but perhaps that wasn't so surprising, Hadley thought, given the smell of the bio-mass generators coming from the steward's overalls: pungent, almost as sickly as silage.

'You don't mind the voice recorder, do you?' Hadley said when they were all assembled by the front door.

Allerton hesitated for a moment but then shrugged.

'Of course not. Why should I? I'm not an Anti-Tech, but the others might object.'

'Not me,' Amos said. 'I hent got noffin to hide.'

The doctor stared vacantly, but on a repeated application he shook his head. Hadley turned to Amos.

'D'you know how much of the drug went into him?'

'Thass ony shock. He say he drew five millilitres, and thass orl in the syringe.'

'We've put out a search for Lady Coulgrane,' Hadley said, 'but the report we received was confused.'

'Tell them not to hurt her,' Allerton said.

'I'm told she stabbed you.'

'Yes, but it's not her fault. She's not well.'

Allerton rubbed his leg and winced.

'So you're not going to press charges?' Hadley said.

'Of course not. I just want her found before she hurts herself — or anyone else.' Allerton fumbled in a pocket and produced a business card. 'These are the details of an excellent clinic in Central City. They'll know how to deal with this situation far better than the police.'

Hadley took the card from him and glanced at it.

'Where's the earl's body?'

'In the study.'

'Then that's where we're going.'

Allerton made an attempt to stand and groaned.

'I don't think I can make it.'

'Fenning,' Hadley said, 'radio in and ask them to contact the clinic.' He handed her the card. She gave a slight nod and walked over to the car. 'Amos, would you mind helping Mr Allerton?'

'No, it's all right,' Allerton said. 'I'll manage.' But Amos hauled him to his feet and practically dragged him up the steps. 'I tell you, I'm all right. Let me go.'

Hadley assisted Dr Carmichael into the study, helped him on to an armchair with a tatty cover that smelt of dogs and went over to the earl's body, which was crumpled on the floor beside the desk. Hadley knelt down, snapped on a pair of gloves and examined the corpse.

In life, the earl had been a middle-aged recluse with grey hair and leathery skin. His hands bore the scars of electrical burns — no doubt mementos from his apprenticeship during the anarchy. The earl was wearing a tweed waistcoat but no jacket. Hadley leant closer and edged the shirt collar lower. There was a raised mark on the back of the earl's neck. Maybe an insect bite or sting.

Hadley bent over the corpse and sniffed, but the air was saturated with the tinny stench of blood from Allerton's bandaged leg and the almond pomade in his slicked-back hair. Fenning had been right about the film-star look. Allerton was draped over a faded brocade chaise longue, the picture of heroic anguish. It was the same sofa that Hadley had once seen his own father lying on, fatally injured by raiders during the anarchy.

Amos stomped over to the other side of the room, trailing mud and moss on the floorboards, folded his arms and glared at Allerton.

'What happened?' Hadley asked.

'I think he was stung,' Allerton said. 'He suddenly cried out, clapped his neck and collapsed. Then he started wheezing and clutching his stomach.'

'It sounds like anaphylactic shock,' Dr Carmichael said. 'Mr Allerton came to fetch me, but it was too late.'

'So he was alive when you went for help, Mr Allerton?' Hadley said.

'Yes.' Allerton was still reclined on the sofa, one hand on his temple. 'I didn't want to leave him, but the lines were down, and there was no one else around.'

Allerton flopped his hand on to his chest and played with a ring on his finger. Hadley eyed the large, green opal on it. Was that kind of thing fashionable in the city? The mixed smells of blood and pomade was like almond syrup gone bad. Despite his country-gent clothes, he was still a newcomer. It couldn't be more than eight years, by Hadley's reckoning, since Allerton had moved to the neighbouring estate.

'What were you doing here, Mr Allerton?' Hadley said.

'The earl phoned me last night and asked me to come round this morning. He was worried about his daughter.'

Hadley turned to the doctor.

'Dr Carmichael, we need to send some blood samples to Central City before you write the death certificate.'

The doctor nodded, winced and rubbed his head. Hadley studied the oak desk and picked up an open chequebook. The stubs showed that it hadn't been used for months, but the remaining slips indicated that the account holder was 'J.E. Coulgrane' — the Earl of Wynherne. The position of the body seemed to suggest that the earl had been seated at the desk and had slipped to the floor when he collapsed. Wouldn't a chat between neighbours be conducted in the sitting room rather than in such a business-like setting?

'What were you talking about?' Hadley said.

'I was suggesting that I contact a clinic to help Lady Coulgrane,' Allerton said.

Hadley put the chequebook back on the desk.

'Were you asking for money for it?'

'Of course not. He was concerned about the cost, but I reassured him that I'd pay for everything.'

'That's very generous of you,' Hadley said. 'D'you assist all your neighbours?'

Allerton struggled to an upright position, propped up by the back and only arm of the sofa.

'Obviously you wouldn't know, as we haven't announced it yet,' he said. 'Lady Coulgrane is my fiancée.'

Amos grunted. His fists tightened. Scars stood out white against his weather-beaten face.

'Mr Allerton,' Hadley said, 'is it true she aimed a shotgun at you last year?'

'Wherever did you hear that?'

'Local gossip.'

'Not the most reliable source of information. I merely surprised her while she was holding the gun, but some people –' he glared at Amos '– misinterpreted what happened.'

'So she hasn't made any threats against you?'

'None whatsoever.'

Hadley picked up a medicine bottle from the desk and studied the label: co-codamol 500mg, Dr P. Barnes. The lid was undone. Pills were scattered on the surface of the desk, but there were also a few left inside the bottle.

'What's wrong with her?'

'She's got a brain tumour,' Allerton said.

The deep resonant chimes of a grandfather clock echoed around the house. Fenning slipped in through the doorway, but her expression gave nothing away. Hadley turned his attention back to Allerton.

'Is she getting treatment?'

'I arranged for her to go to a private hospital, but she's gone into denial and won't accept the diagnosis. That's why I want her to go to the clinic.'

A door creaked in another area of the house. Allerton jerked and nearly fell off the sofa. Hadley looked over at Fenning. She peered into the hallway and shrugged at him.

'Who else is here?' Hadley asked Amos.

'Thass the boy Joe.'

'He's not to wander in and out without permission,' Allerton said.

'We both work here. You're the one who come snoutin' round wi'out permission.'

'If she chose not to tell you we're engaged, that's her business. You're the steward, not her uncle.'

Amos made towards him, his arm sweeping backwards, but Hadley stepped between them.

'That's enough. Amos, how long's Joe been in the house this morning?'

'I sent him directly to Great Bartling to git help. I shink he'll have ony now a-come back.'

'Where were you both before then?'

'At church, like she was, ony we went to the generator shed arter we got back to tricolate the Type 1 bein' as the tempest last night had made the rain run in. We heard a hallerin' and went to see woss dewun. We found the doctor by the beck, but he fared badly and was in a puckaterry, so I came up here and found him –' pointing at Allerton '– dattyin' up the troshel.'

'You mean bleeding,' Allerton said.

'I bandaged his leg.'

'You need to go on a first aid course. You tied it so tight I could've lost my leg.'

'Then I tried the phone.'

'I'd already told you it wasn't working.'

'That dunt signify. He was as duzzy as a shanny mawkin,' Amos said to Hadley. 'Then I sent the boy Joe to fetch help.'

'Any idea where she might've gone?' Hadley asked.

Amos shrugged.

'Maybe she hatta have a mardle wi' a friend.'

'A mardle? She was hardly in a sociable frame of mind,' Allerton said. 'You don't seem to understand the gravity of this situation.'

'Nonetheless,' Hadley said, 'it would help to have a list of her friends, just in case.'

Hadley removed his gloves and looked around the room. The walls were covered with images of Coulgranes throughout the ages — some in uniform, others in evening wear, with hairstyles ranging from powdered wigs to bobs, beehives and curls. There was a mix of miniatures, silhouettes, oil on canvas and photos. One of the photographs was of Lady Coulgrane. The golden ringlets and the porcelain-like sheen to her face made her seem like a china doll, but it would do.

'Fenning, have a copy made of that picture.'

'What wuz she wearin'?' Fenning asked Allerton.

'A white floral print dress, a yellow jacket, black ankle boots and a bergère hat. She always wears the Coulgrane signet ring on her right little finger. It's easily identifiable.'

Fenning and Hadley returned to the car and, after she radioed in for the police photographer, Hadley asked her what she'd found.

'Blond hair clippins,' she replied, handing a bag over to him. 'I coont find evidence of dye in any onem sinks or hutches, and there wunt no discarded packets in the bins. There ent no sign of the clothes Mr Allerton described, so praps she hent changed. A haircut ent much of a disguise, but praps she dint have time to do any more. There's noffin outta th'ordinary in the medicine cabinet, but she mighta took drugs with her. I dint see no sign o' the ring Mr Allerton mentioned, but I found an empty jewellery case.'

'Ask the housekeeper if she can provide a description of any items that might've been in it and get the list circulated to all jewellers.' Hadley looked over to the coppice where Lady Coulgrane had last been seen. 'It might also be an idea if we check with Amos to see if anything's missing from the armoury.'

—2—

A New Migrant

Four lorries were parked in a lay-by. The drivers were gathered around a fast-food stall eating bacon butties. Three of them were large and hairy, their jackets undone and their ties loose. The fourth was taller than the others but he was lean, with a thin, chestnut-coloured moustache. His brown fedora was tilted forwards, casting a shadow across his blue eyes, and he wore a gabardine trench coat over his single-breasted suit.

'That storm last night certainly cleared the air,' he said.

'Yeah, you're right, Jack,' Hector said as he scratched his cauliflower ear.

'Hell of a storm—just like I said it would be.'

Spike removed his sandwich from his mouth.

'Yeah, you sure did,' he said and adjusted the partial denture that took the place of a missing front tooth.

'It's ironic that it took lightning to get rid of those damn Anti-Techs,' Jack said.

He took a bite out of his sandwich. It was greasy, as usual, but at least it would tide him over until dinner. The other three started laughing.

'Yeah, that's real funny,' Alf said.

'Yeah –' Hector's grin was somewhat lopsided due to an old knife wound '– that's a good one.'

'It sure sent them packing,' Jack said, 'but their protest has eaten into my profits.'

The others stopped laughing. Alf scowled.

'Yeah, the bastards.'

Jack looked at him and nodded. Alf's skin was a light brown, apart from the puckered scar on his cheek where Jack had once shot him, but that was in the past when Alf had worked for Slim Hamilton — he was one of Jack's lads now. Spike, once more tucking into his sandwich, was standing next to Alf.

'You've got ketchup on your nose, Spike,' Jack said.

'Sorry, Jack.'

Spike took out a handkerchief and rubbed it over his misshapen nose. Jack finished his sandwich, produced a cheroot from his coat and struck a match against one of the wooden posts of the fast-food stall. While he was lighting the thin cigar, he caught sight of a figure walking along the grass verge with a thumb outstretched. The hitch-hiker was wearing a waxed jacket fastened up to the neck and a pair of hobnailed boots caked in mud. A flat cap overshadowed the youth's eyes.

Jack nudged Hector.

'What d'you reckon?'

'Bet he won't last a month.'

'A fortnight, more like,' Spike said.

Alf shook his head.

'A week. What d'you reckon, Jack?'

'It's hardly fair for me to make a wager, but I'll say at least six weeks to give you lads a chance.'

The kid was a few yards off now, just in front of Jack's truck. His cap looked like it had been stolen from a scarecrow. It was stained and way too big. What little Jack could see of the youth's face was mottled and blistered — had farm labourers never heard of sun cream?
'Where're you heading, boy?'
'Woss the best place to find work?'
The kid didn't have any baggage, not even a little bundle of odds and ends. Jack blew out a stream of smoke.
'If you're looking for a job, you're in luck. I've a friend who needs help in his shop. His last assistant turned out to be no good, but maybe you'll do.'
'I work hard, I do. Dunt you worry about that. What type o' shop is it?'
A truck drove past in the nearside lane and flashed its lights. Jack waved and turned back to the kid.
'It's a sort of junk shop: oddities, a bit of ironmongery and such like. I'm sure I could persuade him to take you on.'
'Thass hully kind o' you, sar.'
'I'm Jack Preston, but you can call me "Jack".' Was it his imagination or had the kid given a start at his name? Maybe his reputation had spread to the country. Sweet. That would be one in the eye for Stan. 'These are my friends: Spike, Hector and Alf. What's your name, lad?'
The boy didn't seem to like eye contact, but maybe he just didn't want to get a crick in his neck.
'Harry.' The kid glanced back over the fields and then said: 'Harry Ferguson.'
'Pleased to meet you, Harry. This is my truck. In you get. Mind the step.'
Jack held the passenger door open. After a moment's hesitation, Harry clambered in, and Jack slammed the door,

grinned at the other truckers, strode over to the driver's side and jumped up.

'You're lucky we met,' he said as he closed the door and fastened his belt. 'I don't usually drive on a Sunday, but the Anti-Techs set up road blocks in Central City last week.' He turned the key in the ignition. 'We were stuck for two days, kicking our heels, so I'm going to take this week off. It's bad for business, but hopefully things will've calmed down by next week.'

Jack pulled out on to the dual carriageway heading east towards Norwich, rested his cheroot in the ashtray and began fiddling with the radio.

'D'you know any cheap places I could stay?' Harry said.

'I've a spare bed at mine, and you're welcome to rent it. I've two other lodgers, but I'm sure you'll get along just fine.'

A voice crackled over the radio.

'What's your status, Jack?'

'On schedule. I have an extra package — the usual.'

He hooked the handset back on its cradle. A twin-cowl Phaeton shot past — must've been doing at least sixty — but its narrow wheels hit a puddle and the car began to skid. It moved over to the nearside lane and slowed down a little. There was a billboard on the verge advertising a brand of toothpaste. The paper was peeling at one corner and one of the wooden posts was snapped. There were fragments of glass and chrome lying on the mud beneath it. Jack eased up on the accelerator. The fields on either side were waterlogged, but it was nothing compared to the flooding further back where the road passed south of The Wash. If it hadn't been for the embankments, dykes and wind pumps, it would've been impassable.

'So how old are you, lad?'

'Twenty.'

'Come off it. You're never twenty.'

Jack picked up his cheroot and tapped off the ash.

'We develop late in our family. My dad dint start shavin' until he wuz twenty-five, and I can't git served nowhere except my local. Well, the landlord know me, so he believe me, but the rest mob me.'

'Yeah? No kidding,' Jack said. 'So how d'you account for the late development?'

'The doctor say thass a faulty gene or some such squit. At school they call me names, and that make me raw. Do they start anything, I lam 'em.'

'Got a bit of a temper, have you?'

'Blast no, bor, I dunt mean that.'

'Did you get much schooling?'

'I larnt to read and write, but woss the use o' school when you hatta work on a farm? My dad — may he rest in peace — was going outta business.'

'That's too bad.'

'Our neighbour hev a big farm, and he skrowge out the smaller ones. We hatta work orl hours, and we still coont break even.'

'Yeah, that sounds familiar.'

'And now my family's orl passed on, and I've no farm. So woss the use in staying? There's no point a-sittin' on my arse. Might jist as well try my luck in the city. Bound to be suffin for a tidy worker.'

Harry continued to chatter: people and places, markets and fêtes, all the inconsequential country affairs strung into one breathless narrative. Jack gave up on the conversation and let his mind wander.

※

It took almost two hours to reach Norwich. The sign welcoming visitors to the fine city had a note proclaiming that it had been proudly rebuilt since the anarchy. Harry stared out of the window at the unfamiliar sights. Pedestrians bustled along the pavements, some stepping out into the road to avoid women's parasols. The men wore homburgs or fedoras, but a few also carried umbrellas, as though they were afraid last night's storm would return, despite the clear sky. The houses were tall with yellow, pink or pastel blue fronts and intricate wrought ironwork on the balconies and across the windows.

'I've never seen such great buildings,' Harry said, 'except praps the town hall, but where are the gardens?'

'Gardens? There aren't many who can afford the extra land, but who needs a bit of grass when you've got everything you need just round the corner?'

'There's a cinema in Great Bartling.'

'That where you lived?'

'No, thass abowt six mile from my farm.'

'Six miles? That's your idea of just down the road?'

Harry turned round and gazed past Jack out of his window. There was a screen fastened to a wall on the other side of the street. On it was a moving image of a woman washing her hair whilst wearing a flimsy, wet dress. So that's what an electronic billboard looked like. The woman on the screen began to shake her hair in the wind. Good grief, she didn't seem to be wearing anything under her dress. No wonder there was so much immorality in the city. Didn't it distract the drivers? Harry glanced at Jack, but he was frowning at the traffic.

The pedestrians on the nearside pavement had become even more bunched up. Harry wound the window down and peered out. The vehicles stank of biofuel. Further along the street, Harry could see banners being held up above the heads of the crowd bearing slogans such as 'No computers!' and 'Don't bring back anarchy!'

'Damn Anti-Techs,' Jack said. 'They'd better not try blocking the roads here.'

'Why are they demonstrating?' Harry said. 'Nowun's thinking o' bringing back puters, are they?'

'Sure they are. What's wrong with that? The authorities use them, why shouldn't the rest of us?'

They turned into a road full of grey warehouses and depots, pulled into a bay and parked alongside another lorry that had arrived just before them. Harry leant out of the window to watch the driver squeezing out of the cab. Particles of food hung on his black beard like insects dangling in a spider's web. His sleeves were rolled up above his elbows, and his forearms were covered in tattoos that danced as he flexed his muscles. His shirt was crumpled around his braces, but he straightened his clothes and put on his jacket and hat. He glanced at Harry and grinned. Jack collected a case from behind his seat, opened the door and jumped down. Harry closed the window and joined them.

'Lo, Eric,' Jack said. 'This is Harry. He's going to be our new flatmate.'

'He's a bit of a skinny runt,' Eric said as he slung a duffel bag over his shoulder.

'He just needs a bit of feeding up. Wait here for us, lad. We've got to put our keys away and sign off.'

Jack and Eric went into the depot office, and Harry stood by the trucks until they returned a few minutes later.

'Come along, lad,' Jack said and strode ahead with Eric.

Harry hurried after them through the gateway where Jack stopped to buy a newspaper from a kiosk before he and Eric merged into the crowd of pedestrians. Harry ducked round the side of the pavement to avoid being jostled but stopped as a disembodied voice spoke from a flickering billboard across the road.

'Unsightly blemishes? Can't afford surgery? Try Dr Masterson's liquid skin.'

Harry looked up and watched a drab woman at a dressing table smear a substance over a face full of liver spots. A moment later she was transformed into an elegant socialite at a party surrounded by attentive men, her skin as smooth as a china doll. The scene changed to a bathroom where the woman peeled off the sheer film without wincing and threw the gummy remains in a bin.

'Only sustainable, natural ingredients used,' the voice said. *'Easy on and easy off. No pain and no fuss.'*

No pain? Ha! Wearing that stuff for any length of time was about as painless as shoving your face in a patch of nettles. Harry was about to turn away when the image changed to a crowd of people who laughed and hugged one another. A smiling mother lifted a baby, and they twirled round in bright sunlight amidst a shower of petals. Again a voice spoke from the billboard.

'The new era. The whole world united in peace and prosperity.'

'Don't worry, lad.' Jack clapped Harry on the shoulder. 'We'll take good care of you.'

Harry's muscles tightened for a moment.

'You all right?' Jack said.

'I fare a mite frazzled and no mistake. I rackon there's a sight more people in this street than there wuz animals on our farm.'

'I'm sure you'll get used to it. Walk between the two of us, and we'll make sure you're not trampled on.'

The three of them left the industrial estate and entered a residential area. The roads grew narrower and quieter and changed from tarmac to cobbles. The terrace houses diminished in size and gaiety until they gave way to grime-covered blocks of flats. Laundry hung in rows above their heads, obscuring the sky.

'Welcome to my neighbourhood,' Jack said. 'I hope you'll soon think of it as home.'

A man lounged against a wall with his jacket undone and his face unshaven. A group of women stood nearby, wearing knee-length close-fitting dresses, boleros and little hats perched on chignons. Some twirled their parasols and others had theirs furled but, as soon as they saw Jack, they straightened themselves, like slovenly privates catching sight of their sergeant-major.

'How's things, girls?'

'Swell, Jack.'

Harry studied Jack's hard-boiled face and then eyed the women. They were smiling at Jack, but not with a touting-for-customers kind of smile. Maybe this wasn't such a good idea. Jack and Eric continued to stride down the lane. Harry followed, but slower. Jack glanced round.

'Tired?' he said.

'I hatta do a lot o' jammin' abowt afore we met.'

'Don't worry, we're almost there.'

Jack turned into one of the buildings. The door had small round marks of painted filler scattered across it as though it had once been infested by giant half-inch thick woodworm. Harry paused to let Eric pass.

'No, after you, kid,' Eric said. 'A skinny runt like you could get lost in a big place like this.'

Harry stepped through the doorway into a lobby with mildew-speckled, faded wallpaper. There was a lift next to the stairwell opposite the entrance and, through the broken grill doors, Harry could see a smear on the back wall leading to a dark stain on the floor. Jack led the way up the stairs, and Eric took the rear. They reached the first floor, and Jack opened a door, letting out a smell of stale beer and rotting food.

'Come on, then,' he said.

For a moment Harry held back but then followed him in. There was a cramped space that aspired to being a hall with three internal doors. Jack opened the right hand one.

'Bathroom,' he said and flicked a switch in the hall.

A light came on through the open doorway and Harry peered in. It was small and windowless with scum lining the sink and bath. An extractor fan juddered into life. Jack switched off the light and pointed ahead.

'Kitchen.'

The counters and sink were full of unwashed crockery harbouring colonies of mould. The net curtain in front of the window was a yellowy grey, with a dead fly entangled in its frayed hem. Jack strode through the third doorway.

'The main room. Come on, don't be shy.'

Eric gave Harry a prod in the back, and Harry stumbled into the room. At one end, there were two sets of bunk-beds opposite each other with a wardrobe along the side wall between them. At the other end, near the window, there was a round table with six chairs in front of a tall, thin cupboard.

The far corner was dominated by a home brew kit and boxes of engine parts. There was a bookcase by the door—its contents were mostly from an era of private detectives drinking bourbon in dingy offices or gangsters wielding tommy guns. The spines were creased and peeling. The floor was strewn with crumpled beer cans, dirty laundry and empty packaging. Jack pointed to the furthest top bunk.

'That's the bed to let. You're lucky I met you before someone else snapped it up. Eric's got the bunk below.'

Harry glanced at the other top bunk where a young man lounged, reading a magazine—*Generator Monthly* by the look of it. His worsted jacket was slung over the end rail, and his fedora was hanging on the nearest bed post. He was in his mid-twenties, as far as Harry could tell, but there were flecks of white in his otherwise black hair. He held a beer can in one hand, but his gaze remained fixed on the page in front of him.

'Adam, my lad,' Jack said, 'this is Harry.'

'He can bugger off,' Adam said without looking up.

Jack smiled at him and winked at Harry.

'Make sure you don't provoke Adam. I suggest you stay away from him unless you want to talk about engines.'

Harry studied the young man or, rather, the magazine in front of his face.

'That look like a Bostock Type 1 generator,' Harry said. Adam flipped over the magazine and glanced at the picture. 'Our farm hev a Type 1 and both the Type 2s: the Mark A and the Mark B.'

'There ain't any Type 1s around no more,' Adam said.

'Maybe they're not hully common, but our farm hev one. That need tricolatin' orl the time, but I useter git it going mostly, though once I was a lummox, and the shock hulled me to the wall. My hair stood anend for rest o' the day.'

Adam tossed his can on to the floor, grabbed the side rail of the bunk with both hands, swung himself over and jumped down, his head missing the ceiling by a few inches. He landed knees bent on an empty cardboard box, which crumpled beneath him. Then he straightened up, strode over to Jack and eyed Harry.

'You worked on a Type 1?' he said.

'I certainly hev, and thass a job to meet someone else who's interested in generators.'

' "Interested" doesn't cover it,' Jack said as he ruffled Adam's hair.

'What type o' generator do this building run on, bor?' Harry asked.

'None,' Adam said. 'There ain't much need for generators in the city now we've got the alcohol sub-stations.'

'I rackon thass better to use readily available fuel, like plants and manure.'

'Not so readily available in the city,' Jack said.

'There's also one that run on animal remains — or human remains if you're not careful.'

'An interesting way to dispose of bodies.' Jack took out a cheroot from his cigar case. 'I'm surprised certain parties haven't made a note of that.'

'So what're the main differences between the Mark A and the Mark B?' Adam said to Harry, but Jack rested a hand on his shoulder.

'Save it for later, my lad. Let the boy get settled first.'

'How much do the rent cost?' Harry said.

Jack twirled the cheroot around his fingers.

'I'll take you to see Bob tomorrow, and once we've found out how much he's prepared to pay you then maybe we can come to an arrangement that will be within your means.'

'But what about ternight? That would craze me to stay the night not knowing how much thass a-gorta cost.'

Jack struck a match with his thumbnail and eyed Harry as he lit his cheroot. Harry adopted an amiable expression.

'I tell you what –' Jack blew out the match '– you can stay the first night free of charge.'

'Thass masterous kind on you,' Harry said. 'What about dinner and breakfast?'

Perhaps that was pushing it a bit. Harry watched, muscles tensed, as Jack flicked the spent match into an ashtray, but he gave a wave with his cheroot.

'This isn't something I'd usually offer, but I like you, so I'll let you have the first dinner, night and breakfast on me. I'm afraid after that I'll have to start charging. I'm sure you understand that times are hard, and I need the extra rent. And there are so many migrants in want of lodgings.'

'Oh, I understand, and I do appreciate it. Thass a tidy thing we met, but dunt you put yarself out on my account. Do you find it an imposition, do you tell me directly. I'd hate for you to change yar mind and mob me later.'

'I don't change my mind. You can use the bottom drawer under the wardrobe for your things — only you don't seem to have any baggage. Leave in a hurry, did you?'

'Those creditors, they take everything. Thass a blessing they left me with the clothes I'm wearing.'

Jack leant against one of the bedposts.

'That sure was low-down of them to not even leave you with a spare pair of underwear but, if you like, I'll arrange a loan to tide you over so you can get kitted out.'

'Blast no,' Harry said, 'that oont be necessary. I'll buy some second-hand ones when I've saved up enough.'

'You're going to get a bit ripe.'

'Nix,' Adam said to Harry. 'You don't want to go around getting second-hand clothes. You don't know what the previous owner might've had. Think of all the infections you could catch.'

Eric nudged Harry.

'Don't mind Adam, kid.' The trucker stank of biofuel and greasy food. 'He's got a thing about infectious diseases. He won't even shake hands with people.'

Harry moved away, crouched down and began to inspect the bottom drawer, all the while listening to the men's conversation and trying to determine the best course of action in this unknown place.

'You bet I won't,' Adam said. 'Sixty percent of people don't wash their hands after going to the can. I ain't catching their germs.'

'How d'you know it's sixty percent?' Eric said. 'I reckon you just made it up.'

'I never made it up. Spud told me and, anyhow, I've seen some bloke go for a piss and then wipe his hands on his trousers.'

Harry stood up and studied the young man. Jack patted Adam on the back.

'There are some lousy people about, my lad, but you know, if germs bother you that much, you might want to help keep this place a bit cleaner.'

'Sorry, Jack.'

'That's all right, my boy. Let's get something to eat. Maybe Harry can tell you about his generators on the way.'

Adam put on his jacket and fedora, tilting his hat forwards so that it was at the same angle as Jack's, and they all left the flat.

— 3 —

ADAM

Adam strolled alongside Harry, with Jack and Eric a few yards ahead. The kid sure knew about the history of generators: dates and everything. Migrants were usually such a dumb bunch. They never lasted long, but maybe Jack might let this one stay a while.

A couple of kids raced around a corner, pulled up when they saw Jack and darted across the road. Jack pointed with his cheroot down the narrow cul-de-sac where the boys had come from.

'Harry, Bob's shop's down that way. Nice and convenient. No need to worry about bus fares, or anything like that.'

Adam watched Harry peer down the lane, but the kid's face remained expressionless. Night always reached Bob's cul-de-sac before the other streets. There were no pavements, on account of it being too narrow, and the buildings stood tall and dirty. There were lights coming from some of the windows, but it was the kind of frail light that seemed to make everything that much dingier.

'Is that true I need papers to git a job in the city, bor?' Harry said.

Where had he heard that from? He must be the first migrant they'd ever come across who'd known that.

'Sure you do,' Jack said. 'D'you have any?'

'No, we dunt hatta have none of that ID dewun back home. Birth certificates are one thing, but to carry about a bit o' paper saying everything about you orl the time, thass jist a load o' squit.'

'Maybe so, but you're going to need ID papers to work here. Fortunately Adam's a sort of part-time clerk, and he'll be able to get you some. Won't you, my lad?'

'Sure, I can do that.'

'Thass hully kind o' you,' Harry said to Adam. 'I expect there's probably a fee.'

Adam glanced at Jack and then shrugged.

'Yeah, that's right.'

They continued walking until they reached a junction. There was a copper on the other side of the intersection. His gut sagged over his trousers and a blackjack hung on his hip. He glanced in their direction, looked around and headed over to them. He inspected the nails on his left hand as he strolled across the road and slid his right hand into a pocket.

'No prizes for guessing what he's after,' Jack murmured to Adam.

The copper stepped on to the pavement, a few yards away, and had another quick look around.

'How's things, Bryson?' Jack said.

The copper sidled over to him and fingered his collar.

'Lost ten grand last night.'

'How'd you manage that?'

Bryson scuffed his shoe on the pavement.

'Poker over at The Blue Diamond. I had it made. I was sure I had it made. High quads with an ace kicker. Then

Long-Odds Verkroost cleaned me out. I can't let the missus get wind of it. You know what she's like.'

'Want a loan to tide you over?'

'That'd be great, Jack. Just until pay day.'

'Call round tomorrow, and we'll sort something out.'

'Cheers, Jack.'

Adam watched the copper walk away, and then he turned to Jack.

'The Blue Diamond's a bit out of his league, ain't it?'

'Sure it is. One of these days I'm going to leave him to his missus. You all right, Harry?'

They had come to a row of shops with neon signs, and the kid was gazing at them like they were at some kind of amusement show.

'This place is a job,' Harry said, 'but I gather that ent as big as Central City.'

Jack blew out a stream of smoke and tapped the ash off his cheroot on to the pavement.

'Central City's bigger, but this place has its charms.'

'I've heard there are some masterous buildings in Central City, like that Sector House. I once saw a picture of it in a newspaper, and that looked a rare place.'

Adam moved away from Harry. If the kid liked Central City so much, he should've gone there instead. Lousy pretentious dump full of lousy government cretins in their dumb new buildings.

'Sector House ain't all it's cracked up to be,' he said. 'They should've given more thought when they built the wall round it. Sure, they made it high, but the mortar ain't flush against the bricks. They must've hired a bunch of cowboys.'

'You mean it's possible to climb?' Harry said.

'I reckon it'd be a cinch.'

Adam broke off as he caught sight of Jack tapping the side of his nose. Jack then slid his finger down, took the cheroot out of his mouth and inspected it for a moment.

'Adam likes climbing the wall down the gym,' he said and drew on the cheroot.

'Yeah, that's right,' Adam said, 'down the gym.'

They continued on their way. A van with a dodgy exhaust drove by leaving a grey cloud trailing behind it. Harry stared after it and turned to Jack.

'D'you rackon I could become a trucker? I've driven heavy agricultural vehicles. I'm sure I could handle a lorry.'

'You're too young to drive a truck,' Eric said.

'Blast, no, bor. I'm twenty.'

'Like hell you are.'

Eric shoved Harry and the kid flew backwards towards a clothes shop. Adam lunged behind Harry, flung both arms around the kid, grabbed him and stumbled back into the wall, just missing the window.

'What d'you want to chuck the kid around for, Eric?' Adam said.

'That was just a prod. He's a featherweight, but what's he think he's doing giving us a load of crap like that?'

Eric poked Harry's left shoulder with a thick, hairy finger. Adam still had his arms around Harry with the kid's back pressed against his chest. Harry's jacket sure seemed to have a lot of padding at the front or maybe there were a couple of deep, full pockets inside it. There was also something straight, hard and about a foot long inside the back of the jacket that dug into Adam's hip. Too rigid for a blackjack. Too uniform for a firearm. Too cylindrical for a knife sheath. A bit of piping, maybe? Harry had grabbed Adam's wrists and tensed up. The kid's hands, tinged with blue from the shop's neon sign, were small with slender fingers. There was a pale band of skin on the right little finger, like people get from wearing a ring most of the time. It occurred to Adam that maybe it wasn't a pocket he'd got a hold on. He loosened his grip.

High heels tapped along an alley at the end of the row of shops. A woman stepped out on to their street.

'Can it,' Jack said quietly. 'Rita's coming. Adam, let the kid go.'

Jack strolled towards the approaching woman with Eric by his side.

'I was just trying to stop you from hitting the wall, that's all,' Adam whispered in Harry's ear. 'I didn't mean to grab your — you there. Okay?' Harry nodded but pushed his hand away from her chest. 'Be careful of Rita. You won't want any job she offers you.'

Adam let go, but as he did so he felt Harry shuddering.

Rita was wearing her usual outfit: a red dress that hugged her figure with a suggestion of underlying structural reinforcements and a wide-brimmed hat covered in rosebuds. Overshadowing that, a tasselled pink parasol swayed, the stalk and hat brim colliding with every step she took. Her left hand always seemed to be on her hip, as though it had been welded in place, and a reticule dangled from her wrist.

'Jack, I see you've finally made it back,' she said as she presented her cheek to him. 'About time too.'

'That's sure nice of you to miss me, Rita love.' Jack's kiss barely reached her cheek. 'Come and meet Harry. Lost his farm, poor kid, but I've let him the spare bunk.'

He beckoned to Adam and Harry, and they came over to join the other three.

'You poor thing.' Rita leant towards Harry, displaying so much of her cleavage in the process that Adam caught a glimpse of the pocket pistol she kept in it. 'It must be hard on you coming to a strange place not knowing anyone, but I know some girls who'd be more than happy to get to know you and help you settle in.'

'I don't reckon Harry would get along with them,' Adam said. 'I know I don't.'

Rita pursed her lips.

'Jack, tell him to butt out and stop insulting my girls.'

Jack glanced over at Adam and looked back at Rita.

'Rita love, I didn't hear any insults. Adam was just trying to explain that he and Harry are developing a bit of a rapport, what with the kid knowing almost as much about generators as Adam. Isn't that right, my lad?'

Adam strolled over to Jack's side and put his hands in his trouser pockets.

'Sure, that's right.'

He grinned at Rita, and she turned her back on him.

'So you're another generator nut, are you, boy?' she said to Harry.

'Our Type 1 is the talk of the neighbourhood.'

'Oh, give me a break.'

'Rita love, you coming to the café with us?' Jack said.

'Yeah, sure. Let's go.'

Rita strutted ahead between Jack and Eric. Adam followed on behind with Harry, and the two of them occupied the rest of the journey talking about generators. They discussed the differences in fuel, efficiency, design, popularity, modern ones versus the older types, and sundry other matters that appeared to be of great interest to Harry and were of definite interest to Adam. He was in the process of quizzing her on the layout of the turbine in the Mark B when they reached the café. Rita turned on them.

'Oh, for crying out loud.'

Adam glared at her and clenched his fists. Jack nudged her. She rolled her eyes upwards but closed the parasol and smiled at Harry.

'So, Harry, Jack tells me you had to leave the country because your dad went bankrupt.'

'Thass true. When my poor old dad died, the creditors took everything.'

Jack dropped his cheroot stub in the gutter and trod on it.

'They didn't even leave the lad with a spare set of clothes.'

'That's too bad,' Rita said.

'Dad wunt even cold in his bed,' Harry said.

'Don't worry, lad.' Jack opened the café door. 'We'll look after you. Let's get you fixed up with a decent meal.'

Adam followed Harry into the café but noticed that Rita was sidling towards her with an expression Adam recognised. If Rita was in the mood for a bit of teasing — when wasn't she? — she'd have to find some other mug. He shoved Harry over to the end of a vacant table, out of Rita's way.

'You sit there, kid,' he said and pulled up the chair next to her.

Rita pouted and went round to the other side of the table. She sat opposite Harry and leant forwards.

'It must've been real tough on you, Harry. I reckon you need a bit of comforting.'

'I dunt need no comforting. Thass jist the way o' things. I know we ony hed a small farm, and the poachers were always a-stealing our hins, but the police are so spread out there's noffin they can do about it.'

'That's a real bummer.'

'Well, what can they do when there's a sight o' land and so few people? And our equipment was old and allus in need o' tricolatin'. My late granfar — may he rest in peace — used to be masterly good with generators. My dad was his prentice, and they both larnt me, but Grandpa Eddie went a bit peculiar in the end.'

'Peculiar?' Jack said as he pulled up the chair next to Rita. 'In what way?'

'Every now and then he rackoned he was a tree. He useter stand out in the field stark naked and sway abowt in the breeze.'

'Were your whole family mental?' Rita said.

'I'm not mad.' Harry clenched her fists. Adam poised himself to intervene, but she remained seated. 'I dunt like it when people say that. I dunt rackon thass polite.'

'I reckon Harry's normal,' Adam said as Eric sat down next to him.

'Everyone's normal compared to you,' Rita said.

Adam leapt to his feet, but Eric jumped up and grabbed his shoulder. Jack motioned him to sit down. Adam thumped back on his seat, but he glared at Rita. She smirked. Jack laid a hand on her arm.

'Let Adam be, Rita.' A waitress came to the table and took their orders. 'How's your brother, Lise?'

'Everything's okay now, Jack,' the waitress said. 'Thank you so much. We're very grateful for your help.'

'That's real nice of you to say, Lise. Let me know if you have any more problems.'

The waitress soon returned with the food and, throughout the meal, Jack only had to glance in her direction to bring her hurrying back to top up his glass or replace Adam's fork. (There was a small bit of who-knows-what on one of the prongs — there was no way he was going to put that in his mouth.) Jack talked for a while about the past week, dwelling in particular on the demonstrations and the resulting traffic jams leaving Central City. Adam was content to listen. Eric supported Jack from time to time with a 'Yeah, that's right.'

'You wouldn't catch me spending my life in a lousy truck,' Rita said.

'It's lucky you don't have to do it then,' Jack said.

'You don't have to either.'

'I like driving. Harry was saying he wants to be a trucker.'

'You're kidding. He's way too small.'

'I'm strong enough. You hatta be, do you want to work on a farm. There's hay bales to shift and tractors to drive, not to mention some o' the animals. We had a pig what was twenty-one stone. He uster eat our hins do they escape into his field, but I slit his throat and chopped him up.'

'That's gross,' Rita said.

'What d'you think happened to the hin you're eatin'?'

'It must be good to know exactly where your food comes from,' Adam said. 'At least you know no one's gobbed in it or swapped it for rat. I mean, look at this —' he prodded a lump of meat with a bone attached '— how can I be sure it's chicken?'

'Thass definitely a hin bone not rat,' Harry said. 'I've killed a sight o' rats — mostly with a shotgun although there was one I decapitated.'

'You can handle a shotgun?' Jack picked up his glass and smiled. 'I like the sound of that.'

He winked at Adam over the glass as he took a sip, but Rita was pursing her lips like she'd swallowed something she'd much rather spit out. Eric dipped a chip in a pool of ketchup and swirled it around on his plate.

'Did you, like, have a field with a bull in it and a sign on the gate with "beware of the bull" written on it?'

'I never saw the point in that,' Harry said. 'Do a duzzy tewl wander off the footpaths into a field with a bull in it, he's ony got hisself to blame.'

Jack put the glass down and ran a finger around its rim.

'You sure have an interesting vocabulary.'

'I dunt talk different from them back home.'

'Yeah? Do they all use long words like "decapitated"?' Jack said.

Adam was sure he detected a slight hesitation, but she grinned again.

'Ah well, that would be my Uncle Barney. He larnt me a good deal, except about generators.' She turned to Adam. 'Wuz that your dad who larned you about generators?'

Jack gave a muffled oath, Rita smirked and Eric gestured at Harry. Adam clenched his fists.

'I don't know who he is, but knowing my mother he'll be a dumb-arsed politician or bank director. Lousy bitch.'

'I'm sorry,' Harry said. 'I didn't mean to upset you.'

He stared at her for a moment and shrugged.

'I ain't bothered. Besides, I could now thump her far harder than she ever hit me if I wanted to and, when she's old and infirm, I'll be the one to lock her up in the cellar, only I won't leave her with the generator: she won't appreciate it like I did.' He smiled. 'It never used to throw things at me or swear at me and tell me I was no good or lock me up because it didn't want to be interrupted while it had company. I wish I could've taken it with me when I left.'

Adam stared at his food and stabbed a chip with his fork. Rita sniggered.

'Button it, Rita,' Jack said.

Blood rushed to Adam's cheeks.

'Thass a rat bone,' Harry said as she pointed at Rita's plate with a knife. 'No, my mistake, thass a hin.'

'What? Jack!'

'Harry, what the hell d'you think you're playing at?'

'I'm sorry, Jack. These hins look like they're been shut up in a barn orl their life, and that deform the bones, which make 'em harder to identify.'

Adam smirked at Rita. She swore at him, scrunched up her paper napkin, threw it on to the table and stormed off. Jack strode after her. They stopped at the café door, but Adam could just make out what they were saying.

'Get rid of him,' Rita said.

'Don't tell me how to run my business.'

'He insulted me.'

'You shouldn't've laughed at Adam. I've told you often enough to let him be.'

'Oh and I suppose you're going to tell me to let Harry be as well.'

'I'll deal with him in my own time.'

'It's bad enough that you let Adam get away with as much as you do. I ain't going to stand for any migrant getting out of line.'

'I don't let anyone get out of line.'

'He'd better not insult me again, because I won't stand for it.'

With that, Rita strutted out of the café. Jack glanced at Adam for a moment. Adam smiled at him, but Jack turned away and went off to settle the bill.

'I'm sorry if I've caused any jip,' Harry said to Jack, after they had left the café. 'That'll larn me, if Rita dunt want no more truck with me.'

Jack leant against a lamp post next to Eric, took out a cheroot and ran it along his moustache, breathing in like he was savouring the last one left in the world.

'For the record, Harry,' he said, 'I know exactly what a rat bone looks like and what rat tastes like. Rita may try to convince everyone she lived a life of luxury during the anarchy, but I sure as hell remember what really happened in those days, and it'll take a damn sight more than thirty years to forget it.'

'I'm sorry, Jack. I didn't know.'

Adam moved over to her side.

'Don't be mad at Harry for stopping Rita from laughing at me. You know I don't like people making fun of me.'

'I certainly never meant to upset you,' she said to him.

'Oh believe me,' Jack said, 'if I thought you'd done that deliberately, you wouldn't still be upright. And Adam, my dear boy,' he added as he stepped away from the lamp post and put an arm across Adam's shoulders, 'it may not be haute cuisine, but they know better than to serve my lad anything unwholesome.'

Adam nodded but then heard distant gunfire.

'That ain't Stan, is it?'

'Sounds like Hershey's guns, but they're close to Stan's neighbourhood — he's not going to like that.' Jack twirled the unlit cheroot around his fingers. 'Harry, you be more careful in future because there are a lot worse things that can happen to you than being kicked out with nowhere to go.' He patted Adam's back and moved away. 'Now, Harry, given that it's your first night here, how about I treat you to a pint of beer at our local? After all, you did say you're twenty and used to get served at your pub back home.'

'But like I said, I can't git served nowhere else.'

'I know the landlord. I'm sure he'd accept your word if you gave him your date of birth.'

'Thass hully kind o' you,' Harry said, 'but I rackon I'm dead on my feet from jammin' abowt so far terday.'

'In that case, I'll get you a beer from the off-licence over the road, and maybe we'll take you along to the pub some other time.'

With that, he strode over to the off-licence. Harry looked, for a moment, as though she was going to call after Jack, but she remained silent. Jack soon returned with four cans of beer tucked in the crook of his left arm and the cheroot, still unlit, in his mouth. He distributed the cans, struck a match and strolled ahead with Eric.

'You're lucky Jack's good-natured,' Adam said to Harry, as they sauntered some yards behind the other two. Street lamps began to flicker on — only every other light, the remainder would come on later. 'So how many generators did you have on your farm?'

'Let me see now...'

She began to count them off on her fingers. Adam smiled as they strolled along together. His can was soon empty, but he caught sight of Harry slipping hers into one of the many pockets of her jacket.

'Watch out,' he said in a low voice. 'Jack'll get offended if you don't drink it.'

'Would he be offended if I gave it to you?'

Adam glanced at Jack's back and then at a newsagent, nestled between a barber's shop and a letting agency.

'There's no sense in it going to waste. Hang on a minute.'

He waited until Jack and Eric had turned into the next street, then ducked into the newsagent, picked up a carton of apple juice from the shelf and took it over to the counter. The shopkeeper, a small balding man from sector one hundred and eighty, bustled over.

'Ah, Mr Trent,' he said. 'I am so pleased to see you. And Mr Preston is back?'

'Yeah, sure he is,' Adam said.

'Perhaps you can talk to him on my son's behalf.'

'I'm in a hurry.'

'But it will not take long.'

'I'll stop by tomorrow.'

'But since you are here —'

'Just the apple juice, or d'you want to piss me off?'

Adam paid and returned outside. He stepped into an alley on the other side of the letting agency and gestured to Harry, who seemed to be inspecting the brickwork.

'Here, hold on to this,' Adam said, handing over the juice carton. 'What're you looking at?'

'I'd always heard the city was full of graffiti, but I can't see none.'

'Maybe in Central City, but not here. We sprayed the last person who tried it.'

'Sprayed?'

'Not in his face. Jack's firm but he ain't vicious.' Adam poured her beer into his empty can. 'The bloke was just a little punk who'd drifted in from somewhere. He was lucky he only got paint sprayed on him. Well, that and a bit of a shaking. And maybe a knock or two. Jack don't stand for people disrespecting his territory. Here, hold my can.' He took the juice carton from her and emptied it into her can.

'The dumb git would've had his hand broken or head blown off if he'd tried it in other parts of the city.'

He discarded the empty juice carton and took back his beer can.

'You can't be too careful,' he said as they left the alley. 'I ain't got nothing contagious, so we could've just swapped cans, but it's best to get into good habits. There're some disgusting people about. Filthy buggers with all their gob and sweat. It ain't no wonder the plague's come back.'

They turned the corner and found Jack lounging against a small brick bus shelter, smoking his cheroot. Eric stood next to him.

'You're being a bit slow,' Jack said. 'We nearly turned back to look for you.'

'Hev the plague really come back?' Harry asked Adam, as they walked over to Jack.

'Sure it has. There was an outbreak of it in sector eighty.'

'Hey,' Eric said, 'that sounds just like that film we saw the night we had the dodgy kebab.'

He crushed his can in one hand and dumped it into a bin fastened below the bus stop sign.

'The film weren't in sector eighty,' Adam said. 'Spud told me he'd heard about it when he was travelling through sector fifty-nine.'

'Adam, my lad,' Jack said, 'Spud's a laugh, but the kind of long distance hauls he does is enough to make a man see pixies dancing with bug-eyed aliens.'

He exhaled a puff of smoke. Adam took another swig from his can. The beer raced to his head like a kid late for a party, and the alcohol fumes danced with the cheroot smoke until they blended in a fog. It brought back memories of late nights. Jack was a good listener, and he wasn't a low-down sneak who'd rat on him. This was a hell of a beer, almost as strong as Jack's home brew. Not that Jack was being mean when he'd bought it for Harry; it was just one of his little life lessons — nothing personal. Harry had chosen not to drink it, so no harm done. She'd just have to learn not to boast about doing things she didn't actually want to do.

'You all right, my lad?' Jack said to Adam.

'Yeah sure, Jack.'

'Come on, Harry, drink up. Haven't you finished yet?'

Harry downed the rest of her drink and tossed the empty can into the bin.

'I didn't mean all in one go.'

She hiccuped and they resumed their walk back to the flat. Adam took another swig.

'I bet it's rife amongst Rita's people,' he said as they approached the entrance to Bob's cul-de-sac. 'I bet they're all covered in sores and boils just waiting to explode pus and blood over everyone.'

'That's enough, my lad,' Jack said.

'Sorry, Jack.'

'How much have you had tonight?'

'Only three cans.'

'Three? You can't have got home much before us.'

'No, I mean two. I lost count.'

'You lost count after two?'

Harry stumbled on a kerb and bumped into Eric.

'Oh, I'm sorry, bor,' she said. 'You've got hully great pavements here.'

'Yeah, well they would be high to a titch like you.'

Harry bumbled along and narrowly missed a lamp post. Eric laughed. She babbled about a trip to market, but her

accent thickened so much that half her words were unintelligible. She veered towards the road, and he shoved her back on course. Jack nudged Adam and leant close to him.
'What d'you reckon, my lad: is he for real or is he yanking our legs?'
Adam shrugged and inspected his beer can. Jack took it out of his hand, shook it slightly and then returned it.
'You pacing yourself, my lad? Don't you drink yours all in one go, will you?'
They reached their apartment block, and Adam followed behind Harry up the stairs. She stumbled on a step, but when she grabbed the rail, he saw her hand shaking. She hesitated for a moment and then continued. The sound of her hobnailed boots echoed along the stairwell. Eric went on ahead and opened up the flat. She staggered into the main room, clasped her temples and moaned.
'What's up with you?' Jack said.
'There's nothing wrong with me.' She clenched her fists, her body quivering. Jack slipped a hand into his coat pocket, but a moment later she smiled. 'I'm sorry. I dint mean to sound so rude. If you dunt mind, I rackon I might turn in.'
She ducked into the bathroom before the others could say a word and closed the door behind her.
'That was interesting,' Jack said as he removed his hand from his pocket. 'Very interesting.'
'Here,' Eric said, 'you don't reckon the kid really is nuts, do you?'
'Nuts, dumb or sick.'
'I reckon Harry'll be all right,' Adam said.
'Maybe, but he needs to know who's boss round here.' Jack stroked his moustache with the tip of his index finger. 'Watch him while Eric and I go to the pub.'

Jack patted Adam's shoulder and left with Eric. Harry returned from the bathroom. Despite the blemishes, her face was pale, and her hands were trembling. She climbed the ladder to her bunk and collapsed on to the mattress, still fully clothed. Adam strolled over.

'You okay, Harry?'

There was no reply. He put his foot on the bottom rung of her ladder. She lurched away and fumbled inside her jacket, but Adam leapt back.

'It's all right,' he said, retreating further towards his own bunk. 'I ain't going to mess with you. I just wanted to know if you needed any help. That can't be from a few drops of beer at the bottom of the can.'

Her head sank on to the pillow. She still had her right hand inside her jacket, but she had slumped on to it. He could just make out her face in the gap under the top rail. Her mouth was slightly open, her breathing rapid and shallow. Maybe he ought to find a bucket.

'It's just a headache, that's all,' she said. 'Everybody gets headaches, don't they?'

'Sure they do. I get them — usually after I've been in a fight or after I've had a few.' He moved forward, until he was halfway along the wardrobe that stood against the wall between the two sets of bunk beds. 'D'you want any paracetamol? Or something stronger? I've got some co-codamol if it's real bad.'

'What will it cost?'

'Nothing. Looks like it's your lucky night for getting things free.'

He went to fetch the pack from the bathroom but, as he opened the medicine cabinet, he heard clattering and thumping sounds from the other room. He turned and saw her stumbling towards him. She clasped the wooden moulding of the door frame with a pale hand.

'You didn't need to get out of bed,' Adam said, 'or are you worried I'm going to give you something else instead?'

'Maybe.'

'I ain't going to do that, but if you don't believe me, it's got the name written on the pill. Well, abbreviated anyway. Look, you sit down by the table while I get some water.'

Adam pulled out a chair for her, cleared some space on the table, put the medicine bottle down and went off into the kitchen. He washed up a glass, filled it with fresh water and returned to find her slumped across the table. He ran over to her, but as soon as he touched her shoulder she flinched and struggled to sit up.

'You may as well trust me,' he said as he put the glass in front of her. 'Sooner or later you'll need to sleep — sooner by the looks of it. What you gonna do? Stay awake for the rest of your life? Run away and doss in a doorway? I've been there and, believe me, I ain't never going back. You'll be a lot safer here, that's for sure.'

She reached for the water and pressed the glass against her right temple. Her cap had fallen off and, when she lowered the tumbler, he had his first clear view of her face. Her eyes were bloodshot, her brow was furrowed and her ragged blond hair stood out in all directions, but her nose was long and thin — a bit like Jack's — and her jaw line reminded him of the smooth curve down the wheel arch to the running board on his Phaeton.

She picked up the medicine bottle but struggled with the safety cap.

'Here, let me do it,' he said.

He took the bottle from her, undid it and shook out a couple of pills on to her hand. She swallowed them, muttered a thank you and, grasping hold of the table and chair back, she pushed herself on to her feet. Adam put an arm around her to steady her, but she tried to pull away.

'I ain't going to make off with you. If you pass out on the floor, I'll have to hoist you up the ladder, and that ain't exactly my idea of fun, so stop being so damn jumpy and let me help you.'

She leant on him, and he led her over to the bunk. She stumbled on a pile of dirty laundry, but he steadied her and helped her up the ladder. Once she had made it up, he returned to the kitchen, washed the beer down with a pint of water and, after a quick trip to the bathroom, he made himself a coffee. He took the mug back to the other room. Harry was lying on her side and seemed asleep. Adam picked up her cap from the table but, as he moved close to her bunk, she opened her eyes.

'I thought you might want your cap back,' he said, holding it up.

She took it from him and dropped it on her head. It flopped across her face.

'That ain't going to stay on all night,' he said, but she didn't reply.

He leant against the wardrobe and sipped his coffee. Outside a dog barked and a car horn sounded. The murmur of a radio programme drifted in from the next flat.

'Who are you running from?' he said.

'What makes you think I'm running from someone?'

'You're as jumpy as a flea on a hot soldering iron, you ain't got no baggage and you've got a piece in your jacket.'

'A piece?'

'You know what I mean: a weapon. Probably a bit of lead piping.'
'It isn't lead piping.'
'Yeah? Then what is it?'
She raised her head and tilted her cap back so that it was no longer across her face.
'Does it matter?'
'Look, I'm sorry about where I grabbed you earlier, but people are going to figure out you're a woman pretty soon and if you're found packing a weapon, you'll be in trouble.'
Harry propped herself up, laid her arms on the bed rail and rested her chin on top. She looked down at him and her mouth twitched at the corners.
'Not as much trouble as I'd be in without it.'
'I wouldn't put it past Rita to get the cops on you just for being in possession.'
'It doesn't look much like a weapon. People have seen it before and not realised what it was.' She closed her eyes and sank back into the pillow. A moment later, her eyes were open again, peering at him from under the rail. 'It is, however, very effective.'
She turned her back on him and rearranged her blankets. He drank some more coffee.
'You ain't an assassin, are you?' he said. She didn't reply. 'What happened to your accent?'
'What accent? I dunt know what you're a-talking abowt.'
'Yeah right.'
He finished his coffee, left the mug on the bedside table and climbed the ladder to his bunk where he found his mechanics magazine. He turned the page and began reading: the Type 1 generator was designed by Dr Edward Bostock, a scientist at Colingham University, just before the fuel crisis

that triggered global anarchy. The holding tank contained enzymes that converted vegetation into liquid, which was then collected in the secondary fermenting chamber. Yeah, Harry had mentioned about that. She also seemed to know a lot about Bostock. Lucky kid growing up with all those generators and having a dad and granddad to teach her. He flicked over the page and turned his back on her. An hour passed and neither of them said a word. He was almost convinced she was asleep when he heard her voice.

'How much rent does Jack usually charge?'

He turned round. Her blue eyes weren't so bloodshot now, and her face was less furrowed. He didn't answer at first, but then he shrugged.

'It varies. Some don't think to negotiate.'

'If I did negotiate, how low do you think he'd be likely to go?'

'How should I know?'

She didn't reply. He returned to his magazine. He read a paragraph, but when he had finished it, he found he couldn't recall any of it. He read it again.

'I reckon eighty a week is the lowest he's ever taken from a migrant.'

They said nothing further for the rest of the evening. Adam changed into his pyjamas, dimmed the lights and fastened his watch around the post near his head. He was still awake when Jack and Eric returned. Adam threw aside his bed clothes, grabbed the side rail of his bunk and jumped down. His bare feet caught on an empty beer can and he swore.

'I don't want to sound like a nag,' Jack said as he hung his coat and hat on a peg, 'but if the two of you were a bit tidier that wouldn't happen.'

'Sorry, Jack.' Adam leant against the bed frame and rubbed his foot. 'I'll clear up tomorrow.'

Eric belched, yawned and sat on his bunk below Harry and removed his shoes.

'Yeah, we can do it tomorrow.'

'Any problems with the kid, my lad?' Jack said to Adam.

'Nix.'

Jack strolled over to Harry's bunk and studied his new lodger in the dim light.

'He hasn't even taken off his hat, coat and boots.'

'Yeah, he looked deadbeat.'

'What d'you make of his accent?'

'We've had migrants with a broad accent before,' Adam said. Jack drummed his fingers on the bedpost. 'He knows a lot about generators.'

Jack turned to Adam and patted his cheek.

'My dear boy, you know very well you can't judge a person by their knowledge of generators. Now I don't like to mention his name, but I reckon you can guess who I'm thinking about.'

'He don't know half as much as he says — not like Harry.'

Jack ruffled Adam's hair.

'Just be careful. Talk all you like about generators and engines, but don't trust him.'

'Can Harry be a trucker?'

'You serious?'

'Sure I am, Jack. I mean, I ain't saying right now, but maybe you could consider it?'

Jack eyed Adam for a moment, but then he smiled.

'All right. I'm not making any promises, but give him some lessons — only in the old quarry. Don't let him loose on the roads.'

'I reckon he's got potential.'

'We'll see. If he's got one hell of a hangover in the morning, then maybe his outburst was just the effect of a strong beer on an untrained gut.'

'Not everyone gets a hangover.'

'Not everyone acts like a headcase.'

— 4 —

New Employment

When Harry awoke the next morning, the flat was filled with cigar smoke and the smell of coffee. She was clammy under her jacket, and she had a crick in her neck. Her feet throbbed inside her boots, and her thigh ached from where she had lain on the penknife in her pocket, but at least she hadn't woken up with a headache — for the first time in weeks. Sounds drifted across the room: crockery clattering, a knife scraping against toast, crunching and conversation.

'I'll wake Harry.'

'Sit down, Adam. I'll give him a shake when it's time to go if he's not up by then.'

'I just thought Bob might not like his new assistant being late.'

'Since when have you cared about Bob? And I'm sitting right next to you. There's no need to shout.'

'Sorry, Jack.'

'If Harry shows any sign of a hangover, Eric can give him the cold water treatment. Isn't that right, Eric?'

'Yeah, sure thing, Jack.'

Harry lay in bed for a few minutes longer, then sighed, stretched and rolled on to her back. The weapon strapped to the inside of her jacket jabbed into her spine, so she turned round on to her front, curled her legs, pushed herself upright and clambered down the ladder. The three men were eating breakfast at the table on the other side of the room.

'Looks like you can hold back on the cold water, Eric,' Jack said as she made her way to the door. Harry glanced back. There was amusement but no friendliness in the smile he gave her. 'You can use one of the towels in the bathroom cupboard, but you're responsible for laundering it.'

Harry nodded, went into the bathroom and switched on the shower. The plumbing juddered and squealed while she washed. It was just starting to knock like a giant death-watch beetle when she turned off the water. She dressed and decided that clean underwear, a toothbrush and toothpaste needed to go high up on her list of expenditures. She then tied her laces, tugged on her cap, checked the contents of her pockets and joined the others.

Jack folded up his newspaper and gestured with it at an empty seat next to Adam.

'Sit down, Harry, and help yourself. The bread's got a few spots of mould on it, but you can pick them off.'

'Most folk dunt realise mould hev invisible roots,' she said as she inspected the bread. 'They pick off the top but eat the rest.'

Adam paused, a slice of toast midway to his mouth.

'What?' he said.

Jack rolled up his newspaper into a tight tube.

'Don't wind Adam up.'

'I wunt trying to,' Harry said. 'Honest, Jack, I was only saying what my Aunt Hilda told me. She was an expert on fungi howsomever even she made the occasional mistake. One time she put magic mushrooms in a casserole, and we orl hed quite a trip. Then she went and ate a toxic one and died.'

Jack held the newspaper as though it was a club for a moment but then tossed it on to the table.

'Not so much of an expert,' he said.

'I rackon that was her poor eyesight what did it. D'you mind if I toast this?'

'Go right ahead.'

Breakfast was soon finished, and Harry set off with Jack towards Bob's shop. He strode ahead, but she caught up and trotted along beside him, although her hobnails jarred against the hard surface. People bustled along the pavement, but they all gave way to Jack.

'You seem to be getting along well with Adam — for the moment,' Jack said.

'Thass a masterley great thing to find someone else woss hully interested in generators. My Grandpa Eddie was the expert in my family, and his death wuz a big loss to the generator community.'

'That the grandfather who thought he was a tree?'

'Only in his latter days.'

'So what did he die of?'

'Hypothermia.'

'No kidding.'

Harry jumped back as a bus bumped up on to the pavement in front of them to make way for a postal van coming in the opposite direction. She ducked behind Jack until the bus thumped back down off the kerb, missing a lamp post by a few inches.

'How long hev you known Adam?' she said as she resumed her place by Jack's side.

'Eight years.' They turned into Bob's cul-de-sac. 'His mother kicked him out when he was sixteen. He got into trouble, but I fixed things for him, and I've looked after him ever since.'

'That do sound like he wuz hully lucky to hev met you,' Harry said.

'You don't know how much trouble he would've been in if I hadn't helped him out.'

He led her down a flight of steps to a basement shop. Thin fingers of sunlight filtered into it through small, grubby windows, and a musty smell permeated the air. A solitary electric bulb hung from the ceiling. The room was filled with stacks of shelves packed with boxes. A stepladder with a handrail running up each side stood in one of the aisles. There was a counter near Harry with an inner doorway beyond. A tapping sound approached from the other side of it, and what looked like a desiccated corpse holding a heavy walking stick emerged. He shuffled around the counter and leered at Harry.

'So you want a job, d'you, boy?' He poked her with his stick. 'Not got much in the way of muscle, have you?'

Harry pushed the stick away.

'I've got more muscle than you. I could easily snap your neck, hang you up and jug you like a hare.'

'None of that, lad.' Jack nudged her jaw with his knuckles. 'Learn some manners, before someone tries teaching you.'

'I ain't taking on someone who gives me that kind of lip,' Bob said. 'I expect a bit of respect from my employees.'

'You're going to give him a chance, Bob. Adam reckons he's got potential.'

Bob bit his lower lip and shrugged. The two of them haggled over her proposed wages until Bob gave in to Jack's higher offer. Jack winked at her.

'You hent told me the rent yit,' Harry said.

'Well, let's say a hundred a week.'

'A hundred? For jist a bed?'

'It's not just a bed,' Jack said. 'It's breakfast as well, not to mention tea and coffee.'

'I was thinkin' more on sixty.'

Jack leant back against the counter and took out a cheroot.

'Sixty? Are you kidding me?'

'Not at orl, Jack, but I need to think about other things, like wittles and clothes.'

'You don't know how lucky you are getting such reasonable accommodation, but I like you, so let's say ninety.'

Harry picked at a bit of dirt under a fingernail and looked back at him.

'That dunt leave me much from my wages. What if unforeseen expenses should crop up? What if I fare sadly? Can't you say seventy?'

Jack stroked his thin moustache with the unlit cheroot.

'Would you bankrupt me? And there's me giving you one night bed and breakfast free.'

'I appreciate your generosity, but I did say at the time I dint want to put you out.'

'Aren't you putting me out right now? I'm hurt, Harry. However, as I said, I like you. You've got a bit to learn, but I reckon you'll do, so let's say eighty, but that's my final offer.'

'Eighty? Well, okay.'

Jack put the cheroot to his lips and struck a match with his thumbnail.

'I usually ask for rent in advance, but I suppose you're not going to be able to manage it until you get your pay check at the end of the week.'

'Dunt you worry about that.' Harry rummaged inside her jacket. 'Spect you probably want a deposit as well.'

The deposit turned out to be the same as a week's rent, but Harry counted out the money and requested a receipt.

'A receipt?' Jack said as he flicked through the bundle of banknotes.

'Thass usual practice, hintut?'

Jack studied Harry, blew out a stream of smoke, tapped ash off his cheroot on to the floor and smiled.

'Sure.'

He took out a pad and pen from the inside of his trench coat and scribbled a receipt. Then he went through the inner doorway with Bob, leaving her behind. Harry wandered about, but the shop wasn't designed for browsing. There were no products on view and the boxes on the shelves just had alphanumeric codes written on them. The two men soon returned. Jack tucked a brown envelope inside his coat and left. Bob shuffled over to her.

'So, Mr Snotty I've-got-more-muscle-than-you, see if you can move that box up on to the top shelf. Or is it too heavy for you?'

He pointed to a box resting on the floor. Harry studied it, looked up at the shelf and fetched the stepladder. She bent her knees, shifted the box on to her shoulder, climbed the ladder and slid the box into place. Then she held the top of the ladder handrails, swung herself round and jumped down. Her hobnails slipped against the stone floor, and she slid over to the opposite shelf. She grabbed it and swung round as though it had been a planned manœuvre.

Bob raised his stick.

'What're you trying to do, boy? Smash through my floor?' The bell on the shop door rang, and Bob shuffled over to the counter. A man with a battered fedora low over his face and coat collar turned up approached him. Bob gestured to Harry with his stick.

'Hey, boy. Fetch the small box at the end of the third shelf, and no acrobatics.'

Harry brought it over. The man began to open the box but stopped and stared at her.

'Don't be so damn nosey,' Bob said to Harry. 'Clear off.'

She returned down the aisle and glanced back. The man peered into the box, handed Bob some money and took it away. There were more boxes to stack on the shelves, but she didn't attempt to find out what was in them.

Lunchtime came round, and Harry was allowed out. She bought a sandwich and drink from the newsagent, returned to the shop and settled down on the floor behind some packing cases where she ate her meal. Afterwards, she took out a document from the inside of her jacket, squinted at it, angled it to catch a few limp rays from the electric bulb but eventually gave up and folded it away. She was about to go back to work when she heard the front door opening. Footsteps approached. Bob's stick tapped in the other direction. Harry remained seated behind the cases and listened.

'Is that you, boy?'

'It's Adam. Where's Harry?'

'Out to lunch. Jack want him knocked about?'

'No. In fact, you're going to keep your stick away from Harry, or you'll get my fist in your face.'

'All right. Let me go. I won't touch the kid.'

'You'd better not.'

The footsteps retreated and the door slammed. There was a sigh and low mumbling. The stick tapped away and all was silent again.

Adam lounged on his bunk that afternoon, reading a history of the modern generator. Coming up next issue: a biography of Edward Bostock, inventor of the Type 1, plus pictures of his prototype, still in use today on his granddaughter's farm.

The front door clicked. It was too quiet to be Jack or Eric. Besides, they weren't due back from the gym yet. He raised the magazine in front of his face and peered around the edge of the page. Harry came into the room but didn't look in his direction. Instead, she sat down at the table, picked up the newspaper and began to flick through it. Adam was debating whether to join her or to adopt a nonchalant attitude and ignore her when she gave a start.

'What's up?' he said.

Harry flicked over the rest of the newspaper.

'All out for a hundred and seventy. I was hoping we would at least hold out for two hundred.'

'What?'

'Cricket.'

'Oh.'

'I'm going to make a coffee,' she said. 'D'you want one?'

'Yeah, all right. Milk, no sugar.'

Harry walked out of the room, and Adam jumped down from his bunk. A can crumpled beneath his shoe — the same one he had trodden on last night. He kicked the empty cans, packaging and dirty laundry under Eric's bunk and strolled over to the table. The newspaper was face down showing the sports results on the back page, but Harry had been looking somewhere in the middle of it. Probably wasn't anything important. She hadn't shut the paper properly. He slid his fingers in the gap and opened it. So what if she didn't want to tell him the truth? It wasn't like they were friends or anything. He sat down and began to skim through the page in front of him.

The Anti-Technology League: Luddites or Protectors of the Future?

Following the demonstrations in Central City against the proposal to allow computer use outside the public sector, our correspondent Ainsley McKee interviewed Fulton Robbins, president of the Anti-Technology League, and Ken de Saulles, chief spokesman for Sector House.

Not those damn Anti-Techs again. Adam skipped on to the next article.

Top Brain Surgeon Killed in Drink-Driving Crash

David Trescothic, leading brain surgeon at Colingham Private Hospital, was killed last night when his car hit a tree. He was taken to his own hospital but pronounced dead on arrival. 'It was most unlike him to drink before driving,' his P.A. Miss Alice Penderbury said, 'but he's been under tremendous strain lately.'

There was a picture of a grey-haired man with sideburns, and next to it was a photo of a car that had a one-way ticket to the scrapyard. Shame about the car — it looked like a Bentley.

Burnt Satellite Fragment
Hits Derelict Airport

A burning chunk of metal — all that was left of an old satellite — smashed into a disused hangar at the abandoned Norwich airport last night. 'It was an enormous fireball,' said Mrs Carpenter, a resident in the nearby housing estate, 'and there was an explosion that shook our flat so violently that the picture of my old mum fell off the shelf and broke. I was sure it was judgement day.'

Perhaps not the apocalypse, but was it a message to the people of our generation? Fulton Robbins, president of the Anti-Technology League, said: 'It's prophetic that one of these artificial abominations hit a symbol of past technology, but how many more of these monstrosities are still up there waiting to fall on us?'

That was a question we put to Professor Wainright at Colingham University. 'The medium orbit satellites may well take at least a hundred years to reach the atmosphere after burning up their fuel,' he said, 'but it was entirely coincidental that it happened to hit an old airport. I'm sure a divine message would have struck the airport in Central City [the only working airport in this sector] not some disused provincial airport. There's nothing supernatural about the incident.'

Others are not so convinced. 'There's something spooky about that place,' Mrs Carpenter stated. 'My neighbour Mrs Bacon swore she saw a ghost plane coming in to land last month, and the very next week she was dead.'

Adam heard Harry returning, so he flicked the newspaper closed and opened up his magazine. She put the mugs on the table and sat opposite him. She was still wearing her jacket and cap, as though she wasn't planning on staying.
'You serious about wanting to be a trucker?' he said.
'Better than being stuck in a basement shop.'
'I can give you lessons, but the chances are you won't get a job.'
Harry shrugged.
'Maybe if I can show I'm up to it, people might change their minds.'
'It's Jack's mind you need to change.'
'How much for lessons?'
'Jack worked out the costs. Hang on while I find it. I'm supposed to let you negotiate, but I can't be arsed, so let's pretend we've wasted ten minutes haggling.'

They finished their coffee and set off through the lanes, out of Jack's neighbourhood and along the streets lined with terrace houses. Adam dodged round a crowd that was spilling out of a bus shelter and, for a moment, he lost sight of Harry, but then he noticed her heading towards an alley. He called her back.
'I'm sorry,' she said. 'I thought I came out of there with Jack and Eric yesterday.'
'Yeah, they go that way, but we're going this way.'
'Is it a short cut?'
'No. You in a hurry or something?'
He walked faster. Harry's hobnails clicked on the pavement behind him, but he didn't look back at her until they reached the depot. He led her through the gates, past the parking bays and into the grey two-storey building.

'We have to sign the keys in and out here.' Adam leant against a hatch frame in the corridor. 'Hiya, Ned. Jack spoken to you about me taking Harry for a ride?'

The man on the other side of the hatch grinned, displaying a gold tooth.

'Sure.' Ned slid Adam's truck key across the counter while Adam scrawled his name in the book. 'You might want to get the kid a pair of stilts so he can reach the pedals.'

Adam picked up the key and looked back at Harry, but she had turned away and was inspecting a wall map.

'I take it this is your route,' she said as she traced the highlighted line with a forefinger.

'Yeah, that's right,' Adam said.

'What's this blob here?'

'That's Betsy's Café.' Adam lounged against the wall next to the map and twirled the truck key around his thumb. 'We stop there on Monday and Thursday nights.' Harry was still staring at the map, her finger resting on Betsy's street just below the junction where Sector House stood. 'Come on, let's go.' He led her outside and over to his lorry. 'Jack's trucks are all based on the Bedford OS model with a van body. Four wheels, as you can see, ten feet long, three ton with spiral bevel rear axle and hydraulic brakes. But it has five gears instead of four, and obviously the engine had to be redesigned for biofuel.'

He unlocked the lorry and, once they were in, he pulled out of the depot and continued talking.

'Jack was thinking about replacing the trucks with the long-wheelbase model a few years ago, but the Anti-Techs keep pressing for further restrictions on vehicle sizes, and he didn't want to risk having to scrap a new fleet of trucks.'

'I'm surprised that a change in the law would make much of a difference to him.'

'You ain't about to get up on your high horse about Jack, are you?'

'No, I just meant that he didn't seem the type to be easily intimidated by such things.'

'Damn right, he ain't, but an over-sized vehicle ain't exactly easy to hide. It's not like we're lawless, Harry. I mean, this ain't the anarchy. I ain't even packing a weapon — well, apart from my knife and sometimes I carry a blackjack and occasionally we need the guns — but what I meant was we don't usually go around waving our tommy guns about in public places just for the hell of it.'

Adam slowed down as he approached a junction.

'My Uncle Barney once told me that lorries used to be huge before the fuel crisis,' Harry said.

'Yeah, sure, that's right. Jack told me when he was a kid he saw one so big it took up two lanes and had to have a police escort.'

Adam drove out of the city and headed south until he reached the gravel quarry. He pulled up in the shadows between two mounds of sand, put the brake on and turned to Harry.

'Out you get then. We'll swap over and you can have a go.'

Harry undid her belt but paused with her hand on the door latch.

'What's up?' Adam said.

'You're not going to let me out and drive off without me?'

'Bloody hell, Harry. You ain't half paranoid.'

'I'm sorry,' she said. 'Empty quarries conjure up all kinds of images.'

'You're nuts, you are.'

'No, I'm not. And I'm not paranoid, either. I just happen to be careful.'

'Are you going to get out or are we going to climb over each other?'

'All right, I'll get out.'

She jumped down and walked around the front, eyeing him. He slid over to the passenger seat and waved the truck key at her so that she could see it wasn't in the ignition. She clambered into the driver's seat, and he gave her the key.

'Step one: turn on the ignition,' he said.

'I've driven lorries laden with hay bales. Long-wheelbase and much heavier than this truck. And it wouldn't have made a difference to us if the Anti-Techs had managed to get the law changed.'

'You know I've half a mind to ask Jack to tell you to pack your bags — if you had any.'

'I just meant that agricultural vehicles are exempt as long as they spend most of the time off-road. I've had plenty of practice driving heavy vehicles, so you don't need to start at the very basics.'

'Well, go on then. Let's see your brilliant driving skills.'

Harry started the engine and drove around the quarry. Adam watched her hands, feet and face. All right, so maybe she could drive as well as she said, and maybe it had sounded a bit condescending when he'd told her to turn on the ignition, but it had just been a joke. She needn't have got so uptight about it. How the hell was he supposed to talk to her? One minute it was like talking to a bloke, next minute she was being all defensive.

'All right, Harry. That's enough or Jack'll be charging for the extra fuel. Swap over and we'll head back.'

— 5 —

WANTED

Adam drove back to the city, with Harry once more in the passenger seat, pulled into the depot and returned his truck key. He then led her to Jack's regular café where they had eaten the previous evening. The glass front door opened into an area that the proprietor liked to designate as the lobby, but it was just a corner of the café that had a latticed fence to separate it from the main room. The lobby contained a collection of potted plants, a large gilt-framed mirror mounted on the side wall, and next to that was a general noticeboard. It was around this board that they found Jack and Eric watching P.C. Donnaghan pinning up a missing-person notice. It looked like the lousy copper was trying to grow a moustache — and failing. Just a few stupid bristles sticking out in all directions like a balding hedgehog.

'Hey, Adam,' Jack said. 'Take a look over here. How's this for a sweet little face?'

Adam glanced at the poster but then stopped and stared. The pale, porcelain-like skin and long, golden tresses were unfamiliar, and the clear blue eyes had a seemingly gentle, innocent expression, but he recognised the long, thin nose and the jaw line.

'She sure is something, isn't she?' Jack said. 'Have we finally found a pretty face that's caught your eye, my lad?'

'I ain't saying she's caught my eye.'

'Sure you're not.' Jack put a hand on Adam's shoulder. 'You're just taking a good look so you can recognise her if you see her hitching a lift.'

'Yeah, keep your eyes peeled,' Eric said. 'Donnaghan says there's a sector-wide search for her.'

Adam risked a glance at Harry. She was standing by a potted aspidistra near the front door. The plant was on a high stand and overshadowed her. A red glow from the neon sign outside filtered through the leaves creating a stippled effect that seemed to highlight her weather-beaten face.

Donnaghan hitched up his trousers. The lousy cop was always doing that. Why didn't he get himself a uniform that fitted for a change or did he reckon it made him look important?

'That's right,' Donnaghan said to Eric. 'Her fiancé is offering a generous reward for her safe return.'

'Fiancé?' Adam said. 'He ain't much good at being a fiancé if he's lost her.'

'That's just what I'd expect from you,' Donnaghan said. 'You wouldn't know how to look after a woman.'

'And you look after them so well,' Adam said but stopped when he felt Jack tapping his shoulder.

The lousy cop was always making insinuations — which was a damn nerve given what he was like — but Adam had Jack with him, so the bastard had better not try anything.

'Donnaghan told us she's nuts,' Eric said.

'Don't be putting words in my mouth, Eric. According to the report, she has a brain tumour that's affected her reasoning. It triggered a delusional state, and she ran away before the doctor was able to sedate her.'

'Yeah, she's nuts.'

'Well, I ain't looking for her,' Adam said. 'It might be contagious.'

'Don't be stupid,' Eric said. 'You can't catch a brain tumour.'

'Don't call me stupid.'

'Pack it in, both of you,' Jack said. 'Anyway, didn't you hear Donnaghan say there's a reward for her return?'

'For her safe return,' Donnaghan said.

'You going to personally see to that?' Adam took a step towards the cop, but Jack tightened his hold and pulled Adam back. 'So what's the reward, anyhow?'

'A generous one.'

'Generous is a relative term,' Jack said. 'How about a number?'

'I don't know. It isn't on the poster.'

Adam laughed.

'Yeah, it's a real big reward, ain't it? So big they can't fit it on the piece of paper. Chances are it's just a handshake, and I ain't touching anyone's hand.'

'Who wrote up this poster?' Jack said. 'It hardly says anything. Where was she last seen?'

'She lives in West Norfolk,' Donnaghan said.

'You're a genius, aren't you, Donnaghan? That's the one bit of information that's actually written on the damn thing. Could you perhaps be a little bit more specific?'

Harry walked over to them and put her hands in her jacket pockets.

'The Wynherne Estate is abowt half way atwin here and Central City,' she said. 'Every one know about the Coulgranes back home. The estate go on for miles south o' the road we come in on.'

'Bet you didn't know that, did you, Donnaghan?' Adam said. 'You ain't as savvy as you think.'

'It's not my fault if they didn't send all the information. Country folk don't seem to realise anything exists beyond their borders.'

'Thass not true,' Harry said. 'We orl know abowt the city back home. Folk often mardle abowt the city. There's a statue o' her great-granfar outside the town hall in Great Bartling. He's on a rearin' hoss with a lance through a raider and another raider crushed beneath the hoss's hooves, and every time we see it, we say, "D'you rackon they'll come back?" And the old blokes have a laugh and say, "Not bloody likely." '

Alf, Hector and Spike entered the café and shouldered Donnaghan out of the way. Eric filled them in, with some embellishment.

'Orl this song and a dance for one mawther,' Harry said, 'but nowun care about a poor farmer woss lorst everythin'.'

'Sure, our hearts bleed for you,' Jack said. 'Isn't that right, lads?'

'I spect she'll be found when someone fy-out the ditches. Only t'other week the old doctor wuz found in one.'

'You sure are an optimist, Harry. You don't think maybe she's running around a field somewhere or hitching a lift? Would you have recognised her if you'd seen her?'

'Ah yis, we orl woulda, but I dint see no fine ladies. Jist a cuppla Massey Fergusons and a Fordson. We hed a Massey Ferguson that belonged to my granfar from afore the anarchy. That lasted us a masterly long time.'

The café door opened again, letting in a blast of cold air, and Rita entered the lobby.

'What's going on? Why the big crowd? Move out the way, Spike, and let me through.'

'Come on, kid,' Adam said to Harry. 'There's too many germs in a crowd.'

He shoved Harry into the main part of the café, nodded at some of the patrons he recognised, sauntered over to a table and slumped into a chair. Harry sat next to him, and they were soon joined by Jack, Eric and Rita. Eric pulled up a seat on the other side of Adam, and Rita took the place opposite Adam. She opened up a compact and smoothed out her eyebrows.

'You want to move down a seat?' Jack said to her.

'I'm not sitting opposite that kid again, thank you very much.'

'Then shift over in front of Eric.'

'I'm not playing musical chairs.'

'All right, but make sure you don't wind Adam up.'

Jack selected the chair opposite Harry, and Lise the waitress came over to take their order. Adam shared his menu card with Harry — not that there was a great deal of variety since all the items seemed to involve chicken or beans or chips or a combination thereof. They ended up selecting the same meal they'd had the previous evening. Lise headed off to the kitchen, and a nineteen-year-old lad slid into the spare seat next to Rita.

'How's things, gorgeous?' he said, leaning towards her.

Rita smiled and nudged him.

'What're you after, Masher?'

'Just came over to meet the new boy. Reckoned he might want help settling in.'

'Beat it, Ralph,' Jack said.

'Aw, Jack, you know I don't like being called that. I'm Masher, I am.'

'I'll mash you if you give me any lip.'

'Give him a break, Jack,' Rita said. 'He's just being sociable.'

'I'll tell you who I'd like to be sociable with,' Masher said. 'That cute little number in the poster.'

'Jack told you to beat it, Ralph,' Adam said.

Masher yawned and went over to join one of the other tables. Adam could see him nudging his neighbour and gesturing at Harry. For a moment, Adam toyed with the idea of going over and smacking him in the face, but he decided that probably wouldn't be such a good idea.

'Why don't you ever give that kid any encouragement?' Rita said to Jack. 'You're always putting him down.'

'I don't like him.'

'And you sure aren't one for hiding your likes and dislikes, are you?'

'Why should I?'

Lise came over with plates balanced on her wrists but, as she passed Masher's table, he patted her backside.

'Hoy, Ralph,' Jack said. 'Keep your hands to yourself. This isn't a damn petting zoo.'

Everyone turned to look at the boy and some of them sniggered.

'For crying out loud, Jack,' Rita said. 'He was just having a bit of fun. She's only a waitress.'

'What's the point in people having my protection if they can't rely on it? Besides, I don't want my dinner on the floor.'

Lise brought the food over, thanked Jack and moved to a different table, notepad at the ready.

'How much d'you reckon the fiancé is prepared to pay?' Rita said. 'I suppose if he's keen on her he might be open to negotiation.'

'Sure, but I reckon you ought to find her before you start haggling over her.'

'She's going to be hard to miss,' Rita said. 'Have someone check out the refuge, and tell your truckers to keep an eye out for her. If your people don't find her, I'm sure one of mine will.'

Adam gripped his table knife so tightly that his knuckles turned white.

'Make sure they treat her nice or he might not want her back,' Jack said.

'Thass true. She do stand out a bit,' Harry said. 'She'd hev stood out on my farm, thass for sure.'

Eric shovelled a forkful of chips into his mouth. He leaned forwards and stared around Adam at Harry, his jaws chomping up and down, but eventually he swallowed.

'Did you ever used to go about with a shotgun saying, "Get orf my land"?'

'Only once that I recall. That wunt long arter my Uncle Barney died, and I wunt feelin' sociable.'

'Did you shoot?' Jack said.

Adam reached for the jug of water and glanced at Harry.

'No, he cleared off hully quick.' She held her glass out to Adam, and he filled it for her. 'We useter be a fare full house when I was young. There was me and my brother, our parents, Uncle Barney, Aunt Hilda, Grandpa Eddie and Grandma Izzy, Grandpa George and Grandma Josey, and there wuz also Great-Grandpa Reggie.'

'That's a full house,' Jack said. 'You must've all been stacked on top of each other.'

'Oh, and there wuz also Uncle Freddy, but he hed an accident with the Mark B generator. Mind you, he kept us well supplied with electricity for a time arter his death.'

'What the hell's that supposed to mean?' Rita said.

Jack signalled to Adam for a top-up.

'Apparently there's a generator that runs on animal and human remains,' Jack said.

'Well, he wuz dead, and we coont find no way to get the body out. Not that we use that generator no more. No one wanted to go near it arter that, so we jist left it in the shud.'

She frowned. 'I should've scrapped it.'

'Has anyone in your family ever died of old age?'

Harry tapped her fingers on the table for a moment.

'My great-granfar died when he wuz a hundred and two.'

'That's a good long run,' Jack said.

'Mind you, he dint die of old age. He fell orf the top o' a haystack.'

'You don't half talk some bull,' Rita said.

'Now, Rita love, don't be like that.'

'Oh come off it, Jack. He's making it up, especially the bit about the generator. That's a load of bull.'

'No it ain't,' Adam said.

'Oh, and you know Harry's life story, do you?'

'No, but I know a damn sight more about generators than you do.'

'You clearly want to know a damn sight more about Harry than anyone else does.'

Adam leapt to his feet.

'What's that supposed to mean?'

'Sit down, Adam,' Jack said. 'And, Rita, just don't go there. I was stuck in Central City for two days thanks to those damn Anti-Techs, and now I'm back I'd appreciate being able to eat my dinner in peace.'

The rest of the meal passed without further bickering. There were sour looks between Rita and Adam, but Jack was used to that, and so far there hadn't been any accusations of either of them kicking the other. At least Harry had remained quiet. The bill was settled, and Jack strode over to the lobby where he found Rita standing in front of the mirror applying cream to her face.

'Rita love, the sun's almost set,' he said. 'You can't need that much cream.'

'There's still some sun out there, and we all know how harmful it is.'

'It isn't that bad.'

Jack leant against the doorpost and waited for the other three. Eric had gone to the gents, and Adam, with Harry tagging along, had stopped to talk to Alf. Rita dipped her fingers into the pot and scooped out another dollop of cream.

'Have you seen Harry's face?' she said. 'That's the sun what's done that. Is that how you want me to end up?'

She remained facing the mirror as she spoke, and the tarnishes where the silver backing had been damaged made it seem as though she had grey blotches over her cheeks.

'Harry's worked outdoors all his life,' Jack said. 'You don't get like that walking in the dusk with a parasol and hat.'

'That kid's mental. You mark my words: he'll end up in a straitjacket and a pair of electric handcuffs, and it'll be the sun what's done it. I ain't taking no chances.'

'Well hurry up.'

Eric came out of the gents and joined Adam and Harry. Jack gestured to them, strode out of the café and took out a cheroot. They followed him outside while Rita remained in front of the mirror.

'Here, Jack,' Adam said, 'd'you mind if I don't come to the pub? Harry'd like to see my car.'

'Sure. Anything for a bit of peace and quiet.'

'Cheers, Jack.'

He and Harry walked away, Harry chatting about cars, but Adam seemed unusually quiet. At least, it was unusual for him to be quiet when the topic was about something mechanical. Jack twirled the cheroot around his fingers.

'It ain't like Adam to let anyone near his car,' Eric said.

'Hopefully it'll keep them both out of trouble for the evening. Maybe it'll do Adam good to have a friend to hang out with.'

Jack struck a match, lit his cheroot and glanced through the window. Rita was now applying cream to her throat.

'I ought to buy shares in that stuff,' he said.

He leant against a lamp post and blew out a smoke ring. Eric put his hands in his pockets and rocked on his feet. The door opened. Rita stepped outside and put up her parasol.

'You got rid of the brat?' she said to Jack.

'I told Adam to take him back. I'm not having a kid cramp my style in the pub. Are we ready?'

'Don't look at me: I ain't holding anyone up,' Rita said and flounced off down the street with her left hand on her hip.

The Crown and Mitre was on the corner between Jack and Big Stan's neighbourhoods and had a mixture of people from both territories. Big Stan O'Brien was already sitting at a table near an inglenook with Seán, Ciaran and Niall on either side of him. He was using his hat as a fan, and his balding head glowed red from the light of the fire. All it needed was for someone to shove an apple in his mouth for him to play the part of a roasting hog. His nose looked as though it had once collided with a brick wall. His ear had a chunk missing.

'How's it going, Jack?' Stan's chair creaked as he leant back and raised his glass to Jack. 'I hear you got stuck in Central City.'

Jack and Eric sat down on an upholstered bench by the window opposite the others, and Rita pulled up a chair at the end of the table.

'Tell me about it, Stan,' Jack said. 'Where'd you get to last night?'

'Hershey knocked off the jewellers down West Street.'

Jack leant back against the wall and blew out a stream of smoke. The thud of darts sounded in the alcove on the other side of the fireplace.

'I heard his guns going. Isn't that place owned by one of your relatives?'

'Sure it is. So as you can imagine, I'm not too happy about it.'

'Hershey's getting to be a cocky little bastard.'

'That's what I was thinking, and I was also thinking that maybe you'd like to help me teach him a lesson.'

The bar behind Stan was beginning to get crowded. Bob shuffled over to it and perched on a stool between a lanky youth and one of Jack's truckers.

'Well, I don't know, Stan,' Jack said. 'It would require a bit of planning to do the job properly, and he hasn't inconvenienced me.'

Stan leant forward, reeking of stout.

'So far, but that might change given the way he's going. We could split his territory half-way. He's got that nice little place down by the river you could have.'

'All right, but it'd have to be done properly.'

'And there's no one better at planning a thing like that than you.'

Jack looked over to the bar, about to catch the landlord's eye, when Masher slid into the seat next to Rita.

'I've got you a drink, Rita.'

'That's real sweet of you, Masher.'

'Yeah, real sweet of you, Ralph,' Jack said.

'I didn't see you offering me a drink.'

'I've only just sat down.'

Jack signalled to the landlord, and a barmaid was dispatched to take his order. The youth next to Bob moved his hand towards the old man's jacket.

'Stan,' Jack said, 'Benny's in danger of losing his fingers.'

'Neutral ground, Jack.'

'Which is why he should be keeping his fingers to himself instead of poking them into people's pockets.'

Stan twisted round in his seat.

'Benny, go play with your brother.' The youth sloped off, and Stan turned back to Jack. 'He can't help it. Half the time his head doesn't know what his hands are doing.'

Pool balls clicked against each other on the far side of the pub. Most of the patrons were grouped according to their territories, except for those around the bar. Occasionally there'd be some jostling, but the landlord only needed to glance in Jack and Stan's direction for things to subside.

One of the logs on the fire crackled and spat out sparks on to the hearth. A shadow fell over the table, and Jack looked up to see Chief Constable Ethan Hall with a face as sore as a kid who'd been grounded for a month. He had an old scar that bisected one of his blond eyebrows, and he was flanked, as usual, by D.I.s van Loame and Cornell. Van Loame also had a scar, but his was across the left side of his jaw, and his nose was bent — a memento from the time he had attempted to arrest Hammer Harmer. The Chief Constable grabbed the back of a chair with both hands as though planning to rip it in half.

'What's up, Ethan?' Jack said. The barmaid brought over a tray of drinks. 'Bring us another three pints, Kitty.'

'Do I look fat?' Ethan said.

'Not a bit. Who's been putting that idea in your head?'

'It'll be the mother-in-law,' Stan said. 'It's always the mother-in-law behind that kind of comment. Tell her it's insulation.'

'Tell her to take a hike,' Jack said.

'Don't mind Jack, Ethan. He's ignorant about in-laws.'

'And I'm happy to keep it that way, Stan.'

'I'm all for the married state,' Ethan said, 'but it would be better if the in-laws didn't live in the same house — or in the same county for that matter.' He sat down, and his D.I.s pulled up the chairs on either side of him. 'She's just trying to stir things up because I didn't like her new hat.'

'Talking about in-laws,' Jack said. 'Stan, your brother-in-law's third cousin's whatsit was over at the café.'

Ciaran thumped his beer mug down on the table. His face bore his usual thuggish scowl.

'Don't say Donnaghan and Adam have had another disagreement,' Stan said. 'They've got to learn to put the past behind them.'

'I was curious about the poster he's pinning up all over the place.'

'Which one?' Ethan said. 'We get so many I lose track.'
'Lady Coulgrane from the Wynherne Estate.'
The pub was full of the usual sounds, but a gasp and a movement by the bar caught Jack's attention. Bob swivelled round on his stool, his front splashed with beer.
'Oh, the china doll,' Ethan said. 'Poor girl. She's the type who's usually found dead.'
'That may cause a problem given her family history.'
Bob was straining forwards in his seat. If the old man's lids opened any wider, his eyeballs would be rolling about on the floor like a pair of marbles.
'Seems like you know more than me,' Ethan said. 'The name rang a bell, but we hardly got any information.'
'Yeah, I noticed the poster was a bit sparse. Her family were big during the anarchy. Apparently there's a statue of her great-grandfather taking out a couple of raiders in one of their market towns.'
Bob slid off his seat and glanced around the pub. The fire shot up a spout of blue-green flame as it reached a nail in one of the logs. Bob jumped, stumbled back and knocked into his stool.
'They're all savages in the country,' Stan said. 'Half of them don't seem to know the anarchy's over.'
'It's coming back to me now,' Jack said. 'Ethan, d'you remember when we were kids we were told of some big old place in West Norfolk?'
'Sure, that's right. A spooky mansion with a high wall, and people who went there never came back.'
Bob ran the back of his hand across his mouth.
'They had everything you could dream of –' Jack waved his cheroot in the air '– but they had their own private army protecting the place.'

'Each soldier was seven foot tall in full armour with two-handed swords and battle-axes.'

'It weren't no laughing matter,' Bob said. He took a step towards their table and then backed away, twisting his stick with both hands.

'What's got you so jumpy, Bob?' Jack said.

'Nothing.'

Bob turned to go, but Eric planted himself by his side, dwarfing the old man.

'Jack asked you a question.'

'They ain't coming here, are they?'

Jack leant back in his seat, drew on his cheroot and breathed out smoke. The old man was squeezing his bad leg with one hand.

'You were a raider,' Jack said.

'It was every man for himself back then. What were we supposed to eat. Bricks?'

'How many of you came back from your raid on the Wynherne Estate?'

Bob chewed on his lower lip, shuffling from one foot to the other.

'Just me.'

'What's eating you? Reckon the old earl's going to come here to take out the one they missed? Well you can relax, the old fellow's dead.'

'It weren't just the old one. It was the other ones—especially *him*.'

'Who?'

'I don't know his name. Maybe he's her father, for all I know. I ain't having nothing to do with any of them.'

He turned round and shuffled away.

※

'What d'you think?' Adam said. 'The exterior's based on the 1930 Ford Model A Phaeton convertible with ten fin per inch radiator. Inside it's got a six cylinder engine with a reciprocating rotary injection pump and electric fan. It's got extra safety features that the original didn't have, such as a collapsible steering wheel, and later I'll fix in the seat belts: two in the front, three in the back.'

He flicked off a bit of dust from the mudguard. The basement car park below their lodgings was mostly dim, but Jack'd had an extra light installed above Adam's place and a fan to improve the ventilation where he worked. The bay to the left had his bike and locker, and the one on the right was always kept vacant, which gave him a fair bit of room to work around the car.

'Have you been working on it long?' Harry asked.

'Couple of years, but I ain't around much.'

Adam picked up a cloth and polished one of the chrome headlamps. He could see her reflection in it, distorted by the curve of the metal. Harry tilted her cap back.

'It must be nice to have your own space away from everyone else.'

'Damn right. D'you want to work on it with me?'

'I'd like that.'

They went upstairs to the flat and brought down Adam's toolbox and a box containing clamps, brackets, hoses and bits of cable. He took out a pair of overalls from his locker, hung up his jacket and perched his fedora over one of the bike helmets on the top shelf. He turned his back on her and stepped into his overalls.

Why had he asked her to work on his car? She'd better not make a mess of it. He never let anyone near his Phaeton — except Jack, of course, only he wasn't interested in engines.

And Eric had given a hand with some heavy lifting, but that was it. She might've said she had some lousy fiancé lurking around in the background. Some bloke with a lot of money and influence, no doubt. Sure, Adam could picture him: a fellow who'd had all the breaks. The kind of git who was just the type to get engaged to a title. Probably had no chin and an affected voice. Maybe they'd had a spat, but he'd find her and they'd make up, and it'd be see-ya, nice knowing-ya.

Adam yanked up his zip. Harry was squinting and shielding her eyes from the light. There couldn't be any truth about the tumour, could there? It'd be just like Donnaghan to get the report wrong. Probably made the whole thing up so he could spin a story to get attention. Adam lifted the cowling.

'How's your head?' he said without looking at her.

'Why d'you ask?'

'There ain't much ventilation down here, so say if you need a bit of air.'

'There's a fan on.'

'What of it? Anyway, I've already made a start on the wiring loom. Can you get under the engine bay? You should see it coming through.'

Harry wriggled under the car.

'Yes, I see it.'

'Here, you'll need the handbrake cable.'

He fetched it from the box and placed it on her upturned palm. Her skin was rough with little scars, like you get when you work with machines a lot. Maybe he'd got it wrong. The similarity between Harry and the missing lady could just be a coincidence, but then he remembered how her accent had slipped from Broad Norfolk to refined tones. He peered through the engine bay and watched her connect the cable.

'So, you've got a fiancé, have you?'

'Since when has "I'd rather been dead in a ditch" been a coy way of saying "Oh yes, I'd love to marry you"?'

'So there ain't much truth in that poster?'

'About as much truth as the report that a herd of pigs have been engaged in aerobatics over The Wash.' She wriggled out from under the car and dusted herself down. 'That's the handbrake connected to the loom. What next?'

'The radiator needs connecting to the pump,' he said. She fetched a hose and clamps from the box while Adam checked the mounting tabs. 'Did the co-codamol help last night?'

'Yes, thanks.'

'D'you need any more?'

'Maybe.'

She held the hose over the lower flange while he clamped it into place.

'How often d'you take them?'

'If you really must know, I've woken up with a headache every morning for the past two months, except today. I think working in Bob's shop triggered one: it's pretty airless in there.'

Yeah, that was true enough. Jack had often joked about Bob's place being like one of those tombs that archaeologists discover, but that didn't explain the last two months. Maybe the would-be fiancé had spiked her water or food, like that story Spud had once told about some bloke who'd poisoned a girl because she'd given him the rub.

Harry pressed the other end of the hose on to the water pump inlet, and Adam leant over to fasten the clamp in place. Her hair brushed against his cheek. There was a lingering smell of biofuel.

'So is he the fellow you're running from?' Adam said, but Harry walked away and fetched another hose and more clamps from the box. 'It ain't surprising you're so jumpy if some sleazy bastard's telling everyone he's your fiancé.' She returned to the car but stopped to rub her forehead. 'You okay?'

'I'm fine.'

'Don't bite my head off,' he said. 'I ain't trying to marry you.' She leant over the engine bay and pressed the hose over the upper flange, and Adam clamped it in place. 'So what happened yesterday that made you leg it without even a change of clothes?'

She straightened up and put a hand on her hip.

'I was forced to embed a pair of scissors into his leg.'

'Scissors?'

'I happened to have a pair in my hand. It was his own stupid fault.'

Adam leant back against the car radiator and folded his arms across his chest.

'What about your assassin's weapon you've got hidden in your jacket?'

'It's not an assassin's weapon.'

'What is it then?'

Harry tucked her hand inside the back of her jacket and pulled out a stick about a foot in length and an inch in diameter with a walnut veneer.

'This is it,' she said.

'Are those bite marks?'

'My dogs got hold of it, but it's useful because if anyone sees it, I can say it's their fetching stick.'

'So it's just a stick?'

Harry held it in front of her. Both ends shot out until they were six feet apart. Adam instinctively reached for the knife strapped to his ankle but then pretended that he was merely scratching his leg.

'That's quite a kick,' he said. 'You could punch a hole in a man's skull with that.'

'Yes. It also goes to half length.'

The stick retracted until it was three feet in length. It then collapsed to its original size. There was a slight swishing sound that suggested some kind of hydraulic system. He couldn't see a control panel, but the tendons on the back of her hand flexed every time she activated it, so there must be hidden buttons beneath her finger tips.

'Sweet,' Adam said. 'Where'd you get it?'

'From someone my Uncle Barney knew.'

'You should get him to deal with that fiancé.'

'Don't call him that. He's not my fiancé.'

'So what shall I call him?'

'I usually go with "the git" or sometimes "the obnoxious bastard".'

Harry tidied the stick away. Adam watched her fiddling with something behind her back and decided that there must be some straps on the lining of her jacket that kept it in place.

'Have your family come down in the world?' he said.

Harry turned back to the engine bay and picked up the unattached end of the second hose.

'Are we going to fix this to the pump?'

'I'm sorry. I didn't mean to be tactless.'

'Allerton lent Dad some money after Uncle Barney died. Unfortunately I was out at the time.'

That went a long way to explaining why she seemed so cagey about money. The bastard had probably failed to mention about interest and other fees to her Dad. Hardly surprising she'd stabbed him.

'The poster didn't say nothing about the cops being after you for assaulting anyone.'

'He has an image to preserve,' Harry said. 'I may not have the influence my family once had, but my godmother's pretty important in our neighbourhood. She believes Allerton is the perfect gentleman who has only my best interests at heart. He's not going to risk losing that impression.'

'Won't she think differently when she hears you had to stab him?'

Harry waggled the free end of the hose back and forth.

'He'll say it's proof that I'm not well. I expect he's being very gentlemanly about it.'

'So get a scan to show you ain't got a tumour. I could have a word with Jack, and he'd fix it up for you.'

'No thank you.' She shoved the hose into his hands. 'Anyway, I've already had a scan and it was negative.'

He handed the hose back to her.

'So what's the problem? You must have some paperwork you can show your godmother.'

'Unfortunately I don't any more. At least, not the right paperwork.'

'What d'you mean?'

Harry laid the loose end of the hose on top of the water pump and stared for a moment at the engine before looking up at Adam.

'The letter I received from the specialist has been replaced by a fake saying that the scan was positive.'

Adam scratched his chin and then fetched a clamp from the box. He tossed it up in the air and caught it.

'So you're saying that it's been swapped by this bloke — what's his name — Allerton?'

'I came back home yesterday to find Allerton running out of the house, saying that my father was having a fit and that he was going to fetch help. I found my father dead and the filing cabinet drawer was ajar. I know my father wouldn't have opened it.'

'Why not?'

'He never touched paperwork.'

'How come?'

'He had some kind of breakdown after my mother died and became a recluse, but even before then he just worked on the generators. Uncle Barney and I dealt with running the farm.'

'I take it you checked the filing cabinet and found the letter had been switched?'

'Yes.' Harry rummaged inside her jacket and produced a letter. 'This is what I found.'

Adam took a look. The top right corner had a logo depicting what was probably meant to be a happy healthy family, only they looked like they were being held in a giant's bodylock. The letter was signed by David Trescothic. Why did that name sound familiar?

'Have you tried asking this Trescothic bloke if he's got a copy of the original?'

'I was going to, but I made the mistake of not going to him immediately. I thought it would be too obvious to go straight to Colingham.'

The image of a smashed Bentley came back to Adam.

'Here, is he the fellow who wrapped his car round a tree last night?'

'Yes.'

'Did you show anyone the letter when you got it?'

Harry tucked it inside her jacket, turned back to the engine and picked up the hose.

'I didn't want to tell anyone in case Dad got to hear about it. I didn't want to worry him.'

She pressed the hose against the water pump outlet. It was a shame Harry didn't seem to want to trust Jack. He'd be able to sort everything out for her. Then again Rita would probably find out and try muscling in. Adam leant over and clamped the hose in place, only this time he decided that it would be more convenient to reach round her with one arm. A blond ringlet trailed down the back of her neck.

'You ain't done a very good job of cutting your hair.'

'I was in a hurry.'

'You missed a bit.' He touched the curl, and she straightened up. 'Jack'll get suspicious if he sees it. D'you want me to cut it for you?'

'Okay.'

He opened the scissor attachment on his penknife and, standing behind her, he snipped off the ringlet and tucked it into his pocket. He closed the cowling and went over to the locker.

'I'm surprised Jack ain't figured out you're a woman yet. Or Rita for that matter.' He opened up a tub of Swarfega and scooped out a glob. 'I'd stay out of her way if I was you. Don't let her into the flat when you're on your own. She's got a key, so you'll have to keep the door bolted.' He worked the dark green, gelatinous substance between his fingers and then took Harry's hands and rubbed it over her skin. 'I've got some old jeans and shirts you can have. I ain't worn them since Jack gave me a suit when I turned eighteen, but they might fit you if you roll the legs up and wear braces.'

He picked up a cloth and began to wipe the Swarfega off his hands.

'Thanks,' she said. 'Jack may have had a point about needing a change of clothes.'

'Yeah, well, you don't want to get second-hand clothes from someone you don't know.' He handed her the cloth. 'I mean, I ain't got nothing contagious, but you just can't tell with other people, can you?'

— 6 —

MEDICAL REPORTS

THE children were supposed to stay inside Wynherne Hall during an attack, but little Charlie Hadley climbed out of a first floor window and down a thick trunk of ivy that clung to the old building. The moon was full but a cloud had drifted across it. Watch fires blazed in the distance. The sound of vehicles came from the South West. The boy tiptoed round the mansion and headed into the coppice. Thin shoots from the alders and birches lashed against his face. He tripped on a fallen branch, but he picked it up and used it to help guide him along the path. He reached a wooden bridge over the stream and grabbed the handrail. The boards creaked beneath his feet and he could hear the water rushing and gurgling below. On the far side, he climbed the bank. Although the moon was still obscured, there were plenty of stars out and in their dim light he could see the low brick building ahead.

He crept up the path and peeped in through a window. No one was about. A lit lantern hung from the ceiling. Charlie eased up the door latch and went inside. Most of the racks were empty as many of the weapons were with the soldiers who were out in the grounds, but there were still some left here: swords, lances and a selection of bows — recurve, compound, long- and crossbows. There was also a stack of shields ranging from small and thin to the thickest, extra reinforced type that only the strongest men, such as Barney Coulgrane, could wield.

Charlie tried one of the smallest shields, but it was too heavy for him. He searched amongst the bows and found a lightweight recurve, slotted the limbs into the riser and tightened the bolts. Then he fitted one end of the string on to the lower limb, put the bow between his legs and bent it, pulling the other end of the string upwards. Inch by inch it neared the upper tip. His body began to shake. He gave an extra heave and pushed the looped string into its notch. Spasms shook his arms. He took a few deep breaths and flexed his muscles, then found a quiver full of arrows. The strap was too wide for his waist, so he slung it over his shoulder and headed out into the night.

The invaders were targeting the section where the boundary wall hadn't been completed. The air was full of the stench of the foul fuel used by the raiders. Charlie Hadley clutched his bow and ran across the meadow. The ground trembled with the thunder of horses' hooves as soldiers of the South West regiment headed over to the breach in the wall. Charlie stumbled on a tussock.

The cloud drifted away from the moon, and the land around him was lit in a white glow, mingled with the orange flames of the watchfires. Vehicles with metal plates fastened to their front and sides bumped over the ground, spewing black smoke from their exhausts. Shots rang out from them. Some missed their mark, some thudded against the extra-reinforced shields of the Wynherne soldiers, but sometimes a horse or rider fell. Crossbow bolts streaked back, their faint thwup sounds barely audible above the clamour. One of the vehicles turned in Charlie's direction. He jumped up, ran over to an old oak tree and scrambled up it. He nocked an arrow to his string, peered out from the branches and fired. It fell short.

An Andalusian horse, its armour glinting in the firelight, galloped towards the vehicle. Its rider had a lion painted on his breastplate, standing proudly on its four paws, its tail in the air. The rider's right hand grasped a lance. Bullets slammed into his shield, but neither horse nor rider flinched. The vehicle swerved round a watchfire. One of the raiders stood in the back, operating a mounted gun. The explosive shots from it stopped and were replaced by loud clicks. The man shouted. The vehicle's wheels began to spin in the mud. Charlie fired another arrow. It struck the leg of the man in the back, and he tumbled out. The vehicle pulled clear of the mud, swung round on to a lane away from the approaching rider, but the vehicle's front tyres tumbled into one of the covered spiked pits. The driver's face smashed against the mangled dashboard. The man next to him was flung out. He rolled around and pulled out a gun, but the rider bore down on him and plunged his lance into the man's chest.

The other raider, still with Charlie's arrow stuck in his leg, tried to crawl away. As the light from the watchfire fell on his face, Charlie realised that he was only a teenager. The rider wheeled round and headed towards him. The youth pulled out a small knife, but he might just as well have brandished a wooden spoon. The rider approached, but he reined in his horse, thrust his lance into the ground, dismounted and removed his helmet. It was Barney Coulgrane. He drew his sword, strode over to the youth and kicked the knife from his hand. He then put the sword tip to the lad's throat.

'If I ever see you on our land again, I will kill you. Go and tell everyone you meet what will happen to them if they try to invade the Wynherne Estate.'

The youth dragged himself backwards until he reached the trunk of the oak tree in which Charlie was hiding. His hands scrambled against the bark, and he pulled himself up and hobbled away. Charlie leant forwards. The branch beneath him creaked. Barney Coulgrane looked up, his sword at the ready. Then he smiled.

'Shouldn't you be in bed?'

Charlie clambered down. The captain of the South West regiment picked up the knife with his gauntleted hand and gave it to the boy.

'A souvenir. Now go back to bed.'

Detective Inspector Hadley sat at his desk and picked up an envelope from the pile of post that had just been delivered. He eased the point of his knife under the flap and slit it open, but he didn't remove the letter inside. Instead he studied the knife. It wasn't much to look at: just a black plastic handle and a two-inch blade. He'd made a leather sheath for it after Barney Coulgrane had given it to him. When anyone asked him why he kept an old blunt knife in his pocket, he would shrug and say that it was his letter-opener. He turned it over in his hands. An open folder lay on his desk. He looked down at the reduced copy of the portrait of Lady Coulgrane. She had the same nose and chin as Barney Coulgrane, and even the same blue eyes and blond hair — although in a completely different style — but her uncle had never had that wide-eyed wistful look.

Hadley and Fenning's office was arranged so that their desks faced each other with the window alongside the space in between. This meant that if Hadley glanced to his left, he could see out across the grassy square in the middle of Great Bartling. The statue of the old earl was at its centre, and the local volunteers were giving it its weekly clean. Even the most tearaway scamp in the district would think twice about scribbling on that landmark. On the other side of the square, the brewery lorry had pulled up outside the Prince of Wales pub, and Molly the barmaid was chatting with the driver.

Hadley heard voices in the corridor outside, the first of which he recognised as the deep brogue of D.I. Williams.

'Have you heard that blooda Quinn's refused our pay rise? The stingy bugger.'

Then came Fenning's merry voice:

'Dint you know he's spent orl the munny on moving the boundaries? Every time he change the constabularies, he hatta pay to make new charts and replace the old logos.'

'Blast it, we're in Norfolk, so we ought to be in the blooda Norfolk Constabulary not blooda Central Constabulary.'

The door opened and Fenning came into the office, but she poked her head back into the corridor.

'I'll be sure to tell Quinn next time I'm in Central City.'

She shut the door, hung her hat and coat on the stand, and slid her briefcase on to her desk. She flipped the catches.

'I've now a-come from visitin' the neighbourhood's most eligible bachelor, or so I've heard him described. Himpin' away on a fancy stick, he wuz, as pensy as a midnight woman the first time she gorn a-nijjertin'.' Fenning came over to Hadley and handed him a sheet of paper covered with names and addresses written in a flowery script. 'Mr Allerton gi' me that list o' Lady Coulgrane's friends. He say they know no more than a crow do bowt Sunday, but I assume you'll want to visit them.'

Hadley looked back at the photo and tapped his forefinger on the desk.

'Why'd she run off like that?'

Fenning perched on the edge of his desk and smoothed out a wrinkle in her trousers.

'I spuz that coulda bin shock,' she said. 'Mr Allerton's convinced she's gorta Colingham, but he dunt know what he's talking abowt. She's likelier to go to Central City do she want to hide.'

'The Colingham lot haven't turned up anything,' Hadley said, 'and it sounds like they've put every man on the job.'

He stood up and turned to the wall map. The Norfolk Constabulary was coloured yellow, but the western part of the county formed part of the pink bubble that defined the Central Constabulary, encompassing Leicester in its westernmost end to almost as far east as Swaffham. Hadley traced the west-east road from Central City to Norwich.

'She could've headed east,' he said.

He turned back to look at Fenning. She brushed a curl away from her eye.

'Yes, she coulda, or she coulda turned north towards Fakenham or south towards Thetford. She could also be hidin' in a barn or abandoned cottage or even in a tree house.'

'Is that where you'd hide?'

'No, I'd hide in yar attic,' she said. 'Do anyone hear the spars creakin', you could say thass high sprites.'

'This is serious.'

'I know, but we dunt hev the resources to go snoutin' round every abandoned cottage. Praps she think Mr Allerton'll press charges for assault, but he oont agree to make a public appeal to let her know she ent in trouble.'

'Why not?'

'He say he witnessed a murder in Central City and came here to escape reprisals from the notorious "Tommy Gun" Preston.' Fenning picked up Hadley's paperweight — an amethyst geode — tossed it up in the air and caught it. 'That dunt quite fit with my idea of an eligible bachelor. Tall, dark, handsome with a sight a munny, but on the run from the mob.'

Hadley moved closer to her. The stray curl fell across her right eye again. He brushed it back.

'No, that doesn't quite fit his image,' he said, 'but I don't understand is why she stabbed him in the first place.'

Fenning turned the paperweight round and about in her hands. The sunlight glinted off the purple crystals.

'Maybe he wunt behavin' in a gentlemanly manner. Dunt you trust them eligible bachelors.'

'The doctor was also on the premises.' Hadley picked up the photo and slid it back into the folder. 'Did you manage to get a description of any of the jewellery she took with her?'

'Ony the signet ring: gold with a carved lion. That was orl the information I could git from the housekeeper. Not even Mr Allerton could supply any information on that front, which is a bit of a rum'um.'

Hadley sat back down and picked up the envelope he had opened. It had the windmill logo of the Fen Bank stamped on it.

'You can't expect men to pay as much attention to jewellery as women.'

Fenning put down the paperweight and leant over the desk towards him.

'Praps not, but he's a bit of a cheapskate if he never buy his fiancée any jewellery — not even an engagement ring.'

'I hope you didn't say anything tactless to such a well-respected member of the community, Fenning.'

'I'm sure I wuz polite about it,' she said. 'Did you contact the pathologist?'

'Yes, but don't hold your breath: that could take weeks. They've got a backlog, and the recent protests have apparently made things worse.'

'What're protesters got to do with the pathologist?'

'He didn't say.' Hadley removed the letter from the envelope. 'I don't see why we can't have our own local expert.'

'Praps you should ask Commissioner Quinn for one.'

'Yes, of course, and I should also ask for a promotion and maybe he might even give me a new car for Christmas.'

He screwed up the empty envelope and threw it at her. She ducked and it missed her.

'Dr Carmichael dint seem to suspect foul play.' Fenning picked up the envelope and tossed it in the bin. 'Then agin, he seemed to fare sadly with that ding to his head and prickin' hisself with a needle.'

'Perhaps we ought to drop in at the surgery: he should've recovered by now.'

Dr Carmichael's surgery was in a small thatched cottage on the edge of the Wynherne Estate. It consisted of a reception area, a nurse's treatment room and the doctor's consulting room, which looked out on to the back garden. One wall was lined with shelves. The top three were packed with books, but the lower ones were empty. There were cardboard boxes piled on the floor, next to a stepladder.

The desk in the centre of the room was cluttered: prescription pads, stethoscope, calender, pen tray and ink bottle, and a framed photo of a middle-aged couple. The doctor was pale and slim with fair hair and round glasses. He was bent over the bottom drawer of the filing cabinet, clicking the folders across the runners. Hadley checked the capacitor indicator on his voice recorder, and Fenning sat by his side with her notepad at the ready.

'It'll be so much better when the health service gets computers again,' the doctor said. 'Although I suppose the rural practices will be the last to benefit.'

'I noticed the label on Lady Coulgrane's medicine bottle has Dr Barnes named as her G.P.,' Hadley said. 'Where is he? Has he moved?'

'No, he died.'

Carmichael clicked another folder forwards.

'How?'

'He drowned in a drainage ditch on his way back from a party.'

'Had he been drinking?'

The doctor closed the bottom drawer and pulled open the top one.

'He'd only had two glasses of wine, but the toxicology report found aspirin as well as alcohol. It wasn't a fatal overdose, but the combination would probably have caused disorientation.'

Fenning scribbled in her notepad. Even Hadley didn't completely rely on his voice recorder, and she was good at shorthand.

'Wuz that definitely an overdose?' she said.

'I suspect he lost count of how many he'd taken. You'd think a doctor would've known better.'

'You look very young,' Hadley said. 'How long have you been in practice?'

Carmichael turned to look at him and pushed his glasses up his nose.

'I qualified a year ago. Up until two weeks ago, I was at Colingham with Dr Gathercole. I'm sure he'll be happy to tell you anything you want to know about me.'

'I certainly didn't mean any offence, doctor, but if you've only been here a couple of weeks, you can't have seen much of Lady Coulgrane.'

'I haven't seen anything at all of her, except for a fleeting glimpse of her back yesterday.'

Hadley glanced at Fenning, and she raised her eyebrows. Carmichael resumed his search through the folders in the cabinet drawer.

'Ah, here's her file.' He pulled out a slim, green folder. 'I was looking for "Wynherne" instead of "Coulgrane". Oh, I sent off the earl's blood samples to Central City for analysis, but I've kept one back in cold storage in case the protesters block the delivery.'

'They've gone home by all accounts,' Hadley said, 'but that's a sensible precaution.'

Carmichael handed over the folder, and Hadley rested his voice recorder on the table, so that he had both hands free to browse through the file.

'But, doctor,' Fenning said, 'do you never meet Lady Coulgrane, when did you first larn about her state o' mind?'

'Mr Allerton described her symptoms while he drove me over there. He was very concerned about leaving her alone with her father in that condition.'

'I thought her dad collapsed time she wuz in church.'

'Mr Allerton told me she returned just as he was setting off to fetch help.'

Hadley lifted a letter out of the file. The top right corner had an image of a man, woman and child being hugged by a pair of large, disembodied arms.

'What d'you think caused the tumour?' he said.
'A genetic disposition.' Carmichael sat down and swivelled his chair round to face them. 'Her mother and brother both died of the same thing.'
Hadley read through the letter. It was addressed to Lady Coulgrane and stated that the scan conducted on the twelfth of the previous month had shown the presence of a glioblastoma intracranial tumour. The letter was signed by David Trescothic, neurologist at Colingham Private Hospital.
Carmichael picked up the voice recorder and peered at it.
'I hope you still don't mind the voice recorder,' Hadley said. 'I asked yesterday.'
'Not at all. I find it fascinating. D'you think that if we had wind-up computers, the Anti-Technology League might be happier about them?'
'I don't think that would work.'
'Perhaps they could be foot-powered,' Carmichael said, 'like sewing machines.'
'I don't thing that would work either. May I have it back?'
Carmichael turned the voice recorder round and pulled out the crank handle.
'If computers were foot-powered, it would counteract the problem of a sedentary lifestyle. You must be in your forties. Did you use a computer when you were a child, Inspector?'
'Yes, I did, but I'm only thirty-eight.'
'Including the Internet? Did you suffer any ill effects?'
'What kind of effects?'
'My supervisor at university did his Ph.D. thesis on the rise of mental health problems associated with Internet use.'
'You sounded keen on computers a moment ago.'
'Oh, they're useful for administrative work, and I'm glad they're allowed in hospitals to aid diagnosis and treatments,

but they need to be properly regulated. There was a very interesting article in the Journal of — what was it? Clinical Psychology? Or Psychological Assessment?'

He stood up and looked over the shelves.

'May I have my voice recorder back?'

'It must be in one of the boxes. I haven't had time to finish unpacking. It was all about how you can't get away from an argument on the Internet. More and more people contribute to it, and it never goes away, so there's no psychological closure. Perhaps you didn't use it long enough to have any lasting effect, or perhaps over time you've suppressed the memories of it.'

Fenning stood up, strode over to the doctor, took the voice recorder with her left hand, grabbed his hand with her other hand and pumped his arm up and down.

'Thank you for sparing us a moment of yar time, Dr Carmichael. We'd better leave you to finish yar unpackin' in peace and quiet.'

Hadley and Fenning stood by the front desk of Colingham Private Hospital. Next to them was the waiting area where people sat in armchairs reading glossy magazines. A sixteen-year-old girl was watering pot plants.

'I'm sorry, you can't see him,' the receptionist said to Hadley, 'Mr Trescothic was moved this morning.'

'Moved where?' Hadley took out his ID and flipped it open. 'This is a police matter.'

She looked at Hadley and then at Fenning.

'Excuse me, I won't be a moment.'

The receptionist opened a door behind her and spoke in a low voice. A man came out of the room, glanced at

Hadley and Fenning, and hurried away to another door. The receptionist returned to the desk.

'The Administrator will speak to you shortly.'

An elderly man came out of the second room, with the younger man following behind him. He leant his wrinkled face close to Hadley. His breath smelt of menthol.

'I'm the hospital administrator,' he said in a low voice. 'I gather you've come about Mr Trescothic.'

'We just wanted a moment of his time to talk to him.'

'Talk to him?' The Administrator glanced at the receptionist and looked back at Hadley. 'My dear fellow, you can't possibly talk to him. Haven't you heard? He died in a car crash last night. The police have been here half the morning.'

'I'm sorry, I didn't know. We're from Great Bartling, not Colingham. Are his patient records available?'

'You'd better speak to Miss Penderbury, his personal assistant. Mrs Arnold, see to it, will you?'

With that, the Administrator returned to his office, and the younger man retired through the door behind the receptionist. She called to the girl with the watering can.

'Jessie, show these people to Miss Penderbury.' The receptionist lowered her voice while the girl came over. 'If you wouldn't mind being discreet: Mr Trescothic's death has made a bit of a dent in the hospital's reputation. We don't want to unduly worry the patients.'

'Naturally,' Hadley said.

The girl led them down the corridor, her head erect, one hand on her hip and the other swinging the watering can back and forth, but not quite far enough to spill the contents. There was a smell of fresh paint, and they passed alcoves with more comfy chairs and potted plants. It made quite a difference to the stark national health hospital on the other side of town.

'Hev you been here long, Jessie?' Fenning asked.

'No, I've ony now a-started my prenticeship.'

Jessie knocked on a door. There came the sound of something clattering and then a voice called them to enter. The girl opened the door and poked her head in.

'Miss Penderbury, a bloke and a mawther to see you.'

'Do they have an appointment?' a voice came from inside.

Hadley and Fenning walked into the room, leaving Jessie to continue the watering. A woman sat by a desk near a sash window. On the wall behind her was a poster of a happy white-haired couple who had enough money to get their hips and knees replaced before they died of old age. Another wall had a poster of a young girl with a bandaged head thanking the wonderful staff for all their support. Miss Penderbury opened an appointment book.

'Your names?'

'D.I. Hadley and D.S. Fenning,' Hadley said, showing his ID. 'D'you mind the voice recorder, Miss Penderbury?'

She stood up, walked round to the other side of the desk and perched against it, her arms folded across her chest.

'I most certainly do mind. Such technology is an infringement of civil liberties.'

'It's just a form of note-taking.'

'It's a matter of principle,' she said. 'I have no objections to a notepad.'

Hadley tucked the voice recorder back into his jacket. There were a couple of comfy chairs in the office, in the same style as those in the waiting areas, but Miss Penderbury gave no gesture that could be interpreted as an offer to sit down. She unfolded her arms and leant back, her hands pressed against the desk behind her. She was wearing a pencil skirt and the top button of her jacket was undone. Colingham was far too close to the city for Hadley's liking. He had a feeling that Fenning would be making comments on Miss Penderbury's dress sense when they drove back to Great Bartling.

'I thought you'd all finally gone. What more do you want to know about Mr Trescothic's death? It's very unsettling for the patients.'

'Actually, we came about Lady Coulgrane,' Hadley said. 'We gather she came to see Mr Trescothic. Can you give us a bit more information about her condition?'

'Patient details are confidential.'

'Perhaps you're not aware she's gone missing. We need to know how ill she is, and how it's likely to affect her behaviour. The Administrator suggested we talk to you.'

'I'll see if I can locate her file.'

Miss Penderbury bent over a drawer in the filing cabinet. Her skirt really was far too tight. He could feel Fenning's elbow nudging him. He considered frowning at her to remind her to be tactful, but that sometimes had the reverse effect so, instead, he stared out of the window. For a moment he saw a shadow moving in the corner of the glass. It was probably nothing, but it might distract Fenning from Miss Penderbury if he went over to investigate.

'What did you make of Lady Coulgrane?' Fenning asked as Hadley walked over to the window.

'I've never met her,' Miss Penderbury said.

The bottom window sash was raised, but the sill had scuff marks on it that seemed out of place in such a pristine building. Hadley gazed out on to a lawn with a stone bird bath supported by a nymph, some flower beds and a few trees dotted about the place with wooden benches under them. There was a faint smell that reminded him of Battenberg cake.

'Dunt you see patients when they arrive?' Fenning asked.

'Yes, but her appointment was before I started work here.'
Hadley turned round. Miss Penderbury was still bent over the drawer. Fenning was tapping her pen against her notepad.

'Haven't you been here long?' Hadley said.

'No.' Miss Penderbury took out a folder, straightened up and closed the drawer with her hip. 'Some job this has turned out to be. I'm only here a week and my boss gets pickled and drives into a tree. How's that going to look on my résumé?'

Hadley walked back to Fenning's side.

'What happened to your predecessor, Miss Penderbury?' he said.

'She left for the city.'

'Whereabouts?'

'Your guess is as good as mine.' Miss Penderbury handed him the slim folder. 'People get the idea that life's more glamorous in the city, and they lose everything chasing after a dream. I doubt anyone here will see her again.'

Hadley opened the folder. There was a copy of the letter he'd seen in Carmichael's surgery, and a sheet of paper with an image from a brain scan. There was a shadow near the front of the left hemisphere. The top right corner of the page had the patient's name: Harriet Catherine Isabella Coulgrane. The last item in the file was Mr Trescothic's report. Chronic headaches, nausea and a change in personality. Fenning looked over his shoulder.

'Nasty way to go,' she said.

Hadley returned the folder. Yes, it was a nasty way to go, but it was a bit of a coincidence that both the G.P. and the specialist were dead and that Allerton was the only one who had known about the tumour. Maybe if they could trace Trescothic's previous P.A., she might be able to supply more information.

'What was her name?' Hadley asked. 'Your predecessor.'
'Jane Lamm.'

— 7 —

A Trip to the Country

Adam saw little of Harry for the rest of the week as she was always up before everyone else and hidden beneath her bedding by the time they returned. Jack and Big Stan had decided to deal with Hershey, so the days were occupied with planning and sussing out his defences. The guns needed to be cleaned and checked for jams. Drum magazines were counted out and distributed. The business was finally over by Saturday afternoon. Jack, Eric and Adam returned to the flat. Harry was sitting on her bunk reading a newspaper.

'Eric,' Jack said, 'Sid wanted you to have his watch.'

'I'm sure going to miss him.'

'Alf's got his wallet, and Hector's got the cuff links.' Jack held up a leather roll. 'Adam, d'you want his set of fine tools?'

'Yeah, they'll come in handy. Thanks, Jack.'

Jack poured out some of the home brew, and the three of them sat on his bunk drinking. Jack lounged against his pillow with Adam next to him, and Eric sat at the other end of the bed with one foot perched on the side frame. They drank to Sid's memory and reminisced. Rain began to hammer against the window. It was lucky it had held off until the shooting had finished. From time to time Adam glanced up at Harry's bunk, but she continued reading the paper until she finally threw it aside and pulled the bed covers over her.

It was one in the morning by the time Adam turned in, but he was woken early by a bang. For a moment he thought it was a gunshot but then realised it was just a vehicle outside backfiring. The first hint of dawn crept into the room around the edges of the curtains. He wriggled round and was adjusting his bedding to block out the dim light when he caught sight of Harry climbing down from her bunk. She paused as Eric muttered in his sleep, then padded across the room, her boots in one hand, and pulled the door to behind her. Adam glanced at his watch. The luminous hands showed seven o'clock. Didn't farmers ever have a lie-in? Perhaps she just needed the can. Yes, it sounded like she was in the bathroom. She'd probably be back in a minute. He closed his eyes and nestled his head into his pillow. But she wouldn't need her boots if she was planning on going back to bed. Was that toast he could smell? So what if she liked getting up early? It was nothing to do with him. He twisted this way and that on the mattress, then flicked off his sheet, unfastened his watch from the bedpost and eased himself down the ladder. Jack stirred but didn't wake up.

Adam threw off his pyjamas and pulled on some clothes. The front door clicked just as he was sliding his braces over his shoulders. He slipped his shoes on, laced them and crept out of the flat, carrying his tie, hat and jacket. He put them on while he hurried down the stairs and out on to the street. He'd forgotten his waistcoat, but there was no time to go back for it.

She was nowhere in sight, but he heard the sound of her hobnailed boots. He ran down the lane and peered round the corner. There she was in her waxed jacket and flat cap looking about as unobtrusive as a boil on the end of a princess's nose. The early morning autumn greyness hung around the street. Harry stood beside a lamp post, inspecting a map in her hands. She folded it up and carried on walking, down Haymarket Street and on past The Blue Diamond nightclub. The body of a failed card sharp lay by the back door awaiting the clean-up team. Harry checked her map again and carried on until she reached the remnants of the old city wall on the border of Jack and Big Stan O'Brien's territories. There was a small room up in those ruins with an unglazed window where lookout men were sometimes stationed. Adam ducked behind a corner and took out his pocket scope, but there was no sign of life. Harry stopped under the shadow of the old wall and unfolded her map. Adam darted across the street.

'What d'you think you're playing at?'

Harry swung round and her hand went to the back of her jacket.

'Adam, you startled me.'

'Startled? You'll be more than startled if Jack finds out.'

'Finds out what?'

He lowered his voice.

'You've got some business in Big Stan's neighbourhood.'

'What d'you mean?'

He clamped a hand over her mouth, checked all directions and gestured back the way they had come. She followed him round the corner.

'Where the hell are you going?'

'To church.'

'What?'

'I'm a Catholic.'

'You're one of Big Stan's lot?'

'I don't know any Stans, big or little.'
The smell of bacon and eggs drifted down from a window above them. Adam hurried her into a bus shelter.
'Jack'll go nuts if you cross over to Stan's.'
'Who is Stan?'
'Don't you know anything? Stan O'Brien is a gangster. Not as powerful as Jack, of course, but Stan's trying to make it big.'
'Is that why he's called "Big Stan"?'
'No, that's on account of his size. Anyway, his people were originally from sector fifty-three. We get a lot of immigrants from there, and they end up in Stan's territory because it's near the R.C. cathedral and they're mostly Catholic.'
'I don't care what he says he is. It's actions not words that define a person's faith.'
'I wouldn't try telling him that.'
Harry leant against the shelter wall and folded her arms.
'I'd never heard of him, and I don't like the sound of him, but I don't see why I can't go to my own cathedral.'
'I ain't your cathedral.'
'I was speaking symbolically as a member of the East Anglian diocese.'
Adam checked the street but there was still no one in sight. He turned back to her.
'Nobody crosses the border without permission,' he said. 'Chances are you'll get shot or beaten up if you try it, or they won't let you back here and then you'll have to work for Stan.'
'How was I supposed to know I was about to cross a border? It's not like there are any signs welcoming people to Big Stan's neighbourhood.'
'Here, give me the map,' he said. She handed it over. It looked new. 'Where'd you get it?'

'I bought it from the newsagent.'

'You know, people on the run don't usually go out of their way to draw attention to themselves.' Adam smoothed the map out against the wall of the shelter. The doorway faced east, so there was just enough light to see by. 'Hold it in place.' He took out a pen. 'This area's Big Stan's neighbourhood.' He drew a loop around it, his pen jerking over the bumps in the brickwork. 'Whatever you do, stay clear of it. This bit's Hershey's, or at least it was. It's now being carved up between Jack and Stan, so keep away from there until the new boundaries have stabilized.' He returned the map but grabbed it back. 'Oh yeah –' he scribbled some more '– and this area's Rita's. You really don't want to go there.'

Harry took the map and studied it by the doorway.

'There's another Catholic church in the north of the city,' she said, pointing to a small cross with the letters R.C. next to it.

'You don't want to go there: it's near the old airport.'

'What's wrong with that?'

'Don't you read the news? I ain't going near it.'

'There doesn't seem to be much option. Is there a bus that goes that way?'

She turned to inspect the bus timetable fastened to the wall. He peered out of the shelter again. He should've worn his waistcoat. It wasn't as effective as a proper bullet-proof vest, but Jack's tailors had come up with a pretty good design that at least reduced impacts. He tugged Harry's sleeve.

'We need to get out of here.' She didn't move. He sighed. 'Look, I know of a place out of town. There's this little village called Weston Snelding, and it's got a Catholic church.'

She turned to face him.

'How d'you know about it?'

'Does it matter?'

'You wouldn't try distracting me with some imaginary church I won't find?'

'Oh great. One minute you're strolling openly into Stan's neighbourhood like you're on a Sunday outing. Next minute you think I'm spinning you a line.'

'I'm sorry,' she said, 'but it seemed a rather unexpected piece of information.'

'You want to know how I know? All right, I'll tell you. Not that it's any of your business. One Friday the traffic was real lousy — there'd been an accident or something — so I thought I may as well stop at a service station until it eased up, but –' he kicked at a corner of the brickwork '– well, Donnaghan was hanging around and the others weren't there. The way that bastard talks makes me want to smash his head in, but that would be bad for Jack, so I went for a walk down some country lanes to cool off. Anyway it's about half an hour's drive from here.'

'I don't have any transport.'

'I suppose I could give you a lift on my bike. It ain't like I've got anything better to do.'

'Thank you.'

'Yeah, well, not a word to anyone. Right?'

They headed back to the basement car park, and Adam fetched his helmet and the spare one from his locker. A vehicle drove past outside. The city was beginning to wake up. Would Jack wonder where he was? Perhaps he should leave a note. Then again, Jack probably wouldn't be up for a couple of hours, and there was no sense in disturbing him.

Adam unlocked his single-cylinder bike, and swung his leg over it. Harry climbed on behind and rested her hands against his waist.

'You're gonna have to hold on tighter than that, if you don't want to fall off,' he said.

She curled her arms around him. He adjusted her grip away from his blackjack and started up the engine. They set off through Jack's neighbourhood, out of the city and along the dual-carriageway, heading west until they turned off at the exit by the service station. The roads became narrower and potholed. Patches of low-lying mist obscured ruts and stones, so he throttled back. Trees arched overhead and the sunlight flickered between the leaves. Thick hedgerows walled them in on either side.

He felt Harry prodding him and saw her reflection in one of the wing mirrors. She was pointing up ahead to a part of the lane where there was a metre-wide strip, a shade darker than the surrounding tarmac, stretched between the muddy verges. Did she think there was something wrong with the road? He'd been this way before and had never had a problem. There was a slight clatter beneath the wheels. They turned a corner and arrived in the village of Weston Snelding. She was probably just a bit edgy.

They arrived at a low wooden building, barely more than a hut set in the middle of a lawn. Adam came to a stop in the gravel car park and flipped down the stand. Five cars were parked there, as well as two open-air carriages and a row of bicycles. Six horses, four of them saddled, were hitched to a wooden rail by the grass. He removed his helmet. From inside the church came the sound of people singing with great enthusiasm but not so much appreciation of tone or rhythm.

'Come on,' Harry said after she had taken off her helmet, 'they've already started.'

He was going to tell her that he'd hang around outside until she was done, but she had already opened the door. He twisted his helmet straps around his hand and then followed her into the porch. Despite its small size, it seemed light and airy. There was a vase of yellow and purple flowers on a windowsill and a cork board with notices and rotas pinned to it. Harry dipped her finger into a small bowl of water, but there was no way Adam was going to copy her if everyone else had been touching it.

They slipped into a wooden pew at the back. The men were dressed in suits and homburgs. Some of the women were wearing felt hats and tweeds, similar in style to the men but with the necessary adjustments in the cut. The other women were wearing floral calf-length dresses, tailored jackets in yellow, green or blue, and wide-brimmed straw hats decorated with ribbons or flowers and tied in a bow under the chin.

Harry flicked through a hymn book. Adam stood next to her and listened. The congregation seemed to be divided into those who thought that singing was a race to see who finished first and those who thought that all hymns should be sung at a funereal pace but, when Harry started, her voice rose above all the others and pulled them into line. Adam was at the end of the pew, so he had a good view of two women standing in the front row on either side of the aisle. They peered round, their faces partially obscured by their wide-brimmed hats, but Harry was too short to be seen over the heads of the people around her, so the women had to be content with staring at Adam. He looked up and inspected the beams holding up the roof until he got a crick in his neck. He then moved his attention to the walls.

There was an alcove behind him where a toddler sat in a nest of brightly coloured cushions with a woman by his side. An older boy, presumably the kid's brother, held up a cloth book for the younger one to look at. The smaller boy screamed. Adam flinched. The mother handed the boy a biscuit, and the brother picked up a patchwork bear and wiggled it about. Adam's helmet slipped from his hand, but he snatched it before it could hit the floor and held it tight. He should walk away, leave Harry here and ride back home. This was the kind of place where she belonged, not in the city, not with him. Everyone sat down and he found himself still standing. He sat down and sidled closer to Harry.

An hour later, everyone piled out of the church. Adam and Harry followed on behind and found the parishioners chatting on the lawn outside. The mist had gone here and the grass was bathed in sunlight. They turned and stared at Harry. With her coat undone, only those with lousy eyesight could possibly mistake her gender, and they surely couldn't have mistaken her voice for anything other than that of a woman.

The priest, who introduced himself as Father Bernard, was young and slender, but his face was sunburnt.

'Thass rare for us to hev visitors, but you're welcome.'

'How d'you do,' Harry said with a smile. 'What a lovely parish you have here.'

'That that is, my bewty, and do you want to stay for a mardle, I'll introduce you.' He turned to Adam. 'D'you play cricket, bor?'

'No.'

'Oh well, but I darst say thass never too late to larn.' Father Bernard indicated to a man standing close by. 'This is Mr Harper, left arm spin, and this is Mrs Harper. She make a masterous sponge cake. Light enough not to slow you down atwin the wickets.'

The two boys Adam had seen earlier were running across the grass. The younger one tripped, but the older one helped him up. They both laughed and chased each other around a small tree that stood alone in the middle of the lawn.

Mrs Harper, one of the women Adam had seen in the front pew, reached out her hand to Harry.

'How d'you do, Miss...?'

'Very well thank you.' Harry shook hands and smiled. 'What a charming little chapel you have, and the flowers looked beautiful.'

'Why thank you.'

'Did you arrange them?'

'Yes, flower arranging is a bit of a passion of mine.'

'This is Major Widrow,' Father Bernard said.

Adam turned to see a stout middle-aged man with a handlebar moustache. He looked as though he ought to have a shotgun under his arm. Instead, he leant on a sturdy walking stick.

'Retired.' The Major pumped Adam's hand. 'Formerly of the Weston Snelding division.'

'The Major useter keep wicket afore his knees gave up,' Father Bernard said. 'This is his wife, Mrs Widrow.'

She was the other woman Adam had seen in the front row. She smiled, nodded at him and shook hands with Harry.

The two boys flopped on to the grass. The mother picked the smaller one up, and a man hoisted the other one on to his shoulders. The family then strolled across the path to the lychgate and headed down the lane.

'Are you new to the area, Mrs...?'

'I used to live near the hamlet of Little Bartling,' Harry said to Mrs Widrow, 'but my father died, and I had to move to the city.'

'I'm so sorry but, my dear, are you sure that's wise?'

'The city's a wicked place,' Mrs Harper said.

'Full of debauchery,' Mrs Widrow said.

'Gamesters.'

'Gangsters.'

There were other children amongst the parishioners, and a boy turned to stare at Adam. He then ran over to a girl, tugged on her sleeve and pointed towards Adam and Harry.

'I can assure you that I keep well away from that type of thing,' Harry said. 'Oh, what a beautiful Maltese cross you have there, Mrs Widrow. Although I suppose I ought to call it a sector whatever-number-it-is cross.'

'Certainly not. I can't abide all this sector nonsense.'

'And it's rather silly to insist the capital should be in the dead centre of the country,' Mrs Harper said. 'What happens if there's a mountain there? Or maybe a lake or a marsh. And why should all the capital cities be called "Central City"? It's very confusing.'

'Damn foolish idea, if you ask me,' Major Widrow said. 'I didn't fight against raiders to be told I live in a damned number. It's all the fault of computers. They used to have computers in everything. I heard they even had the damn things in bottle tops.'

'Are you married?' Mrs Harper asked Harry and glanced at Adam.

'Computers in bottle tops?' Harry said. 'The very idea.'

'Oh, but I see you don't have a wedding ring.'

'This is Mr Simmons,' Father Bernard said to Adam, 'our opening batsman. Hit a masterful six aginst East Belingford.'

Mr Simmons was in his forties with leathery skin and greying sideburns. His suit had flecks of mud around the edges, and he kept tugging at his shirt collar as though it was chafing his neck.

'What bring you to our village, bor?' Mr Simmons asked Adam.

'Unfortunately the area around the Catholic cathedral has been taken over by mobsters,' Harry said, 'and we didn't dare go near it.'

Mrs Widrow's hands flew to her mouth.

'Mobsters? It's just as I said.'

'I've heard the city's full of screens with shocking images,' Mrs Harper said.

'Drunken scenes.'

'Scantily clad people.'

'They've probably got damn computers in them,' Major Widrow said. 'The world's a better place without computers, if you ask me.'

What had possessed Harry to talk about mobsters? She could have come up with a better reason for visiting this church, but it had turned their attention away from her background, and maybe that's all she cared about. At least she hadn't mentioned Jack. Adam watched Major Widrow walking down the lane with his wife's arm through his. Mrs Harper was heading in the other direction with her husband. The congregation on the lawn had dwindled to a few stragglers. Adam moved the straps aside on his helmet in readiness to put it on, but Harry showed no signs of leaving.

'I like it here,' she said.

'It's all right, I suppose.'

'The service station you mentioned, was it the one we passed when we left the dual carriageway?'

'Yeah, that's right.'

'And you walked all the way over here from there?'

'I didn't quite make it this far.'

'So how did you know about the church?'

'What's it to you?'

Harry touched his arm.

'What's wrong?'

He played with the straps on his helmet. One of the parishioners untethered the last of the horses and fastened it to the remaining carriage. Six people were crowded on to the seats in the back, laughing and chattering.

'Sometimes Rita's people hassle me.'

'You mean the –' Harry looked around '– the women.'

'No, not them. They mostly ignore me. I mean the men.' He watched the horse plodding away, pulling the carriage over the gravel drive. 'They wind me up if they catch me on my own, and they say stuff. I don't want to cause trouble for Jack, so I keep buttoned up, but one time I got so mad I got on my bike and rode out of town, so I wouldn't be tempted to take them all out. I probably would've done if I'd had my gun, but Jack don't let me keep hold of it when we're not on business. Well, there I was, riding out on the dual carriageway with nowhere to go, when I remembered how I'd seen some farm machinery round the back of the service station, that time the traffic was bad, so I rode over there to take a better look, only it wasn't in the field where I'd seen it before, so I went on further and kind of explored, and I wound up here.'

'Can you show me round?'

'Yeah, all right. It ain't like there's anything else to do. There's a footpath behind the church.'

Harry slipped her left hand through the straps of her helmet, so that it dangled on her arm like a handbag. He led her round the building and through a graveyard that sloped down into the low-lying mist. Some of the headstones were so old and weather-beaten that the epitaphs were barely visible, but near the boundary fence they came to a newer row with deep-etched carvings proclaiming the valour of those slain during the anarchy. Harry stopped to read them. Adam stood by her side, thankful that none of the villagers could accuse him of having been a raider. The new government had been in place for six years before he'd been born.

The path led them to a stile in the fence. They climbed over and set off along a muddy track bordered by a high tangled mass of brambles on one side and a stream with a field beyond on the other. Adam pointed to a vehicle trundling away in the distance and asked her what it was.

'It's a beet harvester,' she said.

'Did you have any of them on your farm?'

'No, we didn't have any root crops. Allerton grows sugar beet or, rather, he pays people to grow it on his land.'

Harry picked a blackberry and offered it to him.

'It ain't been washed,' he said.

'Yes, it has. It rained last night.'

She popped it in her mouth and jumped over a rut. Adam stopped as he heard words from the final hymn drift over the graveyard accompanied by squelching, slapping sounds. He looked back but at first saw only brambles and mist. Then Father Bernard came into view, mud flying up beneath each footfall. A bag stuffed to bursting point bounced against his back, and his left hand clamped his black capello romano to his head. He smiled and waved as he passed by, but he didn't slow down. He disappeared around a bend, and they ambled along behind.

The path took them into a wood, the stream still chattering by their side. There was a damp smell in the air. Shelves of lichen were fastened to many of the trunks. An oak lay on its side, its roots showing above a hole from which they had once been ripped in a great storm long ago, but the tree still clung to life, its branches reaching up vertically to the height of some of the surrounding trees so that it looked as though a mini forest had sprouted from the fallen bole.

'Look at all those mushrooms,' Harry said. 'Aunt Hilda would've loved it here.'

'What? You mean you didn't make them up?'

'Make what up?'

'All them weird relatives?'

'They weren't weird. Some of them were just a little eccentric, that's all. I thought you believed me.'

'I believed the stuff about the generators, but don't you think you might get fingered if you let out so much about your background?'

'I doubt any of that has made it into a police report.'

'So you really had all them relatives living in your house?'

'Oh yes.'

Harry skipped over a waterlogged rut, and Adam stepped along the grass border. A breeze rustled the leaves above his head and dislodged droplets of water over him. A tree lay across the path a few yards ahead.

'Must've been pretty cramped,' he said.

'Not particularly. Both sets of grandparents had the attic, although in hindsight that probably wasn't such a wise idea as my grandfather took to climbing on to the roof to talk to the gargoyles after my grandmother died. We found him spread out on the path one morning in his pyjamas.'

'Jack said you told him he died of hypothermia.'

'That was my other grandfather.'

Harry jumped over the fallen tree trunk and landed in a puddle. Adam walked around the tree.

'Have you got any family left?'

'No. The house felt pretty empty when it was down to just my father and me. Mrs Burnley-Morris said Dad ought to remarry to propagate the line. She's full of daft ideas.'

'Was he interested in anyone?'

'No, he never got over my mother's death, and I protected him from the kind of scheming young women who like to target titled widowers.' She smacked the side of her boot against a tree, dislodging a clump of mud that had been wedged around the hobnails. 'I just wish I'd been able to protect him from Allerton.'

She whacked her other boot, throwing up more mud.

'Did you say you had a brother?'

'Yes. He died when he was eight.'

'How'd he die?'

Harry picked up a stick and swished at a clump of weeds.

'He had a brain tumour.' She twirled the stick around in her hands, tossed it up into the air and caught it. 'Two years later my mother died of the same thing, so it's hardly surprising my father lost his marbles a bit after that.'

'So is it, like, hereditary then?'

She smacked an overhanging branch with a stick, sending a shower of droplets flying.

'Just because something's hereditary, doesn't mean I've got it.'

'I never said that, but you can see how others might. I'm sorry about your family. I had a little brother.'

What had made him say that? He hadn't even told Jack about it. Harry turned to look at him.

'What happened to him?'

'He didn't make it. So who's Mrs Whatsit-Whatsit?'

'Mrs Burnley-Morris is my godmother.'

Harry tossed the stick again, but this time it didn't come back down. Adam peered up into the leafy canopy.

'I think it's got stuck,' he said.

'Never mind.' Harry hopped over a protruding mass of roots. 'She took a strong interest in my upbringing after my mother died — I was only twelve at the time — but unfortunately we didn't always see eye to eye on certain matters.'

'Like what?'

'Well for a start, she didn't approve of me working on the generators, and she was particularly put out the time I accidentally electrocuted myself as we had a party to go to that evening, and my hair just didn't look right.'

'She'd get a shock if she saw you now.'

'She also insisted I take up singing lessons. I admit that I quite liked the idea — not that I was going to tell her that — but my teacher turned out to be a very peculiar woman.' Harry put one hand on her hip and flourished her other hand. 'I am Belrosa, and I have sung in the most famous nightclubs all across sectors fifty-three through to seventy-five, but now I retire to your charming little village, in this beautiful sector of yours, to teach delicate young ladies to sing in such a manner that will cause all men to become passionately devoted to them.'

'I ain't never heard of anyone migrating to the country. I thought it was always the other way around.'

'It occasionally happens. Uncle Barney helped Belrosa find a cottage, but Allerton used to live in Central City as well.' She planted her boot in a shallow puddle and rocked it back and forth so that it made squelching sounds. 'I don't suppose you've heard of him?'

'No. Why should I?'

'I was just wondering, on the off-chance, if he happened to be notorious.'

'Jack would be the best person to ask.'

'I'd rather not get him involved. Please don't mention it to him.'

She jumped, grabbed an overhanging branch and swung herself up into a tree, scattering water droplets over him. He wiped his face with a handkerchief.

'You got the fidgets or something?' he said.

She peered back at him through the leaves.

'I've been cooped up in a small flat and a poky basement shop all week. Of course I've got the fidgets.' She dropped down by his side. 'Now, where was I?'

'Singing lessons.'

'Oh yes. Mrs Burnley-Morris has the strange idea that young ladies ought to have their talents put on show, so whenever she had a soirée we would all have to go on display.'

'What's a soirée?'

'Mostly music and polite chit-chat,' Harry said. 'A typical evening would go something along these lines: Madeline Burnley-Morris, who's about the same age as I am, sings and plays the harp, and everyone thinks she's angelic, and then there are Rosemary and Violet, who are sisters living near us, and one thumps on the piano while the other warbles. In theory, Rosemary is accompanying Violet, although that would imply they have some kind of agreement as to the rhythm and melody, which unfortunately doesn't seem to be the case, but everybody claps in a polite way and says, "very nice".'

'And you had to sing?'

'That's right. Now, don't get me wrong, I like singing, but those evenings used to make me feel rather like an animal at the market. I half expected someone to come along and inspect my teeth.'

The wood came to an end, and the path was now bordered by the stream on one side and a field of cows on the other with brambles overgrowing the boundary fence.

'I suppose singing badly wouldn't have helped much,' Adam said.

'It certainly didn't help poor old Rosemary and Violet.' Harry plucked a blackberry leaf. 'Although having said that, Mrs Burnley-Morris did eventually stop asking me to sing.'

A smile lingered on her lips. He waited for her to continue, but she didn't seem inclined to say anything further on the matter. They reached a fork in the path. The right hand side led to a footbridge over the stream. Harry took that route but stopped in the middle of the bridge and leant on the wooden railing. The sun came out from behind a cloud and she was bathed in a shaft of light. Adam stood on the bank and watched as she ran her fingers over the veins of the leaf. A breeze ruffled her blond hair.

His mind saw the delicate young lady with the golden ringlets from the missing-person poster singing in front of a group of men, eyeing up a potential wife. Maybe Allerton had been there too. Well, if the bastard tried anything now, Adam would deal with him. She was better off out of that kind of life. He stepped on to the bridge and leant on the railing by her side. The water tumbled and splashed over the pebbles below.

'You never said what happened to your Uncle Barney.'

The leaf was quivering. Perhaps it was just the breeze. She didn't reply.

'What happened to him, Harry?'

'He died.'

The breeze plucked the leaf from her fingers, and it fluttered towards the stream. It spun in an eddy and then floated away. A drop splashed on her hand. He looked up and saw a tear trickling down her cheek. He laid his hand on hers.

'I ain't much good at a lot of things, but I can listen if you ever want to talk about it.'

She turned to him and smiled.

'And the same if you ever want to talk about your brother.'

Like that was ever going to happen. He stared back at the stream.

'Thank you for bringing me here,' she said.

'No problem. I can bring you every Sunday if you like.'

'I'd like that.'

'Just as long as nobody here gets wind of my connections. I don't reckon it would go down well.'

He felt her hand stiffen beneath his. She drew it away.

'I won't say a word.'

She put her hands in her pockets and strode off the bridge. A pheasant scurried across their path, crying with a loud kok-kok sound, and plunged into a clump of ferns. Harry ran down the track and jumped up the wooden step of a stile. She sat on the top and swung her feet while Adam walked over to her. She grinned at him.

'I once walked to one of Mrs Burnley-Morris's soirées across the fields after heavy rain. My muddy hobnailed boots didn't go down at all well, even though I had brought a change of shoes.'

He stood in front of her and rested a foot on the step. She leant towards him and looked as though she was about to speak, but then she glanced over her shoulder and gave an exclamation.

'Oh look. There's a cricket match.'

Harry jumped down on the other side of the stile, and Adam climbed over into a narrow lane that skirted the edge of a cricket pitch. He caught sight of Father Bernard: he had exchanged his collar and cassock for whites and was playing a cut shot to an imaginary ball. He glanced up, waved to them and then practised a defensive stroke.

Adam and Harry wandered along the lane, past the sports pavilion and a small playground, and soon came to a cottage. Bindweed wound its way around the gate and up a lopsided estate agent's board. There was no sign of a path, just tall grass, dandelions and thistles. The thatch was covered in wisteria.

'What a waste of a good cottage,' Harry said.

'D'you reckon it's got a generator?'

'I expect there's one in that lean-to.'

Yeah, that's what he'd figured whenever he'd come here on his bike. The lane was narrow and potholed, but he reckoned his Phaeton would be able to get along it — once he'd finished installing the engine. It looked like the cottage had once had a driveway. It just needed a bit of weeding. There were two dormer windows in the thatch, but the wooden frame around one of them had started to fall apart, and a rotten plank flapped about in the breeze. Maybe Harry might like to live in a nice little place like this. If they both worked on it, it'd be fixed up in no time.

'You used to keep chickens, didn't you?' he said.

'That's right.'

'Reckon they'd be room in this garden for chickens?'

'I expect so.'

There came the thud of ball against bat and the sound of clapping from the cricket pitch. Harry pulled some of the weeds away from the estate agent's board. She stared at it for a moment and then turned and walked down the lane. Adam darted over by her side.

'I expect you'd like to go back to living in the country again,' he said.

'Yes, I would.'

They turned a corner and a garage came into view. It had a board with 'D. Felton, Mechanic' painted across it, swinging in the breeze. There was a tractor on the forecourt, but the place was closed up for the day. Maybe D. Felton was over at the cricket pitch with the rest of the village.

'I used to be a mechanic,' Adam said.

'Why did you stop?'

He dislodged a pebble from the muddy verge with the toe of his shoe.

'Jack told me to quit and join him on the road because I kept getting into fights while he was away. I was eighteen and he reckoned I was old enough to handle the job — and tough enough.'

'Did Jack teach you how to do ID papers?'

'Yeah. He said I had a knack for it.'

'Aren't you ever worried that you'll get arrested?'

What had made her say that? Did she know? No, she wouldn't have come out with that if she knew.

'I'm all right now I'm with Jack.'

'I take it Jack's not worried about getting arrested.'

'You kidding? Even Quinn's people would think twice about nicking Jack. Harry, you're pretty smart, but you need to be a bit more savvy if you want to survive in the city. I ain't never going against Jack, not because it'd land me in a load more trouble than I could handle, but because he took me in and looks out for me. He's all right if you get on his good side. You're much better off working for him than for Big Stan or the others. Alf used to work for Slim Hamilton, and he was psychotic. You never could tell what would make Slim flip, but Jack got him in the end and took over his territory in Central City.'

'Got him? You mean he killed him?'

'Sure he did. Slim must have taken twenty rounds before he finally went down. I got two in the chest, but I was wearing my vest. Then I got hit in the leg. Jack pulled me clear while Eric covered him. After Slim fell, most of his men surrendered, but Jack went easy on the ones who agreed to work for him — like Alf.'

'D'you often get into shoot-outs?'

'Not very often. Well, we had to last week because Hershey had got out of line.'

'But you don't enjoy it, do you?'

Adam kicked the pebble across the lane.

'It's better to shoot someone else than have them shoot you. It's just the way life is, and you can hardly talk, carrying that telescopic stick thing around.'

'I haven't killed anyone with it.'

'You wouldn't keep it in your jacket if you weren't prepared to use it.'

He strode ahead down the lane and over a stone bridge. She hurried after him and fell in step with him. They turned on to a narrow track along the bank of the stream. The cows in the neighbouring field stared at them for a while and then went back to chewing the cud. The cottage and cricket pitch came back into view on the other side of the stream.

'D'you mind if we sit down for a while?' Harry said.

He glanced at his watch.

'Sure, if you like, but not for long or Jack'll wonder where we are.'

She put her helmet down by the side of an old willow tree and spread her jacket on the ground in a nook formed where the thick roots splayed out. Adam got a clear view of her fancy stick strapped to the coat lining. She unfastened it, placed it next to her helmet and gestured to Adam.

'Be careful not to sit on any of the pockets.'

That was easier said than done, but he managed to locate a reasonably pocket-free area. She settled next to him, and he found that his arm was now behind her. She leant back. Her head was close enough for him to detect a faint smell of engine oil in her hair — the helmets had been lying on a dirty rag in his locker. He wondered if she would mind if he kissed her, but then he remembered how touchy she could get and decided against it. Her stick was in easy reach of her right hand, and his right arm was now trapped behind her.

Voices from the cricket pitch shouted, 'good shot', and a ball thudded into the lane on the other side of the stream. Adam wondered if any of the balls ever hit the cottage.

'Could I ask your advice?' Harry said. 'I'd like to sell something, and I've no idea how to go about it.'

'Depends what it is.'

A man in white dashed out into the lane and threw the ball back over the pitch. Harry twisted about and rummaged in one of the inside pockets of her jacket. She produced a pair of ear-rings. They were set with a large pearl and three dangling gems each followed by another pearl.

'I never liked them,' she said. 'They're too heavy, so I thought I may as well sell them.'

'Where d'you get them?'

'Aunt Hetty left them to me.'

'I thought your aunt was called Hilda.'

'That's a different aunt.'

'So what happened to your Aunt Hetty?'

'Oh we don't talk about it. She went a bit peculiar.'

Adam produced a loupe from his pocket. It was a real nice walnut-framed one that Jack had given him, but then he always did get the best whenever he gave Adam a present. Harry held the ear-rings out in the palm of her hand. He picked one up, adjusted the loupe's lenses and inspected it. The stones were real. The sound of clapping drifted over from the cricket pitch.

'I reckon your best bet is to ask Jack to pop them for you,' Adam said.

'How can I do that without explaining who I am and where I got them? He'd think I'd stolen them otherwise.'

'Then don't even think of selling them in Norwich. You'll have to try out of town.'

'I don't have transport.'

Adam slid the lenses back and slipped the loupe into his pocket. A voice called, 'Howzat!'

'I could sell them for you,' he said. 'There's one place we stop off at that Jack ain't too interested in, but if he found out I'd have to tell him where I got them.'

'I don't want you to get into trouble on my account.'

'I'll square it with him if he finds out.'

He scooped the other ear-ring out of her hand, his fingertips brushing against her palm.

'How much commission d'you want?' she said.

'Thirty percent.'

'Okay.'

'Ain't you going to haggle?'

'I don't feel like haggling today.'

✻

Jack sat at the table in the flat, reading a newspaper.

'D'you want some more coffee?' Eric said.

'No, I'm done, thanks.'

Jack checked his watch. Eric helped himself to the last half cup of coffee left in the pot.

'Maybe he's taken Harry to the motor museum.'

Jack didn't reply, but he heard footsteps coming up the stairs accompanied by a tapping sound that indicated the presence of hobnails. The front door clicked open, and soon after Adam and Harry entered the room. Jack lowered his newspaper.

'Where've you been all morning?'

'I wanted t'explore,' Harry said, 'so I asked Adam, and he shew me round. There's a sight o' shops here, and open on a Sunday anorl.'

Jack turned to Adam, eyed his shoes and looked back up at his face.

'You been on your bike, my lad?'

'Yeah.'

Adam shrugged and glanced away.

'How d'you always manage to get so much mud on you when you're on your bike?'

'Muddy puddles, I suppose. I'll go clean it off.'

With that Adam left the room. Jack leant back in his chair and studied Harry, but as always the kid avoided eye contact.

'It's not like Adam to let anyone on his bike.'

'I was tellin' him orl about my tractors back home. He was hully interested.'

'I'm sure he was. Sit down and we'll play cards.'

Eric collected the coffee pot and mugs from the table and headed off to the kitchen. Harry remained standing.

'I dunt rackon I'm much good wi' cards. They hev so many rules. I'm sure I must be duzzy, but I can't keep up with them orl.'

'Don't worry about it.' Jack took a pack of playing cards out of a carved holly box, it's wood as white as ivory. 'I'm sure I can show you an easy game.'

'Thass kind o' you, but I oont want to play for munny bein' as I've not got much to spare.'

Jack stretched his leg under the table and pushed out a chair with his foot.

'You never know, you might win a bit more.'

'Or I might lose what mite I hev left.'

Jack began shuffling the cards.

'It's a wonder you lost your farm given how careful you are with money.'

'I didn't lose it.'

Jack cut the cards and flipped them together. The sound of Eric's tuneless whistling drifted through the open doorway.

'Your dad lost it to his creditors and you couldn't stop it. Yeah? It's a lousy thing to happen, but don't worry, this'll just be for fun.' Jack nodded to Eric as he came into the room. 'Come on, Harry. Plant your backside on a seat. We'll play with matchsticks instead.'

Eric came up behind Harry, placed a large, hairy hand on her shoulder and steered her towards the chair. She glanced up at him, her hand fingering the hem of her jacket, but she sat down and he took the seat next to her. Jack opened a matchbox and emptied the contents on the table.

'You have those ones –' he pushed half the pile over to her '– and I'll have this lot. Now we've got to agree on a stake.'

'Woss that mean?'

'We both put two matches in the middle of the table. Okay?'

Adam returned and pulled up a chair between Jack and Harry. The holly box was in front of him, and he began to run his fingers over Jack's initials carved into the lid. Jack dealt three cards to himself and to Harry.

'Now we inspect our cards. No, don't show me your hand, you twit.'

Jack explained 'threes', 'sequences', 'points' and the importance of knocking. Adam opened the box, took out a pencil and twirled it round his fingers. Harry rearranged her cards.

'So three kings are a good hand?' she said.

'There's no point pretending you've got three kings when you've just flashed your cards at me.'

'I wunt trying to suggest it. I was jist wonderin' what to aim for.'

'D'you want to barter or trade?'

'I hatta give you matchsticks do I trade, dunt I?'

'Sure you do, but if you barter you're more likely to get a lousy card.'

Harry screwed up her nose and counted her matchsticks, straightening each one as she did so. Eric's chair creaked. Jack winked at him. Adam was still twirling the pencil in his right hand, his left resting on the box. Harry looked up.

'Okay, I'll trade.' She handed Jack two matchsticks, and he dealt her a card. 'Oh, thass masterly. I'm glad I traded.'

'You're not supposed to give a running commentary.'

They carried on playing until Harry had traded away all her matchsticks.

'What do I do now?' she said.

'If you want to carry on you'll have to barter.'

'Orl right. I'll barter.'

They swapped cards, and Jack looked at the one she'd given him. It was the ace of diamonds.

'What d'you want to give me an ace for?'

'Thass only one point, hintut?'

'Since when is an ace only worth one lousy point?'

Jack rapped his knuckles on the table and showed his hand: the ace of diamonds and a king and queen of hearts.

'Come on. Turn over your cards.'

She did so: a king and queen of diamonds and the two of clubs he'd given her. Adam clasped the pencil in both hands and began to twist it to and fro.

'You shanny dope,' Eric said. 'If you'd kept the ace you would've won.'

Harry gathered the cards, split the pack and flicked them together with her thumbs.

'I did say I wunt much cop at cards.'

Jack reached out and grabbed Harry's hand. She tried to pull back and glanced up at him. It was the first time he'd got a good view of her face: at the arched blond eyebrows, the blue eyes and the long, thin nose. It might've been pretty if it hadn't been for the reddened weather-damaged skin. There was a snap on Jack's left. Adam dropped two halves of the pencil on to the table. He looked up at Jack with wide eyes.

'Sorry, Jack. I didn't mean to break it.'

Jack took the cards from Harry.

'That's all right, my boy. Harry, you're lucky I've got a good sense of humour. Only someone who's real — what was the word you used? Duzzy? Only someone who's real duzzy would risk messing about with a card game, even one that's just for fun.'

'I certainly dint mean no offence. I woont want to end up like poor old Miguel Alberto del Rosario.'

Harry sat there as though she'd been talking about the weather. Eric was staring at her like he was trying to do some mental arithmetic. Adam drew back a little, glanced at Jack and shook his head.

'Here,' Eric said. 'How come you know about Miguel?'

Harry arranged four matchsticks into a square and began to construct a layer on top of it.

'He came to live near my farm, oh let me see now, that musta been abowt four years ago. He wanted a quiet little cottage orf the beaten track, and my Uncle Barney helped him out.'

Jack began shuffling the cards.

'You know, Harry,' he said, 'Miguel's an old friend of mine, and I'd really like to see him again — for old times' sake. Perhaps you could tell me how to find him.'

'Oh, but dint you know? He's dead.'

'What'd he do? Rig a card game or pull a lame heist?'

'He was shot in his cottage with one onem Thompson sub-machine guns. The police rackoned that was someone from the city.'

Adam edged closer to Jack and returned his attention to the holly box. Jack put the cards down and leant towards her, tapping the table top with his forefinger.

'You didn't come here to get revenge because someone knocked off the little rat, did you?'

Harry drew back.

'I certainly woont risk anything on his account.'

'When'd he die?'

'June last year.'

Jack resumed shuffling the cards.

'So how come the rural cops didn't contact the city?'

'I wuz told they hed. Some o' the old boys say they see furriners they rackoned wuz plain clothes detectives.'

'Foreigners?' Eric said. 'From another sector?'

'I think you'll find they call anyone who's not local a foreigner.' Jack flicked his thumb along one corner of the pile of cards. He had no doubt at all that Ethan would've told him if he'd heard about Miguel, but what about Quinn? He'd been eating into Ethan's territory for too long. 'What constabulary did you come under?'

'Central.' Harry continued building a tower with matchsticks. 'We uster be Norfolk Constabulary, but they changed the boundaries.'

Jack put the cards down and took out a cheroot. What was Quinn playing at?

'Miguel was a right cocky bastard,' Eric said. 'Spud told me as how Miguel once boasted that he was going to do over Sector House.'

'Yeah, that's just the kind of half-cracked idea he would come up with,' Jack said. 'So, Harry, your Uncle Barney helped Miguel out, did he?'

'Yis, thass right,' she said.

'Liked to help people out, did he?'

'He was hully popular, and I rackon Miguel wuz fare in awe o' him.'

'It wasn't like Miguel to be in awe of anyone. How well did you know him?'

'I sometimes see him when I went with Uncle Barney on his rounds.'

'His rounds?'

'He useter visit the cottages round us to check everyone wuz okay, hev a mardle, see if they needed anything.'

Jack picked up a match from the table and struck it.

'That was very neighbourly of him.'
'Miguel hed some rare tales about the city,' Harry said.
'Yeah, I bet he did.'
'He told me about No-Nose Nick, and his raid on a place called The Blue Diamond. Is that true he dunt hev no nose?'
' "Half-Nose" would be more apt,' Jack said, 'although not quite as alliterative.'
'And is that true Miguel stopped him single-handedly?'
Jack laughed.
'Single-handedly? More like no hands. Miguel got so scared he fainted in front of the doorway just as No-Nose was backing out. He had a hair-trigger, and it went off when he tripped over Miguel. That's what blew the remains of Nick's nose off — along with the rest of his head.'

— 8 —

INTERVIEWS

Hadley, with Fenning next to him, turned into the driveway lined with poplars. Behind them, on the other side of the lane they had just left, rose the south-western end of the Wynherne Estate boundary wall. The drive turned and brought them into view of the curving gables and dormer windows of Burnley Manor. A large-leafed variety of ivy climbed its walls. Two horses grazed in the paddock and, as he left the car, the breeze brought him the familiar leather and equine smell tinged with memories of working in the stables on the Wynherne Estate.

They walked over to the door and Hadley yanked on the brass bell pull. An elderly servant showed them into the drawing room. Mrs Burnley-Morris was sitting in a floral print armchair with a spaniel curled around her feet. She lowered the magazine she had evidently been reading and gestured to a brocade sofa on the other side of the oak coffee table that occupied the middle of the room. Hadley and Fenning sat down together.

'You're Charles Hadley, aren't you?' Mrs Burnley-Morris said.

Her hair was now grey and her skin blotchy and wrinkled, but she still had the same stentorian voice that had frequently sent little Charlie Hadley running for cover.

'Yes, ma'am.'

'I remember you. You used to suck your thumb. Nasty habit. I hope you've stopped.'

'A long time ago, ma'am,' Hadley said. 'D'you mind the voice recorder?'

He held it out and she stared at it with the same expression she had once had on encountering him holding a beetle in his muddy hands, but he wasn't a kid any more — or so he told himself.

'What are you thinking of, carrying an infernal device in your pocket?'

'It's only a wind-up recorder.'

'And you turned up in a car. I heard the racket you made.' She tossed her magazine on to the coffee table and pointed to it. 'That has an article correlating so-called technological advancements with increasing immorality. I suggest you read it sometime.' She folded her arms across her stout chest. 'We don't have technology in this house.'

Hadley glanced up at the electric light fitting.

'Don't you have a generator?'

'It's in the shed, not in the house.'

Hadley tucked the voice recorder back into his pocket.

'We came about Lady Coulgrane. It might help us to determine where she's gone if we had a better idea of her character.'

'She's always been a bit peculiar. Her uncle was a very bad influence.'

'Which uncle did you mean?'

'Barnabas Coulgrane. She doted on him, the silly child, but it was hardly a suitable upbringing for a young lady. I tried my best after her poor mother died. Dear Bella, always such a sweet girl and so elegant.' Hadley remembered his first impression of twelve-year-old Bella Bostock wearing filthy dungarees and up to her elbows in grease from her father's generator. The breeze outside the open window rustled through the ivy leaves. 'If only Harriet had taken after her mother, but she was too wild. Her uncle should've hired a governess — someone to teach her to be genteel — but I'm sure that half the time he forgot she was a girl.'

A silly child for doting on a hero? Hadn't they all? He'd find her and bring her home for her uncle's sake. He felt Fenning's foot nudging his.

'Mrs Burnley-Morris,' Fenning said, 'hed you noticed any recent deterioration in har behaviour?'

'She took her uncle's death very badly,' Mrs Burnley-Morris said. 'I'm afraid the shock unhinged her.'

The tambour clock on the mantelpiece chimed twelve o'clock. Fenning waited until the last stroke faded before resuming.

'Do she hev any friends in the city?'

'Certainly not. We all know what type of people live in the city. If she's gone there –' Mrs Burnley-Morris drew in a sharp breath '– well, she's lost for good.'

'Mr Allerton was originally from the city,' Hadley said.

'And he had the good sense to leave. He goes back occasionally to try to persuade the authorities that they must do something about the gangsters, but I'm afraid his pleas fall on deaf ears.' Mrs Burnley-Morris sighed. 'If only her father had remarried. I recommended several possibilities who had all the makings of a countess and who would have known how to keep the house in order. I gather that Mr Allerton helped them out of some financial difficulties.'

'I wasn't aware of that.'

'Naturally he was very discreet about it, but it would never have happened if there had been a reliable woman at the helm.'

Fenning's feet crunched over the gravel driveway back to the car while Hadley looked up at the ivy-clad manor house. Even the Burnley-Morrises had had to leave their home for the safety of the Wynherne Estate. Hadley could remember seeing the newly-wed Burnley-Morrises running across the fields with bags slung on their backs and raiders closing in behind them. Then the horn call had gone up, and his father had ridden out with Barney Coulgrane's regiment to rout the invaders. But it was as though she had blanked that from her memory and relegated the anarchy to the history books.

A young woman with a basket of laundry walked over to an outhouse. She opened the door and Hadley glimpsed a washing machine inside. He turned his back on the house and eased himself behind the wheel.

'I wonder what har idea of a bad influence might be,' Fenning said.

'A bad influence?'

He stopped, took a deep breath and clenched the steering wheel with his hands. Fenning touched his arm.

'Sorry I wunt able to go with you to his funeral.'

He turned on the ignition.

'Don't worry. You would've been squashed. The church was packed.'

'That ent surprisin' nowun wuz around to hear del Rosario being shot during that day,' Fenning said.

'The foreign recluse?'

'Thass right.'

Hadley glanced to his left and saw her straightening an almost non-existent crease in her trousers. Williams and Hale had got the case because Hadley'd had the day off to attend Barney Coulgrane's funeral, but Fenning had been nearly bouncing with excitement when she'd filled him in on his return. He depressed the clutch, put the car into first gear and released the handbrake.

'You're not still sore about missing out on a tommy gun case, are you?'

'That woulda med a change,' she said. 'Did you meet Lady Coulgrane at the funeral?'

'No, I was at the back, and she was at the front surrounded by the old veterans. I wrote a letter of condolence and she sent back a reply, but I've never spoken to her.' He turned the car in the courtyard and drove back down the avenue of poplars. 'Who's next on the list?'

'The singing teacher, Belrosa. No surname given. She live at Rose Cottage, Little Bartling.' Fenning studied the map. 'Rackon turnin' left here is the quickest route.'

'Yes, it is,' Hadley said and turned right.

'We goin' the scenic route?'

'Yes.'

Yes, that's right, they were going the scenic route, the long route, any route that didn't go past the place where his dad had been killed by raiders. Fenning said nothing.

They soon reached the level crossing. The gates were shut. Typical. The train to Central City had stopped just before the crossing to top up the boiler. They could've let the traffic go while they were doing that but, no, they had to hold everyone up — everyone being Hadley and Fenning and a tractor on the other side of the crossing. At least the train didn't need to fill up on fuel as well—the pile of eco-logs reached just above the top of the tender. Hadley drummed his fingers on the wheel. The pipe was finally disconnected and the train pulled off in a cloud of steam.

They eventually arrived at Little Bartling, and he slowed down so they could read the house names. There was an Apple Tree Cottage that had a pear tree in the garden, a Cherry Tree Cottage that had a stump in the middle of the lawn and a Plum Cottage that had a row of raspberry bushes and an old fir.

'There's another cottage further down the lane,' Fenning said. 'Thass got a rose arbour over the gate.'

'Well, that definitely won't be Rose Cottage then.'

He was right: it turned out to be Lilac Cottage. It adjoined The Willows, which actually still had its namesake trees drooping over the boundary hedge, the trailing branches almost brushing the surface of the neighbouring duck pond. The semi-detached cottages looked like half a slice of Battenberg cake: one yellow, the other pink. Hadley's stomach began to growl.

'Would you rather stop for grub first?' Fenning said as he swerved to avoid a puddle near a woman walking two setters along the side of the road.

'No. We may as well find the place now we're here.'

'That look like we've left Little Bartling.' Fenning studied the map again. 'Do we take the next right by the big oak and go down Wash Lane, we'll be able to loop round.'

'You must be joking,' Hadley said. 'I'm not going down there. I wouldn't want to attempt it when it's dry, let alone after all the rain we've had lately.'

'We'd git stuck?'

'Just a bit.' He attempted to turn in the road, but couldn't get the gear into reverse. He swore at it, and it finally clunked into place. Fenning didn't say anything. 'Sorry.'

'D'you want me to ask do that mawther with the dogs know where the cottage is?'

'All right,' Hadley said, 'but if she says anything about heading down Wash Lane, ignore her. Some of the locals have a mischievous sense of humour.'

Fenning jumped out. Hadley reverse the car into a patch of brambles. He rammed the gear lever back into first and drove into a hedge. The front wheels spun on the muddy verge briefly as he tried to move back again, but the car managed to jerk away and he turned it so that it was finally facing the right way. He saw Fenning talking to the woman, but the dog walker seemed to be pointing to Apple Tree Cottage. Had the house had a name change? Or did it have one name for locals and another for furriners? Fenning ran back smiling and climbed into the vehicle.

'There's a turning between Apple Tree and Cherry Tree Cottages.'

'Is there?'

'Apparently thass easy to miss. Anyway, Rose Cottage is down there.'

They headed back through Little Bartling and slowed down as they came to Cherry Tree Cottage. He realised that what he had taken to be a driveway was in fact a lane with a drainage ditch overgrown with brambles along one side. The car bumped over ruts and splashed through puddles. He reached a patch of concrete that had once stretched along the entire lane, but now stood up like an island amid the mud. He was just wishing that he had brought one of the squad Land Rovers when the car thudded into a pothole, and for a moment seemed to get stuck. He revved the engine and the vehicle jerked back out again and skidded until the front left wheel thumped into the ditch. Fenning was thrown sideways into the door.

'You okay?' Hadley said.

'Well that wuz excitin'.' She undid her seat belt and pulled herself towards him. 'Oh look –' she pointed to a gate on the other side of the lane with a sign half-hidden by the surrounding buddleia bushes '– we've found it. We may as well leave the car here. Do we git in anyone's way, they can help pull us out.'

He opened his door, but it slapped back, so he twisted round in his seat, pushed it with one foot while levering the other against the sill and pulling on the frames with his hands until he was able to propel himself out. He turned round and reached out his hand to Fenning and hauled her over. Once out, she adjusted her hat and moved the buddleia branches aside to get a better look at the sign. It was definitely Rose Cottage, but there was no sign of the house.

Hadley pushed open the gate, and they walked along a narrow path between two leylandii hedges until they emerged through a bushy archway on to a lawn in front of a thatched cottage with deep eaves, small windows and roses painted over the white walls. Two rose bushes clung to wooden trellises on either side of the oak front door. A brass bell was fastened next to it, so Hadley wiggled the rope to set the clapper going. After a few minutes the door opened a fraction and a pair of dark eyes peered at them through the gap.

'D.I. Hadley and D.S. Fenning,' Hadley said, showing his credentials.

The eyes widened.

'We came ter ask abowt Lady Coulgrane,' Fenning said.

The eyes looked noticeably less alarmed at the sound of Fenning's voice and the door opened.

'You are local. That is wonderful. Come into the parlour.'

Hadley stepped across the threshold into the dark room on the other side of the door. The floor turned out to be two inches lower than he was expecting. He stumbled, and inwardly cursed himself for not anticipating it. He ought to know well enough that cottages rarely had consistent floor heights. He followed the dim figure ahead of him up a step into the next room, even darker than the first, and down a step and round a corner into a sunlit parlour.

Belrosa positioned herself in front of the French windows, playing with the bangles on her arm. Her hair was too dark for the age betrayed by her wrinkled skin. Her dress was long and close-fitting except where it flared below her thighs. There were vases on the mantelpiece, the coffee table and the windowsill, but the flowers in them were all artificial. The mantelpiece and the occasional tables scattered about the room were full of framed photographs of a much younger Belrosa in sultry poses and the walls had posters advertising that the famous Belrosa would be singing at this, that or the other venue, but the place names meant nothing to Hadley. She gestured with both hands sweeping out towards the red velvet sofa. Hadley and Fenning sat down on it and sank into the upholstery.

'Poor little Harriet,' Belrosa said. 'Is it true that she stabbed a man? He must have been very naughty for her to do that.'

'That doesn't seem to be the case given the presence of her G.P.,' Hadley said. Belrosa began to sway her hips and started to hum whilst playing with a lock of hair. 'When did you last see Lady Coulgrane, Miss or is it Mrs?'

'I have had five husbands, but I am always just Belrosa. No, I am the Belrosa. Are you married, Inspector?'

'No, ma'am. I gather you were Lady Coulgrane's singing teacher.'

'I am the famous Belrosa. I teach all the young ladies to sing. She is my best pupil, but she does not know how good her voice is.'

'D'you have any idea where she might be?'

'I think she has gone to Central City but, if she has, she is lost.'

Mrs Burnley-Morris had said the same. Why should they all give up on her so easily?

'Can you explain, ma'am?'

'She is so naïve. Always going to church every Sunday looking oh so sweet.' She picked up a long, black cigarette holder from a side table and opened a small box. 'I once taught her a song I used to sing in the nightclubs, and she says, "Oh, French, how very cultured." They do not say "sector this" or "sector that" here.'

'I know,' Hadley said.

She took a cigarette out of the box, fixed it into the holder and began to sing.

'Mon coeur est un violon sur lequel ton archet joue et qui vibre tout du long appuyé contre ta joue.' She adjusted the cigarette in its holder. 'The silly child sung it at the Burnley-Morrises' in her contralto that indeed *vibre tout du long*. Can you imagine that?'

It didn't take much imagination to picture Mrs Burnley-Morris's reaction to a night club song.

'Poor little Harriet does not understand why they do not like it. She tells me that she thinks the younger son must have indigestion. I laughed when she told me. They never asked her to sing again after that.'

'But why d'you reckon she's gone to Central City?'

'She often asks about it, but I know in my heart –' she pounded her chest '– that she is not in the country any more. Everyone is looking for her, and she is so well-known that they would have found her by now.'

'Whereabouts in the city might she be?'

'If she is lucky, she will be in the refuge, but maybe she does not know where it is.'

She sat on the sofa arm, next to Hadley, arched her back and put the cigarette holder in her mouth. He edged away. If she was after a light, she'd have to find her own matches.

'Do she hev such a masterous voice,' Fenning said, 'is that likely she might try findin' a job in a nightclub?'

'Maybe. She has the voice, but she does not know the business.'

'Would you be able to contact the people you knew?'

'Oh no. No, I can not.' Belrosa stood up, walked over to the mantelpiece and adjusted the photos. 'I am retired. I come to live in this charming village.' She opened a box of matches, spilling some on to the floor. 'The nice people here do not want crowds of city people wanting to see the famous Belrosa. No, that would not be nice for them.'

'Hent you kept in contact with any o' your friends from the city?' Fenning asked.

'I come to live a quiet life.' Belrosa tried to strike a match, but it snapped. She tossed the ends into the grate. 'You do not tell them you have seen me. You do not know what they are like in the city. No, you must not go there. You go there, the gangsters see you, and bang you are dead. The city police will know where to look for her. Leave it to them.'

※

Hadley left the cottage with Fenning and they wound their way back through the narrow path and into the lane. His car was still there with a wheel in the ditch. He walked around it, wondering if it would be possible to push it out.

'D'you want to radio for help?' Fenning said.

'No, we'll be stuck all day if I do that, and I'll not have Williams telling everyone I can't drive down a country lane.'

He positioned himself in front of the car, bent his knees, grasped the undercarriage and tried to lift it.

'You'll put yarself in horspital a-dewun that,' Fenning said.

He gave up and peered into the ditch. It was a drainage channel, and it had been raining lately, so of course it was half-full of water, but it also had a healthy growth of brambles and nettles up its muddy sides. What was the least objectionable option: get in that ditch or radio for help?

'Get me the crowbar from the boot.'

He tossed his jacket and hat on to the back seats and lowered himself into the ditch. The brambles caught on his clothes, and the nettles stung his hands. Water seeped into his shoes.

'We could allus say I driv it inta the ditch,' Fenning said as she handed him the crowbar.

'You feeling all right? That must be the bravest suggestion I've ever heard you make. But if you think I'm going to let you take the blame over this, you must be soft in the head.'

He slid the crowbar between the patch of concrete and the underside of the car and pulled down on it, levering up the vehicle until the front left wheel was an inch above the level of the lane. Fenning slid a shotgun along the ground under the wheel. She stood on the butt to keep it horizontal.

'I trust that's empty,' Hadley said as he lowered the car so that the wheel rested on the gun barrels.

'Dunt you worry. I ent that desperate for promotion.'

Hadley turned round, braced his feet against the far side of the ditch and pushed his back against the car. The wheel slid along the shotgun and Hadley slipped into the ditch. He fell with a splash in the muddy water amongst the overhanging brambles. He looked up to see Fenning peering down at him.

'You've done it,' she said and held out her hand. 'Here, let me help you out.'

'And have you fall in on top of me?'

She went out of view for a moment and returned with a rope. He grabbed one end, gave an experimental tug and hauled himself upright and out of the ditch but bashed his knee on the concrete. He waved Fenning away. His clothes were soaked and a nettle had become lodged in his braces. He plucked it out, adding to the stings on his hand, and tossed it into the ditch. He then pulled away some branches that were tangled around the nearside headlamp but, in doing so, smeared the chrome with mud.

'Dunt you worry about it now,' Fenning said. 'I'll give you a hand cleanin' it up later. Come on, I'll drive you home, and you can git changed.'

'My other suits are at the cleaners.'

'We'll stop at the second-hand shop in Mundton Green. There'll be suffin there for you.'

She got into the car and backed it off the now dented shotgun and away from the ditch, then fetched an old newspaper from the boot, spread it out on the passenger seat and helped him in. She rubbed some of the mud off his hands with an oily rag, tidied everything away in the boot and returned to the driver's seat.

'Belrosa's right,' Hadley said. 'She'd've been found by now if she was still in the neighbourhood.'

He inspected his tie and found a patch that wasn't quite as sodden as the rest and used it to wipe away a blob of mud he could feel clinging to his chin.

'You'll fare better arter a soak in the bath.'

'Who's she got left to turn to?' He picked up the list of names from the door pocket, leaving muddy fingerprints across the sheet. 'Are they all like Mrs Burnley-Morris or Belrosa?'

'I dunt think they'll be like Belrosa.'

'I'm going to have to phone Central City to ask Quinn's people to help.'

'Do they refuse, I'll tell Quinn we ought to go back to being Norfolk Constabulary, if Central Constabulary's got too big for him to handle.'

'You'd do that as well, wouldn't you?'

'I certainly would.'

— 9 —

A Change in Rental Terms

MONDAY arrived and Harry set off to work. She was accompanied for some of the way by Jack, Eric and Adam as they headed to the depot, but they parted company at the corner of Bob's cul-de-sac.

'Goodbye for now, Harry,' Jack said. 'Stay out of trouble.'

'See you Friday, skinny runt,' Eric said.

Adam glanced at Harry and walked away without saying a word. She hurried along the narrow lane, down the steps into the basement shop and started work. Bob skulked in a corner, muttering and tapping his stick. The morning dragged its heels and the afternoon dragged its knuckles, but five o'clock finally came round. She set out for her lodgings but stopped by at a shoe shop, deciding that it was about time she had some footwear that was better suited to pavements. She also made some purchases at a general store before returning to the flat.

Once inside, she bolted the front door and removed her jacket. She then went into the kitchen and eyed what looked like several weeks', or possibly months', worth of dirty crockery covering all the work surfaces. There was a small pile of coins in a dish on the window sill. Why would Jack leave money lying around while he was away? Was he implying that such trifling amounts were beneath his concern? Or was it a test of his new lodger's honesty? Yes, she'd probably do the same.

A clicking noise made her turn round. The front door jiggled and then shook beneath someone's fist. Harry fetched her stick from her jacket, put the chain on and slid the bolt back. She opened the door a fraction, holding her weapon out of sight. Rita's face peered in at an angle through the gap, her pale blue eyes looking unnaturally large so close up.

'Jack's a-gorn to Central City,' Harry said.

'I know.'

'Then what d'you want?'

'It's what's known as being sociable.'

'Thass nice.'

Rita's face moved so that her mouth was now visible. Her lips were a glossy pink, but the skin around them was downy and showed faint wrinkles.

'Are you going to let me in?'

'Oh, I coont do that.'

'Why not?'

Her fingers edged nearer the door frame, close enough for Harry to see the chips in the pink nail varnish, but far enough from the jamb to be safe from the danger of the door slamming on them.

'Thass not proper.'

'Don't be silly. There's nothing improper about me paying you a friendly little visit. I was worried you might be feeling lonely with the men gone for the week.'

'Thass right kind o' you,' Harry said, without making a move to unchain the door.

'I don't like standing in the hallway talking to a door.'
'Was there suffin you wanted?'
'You really don't seem to have much idea of social etiquette, do you?'
'No, I dunt rackon I do. Never had no call for that afore. Thank you for your visit.'

Harry shut the door and pulled the bolt across, but Rita's voice carried through.

'You reckon you're so smart. Well I know your type. Don't count on Adam protecting you. He knows what'll happen to him if he goes against Jack. You're nothing special. Just another damn migrant, a nobody, and I'm going to make your life hell.'

Harry leant against the door but felt it shake as though it had received a hefty kick from the other side. She returned to the kitchen and counted the money that Jack had left behind — not just the total but also the coinage. She then searched through her own pockets and put aside an exact match in change. She sealed her coins in an envelope and tucked it into a pocket. If Rita intended making trouble by sneaking in and stealing the money while Harry was at work, Harry would at least be able to replace it before Jack came home.

Bob shuffled over to the door. Someone was pounding on it so hard that the bell above it began to tinkle.

'All right, all right. Stop hammering. I'm closed.' He peered through the window and saw Rita, at least he assumed it was Rita judging from the hat and cleavage, but her face was obscured in the shadow of the wide brim and the dark stairwell. He opened the door. 'What's up?'

'Why are you going so easy on Harry?' she said, storming right up close so that she towered over him. Now he could see her face properly, all scrunched up and tight-lipped. 'You getting soft in your old age?'

'Me soft? I ain't soft. Adam said to lay off Harry.'

'Did he now? Well Jack ain't said nothing about it.'

She put her hands on her hips, but she smelt so strongly of perfume and sweat that he took a step back.

'What about Adam?' he said.

'Who's in charge round here? Harry needs taking down a peg or two. You can leave Adam to Jack.'

Rita flounced out of the shop. Bob swung his stick and brought it crashing down on an empty box.

'I'll have none of your lip, boy.' He whacked the box again. 'Thump about my shop in your ruddy great hobnails, would you?' He smashed another bit of packaging. 'Let's see your boyfriend protect you now.' He slapped a hand over his mouth, glanced around and shuddered. No, he'd better not say anything disrespectful about Adam in case it got back to Jack. 'Making filthy great dents in my floor. You could wake the dead with that racket.'

The next morning, Bob lurked by the shop door, still muttering to himself. Footsteps clumped down the stairs outside. He saw legs clad in blue trousers through the top of the dirty window and gripped his stick, but it turned out to be the postman carrying a parcel bound with cord.

'Leave it on the floor,' Bob said whilst staring up the steps.

The postman left, and Bob resumed his position. The sound of whistling faded into the distance. Bob's gaze was drawn to the parcel as he wondered which of his recent orders it might be. The bell above the door tinkled. He jumped back and nearly tripped over a box.

'What the bloody hell d'you think you're doing creeping up on me like that?' He glanced down and saw that Harry was wearing a pair of rubber-soled boots. 'I ain't never met anyone as inconsiderate to an old man like you.'

He raised his stick, but instead of it impacting with a satisfying thump, he felt it twist out of his grasp, and he was hurled against the wall. Harry rammed the stick under his chin, forcing his head upwards. His legs were splayed out, and there wasn't enough strength in them to straighten up. He grabbed the stick and tried to push it away, but her grip was too firm. He looked up at her, intending to spit in her face, but her cap had fallen off and he found himself staring at a completely different face — one that still haunted him in the quiet hours of the night.

'It's you,' he said.

For a moment he thought he heard the sound of a bugle. The old wound in his leg ached. Voices assailed his memory: 'Help me!' 'Drive on. We can't waste fuel.' 'No, don't leave me behind.'

'What d'you mean?' Harry said.

'You're a Coulgrane.' The stick was pushed further under his chin, forcing the back of his head against the light switch. The bulb overhead flickered. 'You run from your family?'

Her eyes narrowed. Blue eyes and blond hair, just like that fellow with the sword.

'No. They know where I am and why I'm here.' She even sounded like him. How come he'd never noticed before? Bits of skin were flaking away from her sunburnt face. 'You were a raider, weren't you?' She gave a little smile. 'Did you meet my Uncle Barney?'

Again he saw the vehicle driving away from him, leaving him behind, but it didn't get far. The knobbly end of his stick was still pressed against his throat. He opened his mouth a couple of times before words finally emerged.

'What're you doing here?'

'I have some business to attend to. And just in case you're wondering, my family aren't the ones who are looking for me. The reward money that bastard is offering isn't anywhere near big enough to compensate for offending the Coulgranes. Do you understand, Bob?'

He tried to nod, but the stick was in the way. He needed a leak. He needed a leak real bad.

'I won't let on, I swear. You'll tell your family I was good to you?'

'Are you being good to me, Bob?'

'It was an accident. I didn't mean nothing. It's all Rita's fault. I swear it won't happen again.'

The stick moved away from his neck. He gulped down some air and rubbed his throat.

'I'm sure it won't,' she said. 'An old man could have a nasty accident if he waves his stick about like that.'

'It won't never happen again. You'll tell them I was good to you?'

Harry returned his stick and backed away. She smiled at him, with the hint of a sneer, slid a penknife out of her pocket and opened out a blade. She then bent down and began sawing through the packing cords around the recent delivery. Bob stood there clenching his stick while the blade rasped, his legs trembling. He could hear the horses. He could feel the ground quaking beneath him as their hooves thundered towards him. Guns were no use once the ammo ran out. Knives were no match against swords. He could hear arrows whistling past him. And the lances: he remembered the lances.

※

Jack stood in his pyjamas and dressing gown on the balcony of Betsy's Café. He exhaled some smoke and gazed at the lamp-studded city night. At the end of the street, Sector House still had lights showing in the top floor windows, just visible above its high surrounding wall. While it was being built, eighteen years ago, he had prevented developers from forcing Betsy out of her property to make way for office blocks, and she had been grateful to him ever since. She was a good-tempered woman: always cheerful, always pleased to see him. She never nagged him. If she wanted anything, she always asked nicely. Rita could learn a thing or two from Betsy. Even out here in Central City he wasn't free of her nagging. Oh no, she had to phone him up and hassle him about Harry. Forget computers, the Anti-Techs ought to be trying to ban telephones.

He finished his cheroot and padded down the hallway. He eased open the door to his room. A sliver of light from the street lamp outside illuminated a mound snoring in one bed and a restless form in the next. He crept over to the third bed and removed his slippers, but he paused as Adam muttered in his sleep. Jack sat next to him and put his mouth up close to Adam's ear.

'Don't keep secrets from me, my lad. I know what you're hiding, but it's going to eat you up if you don't talk to me.'

Adam stirred and, as he did so, Jack noticed that his right hand was holding something. He switched the light on at the dimmest setting and gently uncurled Adam's fingers. There was a lock of blond hair tied together with a bit of string. Jack closed Adam's hand around the hair, tiptoed over to Eric's bed and shook him.

'Huh?' Eric stared blearily at him. 'What's up?'

'Step outside,' Jack said.

'D'you want me to wake Adam?'

'No, leave him be, and keep quiet.'

Eric followed Jack out of the room and down to the end of the corridor. Outside a siren wailed but inside all was quiet, apart from rumbling snorts coming from a nearby room.

'What's going on?' Eric said.

'Have you noticed anything funny about Harry?'

Eric stared at Jack for a moment.

'You kidding me? He must be the weirdest migrant we've ever had.'

'Have you ever noticed Harry getting changed?'

Eric yawned.

'I thought he didn't have no spare clothes.'

'Adam said he gave Harry his old clothes.'

'Did he? Maybe Harry's shy. I mean, teenagers can be a bit funny about that kind of thing.'

'Have you ever seen Harry without that bulky jacket on?'

'No, but then we ain't really seen much of him.'

Eric scratched his chest and poked at a bit of sleep in the corner of one eye.

'Eric, my lad, have you considered the possibility that Harry might be a woman?'

A couple of drunks started a duet in the street outside. Eric's forehead crumpled.

'A woman?' The drunks seemed unsure of the correct tune for their song, but they also seemed to have forgotten most of the lyrics and were ad-libbing. Eric's whole face crumpled. 'Adam ain't going to like that.'

'I have a feeling he's already found out.'

'Hey, good for him.' Eric's bleary eyes widened as he stared at Jack. 'That is good, ain't it?'

'I have to get her away from him.'

Eric's hairy toes scrunched the deep pile of the burgundy carpet beneath his feet.

'He ain't never fallen for anyone before.'

'She's got her own agenda,' Jack said, 'and I'm not going to let her drag Adam into trouble.'

'What you gonna do to her?'

'I haven't decided.'

'It's a shame cos I kinda like her.'

'She hasn't got to you as well, has she?'

'I don't mean like that. She's a laugh, that's all.'

'Then she's definitely got to go, but I need to think about what to do with her. Not a word to anyone, okay?'

Jack rested his case on the ground and lounged against the grey wall of the depot's main building. It was Friday evening and he had arrived back in Norwich. He slid his hands into the deep pockets of his trench coat. The depot gates were hooked open, so he had a clear view of the crowds walking along the pavement outside. This area of the city was the Neutral Territory. Many of the pedestrians were local government clerks heading home for the weekend. They were the type of people who criticised the gangsters, but if it hadn't been for Jack, the city would still be run by those damn cannibal gangs that had formed during the anarchy. He fingered the Beretta in his pocket. They had the nerve to call him lawless. They didn't know the meaning of the word.

Hector and Alf came out of the front door a few yards from Jack. As soon as they saw him, they straightened their fedoras and ties and smoothed out the wrinkles in their suits.

'Hiya, Jack.'

Jack acknowledged them and watched them go through the gateway into the mass of pedestrians. A young man tried to bat Hector out of the way with a briefcase, but Hector gave him a shove with one hand that knocked him into the crowd. No gratitude, that was the problem with these people. The fellow with the case looked like he had been born well after the anarchy was over. He probably didn't even know he owed his job, the food on his plate and his nice home to Jack. It would serve them all right if they allowed Stan to take over the city.

A horn sounded from the road. It honked again, and the crowd started to disperse as a lorry began to turn into them. The last straggler managed to run out of the way, just before it drove through the gateway. It was Eric. He waved at Jack and pulled into a nearby bay. Jack looked around at the vehicles parked in the depot yard. It had been the right decision not to move over to the long-wheelbase model. The whole depot would have had to be redesigned and that would have been more trouble than it was worth. Some of the trucks needed a clean, but Ned would have that sorted out by Monday.

Eric squeezed out of the cab, slung his duffel bag over his shoulder and walked over to Jack's side. The bag strap didn't quite conceal a greasy stain on Eric's jacket. Ned had once suggested to Jack that the truckers wear overalls, but how could he be taken seriously if his men didn't look smart? Image was everything in this game.

'You all right, Jack?' Eric stifled a belch. 'That butty keeps repeating on me.'

'Try to get it out of your system before we get home.'

'I don't reckon it tasted quite right. Did you have the bacon?'

'Oh, it was supposed to be bacon, was it?'

Another lorry pulled in through the gates with its horn sounding. It parked in the bay next to Eric's truck and Spike jumped out. He fastened his jacket, acknowledged them and entered the depot building.

'Did you want something, Jack?' Eric said.

'I'm waiting for Adam.'

Eric started adjusting the straps on his bag.

'You're not going to kick her out as soon as we get home, are you?'

'All I want is a decent meal with good company. Is that too much to ask for?'

'You'll go easy on Adam, won't you, Jack?'

'I always do.'

'He's still a bit of a kid really,' Eric said as he readjusted the straps. 'It's kinda like schoolboy puppy love.'

'Stop fiddling with the damn bag.'

'Sorry, Jack.' Eric dropped it by his feet. 'I hope you don't have to hurt her.'

'So do I.'

Four loud horn beeps sounded from the other side of the gates — that had to be Adam. A lorry turned into the depot and pulled up in the bay next to Spike's. It was a shame to have to upset him, but it was better to deal with things now before he became too attached to her. Adam jumped down from the cab with his rucksack. At least he always managed to look smart and didn't spill food down his clothes.

'What's up?' Adam said

'We thought we'd be sociable and walk home together,' Jack said. 'Put your key away and sign off.'

Eric went with Adam into the building, and they soon returned. The three of them headed off with Eric in front, ploughing a path for them through the crowd. A woman with flabby chins and wearing a navy suit and homburg stood by a bus stop. Next to her was a man wearing a white fedora. What kind of colour was that for a fedora? It was one step away from wearing one of those damn ugly zoot suits.

Jack crossed over the road with Adam and Eric, and they turned into a quieter street. Two men who worked for Rita were leaning against the window of Chataway's Delicatessen. Their faces were unshaven and their clothes dirty with buttons missing. Why couldn't they look as though they'd even attempted to appear respectable? The number of times he'd had to hint to Rita that her people could do with smartening themselves up a bit, but she never did anything about it.

Mr Chataway came out of the shop wearing a blue-striped apron. He pulled down one shutter and moved over to the next window, but the two men were in his way. Chataway cleared his throat, said 'Excuse me' and cleared his throat again, but they paid no attention.

'Eric,' Jack said, 'that fellow looks like he needs a hand.'

Eric tossed his duffel bag to Adam and moved over to the shop. One of the men, an ugly bruiser with a scar across his chin, inspected his nails. The other one yawned. Eric undid his jacket, handed it to the shopkeeper, and rolled up his sleeves, displaying the tattoos on his forearms. He then walked up to the window as though there was no one in the way, and neatly stepped on the left foot of one and the right foot of the other. He leant forward and grasped the metal handle of the shutter. The two men shoved and pulled until they broke free just before the shutter reached the place where their heads had been. Eric took his jacket back from Mr Chataway.

'There was a little bit of a blockage, but I think that got it shifted.'

'This isn't your territory, Jack,' the man with the scarred chin said.

'It isn't Rita's either,' Jack said, 'or has there been a newsflash while I was away? Did Rita forget to mention it when she phoned me for one of her cosy chats last night?'

Not that there had been anything cosy about the phone call as it had mostly consisted of Rita telling him how Bob had suddenly decided that Harry was his new best friend and according to her that was clearly a violation of Jack's authority. And how did she figure that one out? He'd never ordered Bob not to be friendly with Harry. Admittedly it sounded a bit odd, but then Rita was prone to exaggerating. The two men sloped away. The shopkeeper had gone back inside, but just as Jack was about to continue on his way, he dashed back out with a bag.

'Thank you,' he said, handing it over.

Jack peered inside and saw a hunk of ham.

'Well that's real nice of you.'

He set off with Eric and Adam but, once they'd turned into a cul-de-sac, he handed the bag over to Eric to carry.

'I reckon I've got a good chance of getting hold of this area,' Jack said.

Adam was glancing around while he walked and was so close to Jack that their arms were brushing against each other.

'You okay, my boy?'

'Fine.'

But Adam kept looking about him and his hands were flexing. They cut across through an alley into the next street, went past Lin Mai's pharmacy with its pink notice advertising the chemist's discretion, and another couple of junctions later they were back in the narrow cobbled roads with laundry lines stretched above their heads between the buildings. Now that they were in his own territory, Jack slowed his pace and glanced at Adam.

'I've been thinking about Harry,' he said.

Adam shifted his rucksack, put his hands in his pockets and took them back out again.

'What about Harry?'

'I reckon Harry's trouble.'

'No, I'm sure that ain't true, Jack.' He looked away, back again and shrugged. 'I mean, everyone has their funny little ways, don't they?'

'I reckon I ought to kick the kid out.'

A squeal sounded above them. Jack slid his hand into his gun pocket and looked up, but it was only a squeaky pulley from one of the overhead lines. Mrs Marten was bringing in her laundry.

'Harry don't go causing no trouble,' Adam said. 'And you should see all the help she's given me on my car.'

'Ah, you've come out with it at last.'

'With what?'

'The female pronoun, my lad,' Jack said. 'Did you think I wouldn't notice?'

Adam grabbed Jack's arm.

'Please don't hurt her.'

'That, my boy, depends entirely on Harry.'

Adam's grip tightened.

'She's all right, Jack. Really she's all right.'

'Try not to cut off the circulation in my arm, my boy.'

Adam let go.

'Sorry, Jack.'

They passed Mr van Pelt the greengrocer posting a letter in a pillar box. He doffed his homburg when he saw Jack.

Further down the street, some kids were pretending to shoot each other with imaginary tommy guns.

'The thing is, my lad, you should've confided in me as soon as you found out.'

'I didn't want Rita hassling her.'

A freckled kid was employing his loudest voice to mimic the sound of a tommy gun.

'How could you even think I'd allow it?' Jack said. 'It cuts me deep to think you felt you couldn't trust me. Haven't I taken care of you these past eight years?'

Adam held Jack's arm again, but more gently this time, like a child tugging on a parent's sleeve.

'Sure you have, Jack. I'm sorry I didn't tell you, but I never meant no disrespect.'

'I'm glad about that, my lad. I was beginning to think that maybe she meant more than me.'

'No, you're dead. I shot you,' the freckled kid yelled at a small boy.

'Pack it in and clear off,' Adam said to him.

'Calm down, my lad. Don't take it out on them. Here –' Jack gestured to the freckled kid '– you're Jimmy, aren't you?' He tossed a coin at him. 'Go play somewhere else.'

The boy caught the coin and ran off, the other children following him.

'So, can Harry stay?' Adam said.

'Not with us, my boy.'

Jack resumed striding down the pavement. Adam and Eric hurried after him.

'Why can't she stay?'

'Come off it, my lad. We can't have a woman staying with us. It's not a female-friendly flat.'

'Eric's girlfriend sometimes visits.'

'The operative word being "visit". Living with us is a different matter entirely. Women fuss — it's in their nature.' They crossed the lane that led to Bob's shop. 'It's not like she's even got a room to herself. You don't want the woman you fancy to see you in bed all tousled and red-eyed with a hangover. You want her to see you at your best, after you've had a shower and shave and smartened yourself up.'

'She don't seem to mind that.'

'Look, my lad, I'm fed up of Rita nagging me about her. Every night this week she's phoned me up because she says Harry insulted her. Every damn night.'

'Rita must've done something to provoke her.'

'That's irrelevant.'

Up ahead, old Mrs Jenkins was trundling a wheeled shopping bag across the road. Adam looked up at Jack.

'What are you going to do to her?'

'She can go to the refuge.'

'But that's in Central City.'

'And we're in the area two nights a week. Maybe you could stop by and see her from time to time.'

'But, Jack —'

'That's enough. I'll make sure she's looked after for your sake, but I'll not have her causing trouble in my neighbourhood.'

'You won't spring it on her sudden, will you?'

One of the wheels on Mrs Jenkins's bag had got struck between some cobbles and she was struggling to pull it free. Jack strode over, yanked it up and placed it on the pavement. He then went back to Adam and rested a hand on his shoulder.

'Don't worry, my lad. I have way more experience handling women than you.'

'Jack, please be careful. She's touchy and if provoked could do a lot of damage.'

'I thought you were supposed to be on her side,' Jack said with a smile, but it faded when he felt Adam shaking. He tightened his grip on Adam's shoulder. 'She hasn't threatened you, has she, my boy?'

'No, of course not. I wouldn't put up with that.'

'That's good, my lad. I'm glad to hear it.' Jack patted Adam's cheek. 'Listen, my dear boy, you've got a lot of talent and skills that are invaluable to me, but in other ways you're real vulnerable. You're the type of lad who could easily be manipulated by a woman like that. That's why you need me to look out for you, so trust my judgement on this one.'

They soon arrived home. Despite Rita's predictions, the front door wasn't bolted and didn't have the chain on. Jack heard humming in the kitchen so, motioning to Adam and Eric to remain in the cramped hallway, he strode in. Harry wasn't wearing her jacket or cap and had a plain white apron on. Her hair had been washed and brushed, although it seemed a bit ragged around the edges. Well, if she wanted to come clean about being a woman, that was fine by him. It would make things a bit easier. She'd probably cottoned-on to his suspicions when he'd grabbed her hand and had a good look at her last Sunday. It was a shame he had to get rid of her. He could do with a few more smart people working for him.

'Hello, Jack,' she said. 'I hope you hed a good week.'

'Fine thanks.' There was a short stick on the counter next to her with bite marks on it that reminded him of the dog he'd had as a child. Most farmers had dogs. What had she done with hers? He pulled himself out of his reverie and glanced around the empty, gleaming work surfaces. 'You've cleaned up.'

'I hope you dunt mind,' she said. 'I wanted to show my appreciation of yar hospitality.'

'That sure was decent of you.' He gathered together the coins on the window sill. Nothing was missing, but he had expected as much. She was too sharp to fail that kind of a test. He turned back to her. 'Now look, Harry...' He stopped and sniffed. 'You cooking something?'

'Yis, thass much cheaper than eatin' out. I've med enough to go round if you're hungry.'

'Well now, you didn't have to do that,' Jack said, 'but it sure smells good.'

'I wanted to do suffin to thank you for lettin' me hev the first night bed and board free.'

'That was unnecessary, but very decent of you.'

She was a clever little minx, but she still had to go. He ran his finger along a shiny work surface. It wasn't like he now owed her a favour. She was just cancelling his favour, so everything was all square.

'Oh, by the way,' she said. 'You hed some post. I've put it on the table in t'other room.'

'Thanks. I'll go and see to it.'

He left the kitchen. Adam and Eric were still lurking in the hallway. Jack straightened his tie and lowered his voice.

'No sense putting her off while she's cooking. I'll speak to her later.'

They stepped into the other room. There was not a piece of rubbish, mouldy crockery or dirty laundry in sight. The carpet looked not only vacuumed but also washed. Magazines and books had been tidied away and ashtrays emptied. The table had been scrubbed and the only things now on it were the card box, an ashtray and a pile of letters. Even the net curtains were a lighter grey than he had ever thought possible. And she'd had the decency not to add anything, such as doilies or lacy covers, to replace the mess she had removed.

He hung up his hat and coat and strolled around the room, looking for anything out of place. His copy of *Men Without Women* lay neatly on his bedside table. He checked to make sure she hadn't lost his place, then shifted an ashtray an inch to the left but, after a moment, moved it back again. If it had been Rita — ha, like she'd clean up — she would've removed all the ashtrays just to make a point. And she'd probably ditch the Hemingway as well.

'She's even done the laundry,' Eric said as he poked at a neat pile of clothes.

Adam was on the other side of the room inspecting his box of engine parts.

'I'm glad to see she ain't messed with any of this,' he said. 'But that's what I like about Harry. She's got a lot more understanding and consideration than most women.'

'Hey, she's even found the Canaries boxers my mum gave me. I've been looking for them for ages.'

'All right,' Jack said, 'that's enough sight-seeing. Eric, you're not still carrying that ham around, are you?'

'Sorry, Jack. I forgot I was holding it. I'll put it in the fridge.'

Harry came in with a steaming dish. Adam and Eric collected the plates and cutlery from the kitchen while Jack sat down and flicked through his post. He opened a letter from his solicitors. Another problem neatly dealt with. The table was soon laid with food and three cans of beer. Harry set a glass of water by her own place.

'This is very civilised,' Jack said as they set to.

'Yeah,' Eric said, 'and the grub's good.'

Jack hadn't had fish pie since he'd visited his grandparents the Friday before he had started boarding school. Harry had made the mashed potato to just the right consistency and she hadn't overdone the cheese on top. He prodded a prawn with his fork.

'Did you put wine in this, Harry?' he said.

'Yis, but I ony bought a half bottle, so there ent much left, but if you'd rather have some instead o' the beer, I'll fetch it.'

'No, don't bother. The beer's fine.' Well, all right. So she'd done a good job of cleaning the place up and she'd prepared a real nice supper, but she was still trouble. 'So, Harry, you been okay while we were away?'

'Yis thank you, Jack.'

'How've you been getting on with Bob?'

'Masterously. He keep tellin' me I'm the best assistant he's ever hed.'

'You're kidding.'

'We're gittin' on like a house on fire.'

That he had to see. He would definitely be paying Bob a visit in the morning. Adam was mostly silent, but Jack often caught him gazing at Harry. Eric managed the whole meal without abandoning his cutlery in favour of his fingers, and he even refrained from belching. After dessert, Jack leant back in his chair, stretched out his legs and sighed.

'You know, Harry, maybe you should do this more often.'

'And praps you could knock off a bit o' the rent in return?'

She picked up the dirty dishes and whisked them away to the kitchen. Adam and Eric stared at Jack. He finished the last drop of beer, strode over to his coat and began hunting for his cigar case. Perhaps he could find a way to take Rita's attention away from Harry.

'It was a real nice dinner,' Adam said.

'Yeah,' Eric said. 'It's nice to have good grub after a long drive. That's what you wanted, wasn't it, Jack?'

'Maybe.' Jack found his case and took out a cheroot. 'I suppose there are some advantages to having a woman about the place.'

'We can keep her out of Rita's way,' Eric said. 'Especially if Harry ain't going to eat out no more, and she don't go to the pub.'

'And it's real nice the way she's cleaned up,' Adam said. 'Ain't that right, Eric?'

'Yeah.'

'If the two of you tidied up after yourselves, like I'm always asking, it would never have got into the state it was in.' Jack tucked his case into his jacket pocket and returned to his seat. 'At least she doesn't strike me as the kind of woman who's going to litter the place with cushions and pink things and those damn ugly china ornaments.'

'You mean like the ones Rita's got?' Eric said.

'I'd like to use them as target practice.'

'I don't think Rita would like that.'

'No, I don't suppose she would.' Jack twirled the unlit cheroot around his fingers. 'You know, with the place all tidy, I reckon there might be room for a camp-bed. I'm sure I could find another migrant.'

'We don't need anyone else, do we, Jack?' Adam said. 'It'll be nice with just the four of us.'

'It might take Rita's mind off Harry.'

'Yeah, you're right. There would be room. I'll get a camp-bed for you tomorrow.'

'So does that mean Harry can stay?' Eric said.

'Maybe, but if she puts anything pink in here, she's out. I hate the lousy colour. Damn it. I forgot to get out a match.'

'It's all right –' Adam jumped up from his seat '– I'll get it for you.'

He fetched a box of matches from Jack's coat and handed it over.

'Thank you, my boy.'

'What if Harry became a trucker?' Adam said. 'You'd be able to keep an eye on her then, and it would keep her away from Rita.'

Jack paused and then struck a match against the table.

'How's her driving?'

'Good.'

'We could do with a new driver to replace Sid.'

He lit his cheroot.

'Yeah, poor Sid,' Eric said. 'Hershey got in a lucky shot there.'

Jack breathed out some smoke and flicked the spent match into an ashtray.

'But his luck ran out.'

'Yeah, you got him good, Jack.'

'Maybe I'll get Fergal to arrange for Harry to have some extra driving lessons while we're on the road.'

Jack leant back in his chair and smiled at the eager expression on Adam's face. Then he heard a key clicking in the front door. He sighed but at least Harry was in the kitchen. Hopefully she'd have the sense to keep out of sight. Rita entered the room and walked over to him.

'Where've you been?' She ran her fingers through his hair. 'Why didn't you come to the caff?'

'We came home to find that Harry had prepared dinner for us,' he said, 'which was a real thoughtful gesture, and not one we felt we could turn down.'

'Thoughtful, my arse.' Rita curled her fingers until her nails scraped against his skin. 'And I suppose he's been cleaning as well?'

'Don't mess up my hair, Rita love.' Jack pushed her hand away. 'I was thinking of getting a camp-bed and putting up an extra migrant.'

'What for? Migrants are small change for you.'

'Sure they are, but if I've got the space, why not?'

'You really don't like being alone, do you, Jack? Why don't you knock all these flats down and have a nice big house? Then maybe I might move in and keep you company.'

'And what am I supposed to do with all my tenants? Send them over to Stan?'

'Well, if they mean more to you than me, I suppose I'll just have to put up with it. If you deign to come to the pub tonight, I expect I might be there.' She picked up Jack's empty can. 'Or has Harry filled you up with beer as well?'

Ethan sat at his desk listening to his stomach rumble. His bloody mother-in-law! She had a nerve saying how he used to be so slim when he'd been a kid. Slim? Everyone was stick-thin after months of scavenging for food. Being hungry was a constant reminder of a time he'd thought well and truly behind him. He picked up a report from D.I. Cornell, read a sentence and tossed it back on to the desk. Someone was typing in the next office. The few computers that were around these days were big brass chunky machines, with keyboards that clicked almost as loudly as a typewriter.

There was a knock at the door and a police constable showed Jack into Ethan's office.

'Bring up some refreshments, Petersen,' Ethan said to the constable. 'Jack, how's things? Business or pleasure?'

'Came for a bit of advice.' Jack settled into a leather armchair that had seen better days. 'Turns out Harry's a woman.'

'Your new lodger? You're kidding. It's not like you to miss a thing like that.'

'I was dealing with Hershey all that week.' Jack shifted position. 'I noticed the day after I took the little git out — when I had a bit more time on my hands. Anyway, she's not exactly feminine.'

'Well, it's not the first time a woman's tried to pass herself off as a boy. After all, they were doing it back in Shakespeare's day, according to Mrs Lockwood. D'you remember the trouble she had trying to get someone to play the part of Portia?'

'Sure,' Jack said. 'She got that skinny kid to do it in the end.'

'Poor kid. I wonder what happened to him.'

'I doubt he survived, unless he had protection.'

And that, of course, had been the key thing back then. If Ethan hadn't had the protection of Jack's resourcefulness — and ruthlessness — he wouldn't have survived either.

'So does Adam know about Harry?' Ethan said.

'He was the first to figure it out, but they were spending a lot of time on their own together.'

'A little fun on the back seat of his car?'

'I'd like to think so, but knowing Adam I doubt it.'

A woman police constable came into the office with a tray, which she slid on to the desk — her attention on Jack rather than on the contents of the desktop. Ethan straightened up the photo of his wife and kids and then noticed the WPC hovering by the doorway, twirling one of several loose wisps of hair.

'Go on, hop it,' Ethan said. The woman closed the door, but not before throwing a parting smile in Jack's direction. 'You know why she looked dishevelled? They had a fight over who was going to bring your coffee.'

Jack laughed and picked up a cup from the tray.

'She always looks windswept.'

Ethan selected a custard cream and munched on it. Outside, a siren began wailing, and there was a brief blue glow in the window as a car started off on an errand.

'So what d'you want advice about?' Ethan said.

'I called round Bob's this morning.'

'He hasn't been mistreating her, has he?'

'He got the shakes every time he looked at her. It's not like Bob to be scared of a migrant.'

'Not unless the migrant was seven foot tall and dressed in armour. I tell you what it is –' Ethan clasped his hands behind his head and leant back in his chair '– he must've found out she's Adam's girl.'

'If she's been telling people she's Adam's girl, then that's what she'd better be. I won't have her messing him around.'

Ethan dropped a couple of sugar lumps into his coffee, stirred it and tapped the spoon on the cup rim. He thought back to last Sunday evening when Jack had called round and recounted the card game he'd had with Harry.

'What d'you reckon about her connection with Miguel?' Ethan said. 'I had a look through the files, but there's no mention of him since he skipped town. I know my lads would've told us if anything had come to my department about him.'

'Yeah, I know, but it turns out Quinn's people aren't so talkative.'

Ethan was about to take a sip of coffee, but he put the cup down.

'You mean Quinn knew Miguel was dead?'

'Sure he did,' Jack said. 'The rural police contacted his department back when it happened, just like Harry figured.'

'So how come he never let on?'

'He reckoned it was me. Said he thought it would be tactless to bring up the subject.'

'But he could've mentioned what the rural cops were doing about it,' Ethan said.

'Sure he could've, but when I told him the hit had nothing to do with me, he was real curious to know how I'd found out about it.'

'So what'd you tell him?'

'I said it would be real tactless for me to say. But I tell you something, he didn't half have a shifty look on that ugly mug of his when I brought up the subject.'

Jack selected a long, thin ginger biscuit and twirled it around his fingers in a manner with which Ethan had long been familiar. He'd picked up the habit when the two of them had snuck out of their dormitory one night and hidden in a broom cupboard to watch one of Jack's old films on his tablet. Ethan had had the left ear plug, and Jack the right. The next day, Jack had lounged in the school corridors twirling his pencil around his fingers and calling people lousy, dirty rats in a blend of early twentieth century American slang and English private school boy tones. Two months later the whole world had fallen into chaos.

'So you didn't mention Harry to Quinn?' Ethan said.

'No way. It'd end up getting back to Rita, and I'd rather keep her mind off Harry.'

'Does she know Harry's a woman?'

'Not yet.'

'I sure don't want to be around when she finds out. You'd better make sure you don't show any interest in Harry.'

'Oh, believe me, Ethan, she's not my type. Besides, she's Adam's girl.'

'What're you going to do about her?'

'I don't know,' Jack said. 'Thing is, she's a great cook and has cleaned the place up a treat, and then there's Adam, but I reckon she's done a bunk. Maybe she had a good reason, maybe not. I can understand her difference with Rita — hell, there are times when I feel like bolting the door so she can't pester me — but if Harry's planning on making trouble then she's got to go.'

'What's she look like?'

'About five foot four. I'd say she was a blue-eyed blonde, but that would give you the wrong idea. She looks more like a scarecrow that's been out in the sun too long.'

'Can't say I've come across that description in the files, but she could be in disguise.'

'If she wanted to disguise herself, the first thing she'd need to do would be to slap on some liquid skin.'

Ethan's stomach rumbled again. He selected another biscuit, but it was stale, so he flicked it in the bin and prodded the ones left on the plate.

'So she's a good cook, is she?'

'Sure, that's right. Supper last night was the best meal I've had in a long time — and none of this fancy microscopic portions business either. Haven't had sticky toffee pudding since we were kids.'

'That sure was something the school cooks excelled at,' Ethan said. 'How about I come round to lunch tomorrow and check her out?'

'Won't Helen kick up if you miss Sunday lunch?'

'D'you know what I'm going to be eating for my Sunday lunch? Salad.' Ethan picked up a jammy shortbread. 'I'll have my leaves and carrot sticks at one, and then I'll be round yours at two, where I hope there will be some protein on offer.'

'I'm sure that can be arranged. I've knocked a bit off her rent in return for good meals and a clean home, so she ought to be willing to do her best.'

'And if it turns out she's wanted?'

'That will have to depend on what she's done, but I'm sure we can be accommodating.'

— 10 —

Sunday Lunch

Adam took Harry back to the church in Weston Snelding on Sunday morning. Afterwards, they took the same walk as last time and settled down by the old willow on the bank of the stream. The overgrown cottage on the other side was still up for sale. A cricket match was being played again, and he could hear the sound of bat on ball and clapping. Harry stretched out her legs, and Adam watched the sunlight glinting off the polish on her new rubber-soled boots. He wondered how much they'd cost — they were obviously not second-hand. He pulled an envelope out of an inside pocket of his jacket and handed it over.

'That's the money for your ear-rings.'

'Have you taken out your commission?'

'Yeah.'

'Thank you.' She tucked it unopened into her jacket. 'Does Jack know?'

'He ain't mentioned nothing, but if he asks, I'll have to tell him.'

'Well, I suppose now he knows I'm a woman, it's more plausible for me to own a pair of ear-rings, and it is true that Aunt Hetty left them to me. She was my mother's older sister, but she really was very odd. Mind you, she lived in Colingham for the first fifteen or so years of her life, so maybe that accounts for it. There are some strange people living there. Aunt Hetty had a bizarre friend from Colingham who kept getting emanations.'

'She got what?'

'Emanations. Well, that's what she said. She'd go into a room or sit in a chair and go all funny.'

Adam picked up a twig and twirled it round his fingers while she chatted. Would Jack wonder where they'd been? What should he say if he asked? The people of Weston Snelding seemed all right, but he reckoned they wouldn't have been so friendly towards him if it hadn't been for Harry, and they'd turn against him pretty quick if they found out he was a gangster.

'So, anyway,' she continued, 'Grandpa Eddie and his family left Colingham before the anarchy started when he was commissioned by the Coulgranes to develop a compact bio-generator. He'd just got the Type 1 prototype working when the last of the petroleum supplies ran out.'

'Hang about, Harry. D'you mean your granddad was Edward Bostock?'

'Yes, that's right.'

'You're kidding.' No wonder she knew so much about the Bostock generators. A cricket ball thudded into the lane on the other side of the stream amidst a tumult of clapping and shouts. 'There's going to be an article about him in the next *Generator Monthly*.'

'Oh yes, I remember now. They came round a couple of months ago asking to take photos. Amos gave them a long account of Grandpa Eddie.' A man in white ran into the lane and lobbed the ball back on to the pitch. 'My father was too young to fight during the anarchy, so he helped with the generators instead. He fell in love with Grandpa's daughter, and the rest I'm sure you can work out for yourself.' She glanced at her watch. 'We'd better head back or lunch will be late.'

At five to two, Ethan turned up at Jack's place with a bottle of Merlot. The smell of roast beef greeted him and his stomach got all excited. Eric showed him in. The living room seemed a lot bigger than he remembered now that it was tidy.

'Aren't you looking domesticated.' He gave Jack the bottle. 'Table laid and everything.'

'Sure makes a nice change. Pull up a seat.'

Ethan sat down at the table, and Jack fetched a corkscrew while Eric and Adam brought in plates and dishes of food. Then Ethan saw a young woman standing in the doorway, her face sunburnt and her blond hair clean but raggedly cut. Her jeans were too large with the legs rolled up. He recognised the striped shirt and frayed braces that Adam had worn when he was younger. How could Jack not have realised she was a woman?

Eric brought in a carving board with a side of beef, and there was a pop as Jack pulled the cork from the bottle.

'Ethan, this is Harry,' Jack said. 'Harry, my best friend, Chief Constable Ethan Hall. He's in charge of the Norfolk Constabulary.'

She sidled over to Adam's side. Maybe it was just a natural nervousness of someone meeting a stranger, or maybe it was a wariness of the police.

'So how'd you get to be called Harry?' Ethan said.

She picked up a carving knife and began to sharpen it.

'Thass short for Harriet.'

'Harry, give Adam the knife,' Jack said. 'You can dish up while he carves.'

She passed it over and picked up a serving spoon.

'Oh,' Eric said. 'I thought you made up your name cos you wanted us to think you was a boy.'

'Dint say I wuz a boy.'

'All right,' Jack said. 'Drop it. Let's not spoil lunch with an argument.'

Harry put the serving spoon in one of the dishes while Ethan tried to think of questions that wouldn't cause any arguments.

'I gather you're from West Norfolk,' he said. 'Near the Wynherne place.'

'Thass right.'

'Whereabouts exactly?'

Harry paused, the spoon still in her hand.

'Do you start from Little Bartling, keep you a-gorn till you come to the big oak. At the yon side, the rud fork to yar right and that take you into Wash Lane and round by the ruined church, ony you might not be able to see it cos thass behind some trees, and then — oh, no wine for me, thank you, Jack.'

'You sure?'

'Quite sure, thank you.'

Jack filled the other glasses. Ethan wondered if Harry's abstinence was habitual or from fear of relaxed talk. It was odd for Jack to be so curious about a migrant's background, but then he'd always had a soft spot for Adam. Ethan looked round the table. Adam seemed to be spending as much time glancing at Harry as attending to the joint. Eric was holding his knife and fork in readiness. Jack put the bottle on the table and took the seat next to Ethan.

'Is Little Bartling a big place?' Ethan said.

'Oh no, thass ony a hamlet.' Harry scooped some broccoli on to the plate. 'Jist a handful o' cottages and a duck pond. Would you like some Yorkshire puddin'?'

'Don't mind if I do.'

He watched as she deposited a soft slab on his plate. That sure made a change from the rock-hard lumps his wife dished out — or used to dish out before the damn harridan put the dieting idea into her head. How was he supposed to find out about Harry's background with only the name of a hamlet to go on? She had hesitated when he'd asked about her name. Maybe she had made up the name Harriet on the spur of the moment. Eric could've been right.

'I'm sorry to hear you lost your farm,' Ethan said. 'How come your dad wound up bankrupt?'

For a moment he caught a flicker of anger in her face, but she suppressed it pretty quick.

'Arter my Uncle Barney died, some bloke came snoutin' round time I wuz out and persuaded my dad to borrer money. Roast taters?'

'Don't mind if I do.'

Harry heaped potatoes on his plate, and Adam added some slices of beef, but he avoided eye contact with Ethan. Maybe Jack was right to be worried about her influence. Surely Adam would never betray Jack's trust — not after all Jack had done for him? Soon the plates were piled with food, and everyone set to.

'So what's the fellow's name?' Ethan said, but Harry showed signs of having her mouth full, so he took a bite from his plate. 'These are cracking roast potatoes. You should give my Helen a tip or two. No, actually, you'd better not mention it.'

'I hear she's a-makin' you eat salad. Thass not right for an active man, specially not for his Sunday dinner.'

'You try telling her that. Don't get me wrong, she means the world to me, but she gets these crazy ideas into her head. Although I reckon it's her mother who's behind them half the time.'

'Ah, I know the type,' Harry said. 'That sound jist like the old mawther Mrs Weatherby. Allus givin' har son-in-law jip. She talk to him like he wuz a kid puttin' on his parts. First she say he's a slusspot, then she say he smoke like a chimley and that orl he want is jollifircearshuns. She mobbed him so much he say he wuz fit to strangle her.'

After the meal, Ethan set off and Jack accompanied him. There was an ugly brute on the other side of the lane with an unshaven face. That had to be one of Rita's men. It was a bad state of affairs that Jack had to allow them in his neighbourhood, but Ethan knew better than to mention it to his friend. He waited until they were out of sight and earshot of the man before talking to Jack.

'Harry's a real chatterbox once she gets going, isn't she?'

'She's that all right,' Jack said, 'but did you understand what she was saying?'

'I reckon I got the gist of it.'

A copper came round the corner, saluted to Ethan, nodded to Jack and carried on across the road. Jack glanced at the man and leaned close to Ethan.

'Remind Bryson he owes me when he gets his next pay check and advise him to keep away from the crap tables. So, what d'you reckon I ought to do about Harry? I don't want a trouble-maker in my territory.'

'Sounds like her dad's creditor pulled a fast one,' Ethan said. 'Perhaps she retaliated. You can't blame her for that.'

'Maybe. You after more of her cooking?'

'I wouldn't say no, but only if it's okay by you.'

'Sure it is. I wouldn't have my best friend going hungry.'

'That's real decent of you, Jack. In return, I'll send Cornell and van Loame round to Little Bartling to see if they can put your mind at rest.'

They turned into the road where Ethan lived and stopped in front of his terrace house.

'Want to come in for a coffee?'

'No,' Jack said. 'I've got to see Ned about some extra cargo. Besides, the old bat's pulling faces at me out the window. You'd best make out your stomach's rumbling.'

Ethan turned his back to the house.

'You okay with us picking you up at nine tonight?'

'Sure thing,' Jack said. 'Eric's going to head over to Annie's before then, so it'll just be Rita and me who need a lift.'

Harry sat at the table in the flat playing patience while Adam and Jack read — one a mechanics magazine and the other a newspaper. There was a large bouquet tied up with ribbon lying in front of them. Eric came into the room, combing his beard. Harry wondered why Jack allowed such a vast quantity of facial hair on one of his men given how particular he was, but perhaps he had seen Eric clean-shaven and decided against it. Eric stank of the same almond-smelling brand of pomade that Allerton used. She wanted to throw open a window or run outside, but it would only make them ask questions.

'What d'you reckon?' Eric said as he put on an evening jacket and hat.

'You look fine,' Jack said. 'Don't forget your roses.'

Eric picked them up from the table. They seemed to diminish in size when he held them in front of his chest.

'What d'you reckon, Harry?' he said. 'D'you reckon a girl would like them?'

'Sure she would — unless she hev hay fever.'

'Quit that, Harry,' Jack said.

'Here, you don't think she has, do you, Jack?'

'How many times have you given her flowers? And has she ever started sneezing afterwards?'

'Yeah, that's true,' Eric said. 'Hey, but her eyes went all watery last time.'

'Only because you trod on her toe.'

'They look bewful, Eric,' Harry said. 'Are you a-goin' some place special?'

'We're all going to the theatre, except for Adam. He don't like that kind of thing, and he ain't got a bird to take with him. I mean, he can hardly ask you, what with Rita thinking you're a boy.'

'You run along and pick up Annie,' Jack said. 'I'll see you there.'

'Sure thing, Jack.'

Eric straightened his tie and left. Adam continued reading, but Jack went over to the wardrobe and opened it. Harry decided that if he was going to get changed she would leave the room for a while, so she went into the kitchen to make a coffee.

When she returned, Jack was lounging on his bunk in evening wear, except for the jacket, and Adam was reclining next to him. Jack drew on a sweet-smelling cigarette that was unfamiliar to her. The main light was off, and the bedside lamp was dimmed.

'Come and join us, Harry,' Jack said. 'Oh now, don't look at me like that. I'm not trying to lure you into bed with us. Your landlord apologises for the lack of a sitting-room.' He smiled at her for a moment, but then his features relaxed and he seemed to gaze beyond her. 'We had a real nice one back home when I was a kid with sofas and armchairs, but now we have to make do with perching on a bunk.'

She sat down at the foot of his bed and cradled the mug of coffee in her hands. He handed the cigarette over to Adam.

'A nice big old house, it was,' Jack continued, 'in what used to be called the Golden Triangle. Ethan lived nearby, and we both got sent to the same boarding school in Suffolk. When the anarchy broke out we hiked all the way home.' He gave a three-fingered salute. 'We did our best, and then wished we hadn't bothered. We hightailed it out of there, but I went back later with my tommy gun and exterminated the lousy vermin.'

Adam drew on the cigarette and handed it back to Jack.

'They had it coming.'

'Too right they did. It sure as hell isn't golden round there any more. It's in Stan's neighbourhood now, and he's welcome to it.' Jack offered the cigarette to Harry. 'Want some?'

'No thank you.' She glanced at Adam. 'I wunt hev thought thass hygienic, sharin'.'

'It's all right,' Adam said. 'Me and Jack ain't got nothing contagious.'

'I hope you're not going to nag me over a spliff, Harry.' Jack nudged her with a foot. 'I get more than enough of that from Rita, and I'm sure not going to take it from you.'

'I wunt dream o' naggin' you, Jack.'

'That's just as well. Besides, it would be damn hypocritical of you given that you're having your fix.'

'I'm not hevin' a fix. Thass jist coffee.'

'Doc Fisher says caffeine has the same toxicity rating as cannabis.'

'Coffee dunt cause cancer.'

'That's not something to worry about once you've had the jab.'

'What jab?'

'The cancer vaccine. It had only just become available when Ethan and I had it while we were at school, but it was brought back into production a few years ago. I make sure all my people have it. So your argument isn't valid any more.'

Harry gripped her mug with both hands. It wasn't fair that gangsters should be immune from the disease that had killed her mother and brother. The heat from her coffee nearly scalded her, so she adjusted her hold.

'Maybe so,' she said, 'but they have rather different effects howsomever.'

'Sure. You get hyper and we'll get relaxed. It's not like it's crack.'

'Slim was a crack-head,' Adam said.

'He sure was, and look how he ended up. Mind you, I reckon he was cracked right from the start.' Jack blew out a stream of smoke. 'So tell me, Harry, were you shamming the first night you were here — all that staggering about?' He handed the spliff back to Adam, but Adam hesitated before taking it. 'You got something on your mind, my boy?'

'I got Harry an apple juice from the newsagents. We did a swap.'

Adam looked up at Jack like a child who'd just broken a favourite vase.

'I ought to be cross with you, my lad.'

'I'm sorry, Jack, but Harry didn't want it.'

'Harry, I'm offended,' Jack said, lounging back against the pillow, one of his long legs stretched out, the other bent.

'I wuz farin' sadly. I rackon I mighta caught the sun.'

'You look like you've been playing catch with the sun all your life. Don't you have sun cream out in the country?'

'That dunt last orl day. Howsomever, Jack, I hope I've med up for it.'

'Maybe you have. That was a real nice Sunday lunch you cooked for us.' He nudged Adam. 'You got any more secrets you're keeping from me, my lad?'

The spliff trembled between Adam's fingers. Just then there came the sound of a key in the front door.

'Harry, nip into your bunk,' Jack said in a low voice, gently kicking her, 'and hide under the covers.'

She put the mug down beneath Jack's bunk, scrambled up her ladder and pulled the bedding over her. She heard the front door slam and footsteps over the lino in the hallway. Harry peeped out from under the edge of her covers and through the gap below her bunk rail. A pair of stocking-clad legs with firm carves came into view and there was a reek of perfume. Harry pinched her nose to suppress a sneeze.

'You could've waited until you got back home,' came Rita's voice.

'What's it got to do with you?' Jack said.

'What's Stan going to say if you turn up stinking of pot?'

'The chances are he's going to turn up stinking of stout.'

'Don't you care about your reputation?'

'My tommy gun ensures my reputation. I don't need to go to some lousy play with Stan to do that.'

The smell of perfume grew stronger and a hand with pink painted nails gripped the edge of Harry's bunk, the tip of the nails only an inch away from Harry's nose.

'You're losing your grip.'

'Says who? Stan knows he can't risk taking me on without a big fight.'

The hand moved away from Harry's bunk.

'Oh yeah? Maybe that was true a few years ago, but you lost too many men against Slim. What'd you want to take him on for anyway? He wasn't bothering you.'

'He needed taking out, and I was the only one with the guts to do it.'

'Everyone else knew they'd lose too many men.'

'Everyone else had a streak of yellow a mile wide.'

Harry glimpsed Jack's legs striding past. The wardrobe door opened.

'What the hell d'you want your vest for?' Rita said.

For a moment Harry wondered what Rita was talking about, but the corner of a blue bulky object came into view, and she realised that Rita wasn't referring to an undergarment.

'I'm not going to be a target for any upstart git who thinks he can get rid of me,' Jack said.

'Isn't your waistcoat supposed to be bullet-proof?'

'Not as bullet-proof as my vest.' He raised his right trouser leg and strapped on a gun. 'Who came up with the lousy idea of going to a play with Stan?'

'We need to keep in with him.'

'Like we need a hole in the head, which is what he'd try giving me if he didn't know I had a reinforced hat.' A car horn beeped outside. 'Come on. Let's go. Don't keep Ethan waiting.'

'I was ready when I got here.'

They left the flat quarrelling, and Harry jumped down. Adam was sitting on the edge of Jack's bunk holding the tail end of the spliff.

'The lousy bitch,' he said. 'She's always nagging him. One of these days I'm going to take her out. She's got no right to talk to him like that.'

Harry didn't say anything. She went into the bathroom and splashed water on to her toothbrush. Would Adam tell Jack everything? Not that he knew everything. She flipped open the lid of the toothpaste tube. Stick to the original plan: trust no one — except for Amos — and don't owe any favours. She could afford to wait. She squeezed the tube so hard that a blob of paste shot past the brush and hit the sink. It was over a year since Uncle Barney had been murdered. If it took another year to get revenge, then that's what it would have to take. The important thing was to get the job done right. He wouldn't want her to be in debt to anyone — especially not to a bunch of hop-headed gangsters.

— 11 —

STRANGERS

CORNELL checked the map while D.I. van Loame drove the unmarked car along the main road through Great Bartling. They passed houses with pantiles and decorative gables, thatched cottages with hooded dormers, and little rows of terraces with brick cornices. Mostly the buildings were bunched up, just like the group of women with prams who stopped talking to stare at the car as they drove by. A uniformed policeman standing next to a middle-aged woman with a sharp nose looked at Cornell, raised his eyebrows and shook his head. The woman pursed her lips.

'Friendly bunch,' Cornell said. 'I sure hope they just stick to pulling faces at us, and don't start firing arrows.' He caught sight of a street name and checked the map again. 'We should be coming up to a square, and the road to Little Bartling will be on the right.' He looked up again and saw two men standing by a corner. They were wearing fedoras and trench coats and had tommy guns slung under their arms. 'Take a left now!'

Van Loame braked and swerved into a side street.

'Make up your mind.'

'There are some of Quinn's tommy guns up ahead. Pull over. I'll check it out.'

Van Loame parked by the kerb, turned to Cornell and grabbed his arm.

'We didn't come here to get into a fight. We can't afford to have Quinn know we're in his territory.'

'It ought to still be ours, the lousy little backstabber.'

'Yeah I know,' van Loame said, 'but just remember we're not here to take it back — not yet, anyway.'

He let go and Cornell leapt out of the car and ran up the street. A building was flush with the pavement at the junction, which afforded him some cover. He peered round the corner of the building. The two men he had seen earlier had their backs to him, but one turned to toss a cigarette into the gutter, and Cornell recognised the pug-ugly face belonging to Kennedy, one of Quinn's men. Cornell pulled back and pressed himself against the wall. The building on the other corner jutted out, shielding him from the view of the pedestrians they had passed. He took out his pocket scope from his pocket, and risked another look. Kennedy had his back to him once more. Part of the town square was visible behind Kennedy and his companion. There were more of Quinn's men loitering around vehicles. Some of them had sniffer dogs, and they all had guns. Cornell legged it back to the car.

'We need to clear out of here right now.' He shut the door and buckled up. 'Quinn's men are having a party in this town. That may explain the dirty looks we've been getting from the locals.'

A car turned round the corner. They tugged their fedoras over their eyes and sank back in their seats, but the car passed them without slowing and carried on down the road.

Van Loame pulled out and drove along the street past a group of kids playing hopscotch on the pavement.

'Can you find a way out from here?' he said.

'Hang on a minute.' Cornell checked the map. 'It looks like we should take a left at the end of this street. Hold on, that's Harris down that. Take this right.'

Van Loame turned into a narrow lane by a post office.

'Did he see us?'

'I don't think so,' Cornell said, twisting round in his seat. 'What's got Quinn so interested in a little market town?'

'I reckon the boss'll want to know what he's up to. The more we've got on Quinn, the better.'

'There's a pub in the square with a vacancies sign. Let's try the next town –' he looked at the map '– Mundton Green, and check-in with the boss. We may be able to get some country clothes there and come back here after dark.'

Adam raced home from the depot, scattered his pile of post lying on the table and snatched up the new issue of *Generator Monthly*. It had been a fortnight since Harry had told him that she was the grandchild of Edward Bostock. Without bothering about a can of beer, he cast aside his hat and jacket, hastened up the ladder to his bunk with the magazine and searched for the article.

Edward Bostock:
an Interview with the Coulgranes

Dr Edward Bostock, inventor of the Bostock generators, was a biofuel engineer at Colingham University. He was given a grant to further his research by Reginald Coulgrane, the then Earl of Wynherne (celebrated for establishing his own private army during the anarchy), and set up a workshop on the Wynherne Estate.

Bostock's daughter Bella later married John Coulgrane, one of the Earl's grandsons, and the Type 1 prototype is still owned by the family. *Generator Monthly* was granted permission to view the prototype by Bostock's granddaughter, Lady Harriet Coulgrane (pictured below).

Adam turned his attention to the photograph at the bottom of the page of Bostock's granddaughter standing next to his prototype. Despite the long hair arranged in the country style — gathered at the back with ringlets everywhere — she was unmistakably Harry, and not the delicate lady in the posters. She had the smile he sometimes saw on her face when they were alone together. It was a real nice smile, although he hadn't seen it for a while.

He smelt supper cooking and heard humming from the kitchen, which presumably meant that Harry was home. He was about to call her, when he heard the front door open. He stuffed the magazine under his pillow, and Jack and Eric came into the room with a teenage boy in tow. Jack tossed a newspaper on to the bottom bunk.

'Adam, this is Grant,' he said. 'I met him along the road, and the poor lad tells me he has nowhere to go.'

The boy was wearing dirty torn trousers and a shirt with the bottom button undone, revealing his flabby stomach. He thrust his hand into a packet of crisps, scooped it out and sucked his fingers. He reminded Adam of Lackey Larry, the kid who used to swipe his dinner money while Adam was being beaten up by the school bully.

'He can bugger off,' Adam said.

Jack leant against the bedpost and winked at Adam, but then he pulled a solemn face.

'I know we haven't got much in the way of room, but when I heard his sad story, I thought I had to do something to help him out. Isn't that right, Eric?'

'Yeah sure. The poor kid don't have nowhere to go.'

'I remembered we have a camp-bed tucked away in storage somewhere, and I thought he could use it until he found his feet round here. I know it isn't much, but it's a start, and it's a better start than most unfortunates get.'

The boy scratched his belly and picked at his teeth.

'Yeah, that's right,' Eric said, 'and with Harry training to be a trucker, Bob's going to be needing a new assistant.'

'Sure, but it'll help Grant to have Harry around to show him the ropes tomorrow.'

Adam grabbed the side rail, swung himself round and jumped down from his bunk, landing a few inches from the boy's feet. Grant stumbled back against Eric who shoved him away.

'When's Harry going to start trucking?' Adam said.

'As soon as she's passed the HGV test.' Jack picked up Adam's discarded jacket and hat. 'Fergal will arrange it.'

He draped the jacket over the end rail of Adam's bunk and rested the hat on the bedpost. Grant blew into his crisp packet, popped it and dropped the bag on the floor.

'Don't litter the place,' Adam said. 'Pick it up.'

Grant puffed out his cheek, blew out air between pursed lips and tried to kick the bag towards the bin, but it stuck to his shoe, so he hopped over and shook it off his foot into the bin.

Eric ambled over to the dining table on the other side of the room and picked up his post. Harry came into the room with a dish of kedgeree. She no longer wore her jacket indoors and was wearing a shirt and pair of jeans that had belonged to Adam. They weren't too bad a fit — he'd been pretty skinny when he'd left home — and she was wearing his old braces, but she couldn't wear them properly because her breasts were in the way. That sure was a drawback for women who wore trousers. Adam stared at her but quickly tried to find something else to look at. He saw Grant gazing at her and clipped him round the ear.

'If you don't stop gawping at Harry like that, I'll smash your face in.'

Maybe he should've told Harry to get a belt instead, but only uniformed coppers wore belts these days.

'I wunt dewun noffin,' Grant said, rubbing his ear.

Why did Jack have to bring a new migrant home? Not that Adam was criticising Jack — it was Rita's fault. She needed a distraction from Harry, but now the kid knew Harry was a woman, everyone would know.

Jack strolled over to Harry and looked at the contents of her dish.

'It must be Friday. We've got fish again.'

'You don't mind, do you, Jack?' Harry said.

'No, it kind of reminds me of school.' He ruffled her hair. 'It makes a change from the café. They're a decent bunch there, but the menu gets a bit monotonous.'

Jack looked round at Adam and smiled at him, but Adam gestured to him and went out into the hallway. Jack came over and shut the door to the main room.

'What's up, my lad?'

'He'll tell Rita Harry's a woman.'

'We can't hide that forever, especially not if you want her to be your girl. Don't worry, I'll fix things.'

He patted Adam's cheek and returned to the main room. Adam followed on behind. Eric and Grant were already sitting round the table, and Harry was dishing up. Grant pushed his food around the plate with a fork, spilling rice and peas over the edge.

'I dunt like fish.'

'Didn't you tell me how you hadn't eaten all day?' Jack said.

'Well, I hent.'

'Apart from the crisps and the sandwich I got for you.'

'But I dunt like fish. Can't I hev one onem burger and chips meals?'

'Sure, you go out and wander around the city. I expect you might find one eventually, and you might even find different lodgings while you're at it.'

When the meal was over, Jack and Eric took Grant out to the pub. Regulars were lounging around the bar, a mixture of Jack, Stan, Rita and Ethan's people. Some of them stopping by on their way home from work, some of them at work or looking for potential clients. Stan wasn't there yet, but Rita was at their usual table.

'Rita love, it's good to see you,' Jack said as he sat down on the bench next to her seat. He ignored the look of surprise on her face. 'How've you been this week?'

Rita drained her glass.

'You picked up a new friend?'

'This is Grant. He's new in town, so I'm letting him use my camp-bed.'

'Well, isn't that just sweet of you, Jack,' Rita said.

Ralph slid into the seat next to her.

'Hello, Rita. You're looking gorgeous tonight.'

'How's my favourite little rogue?' Rita said, playing with his chin.

'Here, Masher,' Jack said, 'why don't you show Grant round?' He handed over some cash. 'Buy the both of you a drink.'

'Seriously? Thanks, Jack.'

Ralph led Grant over to the crowded bar, elbowing Bob out of the way.

'You're in an unusually good mood tonight,' Rita said to Jack. 'That sure was nice of you to call him Masher for a change.'

'Well, if that's what the kid likes to be called.' Jack touched her hand that was resting on the table near him, but he glanced over at Ralph talking to Grant. 'How about a drink, Rita love?'

'Sure, if you're buying.'

'Sure I am. How about you, Eric?'

'Yeah thanks, Jack.'

Jack signalled to the barmaid. Ralph was still talking to Grant. As long as he hogged the conversation, the less chance Grant had of mentioning that Harry was a woman, but sooner or later he was going to blurt it out. Jack played with Rita's little finger. She pulled her hand away.

'You after something, Jack?'

'Come on, Rita love. I haven't seen you since Sunday, and now I'm home and here we are, together again.'

'You been pining for me?' Rita said.

'You haven't been out of my mind all week.'

Jack glanced back at Ralph. He was demonstrating to Grant how to drink a pint in one go.

'So you've picked up another boy, have you, Jack?'

'He needed a lift and some lodgings.'

Rita touched his cheek. For a moment she pursed her lips as though to kiss him, but then she smiled.

'You usually get all offended when I say that,' she said. 'I make it sound real dirty, that's what you always tell me.'

'And you always say you don't mean it that way, so why should I get angry about it?'

He played with a lock of her hair but again checked on Ralph and Grant.

'Saint Jack's helping out the destitute again? You don't get to do that and keep your tough image.'

'You think I'm doing it out of the goodness of my heart? Every once in a while I find someone useful. Like Adam. I can count on his absolute loyalty and he's a great asset. In fact –' Jack took a bracelet out of his pocket '– he managed to get his hands on this the other day. You like diamonds, don't you?'

Jack fastened it around her wrist. She angled it so that the light glinted off it. The barmaid brought over a tray of drinks. Eric slurped his beer.

'I ain't seen no one else who could've climbed that wall,' he said and belched. 'Ain't that right, Jack?'

'Sure. He's got a real talent,' Jack said. 'And I reckon Harry might prove useful as well.' He caressed Rita's shoulder, but she pulled away. 'Don't be like that, love. You got off on the wrong foot, but there's a reason for it.'

'Oh yeah?'

Jack glanced back at the bar. Grant was now doing the talking.

'Sure there is. Harry was just scared of being found out, that's all.'

'Being found out?'

'I would never have figured it,' Jack said, 'but it turns out she's a woman. Not my idea of a woman, that's for sure. I like an ample pair of breasts.'

He ran his fingers down hers, but she slapped his hand away.

'So you've got a woman living in your little bachelor pad.'

'Adam's quite taken with her, and if my lad wants a girl, then that's what I'll make sure he has.'

Ralph ran over, beer spilling from his glass.

'Here, Rita, you'll never believe this,' he said. 'Grant says Harry's a woman.'

'She's Adam's girl,' Jack said, 'so stay away from her. Go on, the both of you, beat it.'

Ralph glared at him and sloped off with Grant.

'Bet Adam ain't done it with her,' he whispered to Grant. 'I reckon he don't even know what to do.'

'Hoy, I heard that,' Jack said. 'You lay off the both of them.'

Ralph shrugged.

'Come on, Grant. I want you to meet Sal. I reckon you're going to like her.'

It was late at night when they finally returned home. Grant stumbled about the flat and struggled with the camp-bed but eventually gave up and collapsed in a heap on the floor. Jack heard Adam stir, so he went over to his bunk.

'You all right, my lad?'

'Yeah, sure,' Adam said. 'Everything okay?'

'Sure it is. I told you I'd sort it out. They all know that your girl gets my protection.'

'But we're just friends.'

'Has she turned you down?'

'No, I ain't asked her.'

'Then she still gets my protection.'

'Thanks, Jack.'

Adam sank back into his pillow. Jack glanced over to the sleeping form on the opposite bunk. She had better not turn him down.

Harry buttered her toast while Jack kicked the huddled mass on the floor.

'Wake up, boy,' Jack said. 'Don't you want this job? Bob won't take you on if you can't get to work on time.'

Grant moaned and struggled with his blanket. Jack gestured to Eric, and Eric hauled the boy to his feet. Harry dropped some bread into the toaster while Eric dragged Grant to the bathroom. When they returned, the boy's head and half his clothes were soaked, but he seemed more alert. He sat down at the table, his hair dripping and his eyes red. The toaster popped and Harry offered him the slices. He didn't acknowledge her, so she put them on his plate.

'Come on,' Jack said. 'It's time to go.'

'But I hent eaten.'

'You should've got up earlier. Come on, Harry.'

Grant stuffed the unbuttered slices of toast into his pocket and followed Jack and Harry out of the flat. He lagged behind them, and when they reached the stairs leading down to Bob's shop, Jack turned round.

'Hurry up, boy. There's no reason for Harry to be late just because you can't get here on time.' With that he went down the steps, but Harry paused and looked back. 'Don't wait for him, my girl.'

She followed him into the shop. Bob shuffled over to them and greeted them both with a simper. He licked his withered lips as he looked at Harry and clutched his stick.

'Jack told me last night you're leaving, Harry. That's a real shame. I've been good to you, ain't I? We're friends, ain't we?'

'We've got along fine, Bob.'

The bell above the door tinkled as Grant came in. He yawned, fished out a fragment of toast from his pocket and munched on it, spraying crumbs everywhere.

'I ain't getting that to replace Harry, am I?' Bob said.

'This is Grant,' Jack said.

'What use will he be? I bet he ain't half as agile or strong as Harry. You should see the way Harry can scurry up the ladder with a heavy box and jump down like it was no distance at all.'

'Yeah, she's pretty talented, but are you going to take Grant on?'

'If I must.'

Bob shuffled into his office with Jack, leaving Harry with Grant. He stank of sweat, stale cigarettes and beer, despite the dousing he'd been given. His hair was still wet, and a drop of water dribbled down his face until it hung on the tip of his nose.

'How're you farin', bor?' Harry said.

'Like I'm gorta shit over nine hedges.'

'Watch your language in my shop,' Bob said, who had just returned with Jack.

'I think he needs the bathroom,' Harry said.

'He should've gone before he came.'

'He says he's got diarrhœa. I think I ought to show him the way.'

'All right, but no making a mess of my bathroom, boy.'

Harry showed Grant the way and took a few paces back from the door, but to her relief it was vomiting rather than defecation that she heard. She drummed her fingers on the wall until the sound stopped.

'Farin' better?' she said when he emerged.

'You want to know the ins and outs of a duck's arsehole?'

'You're a bit of a nasty one, ent yer?'

Harry soon gave up trying to show Grant what to do and concentrated on her own work. He sloped away early for lunch and was still absent by the time Harry had finished her meal, although that had only consisted of a sandwich and an apple. Bob emerged from his office and looked around the shop.

'Ain't that young layabout come back yet?' he said.

'Not yet. Maybe he's got lost.'

Bob wrinkled his face and shuffled back to his office. When Grant finally returned, he slouched against a wall and looked at a magazine.

'Git you back to work or you'll make Bob raw,' Harry said.

'You're a botty little mawther. What do Adam see in a mawkin like you?'

Grant turned over a page of the magazine. Harry grabbed it but saw a large pair of breasts on the page and let go. Grant waved the page at her.

'Dunt you like that?'

'Were you brought up on the end of a hog-line? Do you put that datty magazine away and mow in. Bob hev a stingy temper. Do you git him in a bad mood, he'll thack you with that stick o' his.'

'You're gittin' on my wick. Do you like the work so much, why dunt you git on wi' it? You can stay in a junk shop for the rest o' yar life do you want, but I'm gorta make it big. I'm gorta hev my own gang, and I'll git them to lam you hard.'

'I'll be hully surprised do that happen.'

'You'll regret givin' me jip, you duzzy old mawther. You dunt want to git on my bad side.'

Bob returned from his office and smacked the knobbly handle of his stick across Grant's back. The boy dropped the magazine and curled into a ball.

'What d'you think I'm paying you for? Go jerk off on your own time.'

Grant flung his arms around his head as Bob struck him again. Harry turned her back on them but, a moment later, she walked over to Bob and laid a hand on his shoulder.

'That's enough. He's not going to be any use to you if you break his bones.'

Bob stopped and Grant struggled to his knees. There were flecks of blood on the boy's vomit-stained top. He screwed up his face as though about to cry.

'Sure thing, Harry. You be grateful Harry's looking out for you, boy. Now get on with your work.'

Bob shuffled off, and Harry held her hand out to Grant.

'Bugger off,' he said so she walked away.

Harry returned alone to the flat that evening and went into the kitchen to prepare the supper. She had just finished tipping some carrots off the chopping board into a saucepan when Grant sauntered in. He opened the fridge and poked a finger into a bowl of chocolate mousse. He sucked his finger and looked in the pan.

'I hope you ent spectin' me to yalm that down,' he said.
'I dunt eat vegetables. They make me fare queer.'

'Then buy yarself some junk food, and git yarself a pod on you, but yar rent includes meals so you'll be payin' extra.'

'I ent payin' for this. Thass reasty, that is.'

He spat in the pan.

'That's going on your rent, you filthy little git.' Jack strode into the kitchen and clouted Grant's head. 'Eric, take him outside and teach him some manners.' Eric came in, hauled the boy up and dragged him out. 'Lucky Adam didn't see that,' Jack said as Harry threw out the contents of the pan. She put it in the sink and started washing it. 'Fergal's offered to give you a test tomorrow. I suggested after lunch since I know you and Adam like going out for a ride on Sunday mornings. That okay with you?'

'That's fine, thanks.'

— 12 —

COLINGHAM

Hadley pocketed his change, picked up the drinks and nearly tripped over the landlord's groenendael. The dog looked up at Hadley and went back to chewing on the leg of a bar stool. Most of the seats in the pub had partially chewed legs. Only strangers didn't first check the structural integrity of their seat before sitting down.

Hadley stepped over the dog and took the drinks to the table by the window where Fenning was staring out at the Great Bartling town square.

'Why do they need guns?' she said. 'You'd think they wuz huntin' a killer, not a missin' mawther.'

Hadley put down a glass in front of her, slopping ginger beer over his hand in the process, and peered over her head. A couple of the Central City policemen were lounging against a car, polishing their tommy guns. On the near side of the square, Mrs Weatherby, her sharp nose twitching, was talking to the vicar of St Mary's.

'That's what the local deputation to the mayor wanted to know this morning, according to Williams,' Hadley said as he sat down. 'They're not a happy bunch, and it's my fault.'

'We hatta ask them for help,' she said. 'They've got much better resources than us.'
One of the city policemen outside slapped a magazine into his gun.
'I thought the point was for them to search for her in the city,' Hadley said.
'That certainly make a change to find them so eager to help.'
The second city policeman looked at Mrs Weatherby and started tossing his drum magazine up in the air so that it span for a few moments before he caught it.
'If they're going to search the neighbourhood, they ought at least to bring some of our people with them,' Hadley said.
'Do they get lost, that'll larn 'em.' Fenning leant close to him. 'Praps we should suggest a few short cuts they might take.'
'We're supposed to be showing our brother officers respect.'
The policeman outside fumbled his catch and the magazine fell, bounced and rolled along the road. He chased after it, caught it and tossed it back into the air again.
'And woss happened to our sister officers?' Fenning said. 'Thass what I'd like to know.'
'Anyway, Williams already had the same idea as you, but it seems someone's warned them which routes to avoid.'
Hadley leant back in his seat and wiped his hand with a handkerchief. There were some familiar lunchtime faces in the pub: gnarled weather-beaten ones, fresh-faced shop assistants, and clerks from the town hall. There were also three secretaries from the police station by the fireplace, giggling over a magazine. In the far corner of the room sat two strangers wearing tweeds and homburgs. They both kept

glancing out of the window while they ate their meal. The furthest one put his knife down to jot something in a notepad by his plate.

The barmaid came over to Hadley and Fenning with their steak and swimmers. Out in the square two more city policemen joined their colleagues. The one who had been playing catch with his magazine slapped it into his gun. The strangers in the corner of the pub put down their cutlery and peered through the window. The far one jotted something else in his notepad.

'Molly,' Hadley said to the barmaid, 'what d'you know about the two men in the corner?'

'They came here last week. They say they're historians from Colingham writing up a book about the anarchy.' She glanced at the two men and leant closer. 'Seem like they allus run off afore the city police come in, and they've been asking about that furriner who was shot last year. Did you want any salt or pepper with that, tergether?'

Hadley and Fenning declined and made a start on their lunch, but Hadley kept an eye on the men while he ate. When they had finished their meal, he nodded to Fenning, and they got up. Hadley stroked the groenendael's black fur and then strolled over to the far corner with Fenning.

'Mind if we sit down?' Hadley said to the strangers, and he and Fenning pulled up seats next to the men.

The table contained remnants of a meal and a pot of coffee. The man next to Hadley reached for his cup and, as he did so, his right sleeve slipped up to reveal a tattoo of the outline of a canary. He put the cup down, pulled his sleeve back in place, and took a toothpick out of his jacket pocket.

'Did the dog eat your seats?' he said.

'We heard you're historians writing about the anarchy,' Hadley said. 'I lived through it, so I was interested.'

The man with the tattoo eyed Hadley. The other one continued gazing out of the window.

'You one of the refugees that hid out at the Coulgrane place?'

'Yes, that's right. I'm Hadley and this is Fenning.'

'McLachlan.' He pointed his thumb at himself and then at his colleague. 'Jeffries.'

The other man glanced up at Hadley and Fenning and returned to staring out of the window. There was a scar across the left side of his jaw, and his nose looked like it might once have been broken. The notepad was by his side, but his coffee cup obscured what was written on it.

'So how long are you staying here?' Hadley asked.

'Why?' McLachlan said. 'You in a hurry to see us go?'

'No, I didn't mean it like that.'

'We're being sociable,' Fenning said. 'We thought you might like a mardle.'

McLachlan chewed on his toothpick for a while before speaking.

'You're coppers, aren't you?'

'How did you know?' Hadley said.

'You hear that?' McLachlan said to Jeffries. 'They want to know how we know? Psychic, aren't we?'

'They might just as well have waved their badges when they came over.' Jeffries looked up at them and jerked his thumb at the window. 'You with them?'

'Who d'you mean?' Hadley said.

'Quinn's lot. You got to be all good buddies together?'

'They're furriners,' Fenning said.

Hadley nudged her foot with his. McLachlan grinned.

'Yeah, that lot are foreigners all right,' he said. 'But we ain't. We're both bred and born in Norw — Norfolk.'

'Norw-Norfolk?' Fenning said.

'North Norfolk. Where Black Shuck roams.'

McLachlan gave a howl. Hadley edged away, but Fenning smiled and there was a mischievous glint in her eyes. The conversation in the pub stopped and people turned to stare at them. The secretaries at the other end of the room stifled their giggles. The landlord's dog began to bark. Fenning leant her elbows on the table, knocked a spoon over the edge and ducked down to fetch it.

'Keep the noise down,' Jeffries said, nodding at the window. 'We don't want to disturb the neighbours.'

Hadley glanced out. A fifth man had joined the group of city police. His gun was slung across his middle and his left hand gripped the front recoil brake. Fenning re-emerged with the spoon.

'I thought Black Shuck was spuzzed to roam orl over East Anglia, not jist North Norfolk,' she said.

'Is that so?' McLachlan said. 'That lot outside would need a change of trousers if it turned up right now. Mind you, I reckon that little doggy over there would probably scare the pants off some of them.'

He began chewing on his toothpick again. The right cuff on his beige tweed jacket was flawed. Hadley had seen that mis-sewn seam in the second hand shop in Mundton Green. It had been hanging next to a blue worsted suit with a stain on the collar, just like the one Jeffries was wearing. Hadley had nearly bought it after his clothes had become coated in mud following his visit to Belrosa, but he had ended up buying a brown suit instead. The strangers' worn homburgs also looked as though they had come from the same shop. McLachlan's was slightly too large.

'I heard they're looking for the missing lady,' Jeffries said. 'So what's with all the artillery? They look more like they're about to enter a war zone.'

'Apparently the city police always carry guns,' Hadley said. 'It's standard practice.'

'Oh sure,' McLachlan said. 'Every copper has to carry a cannon while he helps a little old lady to cross a road.'

'That's so he can mug her when they get to the other side,' Jeffries said. 'Central City's sure gone to the dogs.'

McLachlan chewed on the toothpick some more and then removed it. The tip was soggy and lumpy.

'They're a bunch of pansies,' he said. 'They're scared a sick lady's going to smack them over the head with her reti-thingy.' He turned to Fenning. 'What's the name of the fancy little bag fashionable bints like to carry?'

'A reticule.'

'Sure, that's right. Hey, watch out, boys. She's armed with a reticule. Better get the cannons out.'

Hadley studied the city men outside, playing with their guns, and wondered what kind of an impression they would give a frightened ill lady. Quinn had assured him that his men were always polite when the occasion demanded — not that Hadley had seen any evidence of it so far.

'How do North-Norfolk men end up in Colingham?' Fenning said.

McLachlan picked up his cup, made to drink it and put it down again.

'There's a lot of interesting history in these parts, so we moved over to Colingham to study it. That statue in the square's a Coulgrane, right?'

'That's Reginald Coulgrane,' Hadley said. 'He was the Earl of Wynherne when the anarchy started.'

'He was the one who gave you protection against the raiders?' McLachlan said.

'That's right.' Jeffries sipped his coffee, which gave Hadley a glimpse of his notepad. It seemed to have names written on it, including his and Fenning's. Did the other names belong to the city police outside?

'I hear people round here are still in need of protection,' McLachlan said. 'Like that del Rosario fellow. Were the two of you on that case?'

'No,' Hadley said.

'Know anything about it?'

'Someone with a tommy gun shot him just over a year ago. Commissioner Quinn believes it was Jack Preston.'

Jeffries's coffee cup clattered against the saucer.

'It was Quinn who fingered him? Who the hell does he think he is coming up with a line like that?'

'Commissioner Quinn has a good knowledge of city gangsters,' Hadley said, studying Jeffries. Was it possible that Hadley was talking to two of them right now? 'He seemed to think the murder fitted Preston's style, and apparently he had a grudge against del Rosario.'

'Sure, Quinn's got a real good knowledge of lowlife,' Jeffries said.

'You seem more interested in current affairs than history,' Fenning said.

McLachlan looked at her and wiggled his eyebrows.

'Today is tomorrow's history.' He looked out of the window and jumped up. 'And we need to be getting on with our research.'

Jeffries glanced at his colleague and then out of the window. Hadley followed his gaze. Three of the city policemen were strolling across the square towards the pub, all of them cradling tommy guns.

Jeffries snatched up his notepad. He and McLachlan dodged round a group of farmers with their pints. Hadley and Fenning stood up to follow them, but the dog had ambled over to chew on Hadley's chair, causing him to stumble.

McLachlan paused in the doorway that led to the guest rooms and looked back at Hadley. He put his right index finger to his eye and then pointed at the front door. He ducked out of sight just as the three city policemen walked in. They slung their guns across their backs and strolled over to the bar. Hadley watched as they ordered drinks and then realised that, like everyone else in the room (including the dog), he was staring silently at the strangers. One of them perched on the edge of a stool and reclined against the bar, but the stool toppled under him, sending him sprawling. His colleagues helped him up, and he picked up the seat. One of the legs was chewed at the bottom. He grabbed the barmaid's arm.

'What's the big idea? Set up a trap for us, have you?'

'Let her go,' Hadley said as he and Fenning hurried over. 'It's the dog that damages the seats, not someone playing a prank.'

The man eyed the dog and backed away.

'What do they need a bloody great hound in a pub for?'

'What d'you need guns in a pub for?'

The man walked up close to Hadley. He was an inch taller than Hadley and looked at least two stone heavier.

'And who are you?'

'Detective Inspector Hadley, and this is Detective Sergeant Fenning.'

The man eyed them, sneered and picked up his drink. He and his two colleagues strolled over to the fireplace, leant against the mantelpiece and leered at the secretaries. Hadley drummed his fingers on the bar top. Fenning leant close to him, her mouth near his ear.

'I can't say that I blame those historians for not liking the city police, but the fella I was sitting next to have a gun strapped to his left ankle. Praps he write with his right and shoot with his left, or praps he's got another one on t'other leg as well.'

'Why do they want to know about del Rosario?'

Molly was rubbing the surface of the bar with a cloth, edging closer to Hadley and Fenning.

'Inspector,' she said. 'There ent gorter be a shoot-out, is there? Like that furriner?'

'Don't worry,' Hadley said. 'I'm sure everything's going to be fine.'

A police siren started up outside. Molly twisted the cloth between her fingers. Fenning patted her hand.

'Dunt you worry, my bewty,' she said. 'The city police have more testosterone than brain. Do you give us a call do they cause trouble.'

'What about those historians?' Molly said.

Hadley tapped the bar top. What were they up to? If they really were historians from Colingham, they ought to have some kind of contact with the university. Maybe it would be worth checking them out.

'Do they have visitors?' he said, but Molly shook her head. 'Do they go out at all?'

'Sometimes they go out in their car, but ony when *they* ent around.'

She nodded towards the city police. The secretaries were gathering their things together. It seemed they weren't interested in being leered at. The man who had fallen off the stool moved over to the women but glanced at Hadley and Fenning. He'd better not leer at Fenning, Hadley thought. She'd get her truncheon out.

Hadley thanked Molly and reiterated Fenning's instruction to call if there was a problem, and he and Fenning left the pub. They walked past the statue of Reginald Coulgrane and a horse tethered by a stone trough. The sky was overcast, but hopefully the rain would hold off for a few hours.

'See if you can get hold of a camera with a good zoom lens from the photographic department,' he said. 'We might be able to get a decent shot of the historians from our office window. Let's see if anyone from Colingham recognises them.'

'Rackon we'd have more luck if we took the photo to Norwich.'

'That's out of our jurisdiction now.'

Hadley stood by his office window and peered through the viewfinder. Fenning was next to him with a pair of binoculars. The town seemed to have fallen quiet. There was a muffled sound of clacking on a typewriter or computer keyboard. A dog barked in the distance and then fell silent. Two horses tethered outside gave an occasional whinny. The city police were nowhere in sight. He could hear Fenning breathing gently by his side. She smelt of the rosewater he'd given her for her birthday. Cramp was setting in. He lowered his right hand, flexing it, and it brushed against her leg.

'Thass them in the car,' she said.

Hadley moved his hand back and clicked the camera. He took another shot just as the car pulled out of the pub's driveway. He straightened up and rubbed the back of his neck.

'You okay?' Fenning said.

'Just a bit stiff.'

'You need one o' my Great Aunt Linda's warm herbal bags.'

'No, I don't.'

She grinned at him and took the camera. Hadley picked up a folder.

'Once you get back from the photographic department, you'll have to put historians, gangsters and tommy guns out of your mind,' he said. 'We need to crack the fraud case.'

Hadley opened another folder. There had been a series of bank frauds in the area and a new case had just turned up in a Colingham branch with the same MO. Fenning soon returned and pulled up a chair. They read through statements and cross-referenced details until the photographic department phoned an hour later to say that the pictures were ready. Fenning went off to fetch them and came back with grainy prints of the two men in their car. In the first shot, they were both looking up at the police station, so their faces were uncovered, but the second shot was blurred and their hats obscured them.

Hadley tucked the first photo into his jacket pocket, and he and Fenning set off to Colingham. They parked near the Fen Bank and visited the bank manager. Hadley asked the usual questions, Fenning jotted in her notepad, and the manager mopped his forehead and urged them to apprehend the culprit as soon as possible.

When they were done, Hadley and Fenning left the bank but didn't return to the car. They happened to be close to Colingham University, so they headed over there. It was one of the new universities that had been built shortly before the anarchy, specialising in biofuels, biodiversity and climate science, but over the last thirty years it had developed a thriving history department as well as a medical school with connections to the local hospitals.

They stopped at the porter's lodge, headed past the bioreactor and a series of greenhouses, along a walkway, up a flight of steps and into the main building. They then had to negotiate a maze of windowless corridors until they finally arrived at the history department's general office where they found a middle-aged secretary with white streaks in her brown ringlets and deep crow's feet at the corners of her grey eyes.

'D'you know of a couple of historians from Colingham called McLachlan and Jeffries?' Hadley said, showing her the photo.

'I can't say that I do. I certainly don't recognise their faces.' She opened a drawer and flicked through its contents. 'No, they're not registered here. I'll ask Professor Hayter. He know most of the historians in Colingham.'

She led them down the corridor to the professor's office. He was an elderly balding man, who took a long time looking at the photo and rifling through his notes, muttering to himself.

'No, I'm sorry. I don't have any record of them,' he said. 'They might be amateurs.'

Hadley thanked the professor for his time, and the secretary showed them a short cut out of the university that took them on to a street near the private hospital. An ambulance sped past, its sirens wailing. Hadley and Fenning headed along the road, following the signs towards the town centre, where they had parked. Hadley glanced at his watch. It was almost four o'clock.

'D'you want to head straight back?' he said.

'I'd rather hev some fourses.'

'And me. Let's try over there.'

They crossed over the road and headed towards a small thatched coffee shop adjoining a tiled greengrocers. A tired-looking mother with a baby in a pram and a noisy toddler on a rein ignored her child's pleas for cake and bustled her along. The rack under the pram was full of bulging shopping bags. Hadley moved out of the way to let them pass. Mr Allerton stepped out of the coffee shop, glanced both ways without appearing to notice Hadley or Fenning, and began to walk down the street. A woman came out of the shop, opening an umbrella that obscured her face. She set off towards the private hospital, in the opposite direction to Allerton. She walked fast, even though she was wearing a tight pencil skirt. Hadley called Allerton and ran after him. He had to call a second time before Allerton swung round.

'Inspector Hadley.' Allerton extended his hand. 'What brings you to Colingham?'

Hadley shook hands. Allerton was again wearing his strong almond pomade.

'Business,' Hadley said.

Allerton stared into Hadley's face, as though trying to read his mind. It was odd that a witness under police protection would be happy to go to a coffee shop in a large town, but perhaps the influx of armed city police gave him a greater sense of security.

'Is there any news?' Allerton asked.

'No, I'm sorry, sir. This is an unrelated case.'

'Of course, you must have so many other cases,' Allerton said and turned to go.

If those historians really were gangsters, maybe it was Allerton they were after. Although that didn't explain their interest in del Rosario.

'Wait a minute, Mr Allerton,' Hadley said, tucking his hand into his pocket. Allerton turned back. 'Since you're here, I wonder if you might happen to recognise these men.'

Hadley produced the photo and handed it over. Allerton looked at it. His face developed a greyish hue, and his eyes darted about the street. He shoved the photo back at Hadley.

'Sorry, no idea,' Allerton said.

'You dunt rackonise them?' Fenning said.

Allerton pulled up his collar and tugged his hat over his eyebrows.

'No. It looks like it's going to rain. I'd rather not be caught in it.'

Allerton hurried away, glancing this way and that.

'Thass interestin',' Fenning said. 'If they're the people he's hidin' from, you'd think he woulda mentioned.'

'I was thinking exactly that.'

'Are you going to talk to the city police about our local historians?'

'Let's just keep them under surveillance for now.'

Fenning nudged him.

'Who? The historians or the city police?'

'Maybe both.'

They went into the coffee shop and waited at a table for the waitress. Rain started to splatter against the window. Pedestrians outside broke into a run. Colingham Surgery was on the other side of the road. Perhaps that was where Dr Carmichael used to practise.

'D'you rackon that was Miss Penderbury?' Fenning said. Hadley turned round.

'Who?'

'The mawther who came outta here arter Allerton. That certainly looked like her type of outfit and her figure.'

'I don't know,' Hadley said. 'I was paying more attention to Allerton.'

'That was hully gentlemanly o' you goin' to look outta the window time she was wigglin' her arse at you when we went to see her.'

'I'm glad you restrained yourself from making inappropriate comments at the time.'

On the other side of the coffee shop, a woman sat with a small boy who was eating a slice of Battenberg cake.

'Pomade!' Hadley said.

'Is that a new swear word?'

'When I was looking out of Miss Penderbury's window I noticed a faint smell that reminded me of Battenberg cake. It was just like Allerton's almond pomade.'

A young waitress with dark curls poking out from under her cap came over to them, her notepad at the ready.

'Thass rafty old weather terday,' she said. 'We've got hot corfee, cuckoo or taay to warm you up.'

'Corfee sound like a masterous idea, my bewty,' Fenning said. 'Thass certainly a slow ole dry out. I'm surprised you dunt have a rush now a-comin' in.'

'That'll pick up soon enough. We've now about finished the end o' the school rush.'

'Not just the end o' school by the look of that couple who now a-come outta here,' Fenning said and winked. 'They looked hully embarrassed about bein' seen tergether.'

'The mawther with the tight skirt and the fella who allus sound so primmicky? Two cuckoos and a cake. Thass their usual.'

'My heart alive,' Fenning said. 'How can she have cake in that skirt? She'd tear a seam.'

'Oh, he hev the cake. Allus got suffin to complain about, he hev. Terday he say there's a pishamire in the sugar. Well, I looked, but I dint see noffin. Next thing you know, he'll be sayin' there's pollywiggles in the milk. Wuz that only two corfees?'

'Oh, I rackon we'll hev a slice o' fruit cake atwin us,' Fenning said. 'I rackon my waistline can jist about manage that.'

'What are you talking about, my bewty? There's plenty o' room for it.'

The waitress went off behind the counter. Hadley leant towards Fenning and gestured at the surgery over the road.

'Ask about Carmichael.'

The waitress soon returned with their order.

'D'you know any o' the doctors over at the surgery?' Fenning asked.

'Yis, they sometimes come in here for their fourses.'

'D'you remember Dr Carmichael? Sandy-haired fella with spectacles.'

'Oh yis, a nice bloke, but a few sticks short on a bundle. Allus forgittin' suffin in here, he wuz. Useter be up at the university, but he never spuffled like some onem do.'

'He must've been hully pleased to be given his own practice.'

'He certainly wuz. That was a caution, but one onem blokes on the medical board recommended him. The doctor was hully excited about it, though we orl wondered do the gentleman know what a tewl he is.'

'Did he say who the gentleman was?'

'No, he dint know, but I darst say the doctor'll be fine. You need to make sure he dunt rackon there's suffin wrong with your head, do you know what I mean, as he wanted to be one onem mind specialists, but he wuz good at lookin' arter the screws in my ow mum's fingers.'

The waitress continued chatting for a while about her mother's rheumatic pains until the lady with the boy in the corner wanted to pay her bill.

Hadley and Fenning had nearly finished their fourses when the door opened and two men walked in, their homburgs glistening with rain. Hadley recognised the heavy build of D.I. Jarrett and the pock-marked face of D.S. Regan from the Colingham plain clothes division.

'Lo, Hadley,' Jarrett said, strolling over with his hands in his coat pockets. 'What brings you to Colingham?'

'Hallo, Jarrett. We had to pay a visit to the manager at the Fen Bank.'

'He been misbehaving, or are you after a loan?'

D.I. Jarrett and D.S. Regan pulled chairs over to Hadley and Fenning's table. The waitress had gone into a room behind the counter where there came the sound of crockery clattering.

'They've had a problem with a bit of fraud,' Hadley said.

'And why would Great Bartling be interested in a Colingham bank?'

'It's connected with one of our cases. Your people sent us the paperwork.'

Jarrett picked up a sugar cube from the bowl and tossed it into his mouth. The coffee percolator on the counter gurgled.

'That the only thing that brought you to Colingham?' he said, the sugar cube making a bulge in his cheek.

'Is there a problem with us being here?'

Jarrett prodded the remaining sugar cubes in the bowl and began to stack them one on top of the other.

'Not at all, but if you'd told us, we could've arranged for someone to show you round.'

'The bank was easy enough to find.'

'There's a bloody ant in this sugar bowl,' Jarrett said, picking it out and flicking it across the room.

'Dint you know thass a good source o' protein?' Fenning said.

Jarrett jiggled what remained of the sugar lump in his mouth and brought it in front of his teeth, between his lips. He then sucked it back in again. Hadley wondered how many cavities he had.

'You heading back when you've finished your fourses, Hadley?' Jarrett said.

'That's right. We don't have any other business here.'

'You mind if we join you?'

'Not at all, but we're nearly finished.'

'That's all right. We're not staying long.' Jarrett summoned the waitress and ordered a brownie for himself and a slice of carrot cake for Regan. 'So how's the Coulgrane case coming along?'

'Quinn's people have taken over,' Hadley said. 'I thought you knew that.'

'Sure, that's right. I remember now. You remember, Regan?'

'Sure, it's just come back to me.'

The waitress brought over Jarrett and Regan's cakes. Jarrett picked a lump of chocolate off the top of his brownie and nibbled it.

'Any further developments?' he said to Hadley.

'None that I know of.'

'No suspicious characters hanging around the place?'

'Only Quinn's people.'

'You getting along okay with them?'

'We don't understand why they need to bring machine guns with them,' Hadley said. 'It's unsettling people. If they have to be armed, why not bring hand arms they can conceal?'

Like those historians, Hadley mentally added.

'People who live out in the sticks just don't understand city crime fighting,' Jarrett said.

'You made the right call, Hadley,' Regan said. 'Bringing in Quinn's men. They've got a lot more experience hunting people than you.'

'She's a missin' sick lady not a criminal,' Fenning said.

'Didn't she stab Mr Allerton in the leg?' Regan said to Hadley.

'Mr Allerton's not pressing charges.'

'Don't make her any less dangerous, does it?'

'Mr Allerton doesn't want her harmed.'

'Don't mind Regan,' Jarrett said. 'Quinn's men will look after her with kid gloves, won't they, Regan? She can't help that her brain's messed up.'

A young couple came into the coffee shop and sat down near the counter.

'That's most reassuring,' Hadley said and summoned the waitress to pay his and Fenning's bill. 'We're going to head back to Great Bartling and crack on with this bank case.'

Jarrett and Regan wrapped the remains of their cakes in paper napkins and settled up as well.

'You'll let us know if you have to come back to Colingham, won't you?' Jarrett said. 'We could show you the sights. Where're you parked?'

'Near the bank.'

'We're heading that way, so we may as well keep you company.'

It wasn't far and Hadley was soon behind the wheel with Fenning by his side. He glanced up in the rear-view mirror. Jarrett and Regan were in the car behind them.

'I think we're being seen out of town,' Hadley said.

'Rackon thass a coincidence they turned up arter we met Mr Allerton?'

'He certainly has important friends.' Hadley turned on to the road to Great Bartling. 'But our historians don't number among them.'

'D'you rackon we've stumbled on rival mobs?'

'Try not to sound so excited about the idea, Fenning.'

— 13 —

On the Road

The light at the top of the stairs flickered and buzzed. Adam tapped it and jiggled the bulb in its mounting until the beam became steady. He went down the steps with Harry behind him. The generator took up one side of the cellar of Frank's service station, five miles south of The Wash. There was a sickly sweet smell coming from the rectangular fuel tank.

'The fuel's sugar beet ethanol,' Adam said to Harry, 'but you'll know more about that than me.'

'It's quite similar to Grandpa Eddie's design, except for the holding tank.'

Harry had passed her HGV test the previous day, and Adam had agreed to sit with her in her cab for just this week. It had been Jack's idea for someone to keep an eye on her driving, but it had given Adam the opportunity to tell Harry about this generator, all the way from the depot to Frank's. Now he stood by her side while she inspected the coupling between the tank and generator.

'Who's down there?'

Adam turned to see a large figure blocking the doorway at the top of the stairs.

'Get lost, Donnaghan.'

'Oh, it's you. I might've known. Who's that with you?'

'What's it to you?'

Adam turned back to the generator and tugged Harry's arm, pulling her over to his side.

'And you'll have got permission to be in here, I suppose,' Donnaghan said.

'Frank don't mind me looking at his generator. Don't I fix it for him if I'm around when it goes wrong?' Adam tapped Harry and pointed to a plaque. 'Look, it's one of the series one models.'

'And I fix it as well,' Donnaghan said, 'but you don't find me tramping in and out of the generator room just for the fun of it.'

'Bugger off.'

'You'll be wanting to hit the road before the rush hour. There's tailbacks near Central City.'

'I don't need a lousy traffic cop to tell me my job.'

Adam stomped up the stairs and shoved Donnaghan. The flab on the cop's stomach wobbled, but other than that he didn't move.

'Get out of my way, you great lump of lard.'

But Donnaghan was staring past Adam's elbow. The cop's eyes protruded and his chin drooped. Adam turned and saw Harry standing a few steps lower down in the full light of the bulb. She zipped up her jacket and put her cap on. Adam swung back to Donnaghan and pulled out a knife.

'You stay away from Harry. Get out of my way, or I'll spike you.'

'That would make a pretty bit of trouble for Jack, especially with us being in Central Constabulary right now.'

'Is everything all right, my boy?'

Donnaghan whipped round. Jack was lounging against the wall in the corridor behind him with his hands in his trench coat pockets. Adam slipped the knife away.

'He was looking funny at Harry.'

'I wasn't,' Donnaghan said. 'I came to see who was messing around in the cellar.'

'Oh sure,' Jack said. 'There you were watching out for speeding traffic, and you suddenly got all concerned about Frank's cellar.'

'I'm on my lunch break.'

'Then go eat it.'

Donnaghan stomped away. Jack winked at Adam.

'We've got a bit more time, if you want to play with the generator some more, my boy.'

'No, it's all right,' Adam said. 'I suppose we'd better get going.'

Adam and Harry returned to their truck parked near the biofuel pumps. Adam kicked a tyre.

'One of these days I'm going to accidentally leave the brake off while he's behind the truck.'

He kicked the tyre again and looked up to see Harry staring south-eastwards across the marshes. The wooden sails of a wind pump began to vibrate and pick up speed as the breeze turned into gusts that eddied and swirled until a miniature whirlwind formed, dancing over the flat landscape. Then it faded into nothing and the sails returned to their slow rotation.

Harry put a finger to the corner of her eye.

'You okay?' Adam said.

'Fine. Just a bit of dust, that's all.'

She turned away and climbed into the truck. Behind them, the fuel pump clattered and hummed as someone began to fill up. The smell of the biofuel drifted in the breeze. Jack and Eric came out of the service station café. It was time to go.

'Turn right here. That's the warehouse.'

They were inside Jack's foothold in Central City — but only just. Armed guards patrolled the perimeter of the warehouse. Adam directed Harry to a bay and men bustled around unloading some of the unmarked crates from the truck.

'Come on,' Adam said. 'I'd better introduce you to Ginger Jim. They all need to be able to identify you here.'

Adam took her into the office where Ginger Jim shook her hand with a large, hairy paw. His shaggy beard concealed most of his scars, but his nose was as flattened as a prize-fighter's, and his left iris was paler than his right.

Adam and Harry were returning to their truck when Jack came over.

'How's it going, my lad? How'd she get on with Ginger Jim? I told him to be on his best behaviour. I hope he took down that poster of his before she came in. So, Harry, any questions?'

'Why d'you call him "Ginger Jim"?'

'I would've thought that was flaming obvious.'

'But why not just call him "Jim"? Are you going to start calling me "Blond Harry"?'

'I'm sure I can think of a better name for you, but you can't be "Blond Harry" because there's already a "Blond Jim", which ought to answer your question. Believe me, there are far coarser ways of distinguishing between the two Jims.'

'Why not just use their surnames?'

'Surnames aren't so easy to remember.'

'Who was Blond Jim?' Adam said.

'Don't you remember him? A pretty boy with a mean streak.' Jack patted Harry on the back. 'You're going to do just fine, my girl. Do you ask questions about what's in the crates, where they're going, what's the profit, what's the risk? No, you just want to know how some fellow got his nickname. See you at Betsy's.'

Adam and Harry returned to their truck, and Harry drove through the city until they pulled into Betsy's Café. It was now twilight and the lights were on in the building. Outside a lamp lit up the wooden sign above the entrance. Potted plants and hanging baskets lined the front wall.

'We always stop here for the night when we're in Central City,' Adam said as they stepped down from the cab. 'There ain't a lot of space, so we all have to share. The rooms are mostly twin or triple ones.'

Harry locked the truck, slung her new rucksack over her shoulder and followed him into the lobby. Betsy hailed them.

'You must be Harry. Jack's told me all about you. Has he arrived yet? Hazel, take their bags up to their room. You've got a twin. Jack said that would be all right. I'm sorry, Harry, there are no women for you to share with, but Jack said you wouldn't mind. Not if it was a choice between Adam or a stranger. Not that I'll take in anyone dodgy. We only have decent people here, but it's much nicer to share with a friend. How was your journey? Which of you wants to sign the register? Oh, Jack, there you are.'

Jack had just come in with Eric. Betsy hurried over to them. Jack kissed her and pinned back a lock of her hair that had fallen loose.

'Good to see you again, Betsy my love,' he said.

Adam turned to Harry, but she was studying the missing-person noticeboard on the wall near the reception desk. He tugged her sleeve.

'Come on, Harry. Let's get something to eat.'

They had nearly finished their meal in the dining room when Jack stared over Adam's shoulder.

'Not him again,' Jack said. 'You'd think he was tailing us or something.'

Adam looked round and saw through the window a police car parked outside. Donnaghan hitched up his trousers and walked over to the main entrance.

'What d'you reckon he wants here?' Eric said.

Jack finished his drink, got up and strolled over to the lobby. The other three followed him. Donnaghan was unpinning a poster from the noticeboard.

'Managed to find someone, have you, Donnaghan?' Jack snatched the poster from the cop. 'Jane Lamm. A nice girl if the photo's anything to go by. Offered her your help and protection from all the mean old crooks and villains, did you?'

'What d'you want to know about her for?'

'Oh, I'm sorry. Is it some big secret that a woman's gone missing? Or is it a secret she's been found?'

Donnaghan glanced at Harry.

'I told you to quit staring at Harry,' Adam said.

'Donnaghan,' Jack said, 'just for the record, in case you failed to observe it, Harry's with us now. Savvy?' He looked back at the poster. 'Is it too much to assume that the Central Constabulary police have actually managed to find someone without a cash incentive? Or has she been found in the morgue?'

'Her body was pulled out of the river,' Donnaghan said. 'Probably a jumper.'

'So who is she?'

'Jane Lamm.'

'Yeah, I just read that out, didn't I? Your intellectual prowess never ceases to amaze me.'

'She worked as a P.A. at a private hospital in a town called Colingham, which is maybe about twenty miles east of here.'

'I can read road signs, thank you very much,' Jack said. 'You're a fine one for information, aren't you?'

'I'm sure I could look up her file if you're interested.'

Jack rolled up the poster and whacked Donnaghan across the head with it.

'Don't put yourself out on my account. It was just idle curiosity — a bit of conversation to pass the time. Although I'm sure others could've made it a little more entertaining.' Jack handed over the poster. 'Take care you don't end up on a missing-person board yourself.'

Donnaghan screwed up the poster, swung round and stomped out of the building.

Their room was plain with twin beds separated by a table, but it was neat and clean with a small en suite bathroom. There was a single window that overlooked the busy street outside and opposite was an electronic billboard. Adam threw himself on one of the beds and watched Harry investigating the room, not that there was much for her to find. Just a bible in a drawer and an empty ashtray, which Harry sniffed and moved aside.

'Do you and Jack only smoke those spliffs when Eric's out?' she said.

'What's brought that up?'

'I was thinking about it when you and Jack were smoking last night.'

'Yeah, well, Eric's mum once asked Jack to make sure he never did drugs. Mind you, she didn't say anything about not drinking himself silly or beating the crap out of people or going on shoot-outs.'

Harry opened the window and the sound of the billboard drifted in above the noise of the traffic: buy Nabney's lemonade for that extra fizz; peace and prosperity; buy Rall's toothpaste and dazzle your friends.

'That thing's not going to be on all night, is it?' she said.

'The sound should cut out in half an hour, but the images don't switch off.'

'So it's even more lit up here than in Norwich? I don't think I'll ever get used to how light it is at night in the city. At home, all the generators get switched off at eleven — apart from the one connected to the septic tank, of course.'

'How d'you see where you're going?'

'Wind-up torches, lanterns and candles.'

She leant out of the window. Adam jumped up and went over to her.

'Come away from there.'

'What's up? We're only on the first floor. You're not worried about heights, are you?'

'You kidding? Ain't Jack always said I'm the best climber he's ever known? See that wall down the road. I could get up and over that with no more aids than my climbing shoes and gloves.'

'What's behind the wall?'

'That's Sector House, but it ain't worth getting hospitalised over.' He touched her lightly and pulled her away from the window. 'Don't make yourself such an easy target. We're right on the edge of Jack's territory here.'

She turned around, and he found that he was holding her close to him. At that moment, there was a knock at the door: two rapid taps, a pause, then five more taps.

'I have to go out,' he said. 'Don't wander off.'

Adam stood with Eric a little way behind Jack in Commissioner Quinn's office. Part of Adam's mind was wishing that Jack had summoned him a few minutes — or maybe an hour — later, but most of his concentration was taken up with watching Quinn's every move.

'Stan asked me to bring this over for you,' Jack said, handing Quinn a parcel wrapped in brown paper.

Quinn took it over to the black and silver safe behind his mahogany desk. The other end of the room had a couple of leather armchairs, a chintz sofa and a drinks cabinet. Heavy plush curtains covered the windows. The central heating was on too high for Adam's liking.

'So what's all this I hear about you bullying poor old Donnaghan?' Quinn said, shielding the safe combination dial while he turned it.

'You must've heard that wrong,' Jack said. 'It was just a bit of friendly joshing, that's all.'

'So you didn't hit him on the head?'

'Just a friendly tap.'

'I don't like people teasing coppers, Jack.' Quinn opened the safe door just wide enough to slip the parcel inside. 'It sends out the wrong image.'

'I never tease an honest copper. So how come Stan didn't ask Donnaghan to bring you his parcel, seeing as how he was coming this far?'

Quinn closed the safe door and spun the dial.

'Well, you know how it is for a traffic cop. They've got too much to be worrying about to look after a valuable parcel.'

Adam glanced up at a fancy clock on a shelf. Would Harry still be awake when he got back?

'So what's got you so interested in Jane Lamm?' Quinn said.

A police siren started up outside but soon faded into the distance.

'What's up? Has someone got a guilty conscience?'

'What's that supposed to mean?'

'I know how Donnaghan likes to help women out, as he puts it,' Jack said. 'Although it's help they could well do without. I was just wondering if she was one of them. He had that funny look about him when we saw him removing the poster.'

'Now let's not go through that again. I wouldn't want to speak ill of your best friend, but he does have his prejudices.'

'Well, if that's all, we'll blow,' Jack said.

'Let's not part on a bad note,' Quinn said, walking over to the drinks cabinet. 'You want some amber?'

'Sure, why not?'

Quinn splashed whisky into chunky glasses and shoved a big fat cigar into his mouth with his big fat fingers covered in big fat rings that could double up as knuckledusters. He settled into one of the leather armchairs, lit up with a gold lighter and blew out a cloud of smoke. Jack took the other armchair, which left the chintz sofa for Adam and Eric. It creaked beneath them as they sat down.

The clock chimed a quarter past the hour. Quinn leant over and switched on his radio. A female torcher's husky voice began to vibrate out of it. Adam slipped down a dip in the sofa until he bumped into Eric. He pulled himself back over to his side again.

'You still got your old wind-up radio, Jack?' Quinn said.

'It's not as old looking as your electric one.'

'That's brand new.'

'Sure it is, but it's got that retro style.'

'Must be tiring having to crank up a radio before you can listen to it.'

'It's not like there's a lot of effort involved. You make it sound like I'm cranking up a car.'

'You don't have to wind up your car, do you?'

'Thankfully the Anti-Techs haven't regressed us that far back,' Jack said.

Adam glanced at the clock again. Quinn took a swig from his glass, and Jack made a start on his drink. Adam finally took a sip. It was always best to wait for the person who poured the drink to try it out first — especially when you were dealing with someone like Quinn.

'So what are Cornell and van Loame doing in Colingham?' Quinn said.

'Colingham?' Jack said. 'That's news to me. Where'd you hear that?'

'They're usually never far from Ethan's side, but I've heard they've not been seen for a couple of weeks. What's happened to them?'

A tram rumbled past the window, its bell tinkling. Jack tapped his cheroot over an ashtray.

'They've gone on a touring holiday.'

'Is that so?' Quinn took another puff on his cigar. 'Whereabouts?'

'Well, I think the general idea of a touring holiday is to move around — do a tour, so to speak.'

'But they must have had an itinerary.'

'Maybe they did,' Jack said, 'but they didn't go into the details. I wasn't aware that they were planning on going as far out as Colingham. What's the big deal?'

'Nothing at all. I was just curious.'

There came the distant sound of machine-gun fire and tyres squealing.

'Look, Quinn,' Jack said, 'they're not on official business, but if you've got something private going on there, all you have to do is say.'

'There's nothing going on there at all.'

'So what makes you think they're in Colingham?'

'Just someone mentioned that he thought he might've seen them there.'

'Who mentioned?'

'No one important,' Quinn said. 'Well, I'd better not keep you. I know you all have to hit the road tomorrow.'

Jack finished his drink.

'Sure we do,' he said. 'Thanks for your hospitality, Quinn. I'll be sure to send your regards back to Stan.'

Adam got off the tram with Jack and Eric at the corner of Betsy's street. Once the tram had pulled away and no one was in sight, Adam leaned close to Jack.

'So what are Cornell and van Loame doing in Colingham?'

'Ethan's not mentioned anything about them being there,' Jack said. 'Quinn and Donnaghan were both real sensitive about that missing woman. Maybe there's more to it than Donnaghan's nasty habits.'

'What time are we setting off tomorrow?' Eric said.

'I think we can afford a leisurely start,' Jack said. 'There's no hurry.'

Adam returned to his room. The lights were out and Harry was curled up under her bedding. She was still asleep after he'd brushed his teeth and made a racket with the flush in the bathroom. He went to bed and looked at her silhouette wondering if Jane Lamm was connected with Harry's brain specialist, what Cornell and van Loame were doing in West Norfolk and if Jack was concealing anything from Adam. Didn't Jack trust him any more? Was he afraid that Adam would tell Harry? Maybe he should keep quiet about Cornell and van Loame to show Jack he could be trusted. It wasn't like she really needed to know. Jack wouldn't harm her, even if he did find out about her real identity, and he might even be able to help her. That way Harry would get Jack's help without asking, and Adam wouldn't be betraying either of their confidences.

They set out after a late breakfast the following morning, stopped at another warehouse, collected some crates, and set off north-westwards to Nottingham where they unloaded their cargo and picked up a new batch. They spent the Tuesday night in a truck stop on the outskirts of the city and the following day they headed south to Milton Keynes. On the Thursday they returned to Central City. Harry negotiated the streets, avoiding a kid chasing after a football across her path and a tram coming in the opposite direction, and they finally arrived once more at Betsy's Café where they stayed the night in the same room as last time.

— 14 —

A CHANGE OF CIRCUMSTANCES

Harry stopped the truck at the end of Betsy's driveway, looked right and then left, past Adam who was sitting in the passenger seat. At the end of the road, the wrought iron gates of Sector House were closed. A tram rolled past her.

She had overheard that Jack, Adam and Eric had spent the Monday evening having drinks with Quinn. She hadn't expected Jack to be friends with him but, if he was, then that definitely ruled out all of them, including Adam, as potential allies. A black Bentley roared by.

'You okay?' Adam said.

'I'm fine.'

She turned into a gap in the traffic and headed back east on the return journey. Frank's service station was on the wrong side of the carriageway, so they stopped for lunch at the lay-by where Harry had first met Jack. The sandwiches at the fast-food stall seemed to consist of fat and mayonnaise. Harry made a mental grocery list for when she arrived back in Norwich. She looked southwards across the marshes. Was the blur on the horizon the radio mast near Little Bartling? Were her dogs missing her? At least Amos was looking after them. A blob of mayonnaise oozed out of her sandwich and splatted on the ground.

After they finished eating, they resumed their journey out of the Fenland, heading east, until Harry finally parked in a bay at the depot.

'You've done okay,' Adam said to her. 'I reckon Jack'll agree you're one of us now.'

He fetched his bag from behind his seat, jumped down from the truck and went over to join Jack and Eric who were standing by the front door to the depot's main building. Harry picked up her rucksack and followed them inside.

Once they had signed off and returned their keys, the four of them headed into the crowded street where Jack bought a newspaper and box of matches at a kiosk. The electronic billboard across the road finished telling everyone about the benefits of a particular brand of herbal shampoo and switched to an image of a group of drunken women with flabby arms, thick thighs squidging out from under tiny skirts, and pierced bellies sagging below short tops. They were drinking from bottles and were talking — or slurring — with as much lewdness as the billboards were legally allowed. The fictional street they were stumbling around in was filled with refuse and the wall behind them was covered in graffiti.

'*The old world,*' a voice from the billboard said. The image changed to a montage of fighting, explosions, the dead and dying. '*Out of the ashes of anarchy –*' the screen changed to a view of a clean, well-ordered neighbourhood '*– the new era.*'

A couple walked along this utopian street, the man carrying a baby in a harness, the woman holding a cheerful toddler by the hand. A postman waved to them as he cycled by. The scene changed to a grey-haired man in a suit perched on the edge of a desk with a secretary — the very model of efficiency — typing at a chunky typewriter.

'*Your politicians,*' the voice said, '*protecting not only your future, but the future of your children and your children's children.*'

The grey-haired man smiled in what was probably meant to be a benign manner. The screen faded for a moment and then went to a group of women wearing white dresses, frolicking about a meadow. For a moment, Harry thought it was still part of the same clip until another voice spoke:

'*Dr Masterson's Pluggenplay Cup.*'

Harry turned and realised her companions had already crossed the road. A bicycle bell tinged at her. She jumped aside and was bustled by pedestrians. She darted through a gap in the traffic and followed after the three men. Adam could've waited for her. And it wasn't just because she'd stop to look at the billboard. He'd gone ahead with Jack and Eric on their way to the depot the previous Monday, leaving her to tag along behind. Well, if he didn't want her company that was fine by her. It wasn't as though she was going to care about a little thing like that. One of us? As if she wanted to be one of them.

A bus pulled up alongside a brick shelter that looked more like a little cottage with four windows and fancy gables. Passengers streamed out of the bus across Harry's path. She ducked, weaved and banged her arm against a wheeled bin, but she finally made her way round and broke into a trot until she saw Jack, Adam and Eric passing Chataway's Delicatessen on the other side of the road. A small man in a striped apron ran outside and handed Jack a parcel.

Harry crossed over and fell in behind them. They turned into a cul-de-sac, and Jack gave the parcel to Eric who stuffed it into a pocket. Adam kept glancing here and there and walked so close to Jack that their arms brushed against each other. He was like a kid clinging to his parent.

This was the route Adam had always avoided when he had taken her to the depot for driving lessons. Well, so what? There was no reason why she should concern herself over a young gangster's oddities.

It seemed a quiet road, lined with painted terrace houses. Most of the windows had curtains drawn against the dusk. A thin, red band of sky stretched across the western horizon, just visible above the rooftops. There was no traffic here and no pedestrians except for an old man wheeling out his bin. Saturday was the refuse collection round there, and many of the bins were already out. The old man shuffled back into his pastel-blue house, without paying any regard to Harry.

Further along the street, as the three men passed a cream house, Adam turned up his collar and seemed to shrink into Jack's shadow. No light came through the heavy drapes of that property. On the window sill, a pair of ceramic kittens were frozen in mid-gambol. A muffled cry came from a bin on the pavement outside.

'What's up, Harry?' Jack said, looking back at her.

Adam tugged Jack's sleeve and tried to pull him away.

'Come on,' he said. 'Let's go, Jack.'

Harry remained where she was.

'I think there's a cat trapped in this bin.'

'Leave it,' Jack said.

But she had already lifted the lid. There was a bloody towel heaped on top of the pile of bin bags. Something inside the towel moved. She felt a hand on her left arm accompanied by a gentle pressure.

'Come away,' Jack said. 'There's nothing you can do about it.'

'Of course there is. D'you think I don't know how to look after animals?'

The pressure on her arm increased, but she reached out with her other arm and pulled aside a corner of the towel. It wasn't a cat. In front of her lay a newborn baby covered in blood and mucus. The placenta was still attached, like a liver with red veins running through it. Judging from the colour and the pulsation, it must have been put there moments before they had turned into the street. Next to the baby was a folded piece of paper with a number stamped on it.

'This is the Neutral Territory,' Jack said. 'Don't poke your nose in their affairs.'

'But if it's neutral, surely we can call the police and an ambulance.'

'It's neutral so long as Stan and I butt out of their business. This is the way they do things here. If your name's not on the computers at City Hall, you don't exist. So button it and walk on. Dying of exposure's not so bad compared to some people's lives.'

The bin stank of blood and refuse — sour milk, rotten meat and putrid fish. She turned away and saw Adam staring at the bin. His face was ashen, his knuckles white and his chin was trembling. The baby began to cry again. Harry pulled away from Jack, grabbed the child, dodged round and ran. Her boots pounded against the pavement. A dog barked at a window. A radio blared a jolly theme tune. Heavy footsteps thudded behind her. The baby was slimy and the placenta kept slipping from her grasp. She reached the end of the street. The footsteps were gaining on her. With a extra burst of speed, she dashed into the passageway at the end of the cul-de-sac. The next road was visible up ahead. Over the fence on her right a stone mockery of a garden — complete with a gnome fishing in a puddle — flashed past her. She reached the end of the passageway. The placenta slipped again. She fumbled for it and was grabbed from behind.

'What the hell d'you think you're doing?' Jack said. 'Eric, check the coast is clear.'

Eric stepped out of the passageway and looked around.

'Okay,' he said.

Jack hauled Harry into a nearby bus shelter. This one was dark and poky with a small unglazed window and narrow doorway. He gripped her shoulder and held her against the wall, her rucksack cushioning her back from the bricks. The rim of his hat overshadowed the upper part of his face.

'How can you expect me to just walk on by?' she said.

'I expect you to do as you're told. I wasn't asking you; I was telling you.'

'But you must be able to do something. You have dealings here. The depot's in this territory, and what about the man who just gave you a parcel?'

Jack let go of Harry and stepped back.

'You mean the cheese?'

'Cheese?'

'What'd you think it was? Dope? Sure, I stopped Rita's people from hassling him. But that's different. He's a little man with no protection. If someone round here decides to push him around, he's on his own. The mother of that child, on the other hand, is bound to have protection.'

'How d'you know?'

'Which of us has lived in this city all their life?' The baby began to cry again. Jack lowered his voice. 'Listen, my girl, I gave you a break. I got you a job and a roof over your head.

You don't argue with me. If I tell you not to do something, you don't do it.'

The bus shelter darkened as Eric stepped into the doorway. He leant forwards, strummed his forefinger across his mouth and burbled. The baby stopped crying, turned her head and stared at him with gummy eyes.

'Who's a cute little thing?' he said. 'Can we call her Sam? That's my mum's name.'

'No, Eric. No naming it. We're not keeping it.'

'But you've always said no frails, Jack. We can't kill her.'

'I never said anything about that. We'll dump it at the nearest orphanage.'

'Aw please, Jack. Can't we keep her?'

The baby wriggled in Harry's arms. Jack looked around.

'Where's Adam?' he said. Eric went out and his deep voice called Adam's name. Jack turned back to Harry. 'It's hardly surprising he doesn't want to come near you. All that blood and mucus is probably freaking him out.'

'I'm surprised blood bothers a gangster.'

Jack grabbed her chin.

'You want me to smack your head against this wall?'

'He's here,' Eric said, poking his head through the window.

Adam stood in the doorway, fingering an old scar on the side of his neck. His face was still pallid, and there was a faint smell of vomit.

'You all right, my boy?' Jack said.

'Yeah. We'd better take the baby to the flat before people start gawping.'

'Yeah, and we'd better get her a nappy,' Eric said, 'before she craps all over Harry, and we don't want her catching a chill neither. Don't you think, Jack?'

'Do I look like I care?'

'Sure you do.'

'Like hell I do.' Jack checked outside the shelter, took his newspaper out of his coat and draped it over Harry's arms so that it concealed the baby. 'We get it cleaned up and then find it a home. Adam and Eric, go get some nappies. Harry, you come back with me, and try not to draw attention to yourself.'

Adam made to follow Jack and Harry, but Eric tugged at his sleeve.

'There's a chemist just here,' he said.

'Let's go to one in our neighbourhood.'

'Why? What's wrong with this one?'

'Let's get out of this territory,' Adam said, but Eric had started ambling over to the pharmacy.

Adam bit a fingernail. Eric turned when he reached the shop door and waved to Adam.

'Come on. What're you waiting for?'

Adam spat out a fragment of nail, checked the street for pedestrians and joined Eric. A bell tinkled above the door as they entered the shop. Behind the counter at the far end stood a small woman from sector one hundred and ninety-three with a broad smile beneath her snub nose and dark eyes. Adam tugged his hat down his forehead.

The shop was narrow and long with shelves along the side walls and a double row down the centre. There were bottles ranging from jigger to quart sized with blue, green or brown glass. Eric wandered off down the left aisle, so Adam took the right one. He passed Dr Masterson's cosmetic products, ranging from glossy lipstick to liquid skin. Next to that were items for the incontinent, followed by packets with 'feminine' written in pink curly letters. Sniggering came from the next aisle. There were hangover cures, indigestion remedies, painkillers — what the hell was dysmenorrhœa? — creams to combat hair loss, lotions to remove acne, lung tonics, lozenges, and powders to treat dysfunctions of one form or another. There was a smell of coal tar soap, camphor, iodine and menthol. Adam turned the corner at the end of the aisle and found Eric rummaging through packets of nappies.

'You don't want to see what they've got on the shelf over there,' Eric said.

'Yeah, I bet I don't. Let's just stick with the nappies.'

Three of the packets tumbled off the shelf. Eric tried to put them back, but they seemed to prefer the floor.

'What type are we supposed to get?' he said.

'How should I know?'

Adam picked up one of the dislodged packets. It had a picture of a laughing toddler.

'Do you need any assistance?' the chemist said.

'We're looking for nappies,' Eric said.

The chemist tidied away some blue sachets and came over to them. Her white coat had sharp creases along the seams.

'How old is the baby?'

'She's just been born.'

'Well, those ones will be far too large,' she said, taking the packet from Adam. 'How big is she?'

'About this big,' Eric said, indicating with his hands.

'I meant how much does the baby weigh?'

'I don't know, we ain't weighed her. I mean she's only just popped out.'

'Well the newborn range is probably what you're looking for.' She tidied the loose packets away and looked from Eric to Adam. 'So who's the proud father?'

'She's mine,' Adam said.

'Yeah, that's right,' Eric said. 'Adam and his girlfriend have just had a baby.'

The woman studied Adam with the air of someone trying to recall a face. She must've dealt with thousands of prescriptions over the years. Surely the chemist wouldn't remember him. How many times had he been sent round here to pick up that lousy bitch's pills?

'So which are the newborn nappies then?' Adam said.

'Over here. Didn't you get anything before the birth?'

'She came early,' Adam said. 'We weren't expecting her yet.'

'Was she very premature?'

'Oh yeah,' Eric said. 'It was real early, weren't it, Adam? We were, like, walking home, and then suddenly it all started to happen.'

The chemist gave a stupid little smile, like they were a couple of kids who needed to be humoured.

'In which case you might prefer the premature nappies.'

'No, it's all right,' Adam said. 'I reckon the newborn'll do fine.'

'D'you have any baby clothes?' Eric said.

'There are some just over here.' She picked up a couple of sleep suits from a shelf and held them up. One was pink with sparkling fairies, the other was filled with flowers in various shades of pink: a mosaic of Rita's favourite colour — and Jack's most hated. 'You did say the baby's a girl, didn't you?'

'Yeah,' Adam said. 'I think we'll get the yellow ones. D'you have any milk?'

'You do know that breast is best, don't you?'

Adam stared at her for a moment, but then he noticed that Eric was about to speak so he cut in first.

'She can't — my girlfriend that is — she's sick so can't, you know, do that.'

'Yeah,' Eric said, 'that's why the baby came so early. It's on account of the medication, you see.'

Adam glared at him.

'Anyway, we'd better go. I want to get back to my girlfriend and our baby.'

'Yeah, that's true. So what kind of stuff d'you reckon we need, miss?'

'Well,' the chemist said, 'if you're going to bottle feed, you'll need some bottles.'

Eric picked one up from the shelf. It seemed the size of an egg cup in his large, hairy hand.

'Will this do?' he said.

'You'll need more than one.'

'How come?'

'You need to sterilise the bottles, and I really wouldn't recommend doing them individually. It's best to have four prepared and four sterilising or you won't be able to keep up with the baby's demands.'

'Is that so? We didn't know that, did we, Adam?'

'Yeah well,' Adam said, 'we weren't intending on bottle feeding.'

Jack unlocked the front door and let Harry into the flat. She took the baby into the bathroom, and Jack stood just inside the living room doorway. He took out a cheroot and tapped it on his cigar case. He should never have given in and let Harry stay. He'd always known she'd be trouble. Empty takeaway cartons were strewn around Grant's camp-bed. Filthy little git. He was bound to run along to Rita and tell her all about the baby, and then she'd laugh at Jack, say he was soft. Well, he wasn't soft. He'd pack Harry and the baby off to the refuge. There was no way he wanted a baby near him, especially not a baby girl.

For a moment he could almost see a smiling face with a pair of blue eyes and chestnut curls and hear a voice saying, 'Find me, Jack.' She always hid in the same place, behind the long velour curtains in their sitting room, but he always had to go through the same pantomime routine of looking for her. Was she behind the sofa? The sound of giggling would come from the bulge in the curtain. Was she behind the armchair? The giggling would increase. Every possible — and impossible — place had to be checked before he finally threw open the curtains and she yelled out, 'Boo!'

He looked over at the faded curtains in his flat. Harry had done a good job of cleaning them, but there was a limit to what soap could achieve. Quinn would laugh if he could see them. So what? Let the sap spend all his money on trivialities. Once it dried up, he'd lose all his friends.

Jack opened his hand. The cheroot was crushed. He picked off flecks of tobacco stuck between his fingers. Was that the sound of water boiling? He looked round the living room door frame and had a clear view into the bathroom opposite. The baby was lying on a towel on the lino. Harry was going to get one hell of a slap if she'd left the baby unattended while she'd gone off for a cup of coffee. He turned and peered into the kitchen. A steaming saucepan was on the hob. Harry was moving a pile of dirty crockery out of the sink.

'What're you up to?' Jack said.

'Sterilising some string and a pair of scissors.'

'You ever cut a cord before?'

Harry removed some papers from her jacket and placed them on the window sill next to the dish where Jack kept loose change. She put the jacket in the sink and began to sponge it down. Jack reached over to the window sill. Harry dropped her jacket and grabbed the documents.

'It's all right,' Jack said. 'I was checking the dish.' He picked it up, but it was empty.

'It was like that when I came in,' Harry said.

'You're going to get your bits of paper soggy. Put them back on the window sill. I won't peek at them.' He put the dish back. 'And I know you didn't take the money. You're smarter than that.'

Harry put the documents back on the sill and resumed cleaning blood and mucus from her jacket.

'You didn't answer my question,' Jack said, looking at the contents of the pan. 'D'you know what you're doing?'

Harry hung her jacket on the kitchen door.

'The topic came up when I did my first aid badge when I was a guide.'

'How very grand. Did it come up in any detail? And how many years ago was that?'

'A few.'

'So you've never actually tried it?' he said. 'What about your animals?'

'Pigs don't usually need assistance when they're farrowing, and I have experienced farmhands.'

She squirted some disinfectant into the sink and began scrubbing it. There was a splodge of jam on one of the peeling floor tiles that hadn't been there on Monday morning. Hadn't the lousy boy learnt to clean up after himself? That was going to be tacked on to his rent — along with the money he'd stolen.

'I can fetch a doctor who'll ask no questions,' Jack said. He peered out of the window. How long did it take to buy a packet of nappies? Two of Rita's men were walking down the street — his street — as though they owned the place. Rita was bound to have a go at him the moment she found out Harry had been interfering in the Neutral Territory. Yeah right, like her people never interfered.

'I'll manage,' Harry said.

'So how are you planning on looking after her and keeping down a job?'

'Maybe I can find someone to take her in.'

She removed her watch, placed it on the window sill and made a start on the washing up.

'You mean like I said? Take her to an orphanage.'

'I'll get her a proper home.'

The boiler in the corner of the room began to clatter and judder as water poured into the sink.

'What are you going to do?' Jack said. 'Advertise in the local paper?'

'I'll find her a home in the country.'

'Oh sure. Back home? That would be with all those nice people who didn't take you in after your dad died?'

Her hand jerked. Soap studs flew off it and flicked her in the eye. For a moment she stood with her face buried in a hand towel.

'You're on the run,' he said. 'You think I can't tell?'

The sound of crying came from the next room. She put the towel away.

'Is Sam all right?'

Harry's eyes were red, but that could've just been from the soap.

'She's fine,' Jack said.

The crying subsided. Harry picked up a milk carton and wrinkled her nose.

'Grant must've forgotten to put it back in the fridge.'

'That's his problem so long as he paid for it.' Jack tightened a drawer knob that had come loose. 'You've lost your broad accent.'

'I've acclimatised.'

'Sure you have. It was a fake accent to go with a fake name. Harry Ferguson, you said your name was when we first met. Funny how it sounds like one of your tractors. I don't have to be an enthusiast like Adam to notice a thing like that. What have the West Norfolk police got on you, or should I just ask them?'

Harry scrubbed at some detritus stuck to a table knife.

'It was self-defence.'

'I'm sure it was. Maybe it was your dad's creditor trying to take more than his due,' Jack said. Harry finished with the knife and dipped a mug into the soapy water. Her hair could do with a trim to even up the ends. 'So the louse got what was coming to him. D'you think it bothers me if you did him in?'

'I haven't killed anyone.'

'So maybe you just injured him. But he's got a lot of influence and can swing things his way. Is that right?'

She rinsed off the mug, put it on the draining rack and nodded.

'I figured as much,' Jack said. 'Believe me, I know how hard it is to lose your home and family — and I sure know what it's like to want revenge — but while you're under my roof, you're safe.'

Harry glanced at her bare wrist and then looked up at the kitchen clock.

'I think that's been sterilising long enough.'

She turned off the heat under the pan, washed her hands, flicked off the excess water, fished out the string and scissors with a slotted spoon, and cooled them under the cold tap. She took them over to the bathroom but just stood on the threshold, staring at the floor. Jack watched her for a moment. Then he returned to the living room and ran his finger along the book spines on the case near the door. The battered first aid book was squashed between *Red Harvest* and *The Little Sister*. He tugged it free and the front cover flopped open. His name was on the flyleaf followed by a heavily crossed-out 'aged 10'. He'd been so proud of moving up to double-figures, he'd gone through a phase of writing his age at every possible opportunity. What a dumb thing to do.

He checked the table of contents, flicked through to the section on emergency childbirth and went over to the bathroom door.

'I never thought I'd be needing this chapter. "Make the mother comfortable and reassure her that everything will be okay." I think we can skip this bit.' He turned the page. 'Oh, that's disgusting. Harry, if you ever get pregnant, stay away from me when you're ready to pop. I sure don't want to have to do any of this.'

'The feeling's mutual, thank you, Jack.'

On the following page, there was an annotated diagram of a baby with its cord and placenta. The image didn't indicate any wriggling limbs or crying, which is what Sam had started doing.

'Well, I reckon the cord must've stopped pulsating by now,' Jack said, 'and ten minutes have certainly elapsed. You need three bits of string.'

Harry cut the string twice and looked up at him.

'Tie one of them six inches away from the navel and the other one eight inches. Make sure you do the first one up real tight or she'll bleed to death.'

Harry looped one of the pieces around the floppy tube of skin, but it slipped off when she tried to fasten it. Maybe he ought to call a doctor. Fisher wouldn't ask questions, but that would involve Ethan, which wouldn't be fair on him. Harry wound the string around the cord again and tied it. The baby began to retch and coughed up a black tarry substance.

'I'll call help,' Jack said.

'It's all right.' Harry checked the baby's mouth. 'It's just something she swallowed before she was born.'

'Oh sure. And where'd it come from?'

'It's baby excrement.'

'Harry, that is gross.'

'Jack, you shoot people. How can you be squeamish?'

'I draw the line at swallowing excrement. In fact, I draw it way before then. D'you have to leave it lying on the floor?'

'I'll clean up afterwards.'

The baby cried and kicked her legs while Harry secured the second string. She picked up the scissors and put the blades to the cord.

'You did tie the first one up real tight, didn't you?' Jack said.

'Yes.'

She snipped. Blood spurted out, but not for long. The first string remained tight around the cord. Jack fetched his battered tin medical case from under his bunk and brought it over to the bathroom.

'Here –' he handed her a sealed sterile dressing '– stick that on it.'

She opened the packet and fastened the dressing over the cord and navel, then looked in the medical kit and pointed at a long, thin instrument.

'What's that metal thing?'

'It's for removing bullets.' Jack closed the lid. 'After ten minutes, check the cord for bleeding and tie the third string four inches from the navel. You're on your own now.'

Harry bundled the baby up in a fresh towel and picked her up. Sam had stopped crying and seemed to be trying to suck on Harry's shoulder. The bathroom stank of blood. The black substance still lay on the lino, and the placenta looked like a dead, skinned animal.

'Here, I'll hold her while you clear up,' Jack said, 'but if she soils my suit, you get it laundered.'

He took the baby into the living room. Now that she was cleaned up, she looked a lot like his little sister the first time he had seen her at the hospital. He'd been dragged away from his computer game to view this intruder everyone was fussing over, but his parents gave him a present, 'from your little sister, Jack.' Like a baby could buy anyone a present. It was a tablet with the latest slimline optical drive and superfast video chip. Then he had looked at her, and she had opened her eyes, seeming to look straight back at him. That was when she had ceased to be a wrinkly, pink blob.

Heavy footsteps sounded on the staircase outside, accompanied by Adam and Eric's voices. Jack glanced around for somewhere to put the baby and laid her on the camp-bed. The door opened, and Adam came in, closely followed by Eric — both of them laden with bags.

'No way was she cute,' Adam said. 'She was a nosey, interfering bint.'

'She was just trying to be helpful,' Eric said.

'You were only supposed to buy a packet of nappies,' Jack said, 'not the whole bloody shop.'
'She needs milk and clothes as well,' Adam said as he deposited his bags on the floor.
'And we need this thing to sterilise the bottles,' Eric said. 'And I got a book on how to look after babies.'
'Why d'you need a fancy gadget when you could just use a pan of boiling water?' Jack said.
'But this is specially designed for bottles. It's got slots to hold them in place.'
'Oh well, slots make all the difference, don't they?'
Harry came in with soap-covered rubber gloves.
'How much did it all cost?' she said.
'It's all right,' Adam said as he squatted down in front of the baby. 'Forget about it.'
'You kidding?' Jack said.
'No, I ain't kidding.'
Adam held the baby's hand with a finger. Eric pulled a colourful toy out of a bag and squeaked it in front of the baby. It looked like a psychedelic mutant frog being tortured by a hairy giant.
'Look what Uncle Eric's got for you.' She began to cry again. 'What? Don't you like it, little Sammikins?'
Harry picked her up from the camp-bed and rocked her in her arms.
'I think she's hungry.'
'Oh for crying out loud,' Jack said. 'Eric, go sort out the milk and, Adam, get her a nappy and some clothes. I'm not listening to that all night.' He sank into a chair and took out a cheroot. 'Harry, don't just stand there. Walk up and down the room with her while Adam gets the stuff out.'

※

Jack sat at the table reading his newspaper. He'd had to throw away the cover sheet as it had been smeared with blood, so he wasn't able to do the crossword or check the sports results. He read the tail end of an article that was apparently a continuation from page two and seemed to be about a solar power plant in some desert sector.

> ... and that would mean less dependence on sugar beet for fuel. Instead, farmers could switch to more food crops.

Jack peered over the edge of the paper. Adam and Harry were sitting opposite him. Harry was feeding Sam. Eric was on her other side, staring at them with a dopey expression, still clutching the baby's toy.

'D'you reckon she needs a blanket?' Adam said.

'I think she's warm enough,' Harry said and smiled at him.

Great, Adam gets a nice smile from her, but what did Jack get for helping with the cord?

'Harry,' Jack said. 'I know you've got a lot on your mind, but are we eating in or out tonight?'

'It's all right,' Adam said to her, 'I'll take over feeding Sam while you sort out the dinner.'

'I'd better go to the shop.' Harry handed Sam over to Adam. 'I don't suppose Grant has left anything in the fridge. I'll be back soon.'

'Oh yeah,' Eric said. 'I forgot about the cheese.' He fished it out of his coat pocket and handed it to her. 'You can make something out of this, can't you?'

'I'll get milk and butter and make some macaroni. Is that okay, Jack?'

'Just so long as it's edible.'

Jack moved on to the next article in the paper. It was illustrated with a snapshot of a middle-aged politician with his wife dangling on his arm. She looked a typical politician's wife: motherly. She probably baked cakes for the W.I. Mr and Mrs Bartrum championing probity. Yeah right. Jack had heard a thing or two about Bartrum that didn't get published in the papers.

'What are we going to tell Rita?' Eric said.

'Oh, so now you think about it,' Jack said. 'Just when I finally thought she'd calmed down about Harry.'

'It ain't Harry's fault,' Adam said.

'Oh and how d'you figure that? If you reckon this is a chance to get together with Harry, it won't work. Babies don't fix things, they make things worse.'

'But, Jack — '

'No, I don't want to hear any buts.'

Jack turned the page and lifted up the newspaper. Fulton Robbins, President of the Anti-Technology League, was harping on about computers again. There was a sharp intake of breath. Jack lowered the newspaper. Adam was staring at it with a pale face. Jack sighed.

'Listen, my dear boy,' he said. 'You've got to trust my judgement on these things. I'm only thinking about what's best for all of us. As much as I'd like to, I can't split with Rita. You know the way things are.'

Adam put down the empty bottle and held the baby close to his chest.

'You've got to put her on your shoulder and pat her,' Jack said. 'No, like this.' He put down the newspaper and went over to them. He raised her up and moved Adam's hands round to better support her. Her eyes were closed and she smelt of milk. 'And make sure you don't put any pressure on the fontanelles.'

'The what?'

'The soft spots on the baby's skull. There and there.' He pointed to the back of her head and to the top, where he could see her pulse through her downy hair. 'Have you got a muslin in case she spits up? Because you're not going to want that on your clothes.'

'The chemist didn't say nothing about a muslin.'

'Must be the only thing she didn't sell you. Eric, get a towel.'

Jack sat back down again and watched as Adam patted the baby.

'If Harry doesn't kick up a fuss, maybe we'll be able to put the baby into care before Rita finds out,' Jack said.

'No, Jack,' Adam said. 'I mean, we can think of something, can't we? Maybe we can say Harry's looking after her for someone. You know, like babysitting.'

'Babysitting usually involves giving the baby back.'

'Maybe we could say Harry was pregnant when she left home,' Eric said as he came in with a hand towel.

'Eric, my lad, that jacket of Harry's may have concealed her petite breasts, but it's not bulky enough to hide a nine-month bump. And have either of you thought about where the baby's going to sleep tonight?'

'The cardboard box the sterilizer came in will do as a cot,' Adam said, 'and we could fold up a towel to make a mattress.'

'We're going to run out of towels at this rate.' Jack looked at the scattered packaging on the floor. 'That chemist must've seen you two a mile off. And if you think I want to read in the dark, you've got another thing coming.'

'We could switch on the little light behind you,' Eric said, 'and dim the main one. That'll be enough for you, won't it?'
'We'll see.'
He picked up the newspaper again.

> Mr Robbins is convinced that computers are already being used for more than the allowed state administrative work or medical treatment, but he has so far been unable to produce any evidence for his claims.

Harry soon returned and not long after dished out some macaroni cheese. Sam was now asleep in her makeshift cot, and they ate in peace. Grant still hadn't made an appearance. After supper, Jack headed off to the pub with Eric.

Stan wasn't there, but plenty of his people were. A couple of women were singing a bawdy song. Their faces were flushed, and one of them had a damp patch on her bolero. The fire crackled and spat in the hearth. Grant was cuddling up to a woman in a dark corner. Rita was sitting at their usual table with Ralph by her side.

'Well, look who it isn't,' Rita said. 'You've finally turned up. We were beginning to think you prefer Harry's company to mine. After all, she's a great cook, so I hear, and isn't that what men are supposed to go for in the end?'

'Knock it off, Rita. The traffic was hell, that's all.' Jack motioned to the barmaid and turned back to Rita. 'I see Grant's made himself a friend. Maybe she'll take him in. I'm not having a petty thief under my roof.'

'Who says he's a thief?' Ralph said.

'I do. I left some money in the flat and now it's gone.'

'How d'you know it wasn't someone else? Maybe one of your other lodgers?'

'Are you calling me a thief?' Eric said.

'I didn't mean you.' Ralph inspected his fingernails. 'And I didn't mean Adam.'

Jack pulled up a chair and took out a cheroot.

'I was the last to leave on Monday and tonight I arrived before Harry, Adam and Eric. So go figure it.'

'It's your own fault for leaving money lying around,' Rita said.

'It's a matter of trust, and he's failed it.'

'Grant's my mate,' Ralph said.

'Then take him in yourself.'

'I don't have the room.'

'Neither do I,' Jack said.

The barmaid brought over his and Eric's drinks. Two of Rita's men walked over and leant against a pillar behind her.

'You took Grant in because you felt sorry for him,' Rita said. 'How could you turf him out into the street?'

'I don't feel sorry for thieving little gits.'

'You ought to give him a second chance. The poor boy doesn't have a father figure.'

Jack eyed Rita. Was that a hint? Had one of her people seen him with Harry and the baby?

'Little boys don't know what to do when they lose their mummy and daddy,' she said.

No, she didn't know. She was just having a dig at him — again. He ought to smack her face in for making a crack like that.

'How's it going?' Stan said, approaching the table with Seán, Ciaran and Niall. He pulled up a chair next to Rita. 'How was Quinn, Jack?'

'In good health.'

Rita squeezed Stan's hand.

'We were just saying that Jack ought to give Grant a second chance. The poor boy needs a father figure.'

'Sure he does,' Stan said. 'Everybody needs one. That's what I'm always saying, but I can't see Jack fitting the bill. He's not a family person.'

'But he can't kick Grant out,' Ralph said.

'Of course he can't,' Stan said. 'You don't want your new friend on the street, falling into bad company.' Stan leant back in his chair and gazed around the pub. 'Still no sign of Cornell and van Loame. Haven't they come back from their holiday yet?'

'They're not due back this week,' Jack said.

'That's nice of Ethan to give them such a long holiday.'

'Sure it is, but they deserve a break after all their hard work.'

Jack sipped his beer. An hour later, Grant passed out, slumping into his companion's lap. She pushed him off and he tumbled on to the floor. Jack stood up to go.

'If he thinks we're lugging him back to the flat, he's got another thing coming.'

'We'll help him home,' Ralph said, waving to Rita's men who were still lounging against the pillar. 'Is your lift still broken, Jack? We can manage him up the stairs, and I'll tuck him up nice and snug.'

Like hell he would. The nosey little git just wanted to have a poke about Jack's flat. Jack looked around the crowd of people.

'Spike, Hector, Alf. Give Eric a hand with the boy.'

The four of them took a limb each and carried Grant back to Jack's flat. The living-cum-bedroom was dark. By the sound of it, Sam, Adam and Harry were all asleep. Jack turned up the light just enough to see by, and the men dumped Grant on the camp-bed.

— 15 —

FAMILY MATTERS

ADAM reached past Harry and helped himself to a slice from the toast rack. Jack was standing in front of the mirror, adjusting his tie. Adam caught his reflection, but Jack didn't give his usual wink or smile of acknowledgement. Instead, he smoothed his moustache, strode over to where Grant was sleeping and stamped on the edge of the camp-bed, catapulting the boy on to the floor.

'Come on, you lazy git,' Jack said, 'or you'll be late for work.'

He left the boy in a heap, went over to the wardrobe and took out his waistcoat. Adam moved to the other side of the table and perched on the edge of it so that he obscured Sam's makeshift cot from Grant's view. Not that he was looking at anything, except maybe the carpet. There was a stench of vomit coming from the boy and his bedding.

Sam had woken up during the night, but Adam and Harry had both gone to her. Adam had sorted out her milk while Harry had changed her, and she had soon been settled back to sleep, but her crying had obviously disturbed Grant who had moaned, shouted something incomprehensible and then made retching sounds. The noise must've woken Jack, but he hadn't said anything.

The boy was still huddled up on the floor, but he was now showing signs of life. His top half seemed unwilling to co-operate, but his legs were moving under him as though he was trying to lever himself off the ground. After a while he gave up and remained where he was with his backside sticking up in the air.

Eric's baritone came from the bathroom singing a popular song.

'I don't care if she's got hairy pits, just so long as she's got —'

The clattering and squeaking of the plumbing grew so loud that it muffled the rest of the lyrics. Jack finished getting dressed. Maybe Grant sensed that his backside was presenting an easy target for Jack's foot, or maybe it was a lucky chance for him that he managed to stagger to his feet just in time to avoid a kicking, which was just as well for him given that Jack's cobblers specialised in steel insets.

'Time to go, boy,' Jack said.

'I hent had no food,' Grant said.

His face was covered in flecks of dried vomit and a large lump of snot dangled from one of his nostrils. He lurched towards the table so quickly that the bogey was in danger of flying from his nose. Adam backed away. Grant grabbed the remaining slices of toast from the rack and had just stuffed one of them into his mouth when he stared at Sam.

'Woss that?' he said, spraying crumbs.

'What d'you think it is?' Jack said. 'A puppy?'

'But where'd that come from?'

'I didn't think I'd have to explain that kind of thing to someone of your age.'

'But woss that dewun here?' He turned to Harry. 'Is that yars?'

Jack clipped him round the ear, making the lump of bogey wobble again.

'Don't be so damn personal. Now get along or you'll be late for work.'

Jack shoved him towards the door and then turned to Harry.

'This place stinks. I want it cleaned up by the time I get back.'

With that he left. Adam helped Harry tidy the breakfast things away. She had just snapped on a pair of rubber gloves when Sam began to cry, so Adam made up her milk, put it in the bottle warmer and turfed Eric out of the bathroom so he could change Sam.

'Don't worry, Sammy.' Adam laid her on a towel. 'I'm going to look out for you. I ain't going to let nothing happen to you.'

Sure, he'd made that promise once before, but this time it was going to be different. He wouldn't have gone past that house if he'd had a choice but this more than made up for it. What were the odds on Harry not just finding Sam, but finding her in time to save her? Maybe it was just one of those freak events — like that decayed satellite striking the old airport — or maybe there was something in that whole religious angle Harry seemed so keen on. Maybe he was being given a chance to make up for not saving his little brother.

He finished cleaning Sam and went to check up on her milk. It was warm enough so he took it into the other room and sat down at the table. Harry was scrubbing away at the carpet, and Eric was eating his breakfast.

'Make sure you clear up after yourself, Eric,' Adam said.
'Jack ain't in a good mood.'
'He's just worried about squaring things with Rita.'
'It ain't none of her business.'
'You try telling her that.'
'I'm gonna waste her one of these days.'
'No you ain't,' Eric said. 'Jack's got more than enough trouble what with Stan trying to be number one without you making a mess of things.'
Sam finished her milk and Adam patted her.
'Maybe we could get a car seat and bring Sam with us in the truck,' he said. 'What d'you reckon?'
Harry squeezed her sponge into a bucket.
'I think that's a great idea.'
'You'll be able to look after her while me and Eric are out in the evenings, won't you?' Adam said.
'Of course I will.'
'And we should get her a cot. It ain't hygienic for her to sleep in a box.'
'Ain't there a shop in the city centre what sells baby stuff?' Eric said. 'We could have a look round there.'

They set out once Harry was satisfied that the flat was clean enough for Jack's liking and headed back into the Neutral Territory, bypassing the road where Sam had been found. They took it in turns carrying her and made their way through the mass of Saturday shoppers and leaflet distributors until they arrived in front of the baby store, 'Titty-Totties'.
Adam hitched Sam up his shoulder and stared up at the shop's rainbow façade and pictures of chubby-faced babies who looked as though they had overdosed on Dr Masterson's Anti-Blues Tonic — or giggle-juice as most people called it.

Eric nudged him and sniggered. Adam refused a leaflet from a young man wearing an Anti-Tech badge.

'What's up, Eric?' Harry said.

'It's a bit of a funny name for a baby shop, ain't it?'

'Why's that? "Titty-totty" means very small, and it's a shop for very small people.'

Eric laughed and patted the top of her head.

'Button it, Eric,' Adam said. 'Come on, let's go inside. People are staring.'

They went into the building. It was packed with pregnant women, most of whom had a nervous-looking man at their side. There were also a few toddlers running about and screaming. Adam edged past a woman whose bump was so large she seemed about to explode. A group of women were prodding and poking a selection of prams on display. Eric headed for the biggest one of the lot and jiggled it up and down. It had a shiny chrome frame that glinted in the shop lighting and large wheels with a mass of spokes.

'How about this?' he said. 'It looks real comfy and study.'

'Yeah, and expensive,' Adam said, checking the price tag. 'How are we going to get a pram up a flight of stairs?'

'We could ask Jack to get the lift fixed.'

'Rather you than me,' Harry said. 'Anyway, there's no room in the flat for a big thing like that.'

Eric sighed, squeezed past the pram and reached up for a folded pushchair lying on a shelf.

'What about this?'

Adam checked the label.

'She's too small for that. Look, it says from six months.'

Harry had moved over to another shelf and was gesturing to Adam. He and Eric stepped over a small activity table provided by the shop for bored toddlers and joined Harry.

'We could get a harness instead,' she said.

Eric picked one up from the shelf and dangled it in front of his chest.

'Let's get this one.'

'No, that looks weird.' Adam shifted Sam around in his arms and pointed to another one. 'Harry, try this. It goes on your back.'

'But she won't be able to see the baby,' Eric said.

'But it'll be better for her back. It ain't good to have a heavy weight hanging on your front.'

'Sam ain't exactly a heavy weight.'

'But she's going to grow.'

Harry picked another harness off the shelf.

'I'll get this one,' she said, inspecting the label. 'It can be worn either way. Let's look for a cot.'

They made their way around a herd of wooden rocking horses on display and squeezed past two women discussing the merits of a prenatal educational audio device.

'Do you look at that, Edna,' one said. 'Put that aginst you, and that'll larn the baby to do sums while thass in the womb.'

'Cor blast me, my bewty, but thass a load o' squit.'

Adam shifted Sam's weight in his arms again while Eric headed for an ornately carved wooden cot with pictures of butterflies and fairies painted all over it. Adam handed Sam over to Harry, searched through the travel cots, selected the lightest one that came with its own carry-bag and dumped it in Eric's arms.

'But this cot's got cute pictures on it,' Eric said.

'I don't give a damn about cute pictures — and neither will Jack,' Adam said. 'Lightweight and portable is what we're after.'

'She needs toys to keep her entertained.'

'Go find something that's not as big as an elephant and doesn't make irritating sounds.'

Eric ambled off. Adam found a travel changing mat and a bottle warmer designed for vehicles. Harry tried Sam out in various car seats. Eric returned with his arms full.

'What d'you reckon?' he said, showing a play mat to Adam. 'Harry should like it cos it's got lots of animals on it. Look, there's Mr and Mrs Sheep with baby sheep and Mr and Mrs Horse with baby horse.'

'Yeah, it's all right,' Adam said, before Eric pointed out each animal family in turn. 'Harry, what d'you think?'

Harry put down a car seat and turned round.

'No.'

'No?' Eric said. 'How come? It's got farm animals on it.'

'It's got gender-confused animals on it,' Harry said. 'The bull, or "Mr Cow" as they've called it, has got udders, and "Mrs Duck" is a male mallard. Whoever designed it has clearly never set foot on a farm. What else have you got?'

'Well, there's this sort of octopus thing with different textured tentacles.'

Harry picked it up and turned it round to inspect it. The toy let out a tinny laugh, and amidst various clicks and whirls it started singing, 'One, two, three, four, five, once I caught a fish alive.'

'Okay,' Eric said. 'I didn't know it was going to do that. Jack ain't going to like it, is he?'

'What's in the box?' Harry said, pointing to the last item in Eric's arms.

'It's a mobile with a wind-up musical thingy what turns it round. It plays soothing lullabies.'

'How soothing?'

'I dunno,' Eric said. 'I ain't tried it.'

Adam took the box from him, rummaged around in it, located the musical box component and wound it up.

'It ain't too bad,' he said. 'If Jack don't like it, we can always not wind it up and she can just look at it.'

'So it's okay?' Eric said.

'Sure. Go put the octopus back and swap the play mat for one that ain't gonna miseducate her and we'll meet you at the checkout.'

Adam turned to the car seat Harry had put Sam in and lifted it.

'It's the lightest one I could find,' Harry said.

'That ain't gonna be comfortable to carry. Try her in that one. The handle's got a better design.'

Harry transferred Sam to the next one, and Adam tried it.

'That'll do. Let's go.'

'Wait a minute,' Harry said. 'We need a monitor.'

'What for? She's in the same room as us.'

'If we're at Betsy's we can listen out for her if we go to the lounge.'

'We ain't leaving her alone.'

'She'll get off to sleep better if we're not around to distract her,' Harry said. 'We'll hear her as soon as she wakes up.'

'I ain't having her neglected.'

'It's not neglect to leave a baby to sleep in peace. It's the normal thing to do.'

'Well, all right. But we listen out closely.'

Harry searched through a shelf and selected one.

'This one has the longest range,' she said.

Adam inspected the label.

'We don't need one this powerful. It'd reached all the way across to the other side of the street from Betsy's.'

'It's better to get the most powerful one in case there's any interference.'

'Yeah, I hadn't thought of that. We'd better make sure it's at the bottom of the bag before we leave here in case the Anti-Techs are still hanging around outside.'

Eric returned with a play mat that had colourful shapes, different textures and squeaky bits. He also had three packets of nappies, a stack of muslins and a selection of sleep suits.

'How are we going to get all this home?' he said.

'Are there any buses that stop near the flat?' Harry said.

'Yeah, but we'd have to go all the way over to the castle to pick it up.'

Adam studied the items. Most of the stuff was light but a lot of it was bulky, and the streets were packed with jostling people.

'I'll go back and get my Phaeton.'

'I though it ain't roadworthy,' Eric said.

'Harry and I got it going last weekend.' He took out a wad of cash from his wallet and handed it to Harry. 'Here, that should cover it. You'd better join the queue at the till. Wait for me out front.'

Jack was sitting at the table oiling his tommy gun when the others arrived back at the flat, once again laden down with packages.

'What the hell d'you think you're all playing at?' he said. 'I go out for ten minutes, and you buy up an entire baby store. We're supposed to be getting rid of the kid, not helping her settle in. I might've known Harry wouldn't pay the slightest attention to me, but the two of you ought to know better.'

'Jack, please let Sam stay,' Adam said. 'We can take her along in the truck. We've got a car seat and everything.'

'And you'll only have to share a room with her at the weekends,' Eric said. 'She can go in with Adam and Harry while we're on the road.'

'You should've cleared it with me first.' Jack slammed the drum magazine into his gun and turned to Harry. 'You've thrown everything out of kilter. If it hadn't been for those damn Anti-Techs and their demonstration I'd never have laid eyes on you, and we would've been a damn sight better off.' He put the gun in its strongbox, locked it, slid it under his bunk and turned to look at them. 'When Grant clocks off, it's odds-on he'll go straight to Rita, and she'll be round here like a shot to nag me about it. If you haven't come up with something convincing to tell her by five o'clock, I will personally take that baby to the orphanage. Harry, go sort out the lunch.'

After lunch, Adam left Sam with Harry and locked himself in the bathroom. He took out a crumpled sheet of paper from his pocket and smoothed it out. There was a splodge of dried blood on one corner, but it hadn't obscured any of the text, so he tore it off, removing as little of the unstained paper as possible. The top of the form had 'ADX26' printed on it and a rubber-stamped sixteen digit number. He clicked his pen and wrote 'Samantha' in the first box and 'Trent' in the second. He paused for a moment and appended 'Harriet' to the list of forenames. It then occurred to him that he'd given the child the initials SHT. He could just image kids in the playground inserting a vowel. There were some in his old school who would've enjoyed that kind of thing. The

Generator Monthly article about Harry's grandfather Edward Bostock came back to him. He almost knew it by heart now. It had mentioned Bostock's daughter Bella. Yes, that would do. Sammy could also be named after Harry's mum as well.

Adam continued filling in the rest of the form: 'Stacie Trent' for the child's mother, 'unknown' for the father, and the address where Sam had been found. Adam folded the form and tucked it into a pocket, but when he left the bathroom he found Jack leaning against the living room door frame, smoking.

'Not able to go?' Jack said.

'I was just tidying myself up a bit.'

Jack exhaled smoke into the hallway.

'See that? I'm being considerate. I'm not smoking in front of the baby.' Jack moved away from the doorway, but Adam remained where he was. 'Don't you want to join the others and continue playing at happy families?'

'I'm going out.'

Adam left the flat and ran down the stairs. Happy families? Jack must've been real mad at him to make a crack like that. He hurried into the basement car park, fetched his helmet from the locker and rode his motorbike out into the lane outside. The sky was overcast, but with luck the rain would hold off for a while.

He overtook a dustcart and headed into the Neutral Territory. The streets were packed with cars and buses. There were even more pedestrians crowding the pavements than there had been that morning. He parked near City Hall by the open air market. The place stank of fish, meat, fruit, pastries, paint and leather.

City Hall had undergone extensive renovations after the anarchy, or so Jack had once told Adam. As Adam hadn't even started school when the alterations were finally completed, he had no knowledge of what it used to look like, but now its exterior was covered with barley-sugar columns and arches with fancy carvings. A flight of steps led up to the main entrance above which the words 'Peace and Prosperity' were carved in five-foot-high capital letters.

Gathered outside on the steps was a group of people with placards saying things like: 'No Computers', 'Don't Bring Back Anarchy' and 'Technology Will Destroy Us All'. Adam dodged round them and entered the building. A maze of corridors led off in every direction from the lobby. A couple of city guards lounged by a vending machine.

The city guards, in their well-tailored blue uniforms with shiny buttons, were only nominally in the Norfolk Constabulary. They were funded by the Neutral Territory's ruling élite, which meant they were paid twice as much as regular coppers and had all kinds of extra perks, and they didn't have to answer to Ethan. They also didn't use tommy guns but instead had reconditioned SA80s.

Adam studied the overhead sign posts: tax payments, parking permits, fines, licences, water and sewerage rates, electricity coupons, registrations (birth, marriage, divorce, death). He set off down a corridor, following the registrations signs. The route twisted and turned through the building. At least one armed guard was posted at each intersection.

Some of the doors were marked 'authorized personnel only'. In the distance, a man was shouting, the kind of blustering shout of desperation that had no effect on officials. From time to time a smartly dressed man or woman strode past Adam with the air of belonging, while other people ambled along the corridor, staring at signs. One small harassed-looking man was trying to ask directions from one of the city guards, but he might just as well have asked a statue for all the response he was getting. The tapping of typewriters or computer keyboards came from behind closed doors.

Adam eventually entered a room with a row of grille-fronted counters at one end and a queue of people that snaked back and forth across the room in a roped-off path. He joined the end of it. A large brass clock on the wall ticked loudly. A toddler yelled further down the line. The couple in front of Adam bickered.

'You're not getting the dog,' the woman said.

'He's my dog. I paid for him.'

'I'm the one who always fed him and cleaned up after him.'

An old woman in a black dress joined the queue behind Adam. She kept sniffing and blowing her nose. The last thing he needed was her germs. Someone left one of the counters, the next person was called and everyone in the queue stepped one pace forwards. The clock ticked, the old woman sniffed, the toddler screamed, the couple were still bickering about their damn dog. If they kept it up much longer, he'd cosh the both of them.

'He came to me when we called him,' the man said.

'Only because you'd stuffed your pockets full of treats.'

'Like you didn't as well.'

Adam fingered the blackjack in his pocket. Another person left and the queue moved forwards. The old woman wheezed and coughed.

It was nearly half an hour before the bickering couple were called forwards. The woman with the screaming toddler vacated the next position and Adam was called.

'Can I register my sister?' he said as he slid the form through the gap between the iron grille and the counter top. 'My mother ain't well enough to come in.'

'Can't your father do it?'

'He ain't around.'

The clerk, a woman with cropped hair, a grey suit and grey tie, pursed her lips and studied the form.

'Have you got your ID?' she said.

He handed his papers over. She studied them, tapped the brass keys of her computer, filled in some forms and rubber-stamped them.

'My mother can't cope with a baby at her time of life,' Adam said as he paid the registration fee, 'especially not on her own, so we reckon it'd be better if me and my girlfriend adopted my sister. How do we do that?'

'Have you and your girlfriend considered moving in with your mother?'

Adam considered spinning a tale about how his girlfriend and his mother couldn't stand each other, but decided that might hinder the case for adoption.

'There ain't enough room at her place.'

'Could she move in with you?'

'My landlord wouldn't allow it.'

Too right, he wouldn't. Adam glanced around. There was a guard in one corner of the room. When had he sneaked in? Adam was sure he hadn't been there when he'd joined the queue.

The clerk tapped some more at the computer, rummaged around in a drawer and pulled out a sheet of paper.

'Very well. If that's what your mother feels is best. Since you're related, you'll need to fill form ADX27 and get your mother to sign it.' She slid the paper under the grille. 'You'll have to bring it back with your ID.'

'Does she have to come in as well? It's just that I don't reckon she'll be up to it.'

'It's usual for both parties to come in, but as long as she signs the form and fills in her ID number it should be okay.'

Adam parked his bike outside the cream terrace house where Harry had found Sam. The dark cellar window behind the set of iron railings still had dusty cobwebs, just like there'd been when he'd peered out of there as a child. Some of the grubby marks on the glass might well have been put there by his own fingers, long ago. How long? It had been eight years since he'd been kicked out of this house. And if it hadn't been for Jack — well, Adam knew where he'd be now if it hadn't been for Jack. He'd understand, wouldn't he? But what if he didn't?

One of the china cats in the front window stared at him with glassy eyes. He hammered on the brass knocker. It was shaped like a fairy that was losing its dress in what was probably considered an artistic fashion. The fairy looked like it was winking at him. It probably still sniggered at him behind his back, like it seemed to do when he was a kid.

The door opened. His mother had the same platinum hair, the same infeasibly long black eyelashes, the same sheen on her face. But she'd been careless with the liquid skin that morning. Flakes were starting to peel away around her ears. If he hadn't known her, he would've found it hard to believe that she'd given birth only the previous day. Her stomach was probably being held in by the struts and straps of her corset. Her smooth colourless nails gleamed in the sunlight. He still had the scars from them. He put his foot in the doorway.

'Sign this,' he said, holding out the form.

She turned to one side and adjusted her lace-trimmed black velvet bolero. She must still have her full-length mirror by the door.

'I ain't going until you sign it,' Adam said.

'You still talk like a retard.'

'You taught me. Oh, no, actually it was the radio not you, weren't it?'

'You always were a whiner.'

She tilted her head to one side and ran a nail down her face, just in front of her ear, dislodging flakes of dried liquid skin. She then inspected the nail and scraped away the detritus from under it with her thumbnail.

'Sign it,' Adam said.

She looked at him, and her thick, red glossy lips curled into a smile.

'Another school trip, is it?'

'It's adoption papers — for my sister. You're going to sign her over to me.'

She turned to the mirror again and adjusted an eyelash.

'Have you come down so far in the world that you've resorted to rummaging in bins?'

'I'll have you done for attempted murder if you don't sign it.'

'You always were a moron. Don't you remember how many nice friends I have?'

She clawed her hands. Her rings looked like knuckle-dusters.

'Sure, I remember,' Adam said. 'And maybe you remember there's a window in the cellar. I liked climbing up to look out of it, and sometimes I got a good look at your best pals. I saw one of them in the papers yesterday with his wife on his arm, and he was spouting high-moral politician crap. Sign the form or I start talking about your pals and just what kind of morals they've really got.'

She took the form with a hand that seemed delicate but was strong enough to twist a boy's arm behind his back. She looked over the document.

'I could tell people how you terrorised me,' she said. 'I know a couple of doctors who could diagnose you with some violent mental health problem. I did all I could, they'll say, but I had to send you away for my own safety.'

'If that's the way you want to play it –' Adam pulled a blackjack out of his pocket '– I'll give you something to back up that claim.'

She eyed him, turned and there was the sound of a pen scribbling on paper.

'Enjoy the screaming and sleepless nights.' She handed back the form. 'Remember me when you cuff her.'

She pouted her lips as though about to blow him a kiss, laughed and shut the door. Adam kicked it. The woodwork cracked. There was a scuff mark on the leather covering his steel toecap, but a bit of polish would soon take care of that. A net curtain in next door's window twitched. Adam tucked the form in his pocket, checked his watch and walked back to his bike.

Jack had a map of the city spread out on the table and was pencilling around an area adjoining the northern end of the Neutral Territory. It had been a wasteland of disused warehouses and abandoned flats, but it had just been bought up by a Colingham firm. Colingham again. How come he was hearing that name so much lately? What did Quinn have going on there?

Harry and Eric were in one corner of the room with instruction sheets and packaging scattered across the floor. The cardboard box nearest Jack's foot had 'easy-assembly travel cot' written on the side of it. Sam was asleep in her car seat on the floor at the far end by the bunk beds, away from the mess. Although it was a wonder she was sleeping given how much Eric and Harry had been quarrelling. Jack kicked the box. Happy families? What had possessed him to make a crack like that at Adam? The look on his face — Jack would've beaten the life out of anyone for saying a thing like that to Adam. Where was he? He'd been gone well over an hour.

Jack drew a line along the old road to Drayton and then curved it over to the north-western edge of Stan's neighbourhood.

'No, it goes that way,' Harry said.

'Like hell it does,' Eric said, shoving the instruction sheet in Harry's face. 'Look.'

Jack's pencil tip snapped. He flicked open his knife and began to shave off the wood. What business did a company from Colingham have coming here to his city? Did they have any connection with Quinn? They could be trying to bolster Stan's neighbourhood. Or maybe the Neutral Territory was trying to bring in some allies. Harry would choose now of all times to interfere with them. A baby in the bin meant a single woman living on her own, and in that kind of neighbourhood that meant someone's mistress. And that someone would be the kind of man who'd pull strings to keep his sordid little secrets quiet. Jack brushed away the flakes of wood and carbon dust from the table with his hand.

'You've got it upside-down,' Harry said.

'That ain't never upside-down,' Eric said.

Jack slammed his fist on the table.

'Button it, the both of you. It's bad enough Adam and Eric bickering all the time, but I'll not have you at it as well, Harry.'

Harry took the instruction sheet from Eric.

'I'll manage on my own.'

'Oh sure,' Jack said, standing up. 'Little Miss Independent can manage on her own. You cause trouble for us all, you rope Adam and Eric in, but all the time you just want to go it alone.'

'Where is Adam?' Harry said. 'Why did he walk off like that? What did you say to him?'

Jack slapped her. She staggered back, dropping the instructions. Eric caught her and steadied her, but she held a hand to her cheek, staring at Jack. Why'd she have to look at him like that? Hadn't anyone ever slapped her before? He wasn't going to fall for that big, blue-eyed routine.

'You don't talk to me like that. This is my territory. Think you got lucky knowing Miguel? So you met a petty thief, a little card sharp, and you think you know my world. Did that little slice of underworld colour add a bit of glamour to your dull rural life?'

'Lucky?' she said. 'If that little rat hadn't turned up, my Uncle Barney would still be alive and I wouldn't be here. Underworld colour? He was a damn coward who hid and let himself be killed rather than giving evidence. He could've proved my uncle was murdered. My uncle, my godfather, the only one who was there for me, the only one who didn't fall sick or go mad.'

Tears trickled down her face. There was a smudge of carbon on her reddened left cheek. She sat down by the table and hugged her knees. Jack leant against the back of his chair. Why should he apologise to her? Everyone had had something lousy happen to them in their life. She was nothing special. She had to learn not to get out of line.

'Ethan's got some lads who are pretty good at ferreting out evidence,' he said.

'I don't need help.'

'Sure you do. You're not the type to let someone get away with a thing like that. You want to get your own back. Who wouldn't? But how are you going to find out anything on your own? You're a farmer, not a detective. You don't have contacts. You don't have resources. You're all on your own, trying to survive in a big, bad world.'

'I'm not getting help from a gangster who's ... '

'Who's what? Everyone bends the rules in the city. I'm straight as a die compared to the pen-pushers in City Hall.'

'At least they're not involved in the prostitution racket.'

'What? And you think I am? Says who?'

'Isn't that Rita's line?'

'What's that got to do with me? You think I'm going to hand you over to her? Oh sure, what would I get for a nice girl like you?'

'Don't. That's horrid.'

'Don't you insult me. I may be a lot of things, but I'm not some lousy pimp. I don't have anything to do with her business. Not a client, not a shareholder. Nothing. All right?'

'Then why d'you put up with her?'

'You're asking for another slap.' Jack perched on the edge of the table and took out a cheroot. 'Rita and I got together a long time ago, during the anarchy. It's nice to have a bit of comfort to take your mind off the crud life throws at you. You want to know what life was like back then? You're not the only one who's lost loved ones. Your uncle was murdered. My family were killed by cannibals.'

He struck a match and lit his cheroot. She was staring at him liked she'd seen a gorgon. He blew out a cloud of smoke.

'I told you I hiked back home with Ethan,' he said. 'Well when I got there, I found what was left of my family in a heap outside. They were mostly bone, but the heads were left. In bad shape, but just about recognisable. By the time I was twelve, I'd already killed the bastards who'd done it, and I'd taken over the castle in the city and was protecting a large group of people.'

'Yeah, that's right,' Eric said. 'Jack looked after me and my mum and lots of the others, as well.'

'Sure, I did. I was the one who turned this city around. I got this place back on its feet. Maybe I should've paid more attention to what she was doing, but I had a lot on my mind. Rita carved out her own career without any help from me, and she's got a lot of clout these days. Some of her clients are influential, and she isn't averse to a spot of blackmail. The anarchy taught us that it's the strong who survive, and the same was true for the people round your home.'

'The Coulgranes protected everyone in the neighbourhood during the anarchy.'

'So they looked after their surfs, did they?'

Jack flicked his match into the ashtray. Harry's hand went to her left cheek, but she pulled it away. It didn't look quite so red now, but the carbon smudge was still there.

'My Uncle Barney fought for the old General,' she said. 'He was made a captain of the South-West regiment.'

'Yeah, I should've figured that. The old General? Was he the earl with the horse and lance?'

'Yes.'

'And the seven-foot-high soldiers in shining armour.'

'Seven foot?'

'That's how the stories go. Haven't you ever heard Bob talking about it?' Jack held the cheroot between his fingers and watched the smoke curling up to the ceiling. 'Would that be why he started being so nice to you? Did you tell him about your uncle?'

'I didn't have to. Apparently there's a strong family resemblance between us.'

'You're certainly not feminine, are you? You've got an androgynous look about you.'

'I'm not butch.'

'Oh, have I hurt your feelings? I never said you were, but you've got to admit I'm right about the need to be strong. I've seen you with Bob. You're stronger than him. Not just physically, but psychologically. And you know it. The way you talk to him, the way you act around him, reinforces it. He's a small, mean, bitter piece of work. You either crush him or you're his victim. You survive by being strong. So do I.'

'I've never killed anyone.'

'What will you do when you find your uncle's murderer?'

'I know who's responsible. I just don't know who he got to do the actual killing.'

'So, what, you came to the city in search of a hit man? What were you planning on doing when you found him? Give him a spanking?'

'I shall expose him.'

Jack laughed and patted the top of her head.

'It's not funny, Jack,' she said.

'You kidding me? How are you going to expose him? Strip him naked and tie him to a post?'

'That's not what I meant.'

Jack took a puff of his cheroot and blew out a cloud of smoke towards the open window.

'Listen, sweetheart, your old General wasn't called that because he ran a hippie commune, and your uncle didn't get to be a captain by exposing villains. Your precious Coulgranes had an army. They killed to protect their people. I kill to protect my people. They protected the women, the children and the elderly, but only those within their own walls. I protect the frails in my territory, but only the ones in my territory. Like Eric's little old ma. She's in a nursing home. Who d'you think pays for her treatment? That baby, on the other hand, is from outside my territory so I don't interfere. Not any more.'

Jack took another drag of his cheroot. The sound of a vacuum cleaner started up in the flat below. That would be Mrs Daly. Outside Mrs Wellings was calling in her kids, and deaf old Parker was passing the time of day with someone at the top of his voice. Jack's tenants, all of them. His east-facing window was growing dim. Jack glanced at his watch. Four o'clock. He looked back at Sammy asleep in her car seat. He turned to Harry.

'Listen to me, Miss Independent. In case you hadn't noticed, my lad is sweet on you. He was never able to look at a woman without being reminded of his damn mother until you turned up. You don't hurt him. You don't string him along. When he gets back, we'll sort out what to do with the baby, and you will accept my decision. I won't have you challenging my authority.'

Jack stayed perched against the table with one foot on his chair, smoking. Harry stared at the ground. Sam began to stir. Eric went over to her and rocked her seat. The sound of a motorbike engine drew up outside and then became muffled as it headed under the building. A few minutes later there were hurried footsteps coming up the staircase, a key turning and the sound of the front door to the flat closing with a click.

Adam came into the room and went straight over to Sam.

'Where've you been?' Eric said.

Adam turned and walked over to Jack.

'You okay, my boy?' Jack said.

'Yeah.' Adam looked at Harry. 'You all right, Harry? You've got something on your cheek.' He took out a handkerchief and rubbed the carbon off. He peered at her eyes. 'What's up?'

'Nothing. I just got a bit of dust in my eyes, that's all.'

'You didn't answer Eric,' Jack said. 'Where'd you get to, my boy?'

'I'm sorry, Jack. I had to do it.'

Jack tapped his cheroot over the ashtray.

'Do what?'

'Save Sammy. I couldn't let it happen again. I should've been the one to pick her out of that bin, but it was like I was frozen solid. It was like I was a kid again.'

'Couldn't let what happen again?'

'She killed my brother.'

Jack rested his cheroot on the ashtray and gently held Adam by the shoulder.

'What are you talking about, my boy?'

'I promised I'd look out for him. I promised he'd never be alone, but then she suffocated him. I saw her do it and I didn't even try to stop her. Sam's my sister. That was my mother's bin. You know how Verkroost over at The Blue Diamond always says long odds ain't so long if you've got luck on your side? Maybe it was a million to one chance and we just had a bit of luck, but maybe it was my brother giving me a way to square with him.'

Adam was trembling so much, he almost looked like someone with DTs.

'My dear boy, why didn't you tell me? I'd've got the very best for her if I'd known she was your sister.'

'So she can stay?'

'What? You think I'd kick your sister out?'

'And I can square things with my brother, can't I?'

'I'm not so sure about the whole supernatural angle, my lad,' Jack said. 'I've been around long enough to have seen some pretty long odds.' Adam looked like the lost sixteen-year-old kid Jack had first met at the police station eight years ago. 'Don't worry, my boy. I'll fix things up for you.'

'It's all right. I've just registered her. I got her papers out of the bin after Harry ran off with her. And I made my mother sign the adoption papers. That's where I've just been.'

'Here, Adam,' Eric said, 'you ain't gone and got Jack into trouble, have you?'

'I never mentioned Jack. And I thought you were all for looking after Sam, or have you changed your mind?'

'I ain't changed my mind, but you should've let Jack deal with it.'

'I was keeping Jack out of it. D'you think I don't know better than to cause trouble for him? She don't know I work for him.'

'Everyone who's anybody knows you're Jack's lad.'

Adam picked up yesterday's newspaper from the table.

'See him,' he said, pointing to a picture, 'that may well be Sammy's father.'

'Who is he?' Harry said.

'Bartrum. A lousy politician, but he ain't gonna want no bad publicity so he ain't gonna cause no trouble.'

'You kidding?' Eric said. 'Don't you know how big he is in the Neutral Territory? He'll turn them against Jack, just to shut you up.'

'But they won't do that. Will they, Jack?'

Jack ran his fingers through his hair. From what he had heard on the street, Bartrum was good buddies with some of Rita's more affluent clientèle. Combined, Adam's mother and Rita had enough backing to persuade Stan to have a go at being the number one gangster. And Rita hated Adam enough to try a stunt like that. She still hadn't forgiven Jack for wasting a favour, as she had put it, for the sake of an out-of-luck kid. When Jack looked up he saw that Harry was holding Adam's hand.

'It's okay, my boy.'

Eric made to speak, but Jack motioned him to stay quiet.

'You sure, Jack?' Adam said.

'Sure, I'm sure. Like you said, he won't want any bad publicity. At least now I know what to say to Rita. When she gets here, leave me to do the talking and you all stick to my story. Understood?'

'Yes,' Harry said.

'Yeah, sure thing, Jack,' Eric said.

'And, Harry, you help Adam look after Sammy. Don't you even think of leaving him in the lurch.'

'Of course I won't. What kind of person d'you think I am?'

'A pain in the arse. All I'm saying is that if you disappear without a trace, I'll have someone find you.'

'If I disappear, it won't be of my choosing.'

'Any time you feel like confiding in me, just go ahead.'

'I've caused enough problems for you.'

'Well that's real sweet of you to finally start thinking about it.'

'But, Harry,' Adam said as he picked up the cot instruction leaflet, 'Jack can fix things for you.'

He studied the pieces on the floor and began to assemble the cot.

'I'm not giving you another enemy to worry about,' she said. 'It looks like Sam's stirring. I'll sort out some milk.'

Jack set Eric by the window to watch for Rita and in due course he signalled her approach. Jack ordered Harry to stay out of sight in the kitchen, and she obeyed without a word. Adam stood in front of the now-assembled cot with his arms folded. Jack sat at the table and opened the newspaper at random. There was an article about an arson attempt at the abandoned airport. Rita entered the room in a haze of perfume, with a reticule dangling from her wrist. Grant sauntered along behind, picking at his teeth.

'This is an unexpected social call, Rita,' Jack said, glancing up from the paper. 'That's real nice of you.'

'Yeah right.' Rita pushed Adam to one side. 'I didn't realise you were planning on picking up any more migrants, Jack. Hitched a ride, did it?'

'She's Adam's sister. He's adopted her.'

'Why?'

'Because she's his sister, and his mother isn't exactly the maternal type.'

'Her name's Sam,' Eric said. 'That's my mum's name.'

'So?' Rita said.

She picked up Sam's psychedelic toy frog, looked at it and tossed it to one side.

'I like my mum.'

'And there's me thinking you had "Mum" tattooed on your arm because you couldn't remember her name. She's irrelevant.'

'He's just pointing out that my sister is named after decent people,' Adam said. 'She's also named after Harry and her mum.'

'Oh my, how twee.'

Grant screwed up his face.

'I dunt want to share a room with a blarin' baby.'

'There's nothing to stop you from walking right out that door and sleeping on the street,' Jack said.

'Don't take that tone with him,' Rita said.

Jack slammed the newspaper down on the table.

'Why shouldn't I? We have to put up with his lousy habits. Don't try making an issue out of this Rita. Sam's registered, and Adam's legally adopted her, so everything's all square and above board. Stan won't side with you on this one.'

— 16 —

THE ANTI-TECHNOLOGY LEAGUE

Heads turned when Adam and Harry arrived in church with Sam. Adam's first impulse was to avoid eye contact, but then he decided to give a nod of greeting as though nothing unusual had happened. After the dismissal, they found most of the parishioners chatting on the lawn outside the church. Mrs Harper and Mrs Widrow came over to Adam and Harry.

'What an adorable baby,' Mrs Widrow said and raised her eyebrows at Harry.

'She's Adam's sister,' Harry said, turning the car seat so they had a better view of the baby.

A girl from the congregation ran past them, chasing a boy who was waving a straw hat.

'Do you give that back, Billy,' the girl said, 'or I wunt half lam you.'

'Are you looking after her for the day?' Mrs Harper asked Adam.

He toyed with a story about his mother having been in a car crash — a particularly gruesome one where she had suffered in terrible agony — but in the end he reckoned it would be best to stick with Jack's story.

'I've adopted her. My mother didn't want her, and there ain't no father around.'

There was a collective gasp. Mrs Harper shook her head.

'Well, that's the city for you.'

'A terrible place,' Mrs Widrow said.

'But so good of you to adopt her.'

'Yeah well, I couldn't have her put into care,' Adam said.

'You're so right.' Mrs Harper leant over Sam and stroked the baby's fingers. 'You're a sweet little darling, aren't you? Yes, you are.'

'It's reassuring to know that there are a few decent folk in the city,' Mrs Widrow said. 'I don't much care about having children outside of marriage as there's nothing that can be done if the father leaves mother and child in the lurch, but for both parents to not care about the child is quite appalling.'

Mrs Harper tickled Sam's tummy.

'The postmistress looks after her son very well,' she said. 'A nicely turned out little boy. Of course, we all know who the father is. Not that he cares tuppence about it.'

Major Widrow gave a snort.

'You'll find there are no secrets in this village,' he said to Adam. 'Very active grapevine. Good man for taking your sister in.'

Before Adam realised what was happening, the Major had seized his hand and pumped his arm.

'I suppose you have to give her bottled milk,' Mrs Harper said to Harry. 'You'll have to make sure you give her lots of boiled water to prevent her from getting — well, you know.'

'Bunged up,' a woman in a tweed suit said. 'Carrie Bramley, local midwife. You want any advice, just ask.'

Major Widrow had turned away from the women and was looking at Adam's car, which was parked close to the church, next to one of the horse-drawn carriages.

'That's a Phaeton, isn't it?' the Major said to Adam.

'Yeah, that's right.'

Adam fetched a rag from the car and wiped away some mud from the paintwork. The Major peered in through one of the windows.

'Nice finish. Build it yourself?'

'Yeah. I used to be a mechanic.'

The Major straightened up and nodded. His face was reddened and weather-beaten, much like Harry's. His grey eyebrows were bushy with stray wiry hairs, and there were a couple of deep scars across his left temple.

'It's good to have proper cars built by human hands,' the Major said. 'None of this machines making other machines business. And then what happens? They fill them full of computer chips and the damn things break down and you can't fix them.'

'A car's much safer than a motorbike, if you ask me,' Mrs Harper said. 'And far more dignified. Now, my dear, don't tell me the poor child didn't even get any colostrum.'

Father Bernard finished talking to a parishioner and came over to Adam.

'Not a-goin' for a walk terday, bor?'

'Looks like it might rain,' Adam said. 'I don't want Sam to catch cold. You got cricket today?'

Father Bernard sighed.

'The season's over,' he said. 'Do you watch out for that hoss manure, Billy.'

The girl had reclaimed her straw hat and was now charging after the boy with a stick. Father Bernard turned back to Adam.

'Did you want the child baptised?'

'What? Oh, sure. Okay. What do we have to do?'

'There are some preparations. That dunt take too long, jist a few hours on a cuppla days.'

'We can't make a weekday.'

'Do you want to come in the evenin' arter work, thass orl right,' Father Bernard said.

'No, we're out of county during the week. We don't get back to Norwich until Friday.'

'What line of work are you in now?' Major Widrow asked.

'Trucking,' Adam said. 'How about Saturday afternoon, Father Bernard?'

'Ah no, bor, the rugger season start next Saturday arternune. We've a match against East Belingford. How about Saturday mornin' at eleven o'clock?'

'Sure.'

The boy Billy now had a stick as well, and he and the girl had started a play sword fight.

'So we have to choose godparents, ain't that right?' Adam said. 'Is it okay if the godfather ain't a church person?'

'Do you stop your muckin' abowt, Irene,' a woman said to the girl.

'But mum, Billy's being a city gangster so I've gotta kill him.'

'You'll get your dress orl datty. Time to go. That do look like rain.'

'Praps you'd like to bring yar friend along with you on Saturday,' Father Bernard said to Adam.

'Actually, maybe that ain't such a good idea,' Adam said. 'I mean, he's kinda busy, and like I said he don't go to church.'

Major Widrow turned from the car to look at Adam. The scars on the old man's temple stood out white against his weather-beaten skin. Harry came over with Sam.

'You okay, Adam?' she said.

'Yeah, sure.'

'We were now a-talkin' about gittin' the child baptised,' Father Bernard said. 'We were thinkin' on Saturday morning for the first of the preparations.'

Harry smiled and slipped her hand through Adam's arm. 'Oh, Adam, that's great.'

'Yeah,' he said. 'Let's get Sammy in the car. It's starting to rain.'

The windscreen wipers juddered across the glass. He'd have to adjust them when they got home. Harry was sitting by Adam's side, and Sam was in her car seat in the back.

'What made you decide to get Sam baptised?' Harry said. 'Not that I'm complaining. I was just wondering.'

'Well, you know. I thought it'd be the right thing to do.'

Adam pulled on to the muddy verge to give way to an oncoming tractor. The driver waved and trundled past. The Phaeton's narrow wheels skidded as Adam tried to drive on. He eased up and, amid a slew of mud and clatter of pebbles, he managed to get back on the lane again.

'Look, Harry,' he said, 'it might be best if you don't mention about Sam's christening to anyone.'

'Sam will start talking about going to church when she gets older.'

'Yeah, but you see, the thing is we can't let Big Stan get to hear about it.'

'It's none of his business.'

'Jack always gets an invite whenever Stan's relatives get christened, married or buried. Stan'll take offence if there's no reciprocal arrangement.'

'We can't have someone like Stan O'Brien in Weston Snelding,' Harry said. 'I'll not have his hypocrisy tainting the place. Besides, imagine how the villagers would react.'

'Yeah, I've already been imagining it.' Adam steered around a muddy pothole. 'You still ain't told them your name. Ain't you gonna have to say if we get Sam baptised? Are you gonna give them your fake name? Only we ought to keep our stories straight.'

'I won't lie in church. Of course, you'll have to tell them your name and Sam's, but there's no need for mine, is there?'

'In which case, they'll end up calling you "Mrs Trent".' Adam grinned. 'Maybe I should get you a wedding ring.'

'Don't make fun of that kind of thing.'

They had reached a junction, so Adam stopped to look at her, but she'd turned her back on him. She sure was touchy about the strangest things.

'What have you got there?'

Jack made some space on the table so that Ethan could put down his bag.

'When I got back from the pub last night, I mentioned about Sam to Helen, and she immediately hunted in the attic for our old baby stuff. She wouldn't even wait until morning. Anyway, she wanted Adam to have it.'

Ethan opened up the bag, displaying its contents. Eric peered inside it. Adam finished winding Sam, laid her in her cot and came over to have a look.

'Not planning on having more?' Jack said.

'Four's plenty.' Ethan took out a dress and held it up. 'What d'you think?'

'That's real sweet. What d'you reckon, Adam?'

'I thought you didn't like pink.'

'There's nothing wrong with a little bit of pink on a baby girl.' Jack took the dress and studied it. Then he dumped it back in the bag. 'Harry, are we just going to smell the lunch today, or do we get to eat it?'

'It's almost ready,' Harry said and left the room.

Adam added the contents of the bag to the box containing Sam's things. Ethan went over to look at the sleeping baby.

'You can have our old cot if you like, and keep this one for travelling. I'll bring the pram over as well. I reckon it'll fit nice and snug in that corner there.'

'We thought about getting a pram,' Eric said, 'but we reckoned we wouldn't be able to get it up the stairs.'

'That's not a problem,' Ethan said. 'Jack, you can get someone to fix the lift, can't you?'

'Yeah, sure.'

'I've found out more about Harry,' Jack said as he and Ethan strolled along the pavement after lunch.

'You sure have become domesticated. First Harry, now Sam.'

'She's a loose cannon.'

Jack glanced around. Old Mr Cooper was shuffling along the road towards them. He was the type who couldn't hear so well when it was the rent that was being talked about, but his hearing seemed to improved when more private topics were being discussed.

'What d'you reckon about Adam and Harry's idea to take Sam on the road?' Jack said.

'Might be okay for the first month, but I reckon it'll soon get too much for them. Why don't you fix up a place for the three of them? Near enough so Harry can still cook for you, but with enough distance so Sam doesn't disturb you.'

'I'm not letting Harry out of my sight.'

Mr Cooper had stopped to read the community noticeboard just ahead of them, so Jack nodded to Ethan and they strolled over to the other side of the road.

'She's after a hit man,' Jack said.

'Seriously? She asked for help?'

'Nope.'

Mr Cooper finished perusing the notices, ambled over to the door of the block of flats where he lived and dropped his keys. He bent down for them with as much speed as a rusting tin man. Ethan ran over, picked up the keys, let the old man into the building and returned to Jack's side.

'So what's with the hit man? Who'd he knock off?'

'Harry's Uncle Barney. Seems he found out something from Miguel, but Miguel buttoned up real tight and wouldn't help with the investigations.'

'And now Quinn's thugs are all over that region,' Ethan said. 'Reckon there's a connection?'

'Quinn sure was touchy about Colingham. He seemed convinced Cornell and van Loame were poking around there.'

'Cornell said they hadn't been anywhere near Colingham, but he did find out something you're not going to like.' Ethan waited while a mother and child walked by. 'Quinn fingered you for Miguel's killing.'

Jack stopped. He gripped the pistol in his coat pocket. A couple of kids raced round the corner, pulled up short when they saw him and ran back the other way. Jack let go of his gun.

'I might've guessed. That's sure his style.'
'Cornell reckons the search for the missing lady is a blind. It's a manhunt and not a tactful one. Miguel and Harry's uncle get knocked off because they know too much. Maybe there's someone else in the know? There's more at stake here than fixing things for Harry. Quinn's up to something in West Norfolk, and whatever it is it won't be good news for us.'

'Mary, warm up the baby's milk. Tess, help them with the baggage. Here's your key, Jack.'

Betsy left it on the counter and hurried over to Adam and Harry. Jack signed himself in and picked up the key. Great, not even a peck on the cheek today. Eric came into the lobby with some more of Sam's luggage. Jack took his own case up to his room. You'd have thought they were embarking on a six-month expedition that morning with all the paraphernalia they'd had to bring with them to the depot. Harry had pushed Sam along in Ethan's donated pram with the travel cot all folded up and packed away in its bag, which she had slung on her back. The rest of Sam's baggage had been divided between Adam and Eric. They had taken the longer route to the depot, by-passing the road where Adam's mother lived.

At least the weather had been clear, if cold, and the traffic reasonable. Jack locked up his room and returned downstairs. There was the usual clatter of crockery and hubbub of voices in the dining room. Truckers called out greetings to him as he entered, but the conversations faltered. Jack turned and saw that a young man and woman had come into the room behind him.

They were a gawky pair with steel-framed glasses and both were wrapped up in a scarf and bobble hat. Their lapels were covered in badges and they stood by the doorway, fidgeting with a handful of leaflets. One good sneeze from a trucker would probably blow the pair halfway across the city.

Jack pulled up a chair at the table opposite them, poured himself a glass of water and studied them. They jumped aside as the door swung open and Eric came in. He glanced at them and came over to Jack.

'What's going on?'

'Anti-Techs, by the look of them,' Jack said. 'What d'you reckon? Guts or naïveté?'

'Just plain dumb.'

Eric sat down next to Jack and picked up the menu. The young man cleared his throat. Adam and Harry came in with Sam. Jack gestured to Adam while Harry cleared a space at the end of the table for Sam's seat.

'Don't get too settled,' Jack said to Adam. 'We're going out tonight.'

The Anti-Tech man cleared his throat again.

'Many of you will remember the anarchy.'

'Oh great,' Jack said. 'They want to give us a speech as well as leaflets.'

'They must be nuts,' Adam said. 'Don't they know this is your territory?'

'Apparently not. But they soon will.'

'The fuel crisis was caused by too much technology.'

Alf stood up and strode over to the Anti-Techs. He was at least six inches taller than them and wider than the pair of them put together.

'How'd you produce those leaflets? Carve them in stone, did you?'

'It's excessive technology that's the problem,' the woman said. 'That's why we're calling for legislation to limit available technology to sustainable levels.'

Spike and Hector left their seats to join Alf, casting the Anti-Techs into shadow.

'We were stuck here for two days because of your lousy demonstration,' Spike said.

'If we don't learn from the past –' she edged behind her companion '– the anarchy will happen all over again.'

That sure was typical of a woman. Asking for a fight while sheltering behind a man. The sap.

Harry stood up and strode over to them, her hands in her pockets. The truckers glanced at her and then at Jack. Adam half-rose from his seat. Jack gestured to the truckers, and they stepped back. Harry took her hand out of her pocket, leant forward and plucked a leaflet out of the man's hand.

'May I have one?' she said and returned to her seat.

The three truckers looked at Jack. He shrugged and they returned to their seats. Conversations restarted in the room and a waitress came over to take Jack's order. The Anti-Techs seemed to consider the distribution of one leaflet a success and sidled away.

'Let's have a look at it then,' Jack said to Harry after the waitress had left.

Harry handed over the leaflet. It was a typewritten mimeographed copy with an outlined logo of a hand pressing down on a computer — one of the modern chunky ones. That young pair probably wouldn't be able to identify any of the old slimline types. The prose was full of the usual hyperbole about anarchy and food shortages. The exclamation key on their typewriter must've got pretty worn down with so much usage.

'You're not planning on joining them, are you?' Jack said.

'It's true that farmers can't produce more sugar beet without causing a food shortage,' Harry said.

Jack gave her back the leaflet.

'We won't need so much ethanol once they've finished the desert solar panels.'

'Harry's right,' a voice from behind said. 'And we can't be relying on something from other sectors, especially not ones so far away.'

Jack glanced round: it was Donnaghan. The lousy little bastard was always creeping up on people and listening in. The slob couldn't even tuck his shirt in properly, and his attempt to grow a moustache was pathetic.

'Where were you when the Anti-Techs were demonstrating?' Jack said. 'Are coppers scared of a bunch of kids?'

'We stopped it from getting out of hand.'

Donnaghan hitched up his trousers and ambled off, tracing a circuitous route around the tables.

'Yeah right,' Jack said. 'What's the betting he hid somewhere safe until the lightning frightened them off?'

'But, Jack,' Harry said, 'don't you think it's possible the Anti-Technology League have got a point?'

'Now don't get me wrong, my girl, I agree there's a lot to be said for good old-fashioned mechanical things. Like my tommy gun: it doesn't have fancy gizmos, and it's got a kick like a mule, but it was straight-forward to make, and it's got style. I don't like the Anti-Techs because they interfere with my business, and I won't stand for that.'

The young Anti-Tech pair came into view through the window opposite Jack. It looked as though they were trying to foist a leaflet on to Betsy who seemed to be shooing them off her property.

'You don't mean you made your tommy gun, do you?' Harry said.

'I've got other people to manufacture them now but, sure, I made my first one during the anarchy. Although I'm surprised it didn't fall apart or blow up in my face. I did most of it in the technology lab in school before Ethan and I left. I managed to swipe some saltpetre from the chemistry supplies and charcoal from the art classroom, but it wasn't until we got back to the city and were doing a bit of salvaging before I found the sulphur. What kind of science teacher doesn't keep sulphur in his cupboard?'

The waitress brought over their orders. Eric topped up the glasses while Adam adjusted Sam's seat.

'Where did you learn how to make it?' Harry said after the waitress had gone.

'I had a thing for tommy guns when I was a kid. My parents had a collection of old gangster films, which got me interested, and I read a lot of books from that era. The Continental Op sure stirred things up in Poisonville. Anyway, when I was at school I had a look on the computer and found the specs. I've still got the printout.'

'What? You mean computers would tell children how to make guns?'

Jack cut a piece of his steak.

'You'd be amazed at what you could learn from the Internet. In fact, I'd already started getting hold of the parts before the anarchy happened. Not that I was planning on shooting people back then. It was just a hobby. Like building a model aeroplane.'

'Well, it sounds to me that the Anti-Technology League are right.' Harry sniffed and put her cutlery down. 'Oh, Sam, I've only just changed you.'

'You're going to have to change her again. I'm not having that in the background while I'm eating my dinner.' Jack eyed Harry as she picked Sam up and took her out. He smoothed his moustache with his thumbnail. 'I hope she's not planning on getting involved with the Anti-Techs. We're going to have to keep an eye on her.'

'What about this evening?' Adam said. 'Didn't you say we had to go out?'

'Yeah, that's right. We'll just have to hope she behaves herself. I need a climber, and you're the best I've got.'

'What's the job?'

Jack leant forward to reply but noticed a reflection in the window. He glanced round. Donnaghan was now sitting at a nearby table, seemingly engrossed in a magazine.

'Tell you later. Anyone would think Donnaghan was tailing us, the way he keeps popping up.'

'You don't reckon he is, do you?' Eric said.

'Not even Stan or Quinn are stupid enough to use him for a tail job. He's just skiving, that's all. Frightened he's going to catch a chill outside.' Jack turned back to Adam. 'Anyway, my boy, don't worry about leaving Harry alone with Sam. She put a lot on the line to save her. Whatever her interest in the Anti-Techs is, she knows her priority is looking after your little sister.'

'Oh, I know that,' Adam said. 'She'll be a good role model for Sammy, won't she?'

'Once she gets off her high horse,' Jack said. 'But I'm glad to see her face has cleared up.'

'Who? Harry?'

'Sure. Who else?' Jack said. 'It was covered in lesions when I first saw her.'

'It was never that bad.'

'Well you would think that — she's like a rare generator to you — but I'm more objective. Her cheeks are still a bit red, but there's a definite improvement. Eric, didn't her face look a lot worse when she first arrived?'

Eric finished his mouthful.

'Well actually, Jack, I think Adam's right.'

'You both know I'm the one with the best memory around here. I'll allow for partiality, Adam, but Eric, I'm surprised at you disagreeing with me like that.'

'Sorry, Jack,' Eric said. 'Yeah you're right. Her face has cleared up a lot.'

Jack pushed his plate away.

'I don't know why you're both making such a fuss about it. I'm going out for a smoke. Make sure you're ready in half an hour.'

Betsy finished watering the hanging baskets and neatened the flowers. An alarm began to wail up the street, near Sector House, but that was outside Jack's territory. She stood back and eyed her property in the light of the street lamps. The sign still needed a lick of paint. She'd have to ask Jack if he wouldn't mind chasing up the decorator. Something white fluttered in the branches of a potted rose bush by the driveway entrance. She went over to investigate and found that it was one of the Anti-Tech leaflets caught on a thorn. She eased it out of the plant and scrunched it up. She was about to turn back when she stopped. There was a familiar figure in a telephone box across the street, back towards Betsy and head low over the instrument, but there was no mistaking that waxed jacket. Was there something wrong with the phone in Harry's room? How did people expect Betsy to get things fixed if they didn't report the problem?

'Betsy, come quick.'

She turned and saw Tess stumbling towards her, sodden and panting. Betsy ran over.

'What's happened?'

'Burst pipe in the kitchen.'

'Have you turned off the stopcock?' Betsy said as they sped up the driveway.

'Yes, but it's made a mess everywhere.'

The girl's shoes slapped against the ground, sending up a shower of droplets that splashed Betsy's stockinged ankles. Betsy jumped up the stairs leading to the front door, dashed across the lobby, through the dining room and one step down into the kitchen. Water had spread across the tiles, reaching just below the level of the dining room floor. The cook and waitresses were scooping up water with buckets and emptying them down the sink.

Betsy phoned the plumber, then donned an apron and found another bucket. It was lucky everyone had finished eating. And that step down into the kitchen, which the waitresses were always complaining about, had proved useful. At least the dining room floor wouldn't get ruined. Maybe she should check the phone in Harry's room just to make sure it was okay. Betsy tipped another bucketful down the sink. Who would a migrant with no family be phoning? She had looked quite furtive. This water was freezing. Betsy should've changed her shoes.

The plumber arrived and dumped his tools on a worktop. The water was now too low for the buckets so Betsy got out some mops. How did Harry fit into Jack's organisation? One minute he was grumbling about her, the next he seemed to be treating her like he treated Adam. Well, Betsy knew better than to criticise Adam in front of Jack, so maybe she ought to be careful saying anything about Harry.

'Tess, there's a pile of old towels in the cellar.' Betsy squeezed out the mop. 'Go fetch them.'

Harry hadn't left Sam unattended, had she? The plumber dropped his wrench on the floor. It landed with a soggy thud. Water splashed up against the chrome cupboard doors. The plumber retrieved the wrench and continued working on the pipe. Betsy went over to inspect the floor tile to see if it had been damaged.

Eric's deep booming laugh rang out from the entrance, so Betsy dashed out through the dining room into the lobby, removing her apron. Jack was heading towards the staircase with Eric and Adam.

'What happened to you, Betsy?' Jack said.

'A pipe burst. It's flooded the kitchen. The plumber's here, but I've spent all evening mopping up.'

'That's a lousy piece of luck,' Jack said, straightening her bolero. 'You let me know if the plumber gives you any trouble. You ought to change your shoes and stockings or you'll get a chill.'

With that he kissed her and turned to go. He put an arm on Adam's shoulders.

'You did real good, my lad. I'm real proud of you.'

Eric bent down and picked up a piece of paper lying on the floor.

'It's another one of them Anti-Tech leaflets.'

'Lousy litter bugs,' Jack said.

'I've been thinking,' Eric said. 'I don't reckon you need to worry about Harry being interested in the Anti-Techs cos she bought that fancy baby monitoring gadget for Sammy.'

'Keep your voice down, Eric,' Adam said, 'or you'll wake her up.'

Betsy watched the three men turn the corner at the top of the stairs. Of course, that must've been why Harry hadn't used the phone in her room. She hadn't wanted to disturb the baby. Just as well Betsy hadn't bothered Jack about the incident.

The week went smoothly and, to Adam's relief, Sam seemed to like the vibrations of the truck. Harry had offered to take Sam in her vehicle, but Jack had refused until Harry had clocked up more mileage. So Adam had tied the psychedelic frog to his passenger head rest for Sam to look at. The activity bar fastened to her car seat had a small bell that jingled with every bump in the road.

They headed home on Friday evening as usual, and the next morning Adam parked his Phaeton in the church car park in Weston Snelding. Harry went to take Sam out of the back while Adam looked around, wondering where the baptism preparations were supposed to take place. In front of him was the lawn that surrounded the church. On the other side of the car park was a small cottage with bean poles in the garden. The front door opened, and Father Bernard waved to them.

'How are you a-gorn on, tergether?' he said. Adam went over and shook hands. 'Come on in. I've now a-made a pot of taay.'

'I'll just lock my car first.'

'What d'you want to do that for, bor? Nowun here's a-gorn to steal it.'

Adam glanced over his shoulder. Harry came up beside him with Sam in her seat.

'Do that make you fare better, jist you go and lock it,' Father Bernard said to Adam and turned to Harry. 'Do you come in, my bewty. I've lit the stove in the parlour.'

Adam ran back to his car, locked it and returned to the cottage to find the front door wide open. He closed it behind him. Just a ward lock and a loose-fitting bolt. The hallway was dark with dried mud on the floor tiles. By the wall, there was a tumbled mass of boots, bats and balls of various shapes and sizes. Adam followed the sounds of voices and clinking of crockery, ducked under a low lintel and found the others in the sitting room. A fire crackled in the wood burner. Hanging on the wall above was a large painting of a cricket scene. Next to it was an old sepia print of some bearded bloke in a striped cap holding a cricket bat. Eric's beard was like stubble compared to that fellow's. A bookcase fitted snugly in an alcove. Its shelves were filled with a mixture of religious and sporting titles. There was a wooden cross and three small statues at one end of the mantelpiece, and at the other end were two trophies: one a cup, the other a silver batsman in mid-swing. In the centre of the mantelpiece was a brass carriage clock. An old springer spaniel came over to Adam, sniffed him and then settled down on the rug in front of the hearth.

'Do you sit down, bor,' Father Bernard said. 'I dunt think I heard yar names.'

'I'm Adam Trent, and this is Sam.'

'And I'm Harriet,' Harry said with a smile. 'This is a lovely little presbytery.'

'Thass a masterous cottage, hintut, my bewty?' Father Bernard turned to Adam. 'Did you think more abowt asking yar mate to be godfa'r?'

'I didn't realise you had someone in mind,' Harry said.

'Oh, it was just a thought, but I ain't got no Catholic friends. Well, apart from you.'

Father Bernard studied Adam for a moment and then picked up a thin book from the coffee table.

'I've got you a preparation book. That explain orl about it. Do you want sugar with yar taay?'

The next morning Adam returned to Weston Snelding with Harry and Sam for Sunday mass. Father Bernard preached about some repentant tax collector, who'd been taking a cut for himself. Yeah, there were people down in City Hall who were just like that, only Adam couldn't see them repenting any time soon.

'Thass nice to see you agin, Mr Trent,' Father Bernard said as Adam came out of the church after the dismissal.

Major Widrow was nearby with his wife who was chatting to another parishioner. He came over to greet Adam. Harry came out of the church on to the lawn with Sam. The women from the congregation drew round her.

'And how's the dear little thing today?' Mrs Widrow said, with a glance at Harry's left hand. 'Mrs Trent?'

Adam looked at Harry's face, but it was difficult to tell if the redness of her cheeks was embarrassment or her usual weather-beaten colouring.

'She's doing very well,' Harry said. 'I think she really likes coming here. It's such a neat and tidy church. Someone must spend hours cleaning it.'

Mrs Widrow brushed a piece of fluff off her shoulder.

'Thank you, dear. It's so nice when people notice.'

'Oh, so this is your marvellous handiwork?'

'I've been on the cleaning rota for forty years.'

'So have I,' Mrs Harper said, 'and dear Miss Maitland over there.'

Adam looked over at the grey-haired woman with a walking stick and tried to imagine her with a dustpan and brush. Surely she'd just fall over or seize up.

'Well, I think you do a wonderful job,' Harry said. 'Don't you, Adam?'

'Yeah sure.'

He slipped his hand around her waist. She didn't pull away and continued talking for a while longer.

'How d'you always know what these people do?' Adam asked as they pulled out of the church driveway. 'You can't kid me that's a coincidence the way you always turn the conversation like that.'

Harry waved to Mrs Widrow and Mrs Harper.

'The rotas are on the noticeboard.'

'You're a bit like Jack.'

'I'm nothing like Jack,' she said. He glanced at her. This time her cheeks definitely seemed redder than usual. 'Slow down for that horse.'

'Yeah, all right. I'd seen it.' He stopped and waited for the oncoming horse and rider to pass. 'I told you they'd start calling you "Mrs Trent".'

'I can hardly say, "How d'you do? I'm Lady Harriet Coulgrane."'

Adam drove down the lane and turned the corner out of the village. The wheels rumbled over the uneven section of road. The hedgerow was tall and thick on either side. A line of chestnuts overshadowed them.

'I can't see anyone in Weston Snelding turning you over to Allerton,' Adam said. 'I reckon you can trust them.'

'They're not my people.'

'You kidding? Sure they are. Some of them are farmers, and some of them are a bit posh.'

'I hate that word.'

Adam steered round a pothole and braked as a pheasant wandered into the lane.

'What word?'

'"Posh." It sounds terribly vulgar.'

'Seriously?' he said. 'That ain't nothing, but I weren't exactly brought up in fine society, so sometimes I do say things that are a bit vulgar.'

'I'm sorry, Adam. I didn't mean it like that.'

She rested her hand on his shoulder. He turned to look at her and then leant back towards the rear seats.

'See, Sammy. Harry'll bring you up proper.' He patted Harry's hand and faced the front. 'Damn stupid bird. What's it doing just sitting there in the middle of the road?'

He revved the engine and edged forward until the bird pattered away into the hedgerow.

'It's a shame your papers ain't legit,' Adam said, 'or we could make you jointly responsible for Sammy.'

'I already consider myself jointly responsible for her.'

'Yeah, but it's better to tie things up legally, just in case anything happens to me. Not that you need to worry. I know Jack would look after the both of you if I bit the dust.'

'Would he?'

'Sure he would. He's always been good to me, and he likes you.'

Adam stopped at a junction. Yeah, Jack sure seemed to like Harry now.

'I'd rather you didn't get yourself killed,' Harry said. 'How do I get registered properly?'

'You'd need your birth certificate.'

Sweet, she didn't want him to get himself killed. That sure was a declaration from someone like Harry — or was she just being practical?

'I brought it with me,' Harry said, 'and my driving licence, but Allerton might be able to trace me if I'm registered.'

'And what would he do then? He'd be real dumb to try a snatch in Jack's territory.'

A tractor drove past along the main road, its trailer full of muddy beet.

'He's still claiming I've got a tumour,' Harry said.

'So we get you another scan.'

'I'd thought about it, but I'd have to give away my identity to do that, and he's bound to have people watching all the hospitals in this sector.'

'You reckon he's that big? Just lay all your cards on the table with Jack, and he'll sort it out for you.'

'I'd rather he didn't.'

Adam shrugged, checked both directions and pulled on to the main road. The sky was clouding over. It was a shame it had been too cold and damp to go for a walk again.

'How's things with Cornell and van Loame?'

Jack was settled in the old leather armchair in Ethan's office with a cup of coffee. Harry had made a fine lunch again, and the top floor of the police station was always quiet on a Sunday afternoon. A siren started wailing outside as a squad car was dispatched. Sure, downstairs wasn't so peaceful, but at least no one was bothering them up here.

'They got stuck in the mud and had to be hauled out by a friendly farmer with a tractor,' Ethan said.

'You're kidding.'

Ethan took out a box of mint chocolate sticks from his desk drawer and offered it to Jack.

'Is Helen showing any signs of giving up on the diet idea?' Jack said as he took a chocolate.

'It's the old battleaxe who won't let go of the idea.'

'She's getting on in years. One day she might take a tumble down the stairs.'

Ethan dropped the box, scattering chocolate sticks everywhere.

'Don't even joke about that.'

'Here –' Jack put down his coffee cup '– you want a hand cleaning that up?'

'You wouldn't, would you, Jack?'

Jack scooped up a handful of chocolate and tossed it in the box.

'What? Rub out your mother-in-law? You know I don't waste frails.' Jack wiped his hands with his handkerchief and returned to his coffee. 'So how did Cornell and van Loame manage to get stuck?'

'You remember how Harry started giving directions to her farm from Little Bartling? They thought they'd give it a try. Figured the worst that could happen would be going round in a circle.'

'I thought they were supposed to be your best detectives.'

'Don't be like that. You know they are, but they're city coppers. What's eating you today?'

'Nothing.'

'Quinn hasn't been winding you up again, has he?'

'No.'

'It's Harry, isn't it? So what if she took an Anti-Tech leaflet? She's a smart girl. She must've figured it was the best way to stop a bunch of truckers beating up a pair of kids.'

'They weren't kids. Besides, I wouldn't have let it get out of hand.'

'She's probably thrown it away by now.' Ethan dumped the chocolate box in the bin and returned to his seat. 'Adam given you any leads about her?'

'No, he's keeping buttoned up.' Jack lifted up his cup, then put it back down on the saucer. 'And as if I haven't got enough on my plate, that bastard Donnaghan always seems to be in our shadows between here and Central City. He'd better not have any designs on Harry.'

'He's living on borrowed time, that one,' Ethan said.

'He ought to know that Stan and Quinn's combined protection won't be enough to save him from Adam if he makes a move on Harry.'

'And then the shit will hit the fan, and we'll have a bloodbath on our hands.'

The sound of chanting came in through the open window. Jack glanced out. Down on the street there was a procession of Anti-Techs with their placards. He returned to his coffee.

'Can you change Donnaghan's shift?' Jack said.

'I'd change his quarters to a nice grey cell if I could. We need to deal with his buddy Quinn, and I reckon this West Norfolk business is the key.'

'We don't know that. Quinn and his men could just be after the reward money for the missing lady.'

Ethan pushed his cup to one side.

'They'd need to find her in one piece for that,' he said. 'And that's not going to happen with the firepower they've brought along with them.'

'They're scared of the seven-foot-tall soldiers in shining armour.'

'Be serious, Jack.'

Jack leant back in the chair. On the corner of Ethan's desk was a wedding photo in a silver frame. A much younger Ethan was standing with Helen on one side and Jack — the best man — on the other.

'All right,' Jack said. 'Granted there's something going on in Colingham, and Miguel was wasted because he poked his nose where it didn't belong. Quinn tried pinning it on me, so that means he's responsible for it. But where does that get us? If Harry's anything to go by, the people out there aren't over-fond of the city. Cornell and van Loame haven't made much progress.'

'They've found out the local coppers don't like Quinn's men.'

'We can't trust them,' Jack said. 'They're in Central Constabulary.'

'They're police officers, possibly honest ones.'

'Not for long under Quinn. Look, Ethan, I know you want to do the right thing. If someone like you had Quinn's job, there wouldn't be any need for shoot-outs.'

'We can't take Quinn down in a shoot-out.'

'I know,' Jack said. 'I lost far too many men taking Slim out.'

'Don't get me wrong. I'm glad Slim's gone. I never would've figured that even Quinn would turn a blind eye to that kind of thing. But I want to do things by the book.'

Jack got up, went round and perched himself on the desk in front of Ethan.

'Sure you do,' he said. 'D'you think I don't know that? Haven't we been best friends for as long as we can remember?'

'Sure we have.'

'And haven't I always looked out for you?'

'Sure you have,' Ethan said. 'I wouldn't have survived the anarchy without you.'

'And I would've gone nuts without your company. We pulled each other through, and there were no rule books to go by.'

'There are now.'

Jack leant down close to Ethan.

'Only because we made it happen.'

The chanting outside had died down. The Anti-Techs were probably doing their usual circuit of the city via the police station and City Hall.

'We could get Great Bartling's help without them knowing what it's about,' Ethan said.

'How?'

'Remember that job Miguel pulled here?'

'Sure I remember,' Jack said. 'I'm not likely to forget that — the lousy little rat.'

'So I get Cornell to write to Sergeant Fenning and say we've been looking for him, but we've only just heard that he moved to West Norfolk.'

'Why Fenning?'

'Cornell's recommendation,' Ethan said. 'He reckons she's on the level.'

Jack returned to the leather armchair.

'Does he also reckon she's pretty?'

'He didn't say, but apparently she didn't hide her dislike of Quinn's men.'

'Does she like Cornell and van Loame any better?'

'There's an alternative,' Ethan said, leaning back in his chair. 'We could always ask Harry for help. She'll know her way around the locals.'

'You kidding? Like I'd ask Harry for help. So what's the plan? Cornell asks Fenning for the dope on Miguel. Then what?'

'Let's see what she turns up.'

'And if Fenning talks to Quinn?' Jack said. 'And he asks me why you're interested in Miguel?'

'Say you don't like being fingered for someone else's hit, only don't mention anything about knowing it was Quinn who did the fingering.'

— 17 —

SECTOR HOUSE

Harry arrived at Betsy's on Monday evening to find the front desk empty and the lounge full of truckers. All Harry could see were their backs: some jacketless with shirt sleeves rolled up, some with waistcoats, some without. All silent, except for one deep voice in the midst of them.

'So Kurt and I helped get the women and kids into the truck while Frimunt covered us, but then this bloody great armoured car turns up, but there's this little three-year-old girl who's wandered off, so Frimunt legs it over to her, just as they let loose mortar rounds. The corner of the building took most of the impact, but a chunk of brick smashed the back of Frimunt's head. He was gone, but he'd managed to shelter the kid. Only trouble was, she's trapped under his body.'

Harry put down her rucksack and stood up on tiptoes in the lounge doorway, but she wasn't able to see the speaker.

'Coming through, coming through. Let me pass, lads.'

Betsy came into view, squeezing through the mass of bodies. Her face was flushed and her bolero rucked up around her shoulders. She pushed past the last row of truckers and emerged into the lobby by Harry's side.

'What's going on?' Harry said.

'Spud's back from foreign parts.' Betsy patted her hair and adjusted her bolero. 'Has Jack arrived?'

'He had to talk to Ginger Jim. I don't know how long he'll be.'

'That was Helmut gone as well,' the deep voice continued. 'So Kurt put his foot down, only there was wrecked vehicles all over the place. The shell craters knackered the suspension, but we kept going. There were plumes of smoke billowing across the city skyline, and there was a column of flame where the refinery used to be. Fifty foot at least, it must've been.'

'Where's Sam?' Betsy said, glancing out of the front window.

'With Adam, but I've got her stuff, so if you can give me a room I'll set the cot up.'

'I'll sort it out in a moment.' Betsy took out a bunch of keys from her pocket. 'I've got to fetch another cask from the cellar.'

'D'you want a hand?'

'Yes, I would. Thanks, Harry.'

Betsy went over to a door between the lounge and dining room, unlocked it and flicked a switch. Harry followed her through and then down a wooden staircase. Long threads of dusty cobwebs dangled from the ceiling joists. The bare brick walls were lined with shelves on which were stacked piles of cans: carrots, beans, potatoes, ham, beef, soup, pasta, fruit. There were also cartons of long-life milk and foil sachets of dried herbs and dried fruit.

'I didn't think you used canned food in your meals.'

'I don't.' Betsy went over to a row of wooden barrels. 'Those belong to Jack — just in case the anarchy returns. He likes to be prepared.'

'How old are the cans?'

'He refreshes the stock from time to time.' Betsy bent down and inspected the barrel labels. 'Anything that has less than six months on the best before date gets sent to the refuge.'

'A bit of extra profit?'

'Of course not.' Betsy straightened up and looked at Harry. 'You do know that it was Jack who set up the refuge, don't you?'

'Really?'

Harry went over and helped Betsy shift a barrel away from the others to where the floor was clearer.

'Rita kicked up quite a stink over it,' Betsy said as she trundled a trolley over. 'Said it was a waste of money and resources.'

'I can just image she would.' Harry helped shuffle the barrel on to the trolley. 'I'm glad he didn't give in to her.'

'He had to compromise and allow her people into his territory. You must've seen them lounging around looking like they've been pulled through a hedge backwards.'

Betsy rolled the trolley over to the hatch of a dumb waiter, and Harry helped her hoist the barrel on to the platform. Once it was securely in place, Betsy tugged on a cord and shut the hatch door. A few moments later, there was a sound of squeaking pulleys and creaking ropes. They returned up the wooden staircase. After Betsy had switched off the cellar light and locked the door, she went over to the lobby desk, wrote in the register and handed Harry a key.

'If I wasn't so rushed, I'd help you with your luggage now. If you don't mind waiting, I'll give you a hand later.'

'It's all right, I can manage.'

Harry picked up her rucksack, fetched a bag of baby things and the travel cot from her truck and took them to her room. She dumped her jacket on one of the beds and set up the cot. Once that was done she returned to the lobby. The truckers were still packed in the lounge, listening to Spud. The front door was flung open and Eric came in with his duffel bag slung over his shoulder.

'Some lousy little git in a coupé cut me up. Then the stupid bastard nearly hit a tram.'

'Is Adam still at the warehouse?' Harry said.

'No,' Eric said, 'he was behind me, but the lights changed after I pulled out so he may be a while. Is that Spud? Why didn't you tell me?' Eric dropped his bag by the lounge door. 'Here, let me through.'

The other truckers made way for him, and he was soon out of sight. Harry wandered over to the lobby window to look out for Adam.

'All alone?'

She turned. Donnaghan was picking at his stubbly moustache. There was a ketchup stain on his lapel. He glanced over his shoulder at the lounge door. The truckers were still engrossed in Spud's story.

'I worry about you being in the company you're in,' he said.

'I can look after myself.'

'A nice girl like you shouldn't get mixed up in the kind of things they get up to.'

'And what are you planning on doing about it?'

'What can I do about it on my own? Sure, if the police were all straight, that would be different, but what can a lowly traffic cop do?'

He took a step forwards. She backed away.

'Thank you for your concern, but I don't need your help.'
Harry glanced out of the window, but there was no sign of Adam or Jack. Maybe she should join Eric in the lounge.

'Doesn't it bother you what kind of life that little girl will grow up in?' Donnaghan said.

'Adam and I will keep her safe.'

'Can you keep her safe from him? I've seen his temper: a vicious, murderous rage. He once smashed in a man's skull with a wrench just on account of a little shove. You can't escape bad blood.'

'He won't ever harm Sammy.'

Donnaghan took another step towards her. She backed into a potted plant.

'He's a killer.'

'Haven't you ever killed anyone?' Harry said.

His cheeks twitched. He stank of onions.

'Why did you say that?'

'You have a gun and a blackjack on your belt.' She edged around the plant. 'Haven't you ever used them?'

'In the line of duty, but I never use dope. D'you know what that stuff they smoke does to you? What it'll do to the baby? Phobias, paranoia, birth defects. She'll become an addict.'

'If you don't shut up –' Harry pushed the plant's leaves out of the way '– I'll tell Jack what you said.'

With that, she turned and strode across the lobby, threw open the front door, ran down the steps and along the driveway until she reached the pavement outside. The rush hour was over and there were no lorries to be seen. It was getting too cold to be out without a coat, but she wasn't going back in until Adam turned up — or Jack. She paced up and down. The nasty piece of work. No wonder Adam didn't like him.

Besides, they hadn't smoked a spliff in front of Sam. Not yet, anyway. A tram trundled by. Did it really have those side effects? The electronic billboard opposite was showing an image of a happy family. Harry reached the edge of the pool of light thrown by the overhead lamp and glanced at the shadows further up the street. Was that someone by Betsy's side gate? She shivered. Was it her imagination, or was someone watching her? She moved her right hand round to her back, but there was no stick there. Her jacket was still in her room. A van came down the road and pulled up by the side gate.

Not another red light. A tram trundled across the junction. Adam drummed his fingers on the steering wheel, and Sam began to cry.

'It's all right, Sammy,' Adam said, 'we're nearly there.' The lights changed. 'At last.'

He turned the corner and saw Harry standing under the lamp outside Betsy's, her back to him. The street was empty, apart from a van parked further up on the wrong side of the road with its lights still on. The billboard opposite Betsy's flickered. The last remnants of daylight glanced off the metal roof of Sector House.

Harry turned, looked up at him and gave him such a smile that his foot slipped across the clutch as he changed gear. The van pulled out, accelerated, swung round in a U-turn in front of him, its tyres squealing, and stopped outside Betsy's driveway. Adam slammed his foot on the brake and hit the horn. The van's back doors were flung open, two men jumped out, grabbed Harry and dragged her inside. The van sped to the end of the road and on through the gateway into the precinct of Sector House. Adam rammed the gear from neutral into first, but Sam screamed. The gates closed behind the vehicle. Adam snatched his radio.

'Jack! Jack, d'you read me?'

But all he could hear was static and Sam's cries. He pulled into Betsy's Café and ran inside, calling to Eric. Adam saw the crowd in the lounge and dashed over.

'Is Eric here?' He shoved the nearest truckers. 'Get out of my way.'

'Hey, Adam,' one of them said. 'Can't you see Spud's back?'

'Eric, get your arse over here. Get out of my way, you lot. Eric! Harry's been nabbed. Look after Sam.'

Adam ran back to his lorry and tugged his rucksack from behind his seat.

'Where's Jack?' Eric said, hurrying down Betsy's front steps.

'I can't reach him. There's no time to wait. Have you got the guns?'

'Jack's got them.'

Adam tossed his hat and trench coat into the cab.

'Keep Sam safe.'

He slung his bag on his shoulder, ran out into the street and raced down the pavement, but once he had crossed the road he walked past the wrought iron gates of Sector House and glanced through the bars. The van was parked in the driveway. Two armed security guards stood by the steps leading up to the large double-doors at the front of the building, and there were at least four more patrolling the grounds that Adam could see. He continued walking and headed down a side alley, following the perimeter wall — maybe about forty feet high, by the look of it, with iron railings along the top. No one was about. He took his climbing gear out of his bag, changed his shoes, put on his gloves, and clipped and tightened the straps of his rucksack.

He ran his fingers over the wall, feeling the gaps between the bricks. He reached up and began to climb. Lousy workmanship. The mortar crumbled as he probed for a secure hold. No shouts yet. Just the usual city sounds. Traffic and distant alarms. The corner of a brick gave way beneath his foot and clattered down the wall until it hit the path below. Don't rush it. Just another climbing job, like he was always doing for Jack. A breeze ruffled his hair. Masonry dust flew up his nose. He held tight, his body close to the wall, and snorted the dust back out before it could trigger a sneeze. He remained stationary for a moment. Still no shouts. Just the electronic billboard down the road persuading everyone to buy a new brand of shampoo.

He stretched his hand and took hold of one of the wrought iron railings fastened to the top of the wall. It wobbled and flakes of rust drifted on to his face. He blinked as some fell into his eyes. He tried the one next to it. This one was a little better. He hauled himself up. The rail shifted with the sound of metal grinding against brick. He lunged upwards, caught another bar and pulled himself up on to the top of the wall and over the ironwork.

The wind was stronger here, pushing him back against the railings. He perched on the wall, his heels on the edge of the topmost row of bricks. The last light of day had gone. The moon, nearing its first quarter, was partially obscured by ragged clouds. A yard away from him gleamed the outermost edge of a metal roof. Its smooth, shallow pitch was covered with vents and pipework. Fumes wafted towards him. The smell was unfamiliar — neither beet-based fuel nor wood smoke — but it was the kind of stench you didn't want lingering in your nostrils. Below his feet the wall soon disappeared into the darkness. The wind picked up.

He jumped, landed with a clatter, caught hold of a stack vent and clung on, listening. A vehicle engine started up. The electronic billboard gave its signature peace and prosperity speech, bidding everyone sweet dreams before switching off the sound for the night. Adam crawled over pipes, upwind from the fumes. There were pockets of warm air around a few of the vents, but he avoided those areas. Every now and then steam would spout out of them. The metal roof was damp with condensation. He slipped and stumbled across it, grabbing hold of pipes for support. Some were only a few inches in diameter, some at least four feet. He was surrounded by whooshing, rattling, gurgling noises.

This was only a peripheral building, but it was linked to the main structure by a narrow span that looked like it contained a connecting corridor. The windows along the side of it were dark and empty. He crouched near the edge and took out his pocket scope. The clouds drifted away from the moon. He could make out a guard walking in the courtyard, four stories down. Adam waited for him to turn the corner and then ran along the arch. On the other side, he found a skylight lit from below. He peered down and saw a man in a lab coat writing on a spiral-bound notepad. Adam remained still for a couple of minutes until the man put the notepad down on a bench and left the room.

There was a metal strip on the inside of the skylight all around the perimeter that was undoubtably part of the security system. Adam swapped his climbing gloves for a supple leather pair, took a battery-powered drill out of his rucksack, selected a spade-shaped carbide bit, secured it in the chuck, put on his safety goggles, and bored through the glass and metal on opposite sides of the window. He brushed away the residual white powder, inserted a spring toggle bolt in each hole and connected them with a piece of wire. They'd better not hurt her. His hands shook as he replaced the now hot carbide bit with a hollow-core diamond one. What were they doing to her? He drilled through the glass. The high-pitched whine seemed louder than usual. The muffler ought to be doing a better job than that. He put the tools away and slipped a looped wire through the hole. He'd kill them if they hurt her. The loop hooked on to the catch. If he only had his tommy gun, he'd pump the bastards full of lead. He eased the skylight open. No alarms — the bypass was working. He gave the room another quick check and let himself down.

The lab door was shut. There was a row of white coats hanging on the wall next to it. He could hear a humming sound but couldn't make out where it was coming from. Scattered on the lab benches were bits of wire, circuit boards, soldering irons and small mirrors: some concave, some convex and one that seemed to be made up of thousands of tiny mirrors. Above the bench nearest to him there was a glass-fronted cabinet. He was about to walk past when he stopped and stared at it. He tried the handle. At first he thought it was locked, but after a few tugs the cupboard door flew open. He reached up and took a stick off the shelf. This was Harry's — no, it wasn't. This one hadn't been chewed by dogs. If only Harry had told him how to operate it. How had she held it?

There was something else in the cabinet. It looked like a gun. Now that was more like it. He picked it up. The barrel was half the length of a shotgun, and the butt was twice as thick, but the calibre was no more than a couple of millimetres. What did it shoot? Pellets? There was a button where the trigger ought to be, but he couldn't see how to load it. Perhaps it was already primed, but if all else failed he could use it as a club.

He found a large satchel lying on the floor, emptied it and stuffed his rucksack and the stick into it. Where was that humming sound coming from? There was another bench behind him. On it was a similar gun next to a pair of gauntlets, safety glasses and a smooth, black object about the size of a paperback, but no more than a quarter of an inch thick. That was the source of the noise. It was connected via a cable to the gun. Adam touched the shiny black surface. An image appeared, as clear as the ones displayed on an electronic billboard, showing an array of numbers and a graph. He moved away, selected a loose-fitting lab coat from the row of hooks near the entrance, cut a slit in the right pocket, slid his hand through it, held the gun from the cabinet inside the coat and lifted the satchel strap over his head.

Perhaps he should have waited for Jack's help, but it was too late now. He picked up the spiral-bound notepad with his free hand and put his ear to the door. He eased the handle down and peered round the jamb. Outside the lab there was a windowless corridor that extended in both directions. Doors lined either side of it. Strip lights buzzed overhead. To Adam's right the corridor linked up with another passageway, but that way was unlit. To his left, it led to a set of double doors with slit windows and a fire exit sign. He chose that direction. There was a high-pitched whine, like a drill, coming from one of the rooms. The walls were covered with posters reminding people of safety regulations, what to do in the event of an emergency and instructions not to enter a room when the red light was on. There were pairs of red and green bulbs above some of the lintels. They were mostly showing green.

Two men in lab coats emerged from a doorway further down the corridor, each wheeling a canister. Their ages could have been anywhere between thirty and fifty. They had the bearing of men who'd never seen the inside of a gym. Both had name badges clipped to their lapels.

Adam continued walking but raised the notepad so that it obscured his bare lapel. He stared at the page as though it was immensely interesting. Not that it was. It was full of weird symbols and words like 'stimulated emissions' and 'free excited radicals', whatever that meant.

'I still don't think it's a viable option,' one of the approaching men said to his colleague.

'All right, so we've still got a problem with blooming and shading, but the adaptive mirrors will compensate.'

'That's not much use if we can't solve the overheating.'

The nearer man nodded at Adam as they passed. Adam returned the nod in what he hoped would appear the distracted manner of a scientist engrossed in his work. One of the cylinders was marked ^2HF and the other C_2H_4. The door they had come out of was covered in chemical hazard symbols and was labelled 'stores'. Next to that were two lifts — the fancy type with sliding panels instead of a grille. Opposite was a half-open door. Adam glanced behind him. The two men went into the lab he had broken into. Would they notice the missing stuff or the hole in the skylight?

He stopped as he saw what lay beyond the doorway opposite the lifts. It looked like an operating theatre, only the bed had restraining straps. He walked on and pushed open one of the doors at the end of the corridor. He had arrived at the top of a staircase. He looked down the stairwell, then back at the corridor through the slit window in the door.

Why had Harry been snatched? What were they planning to do to her? Was Allerton behind this? The man who had convinced her friends that she had a brain tumour? Why was there an operating theatre here? Who were they going to operate on? Did those two scientists know anything about it? He put the notepad down and took the stick out of the bag. With it in one hand and the gun in the other, he peered through the window into the corridor.

He inched the door ajar. There was a ping in the corridor. The lift doors opened. Harry lurched out. Her wrists were fastened with a pair of handcuffs — not the little bracelets the police used. This pair looked as though they'd been designed for an ogre like Hammer Harmer: electronic cuffs, supposedly banned except on the criminally insane. Her arms hung down her body like they were about to be pulled out of their sockets.

Two security guards stepped out behind her, followed by a man holding a control panel. Harry staggered but then ducked to one side, towards the stairs. For a moment, Adam saw her face clearly through the window. The man with the control panel flicked a switch. She screamed and collapsed on to the floor. At the same time, a door further down the corridor was flung open and the two scientists ran out, one of them yelling, 'Intruder!'

Adam kicked open the door, brought up the gun, aimed at the handcuff operator and pressed the button. There was no sound or recoil from the gun, but the control panel exploded — as did the man's stomach. A hole burnt through the door to the chemical store room behind him. The gun became scalding hot, even through the leather gloves. Adam dropped it. At the same instant a ball of fire blasted out of the store room, engulfing one of the security men. The other caught fire. Flames leapt up his arm as he ran screaming towards Adam.

Adam transferred the stick to his right hand, but as he gripped it he felt the surface depress under his index finger. The stick shot open, smacking the man in the head. The overhead light popped in a shower of sparks as flames billowed across the ceiling. Another explosion burst through a wall. Something struck Adam in the chest. He reeled backwards. A klaxon rang out. Thick black smoke stung his eyes. He threw himself on the ground.

Harry was still lying where she had fallen. He crawled over to her, using the stick to knock aside burning debris. People were screaming, but whether they were in the corridor or one of the rooms off it, Adam couldn't tell. He dragged Harry backwards. Every breath seemed to scorch his lungs. The ceiling started to crack and sag. Just as he pulled her into the stairwell, a mass of tiles and metal duct work crashed down into the corridor. Harry coughed and retched.

He retrieved the bag and helped her to her feet and down the first few steps. Another explosion ripped through the upper floor. The stairs heaved beneath them. The metal banister buckled.

'Come on, Harry, keep going. You can make it.'

His voice rasped in his dry mouth. There were shouts and screams lower down the stairwell. Adam felt around the centre of the stick, pressing his fingers against its surface until he felt a click and it telescoped back to its smallest size. He tucked it into the satchel but left the bag unfastened. He removed his singed lab coat and draped it round her shoulders to obscure the handcuffs as much as possible. Cracks spread out down the steps. Chucks of concrete tumbled down around them.

They reached the next landing where they were jostled by people streaming out of a corridor. Harry stumbled. Adam grabbed her. A woman in a suit tripped and fell with a scream through a gap in the broken banister, tumbling on to the people below her. There was a security guard in the crowd close behind Adam. Now he was level with him. Adam shoved him into a knot of scientists, increased his hold on Harry and hurried her further down.

At last they reached the ground floor and staggered out into a crowded lobby full of ornate columns. Security guards were directing people. One gestured to Adam, then stared at Harry and reached for the gun on his belt. Another explosion shook the building. The pillar behind the guard tumbled and fell on him. Adam dodged round as another pillar split in two. The crowd was bottlenecked in the exit. The double doors were wide open, but there were too many people.

Harry began to sag in his arms. He heaved her up over his shoulder. The cuffs dug into his chest. Bodies pressed against him on all sides. A crack ran down the wall from the ceiling to the exit door lintel. Adam ducked to one side, barging people out of the way, picked up a lump of masonry and hurled it at a window. The glass smashed. He knocked at the remaining fragments with the stick and eased Harry out. He jumped down by her side and lifted her up.

There seemed to be just as many people in the driveway as there had been in the lobby. Then Adam realised why. The gates were still shut. The crowd surged against them. One man tried to clamber up the bars, but he slipped and fell into the throng below. Security guards with truncheons were trying to push people back.

Adam held Harry close to him. Were the gates closed because they didn't want her to escape or was it just that the keys had been lost in the confusion? His arms ached and his chest throbbed. At the moment, he wouldn't even manage it back up the wall on his own, let alone with Harry, and he wasn't going anywhere without her. The gate was the only way out.

Another blast from the building catapulted burning debris over the wall into the street beyond. One of the security guards was overwhelmed and dragged to the ground. Shots rang out but at last the gates were opened and the crowd pushed through. Adam tried to hoist Harry on to his shoulder again, but he sank to his knees. He staggered back up and propped her against him. He held her around the waist and joined the jostling, shoving mass until they were through the gateway and on to the pavement outside the wall.

The traffic was jammed, horns were beeping, sirens were blaring and people were running in all directions, getting in each other's way and tripping over one another. Adam helped Harry across the street, through an alleyway and into the parking area at the rear of Betsy's Café. He peered around a truck, then staggered with Harry over to the back door of the building.

'Have you got a key?' he said.

'Pocket.'

Adam supported her with one hand and searched her pockets with the other. He found the key ring. It had two keys on it: one for the room and one for the back door. He glanced round, unlocked the door and eased it open. No one was about. He led her inside and the lock snapped shut behind them. They went down the narrow passageway. Harry was like a dead weight in his arms.

They reached the service lift. He slid open both grille doors and dragged Harry in. He closed the doors and pressed the button for the next floor. The cage clanked and rattled as the lift ascended. It stopped with a lurch on the first floor.

Adam peered through the grille, then opened the doors and helped Harry out. He checked the key for the room number — only a little way down the corridor.

'Come on, Harry. We're nearly there. You can do it.'

He leant her against the wall to help take the weight off his arm and shuffled her down the passage until they reached their room. He unlocked the door and heaved her on to the bed. Her wrists were red and chafed around the cuffs. The top of her left sleeve had been ripped, and there was a bruised area with puncture marks on her arm.

'What'd they inject you with?' he said.

'Sedative I think.'

'They made a right mess of it.'

She smiled faintly.

'I'm not going to lie still while strange men try to jab me.'

'Is that why they put the electric cuffs on?'

She closed her eyes for a moment, then opened them again.

'Thank you for rescuing me.' She tried to raise herself on her arm but slumped back. 'Where's Sam?'

'With Eric. Stay here. I'll get her, and I'll fetch the rest of my kit from the truck.'

He changed out of his climbing gear, locked the door behind him and found Eric outside with the other truckers. Emergency vehicles had arrived, but traffic was backed up in all directions. There were still explosions bursting out of the building. Windows reflected the light of the roaring flames.

'Where've you been?' Eric said.

'Where's Sam?'

'With Betsy. Where's Harry?'

'She's fine.'

'Jack's looking for you. He bawled me out for not going with you.'

'Someone had to look after Sam.'

'He said you should've left her with Betsy.'

'That would've slowed me down,' Adam said. 'I only just got there in time.'

A shower of sparks rained down on the street. Alf and Hector broke away from the group of truckers and ran over to Adam.

'Adam, you're okay,' Alf said. 'Where's Harry?'

'Safe.'

'Find Jack,' Eric said to Alf and Hector.

'Tell him everything's okay,' Adam said.

'You going to tell Jack what happened?' Eric said to Adam as the other two headed back into the crowd. 'He ain't happy with you running off like that.'

'Where's Betsy?'

'In the lobby last time I saw her.'

Adam ran back inside. The lobby was empty. The commotion outside was still audible, but above it he could hear the sound of crying coming from the lounge. He hurried over and found Betsy there, rocking Sam in her arms.

'There you are,' Betsy said. 'At last. What's this about Harry being snatched?'

'Just some punks.' Adam took Sam. 'I've dealt with them.'

He took Sam upstairs and unlocked the bedroom door. Harry's eyes were closed, and she was motionless. He laid Sam in her cot and went over to Harry and tried to feel her wrist for a pulse but the handcuffs were in the way. He shifted them up her arms. Sam wailed. Harry stirred and opened her eyes.

'Sam,' she said.

'Stay there. I'll calm her down.'

Adam picked Sam up and jiggled her around. Then, holding her in the crook of his left arm, he prepared her milk. She wriggled, pressing against his bruised chest. He laid her down on the floor, changed her and dumped the soiled nappy in a bag. At first she screamed too much to drink but finally quietened down and drained the bottle. Adam laid her in her cot and wound up the mobile.

He rummaged through his rucksack and found a shammy. He cut it in half, attached strips of insulating tape to both parts, slipped each piece between the handcuffs and Harry's skin, and eased the cuffs and the insulation further up her arms. He bathed and bandaged her wrists, rested them on a pillow, put on his gloves and fetched a roll of fine tools.

'There may still be a charge left in the capacitors,' he said, selecting an awl. 'If I can't get them off, I'll have to ask Jack for help.'

'No. I'm not owing him a favour.'

Adam switched on the ceiling light and moved her arms a little so that he had a better view of the lock in the centrepiece of the cuffs. She smelt singed, but then so did he.

'Keep still.' He leant close, inserted the awl into the keyhole and probed the locking mechanism. 'We may not have a choice. He knows you were snatched.'

'What did you tell him?'

'Nothing yet, but he'll be here soon enough asking questions, and electric cuffs ain't exactly available from your local hardware store.' A spark flashed out of the cuffs. Harry flinched. 'You okay?'

'Fine.'

'Quinn will go for Jack if he finds out I blew up Sector House.' He rubbed his eyes with a knuckle, then inserted another awl and wriggled it about. 'It's outside Jack's territory.'

'They started it,' Harry said.

'Why? What did they want with you?'

'Allerton was behind it. They had this thing — like one of those electronic billboards, only much smaller. I saw him on it, only he could see me as well. He said, "Yes, that's her" when they pulled me in front of it. He said they were going to make me better and then I could come home.'

Make her better? And they'd got her within feet of that operating theatre. Adam wiped a drop of sweat from his forehead and continued on the lock. His chest throbbed from where he'd been hit by the debris from the blast. Something gave a little under the awl. He pushed further. There was a click and the cuffs opened.

'Look at that. I did it.'

There was a knock at the door. Adam wrapped the cuffs in Sam's soiled nappy, retied the sack, stuffed the satchel under the bed and answered the door. Jack was there with Eric. Jack peered over Adam's head.

'You took your time, my boy.'

'Sam needed a nappy change.'

Nuts. He'd forgotten about the shammies he'd left on Harry's wrists.

'You going to let us in then?'

'Yeah sure.'

Jack pushed Adam to one side. Eric shut the door and leant against it. An explosion sounded outside. Jack took his Beretta out of his coat pocket and peered out of the window. The bag containing Sam's soiled nappy and the cuffs still lay on the floor. Adam edged towards it. Jack opened the window.

'Alf, get the lads back behind Betsy's wall.'
Jack closed the window and turned round. Adam moved his hand across the charred patch on his jacket. Jack strode past the nappy sack, sat down on the bed and removed his hat.
'You don't look so good, Harry. You been giving someone a piece of your mind?' He tapped her cheek with the pistol barrel. 'Not everyone is as tolerant as me.'
'She weren't doing nothing,' Adam said, eyeing Jack's Beretta. 'She was just waiting outside Betsy's gate for me when they grabbed her.'
'What? In my territory? Who were they?'
'I didn't get around to asking them. They were hurting her, so I took them out.'
Another explosion erupted from up the road. Alarms mingled with the sound of shouts and car horns.
'So you were in my territory when you took them out?'
Adam picked at a piece of lint.
'No, they'd dragged her up the street.'
'Any witnesses?'
'No. The fireworks at Sector House started up. That kind of distracted everyone.'
'What'd you do with the bodies?'
'They're under a load of rubble. They'll have plenty of company with the way that place blew up.'
'What's happening to this lousy city? One of my people snatched in my territory. Sector House blowing up. We need to stay sharp. Someone may be trying to muscle in.'
Jack put the gun back in his pocket, fingered the rip in Harry's shirt and ran his hand down her arm. Adam moved closer. Jack turned back her sleeve. The shammies were gone.
'What happened to your wrists, my girl?' Jack said as he touched the bandages.

Harry struggled to open her eyes, looked at Jack, then closed them again.

'They tied me up.'

'Looks like they jabbed you as well.'

'They tried to sedate her,' Adam said. 'D'you reckon she'll be all right?'

'She's a survivor. Who were they?'

Adam scratched at his jacket.

'A bunch of pervs, I guess.'

'Operating in my territory? No way.' Jack turned back to Harry. 'No messing with me, my girl. Who were they?'

She tried to speak. Jack leant closer.

'Friends of someone,' she said.

'Would that someone be the fellow who hires hit men?'

'Hit men?' Adam said.

'Didn't she tell you, my boy? Seems her Uncle Barney was killed by a hit man.'

'Sorry, Adam.' Harry's voice was barely audible. 'Tried not to get you involved.'

'I'm sure we all appreciate the sentiment,' Jack said, 'but it seems to have failed in practice. So how'd they find you?'

'They got lucky, I suppose,' she said. 'He has friends here.'

'And you didn't think to mention? Oh no, little Miss Independent likes to keep buttoned up.' A shot sounded outside. Jack reached for his pocket, but there was no further gunfire, only yells and the sirens. He turned back to Harry. 'You hurt anywhere else?'

'Just my pride.'

Jack smiled, but he checked her pulse and looked at her eyes.

'Kill the lights, Eric.'

Eric flicked the switch by the door, but the room wasn't plunged into darkness. Instead it was lit with an orange glow from the fire up the road, mixed with the flashing blue of the emergency vehicles. Jack moved closer to Harry so that he was only a few inches from her face.

'What're you doing, Jack?' she said.

'Checking your pupil dilation. Did you think I was about to give you a big smoochy kiss? You can hit the lights again, Eric.' He patted her cheek and looked at the floor as the light flickered on. 'What's in the bag?'

'Sam's soiled nappy.' Adam went to pick it up. 'Like I said, I was changing her.'

'I'm surprised at you, my lad. That's hardly hygienic. What happened to your jacket?'

Adam picked at the charred threads on the front of his suit.

'I got hit by some debris.'

'You want to give me a bit more detail?'

'I saw them jump Harry as I pulled into Betsy's, so I asked Eric to look after Sam and ran after them.'

'There was a whole lounge full of my lads, and you didn't ask a single one of them to back you up? So then what?'

'Well, I was pretty mad,' Adam said. How long had it taken between leaving Eric and blasting those men? 'We got into a fight. Harry managed to get out of the way.'

'How many of them were there?'

'Three. Things didn't look so good but, like I said, the explosion happened. I got hit by something, but so did they, and I managed to finish them off. I'll just throw this nappy away. If that's okay.'

'I don't want it for Christmas, that's for sure.'

Adam took the nappy sack into the bathroom, dumped it into the bin and washed his hands. When he returned, Jack was still sitting on the edge of Harry's bed. He was playing with a lock of her hair with one hand. He had his pistol out again in the other hand, but it was resting on his leg.

'Harry, from now on when we're in Central City you don't take a step outside without us. Stay indoors and if we're not around, stick close to my lads.' Jack picked up his hat and went over to the window. 'Quinn's lost control of this lousy stinking city.'

'D'you reckon we should move out?' Eric said.

'With that gridlock? We wouldn't get further than the end of the drive. Our best bet is to stay put and keep the windows closed. Adam, come with me.'

Adam followed Jack out of the room. The corridor was empty. Jack held Adam's shoulder and pulled him close.

'If it was just a sedative they jabbed her with, she'll be fine once she's slept it off, but I'll get Fisher to check her out when we get back, just to make sure.'

'Thanks, Jack.'

Adam smiled, but Jack's grip hardened.

'Don't you ever run off without backup again, my boy. Get her to talk. Now would be a good time. She's less likely to hold back when she's half-doped.'

Once Jack and Eric had gone, Adam locked the bedroom door and went over to Harry. He removed her boots and pulled the bedding over her. As he tugged the sheet around he found she had been lying on the shammies. She might be half-doped, but she still had some wits about her.

'It was Miguel who gave you that stick, wasn't it?' he said.

'I found it after he died.'

'So you swiped it?'

'He owed us rent.'

'I ain't complaining,' Adam said. 'Did he ever mention Sector House?' Harry twisted a corner of the sheet around her fingers. 'Come on, Harry. You mentioned Miguel to Jack for a reason that time you played cards. And didn't Eric say something about Miguel boasting he was going to do over Sector House? And what do I find there? A stick identical to yours.'

'I'm tired.'

She turned away from him. He leant over her.

'I know you are, but I can't help you if you ain't straight with me.' He played with the same lock of hair Jack had played with. She looked pale, but she sounded less spaced than she'd been when answering Jack. 'I'm sorry about your Uncle Barney. I know he meant a lot to you. Remember how you told me I could talk about what happened to my little brother and I told you how you could talk about your uncle? Tell me about him, Harry. What happened?'

There was a catch in her breath. A tear glistened in the corner of her eye. He wiped it away with the tip of his finger. Her hand scrunched the edge of the pillow.

'It was last year.' Her voice was little more than a whisper. He leant closer. 'I went with Uncle Barney to visit Miguel. It was summer so we were outside in the garden. There was a tall hedge around it, but we could hear people talking in the lane on the other side. I recognised Allerton's voice. Miguel went pale. He peered through a gap in the hedge. Then he ran into the cottage. Uncle Barney told me to keep watch, and he went inside. The windows were open, and I heard a few words. Something like, "he was there in Sector House" and "they'll kill me if they find out". That's all I could make out, apart from the odd word like "frail" and "blond".'

'Did your uncle talk to you about it afterwards?'

'No.'

She tugged at the sheet. He straightened it for her.

'Get some rest.' He drew the curtains, but they were too thin to cut out all the lights outside. A short burst of gunfire sounded. 'Let me know if you need anything.'

Adam stayed by her side until she fell asleep. It must have been either the sedative or exhaustion. No one else could've managed it with the noise outside. Even with the windows shut, he could still hear the fire roaring and loud cracks and explosions.

Sam started to cry. He changed her, fed her and walked her up and down the room until the explosions died down and only the roaring remained. She eventually fell asleep in his arms, and he laid her in the cot. He undressed in the bathroom and pressed a cold, damp flannel to his bruised chest. Jack's specialist tailors sure knew their job, but his skin was already swelling and purple in an area at least six inches in diameter.

He changed into his pyjamas and returned to the bedroom. Harry's jacket was lying on his bed. He could make out the bulge where her stick was kept. He moved the coat so that the tartan lining was showing. The stick was strapped in place. There were inner pockets of various sizes on either side of it. He ran his fingers over them. Harry stirred. He paused, checked she was still asleep and unzipped a pocket. It contained her fake papers and some cash. He tried another one: it had a couple of pairs of ear-rings, three bracelets, a necklace and a ring. In the next one he found more cash, her real driving licence and birth certificate, and a photo of a younger Harry and a man with a strong facial resemblance. They both had a shotgun over their shoulder, and a large dog stood in front of them.

The final inside pocket contained two documents. Adam eased them out. The first was the specialist's letter Harry had shown him the day after they had met. The other document had the kind of stiff paper solicitors used. He took it into the bathroom and held it up to the light. It had a watermark that look a bit like a fried egg. He'd seen that work somewhere before. Sure, that was one of the Central City shysters.

His eyes were blurred and stung like someone had rubbed raw onion into them. His head pounded, screaming at him to go to bed, his chest ached as though a truck had been parked on it, but he had to figure out what was going on. Harry was going to get protection, whether she wanted it or not. He sat on the floor, his back against the wall and focused on the paper. Yeah, this had been written by a loan shark, no doubt about it. Harry's dad had put everything he had down as security. The amount he'd borrowed didn't appear anywhere. It was signed and dated the previous year.

Hadn't Harry once said something about Allerton loaning her dad some money after her Uncle Barney had died? From what Adam had heard about her uncle, he wouldn't have let his brother sign a dodgy contract like this. What exactly had happened? Miguel had told Harry's uncle something about Sector House, then her uncle had been killed by a hit man, and then Allerton had persuaded Harry's father to put pen to this cockeyed rag. And somewhere in that time Miguel had also been shot. Before he'd left the city, he'd tried his hand at a bit of petty pilfering and had stumbled on a top-secret lab. If Miguel had told the Anti-Techs what he'd seen, it would've been like a superheated boiler going critical.

Adam returned the papers to Harry's jacket and checked the outside pockets, but they didn't reveal much: a penknife, a pair of gloves, an Anti-Tech leaflet, a handkerchief, bits of string, some dog biscuits, a notepad and pencil, and last Sunday's church newsletter — was it only yesterday? It might even be the day before now, though it felt more like a month ago. He tidied the jacket away and went to bed. Ten minutes later he heard a knock at the door.

'Everything okay?' Jack said when Adam opened the door. There was a thin layer of ash on his hat. 'You look beat, my boy. How's Harry?'

'Asleep.'

'I've been over to see Quinn.' Jack closed the door behind him. 'He says he doesn't know what started the fire or why it sounds like a war zone. You'd think they had an arsenal hidden in their attic.' Jack steadied Adam as he stumbled over a bag. 'Here, my lad, get back into bed.'

'Don't trust Quinn.'

'I'm very careful about who I trust.'

'You reckon Quinn's in on whatever's going down in Sector House?'

'He'll pally up with any lowlife who's got enough money.' Jack sat by Harry's side and pressed his fingers against her wrist. 'Have you noticed any problems with her breathing?'

'No.'

Jack laid a hand on her forehead. Then he bent down so that his ear was close to her mouth, his cheek almost touching her face.

'Jack.'

'What?'

'Nothing.'

'Don't worry, my boy,' Jack said as he sat up. 'She's tougher than she looks. How come you haven't changed her into her pyjamas?'

'I ain't undressing her.'

'Haven't the two of you got together yet?'

'I don't want to rush her.'

'There's not rushing and there's standing still,' Jack said and stroked her cheek. 'You don't want to let her slip through your fingers.'

— 18 —

The Aftermath

'I heard it was the Anti-Techs.'
'What? Like that geeky pair who was here last week? Nah.'

Adam walked past Hector and Spike who were sitting with Alf and Spud. Hector nodded to Adam, squirted some sauce on to his sausages and turned back to Spike.

'Sure it was. That's just a step up from their demonstrations.'

The dining room was full of chatter. There was a coating of ash on all the windows and an acrid tang in the air. Adam rested Sam's seat on the next table and checked it was stable. Eric pulled up a chair next to Adam and took a slice of toast from the rack.

'It's the sugar beet farmers,' Spike said, reaching for the milk jug. 'They don't want us getting electricity from abroad or their profits will fall.'

Harry sat down opposite Adam. She looked pale. Adam rubbed his chest. It felt like he'd slept under a slab of cement.

'I heard it was the beet farmers who were financing the Anti-Techs,' Alf said.

'Yeah?' Jack said as he sat next to Harry. He nudged her. 'Go on, 'fess up, Harry. You a subversive beet farmer?'

'I don't — didn't grow beet.'

A waitress handed Jack a plate of bacon and scrambled eggs.

'You're the type who keeps an ear to the ground,' Jack said. 'You must've known some beet farmers. Go on. Spill the beans. The lads like a good story.'

'Yeah,' Alf said. 'Would any of them do a deal with the Anti-Techs?'

'I know one who'd sell his grandmother to make a profit.' Harry poured herself a coffee. 'If he hasn't already. But I can't see him getting along with the Anti-Techs. He likes his fancy electrical gadgets. He's got a tropical fish tank, a fridge, a freezer.'

'Who was that fellow who had a thing for tropical fish?' Eric said to Adam. 'It must've cost him a packet to power their tank.'

'What d'you mean, he has a fridge?' Jack said to Harry. 'Doesn't everyone?'

Harry reached for the jam pot.

'You can get by without one if you've got a decent pantry.'

'What fellow?' Adam said to Eric.

'You must remember him.' Eric slurped some orange juice. 'There was all that ruckus over those frails.'

'Did you wash your laundry in a river as well?' Jack said to Harry. 'I can just see you bashing your socks on the rocks.'

'No, of course not.' Harry scraped her knife against her toast. 'A washing machine doesn't need the generators to be switched on all the time.'

'So washing machines are okay but fridges aren't? Well, I can see why you were so interested when those Anti-Techs came here.'

Adam glanced up at them. Jack was sitting so close to Harry that their elbows were brushing against each other. But perhaps that was just because Sam's seat was taking up so much space.

'He was a nasty piece of work,' Eric said to Adam. 'One of Quinn's buddies. He used to hang out with Blond Jim.'

A waitress brought a fresh pot of coffee over to the next table.

'Let's just hope there's not going to be any rioting,' Spud said.

'Rioting?' Adam put down his cutlery. 'You ain't serious, are you?'

'You kidding? There's been a coup in sector seventy. I was telling everyone about it last night.'

'A coup's not the same as rioting,' Jack said.

'There was rioting in sector fifty-nine last month.' Spud cut up a piece of bacon. 'It was le Movement Contre la Technologie that started it — that's their version of the Anti-Technology League.'

'Last month?' Adam said. 'That ain't been in the news.'

'When was the last time you heard about other sectors in the news? Sector one are trying to keep a lid on it.'

'Whoever or whatever started the fire, we need to be out of here as soon as possible,' Jack said. 'We don't want to get stuck in a crowd of sightseers. I had a look out earlier. It's cleared up a bit, but there are already some Anti-Techs out with their placards. Harry, you up to driving?'

'I'm fine.'

'Keep your breakfast short, lads. We're hitting the road within the next half-hour.'

Horns honked. The wipers smeared the glass. It had started to drizzle, but the rain was mixed with dust and ash. Condensation misted up the inside of Adam's windscreen. He turned up the fan. A cloud of smoke stretched across the sky, blotting out the sun. It seemed like everyone was heading out of the city on this route. Here and there a car lay upturned in a ditch or the mangled remains of two or three wrecks straddled a lane, but the traffic had eased by the time he arrived in Nottingham that evening. The journey on Wednesday to Milton Keynes was relatively clear, but the congestion returned later that day as reports came in over the radio of disturbances in the capital. By late Thursday afternoon, the tailbacks into Central City extended for miles, but they were worse in the opposite direction.

Warning lights flashed on the dual carriageway as Adam neared the slip road that led off into Central City. Sam, secure in her seat next to him, began to cry. Adam jiggled her toys and tried to reassure her, but he fell quiet when he saw vast columns of smoke across the skyline as though a multitude of incinerators had sprung up in his absence. The streets were filled with debris, cars were damaged and windows were broken. A tram had overturned, blocking half the road, its metal arm stuck in the shattered orange globe of a Belisha beacon. The electronic billboard opposite Betsy's Café had been smashed. Adam turned into the driveway, pulled up in a parking bay and waited for Harry to arrive. He drummed his fingers on the steering wheel and picked up his handset.

'Harry, where are you?'
'Approaching Betsy's.'

He stared at the driveway entrance. The potted plants that used to be on either side of it were gone. There were piles of bulging black sacks around the dustbins. The acrid smell was still present, mixed with the stench of burnt rubber and biofuel. Adam's heart thumped, counting away the seconds while he gazed at the empty gateway. Gunfire sounded in the distance. Was that a grenade?

A lorry pulled in. Harry was at the wheel. Adam jumped out of his cab and fumbled with the catch that held Sam's car seat in place. He wiggled it, pressing the button, until it clicked free. Harry parked her truck in the next bay while Adam slung his rucksack on his back and eased Sam's seat out. Harry collected her baggage, and they dashed inside.

Alf and Hector were positioned on either side of the front door with their guns at the ready. A window had a jagged star of splintered glass. Another explosion sounded in the distance. Hazel, one of Betsy's staff, sat on the lobby floor crying, her hands clasped to her ears. Betsy knelt by her side, with an arm around her. Spike was by the edge of the broken window with his gun. Mary the waitress sat behind the reception desk, her arms folded on its surface, pillowing her head. Sam was screaming, her cheeks soggy and bright red. Mucus was bubbling from her nose. Adam put her seat down at the other end of the desk and unstrapped her from it.

'Is Jack with you?' Betsy said, hurrying over to him.

Adam put Sam on his shoulder and patted her back while rocking her.

'He was only a little way behind me,' Harry said, rummaging in Sam's bag.

The front door was flung open. Jack strode in with his tommy gun under his right arm and Eric by his side.

'Quinn's sure got this city under control, hasn't he?' Jack said.

Betsy ran over to him and threw her arms around his neck.

'Oh, Jack. You won't believe what's been going on here. I thought it was bad enough when Sector House blew up, but now it's like that coup Spud was telling us about.'

Harry handed Sam's bottle of water to Adam. He tried to put it in Sam's mouth, but she was screaming too much to drink it. Mary raised her head from her arms.

'It was worse than that,' she said. 'They didn't have laser weapons in sector seventy.'

'Lasers?' Jack said. 'Where'd they come from?'

'Sector House,' Mary said. 'They think it was one of them what caused the fire.'

Harry took out Sam's milk from her bag and plugged the bottle warmer into a wall socket.

'And they found old high-tech computers,' Betsy said. 'And some kind of medical lab.'

'I heard them talking about it when they came in for a bite to eat,' Mary said.

Adam tried to give Sam her dummy, but she continued screaming, so he paced up and down the lobby.

'Who're the "they" and "them"?' Jack asked.

'The firefighters,' Betsy said. 'Then the Anti-Techs got to hear about it and flipped. Someone smashed the billboard outside, and that's when the rioting started. Spud and the others got the guns out and told them to clear out of your territory. That scared most of them off, but some came back with alcohol bombs. They were shot, but the rest of the rioters moved into the neighbouring territories and spread out across the rest of the city.'

'Betsy,' Adam said. 'Give us a key. I'll sign the register once Sam's had her milk.'

Sam's milk was soon ready. At first she was crying too much to drink but at last she calmed down, guzzled it and fell asleep in Adam's arms. He laid her in her bed after Harry had put up the cot and gone into the bathroom to wash the bottle. Then he went over to the edge of the window and peered out. The skeletal, twisted remains of Sector House smouldered at the end of the street. The memory of the blast he had caused was still vivid. If Harry hadn't been lying on the floor at the time.... He could hear her humming in the bathroom above the sound of splashing water. Did Allerton have any more friends with a secret medical lab that had restraining straps on the operating couch? Maybe he should just rub Allerton out. A gun would be the easiest way, but he wouldn't be able to get one from Jack without an explanation. But there were plenty of other methods he could think of. The only problem was how to locate a man he knew nothing about who lived in the depths of the West Norfolk countryside. He could hardly turn up with a map and ask for directions, and how was he supposed to get there and back without Jack or Harry asking him where he'd been?

A hand touched his arm. He turned. It was Harry. He hadn't even noticed that she'd stopped humming.

'Are you all right, Adam?'

'Sure.' He put his arm around her and drew her towards him. 'Here, I've told you before not to make a target of yourself, standing directly in front of the window. Come round this side. There might be snipers out there.'

She moved round him. He rested a hand on her shoulder.

'I owe you my life,' she said.

'You saved my sister, so we're quits.'

Dusk was deepening into night, veiling the columns of smoke across the city. Street lights flickered on, but there were dark gaps where bulbs had been smashed or where bent lamp posts leaned across the pavements. The damaged billboard was grey and silent. Harry rested her head on his shoulder.

'I have bad dreams where I'm back in that place,' she said, 'but you're not there.'

He looked at her blond curls. Should he pat her head or stroke her hair? What would Jack do?

'I'm going to protect you, Harry. Allerton ain't going to get away with kidnapping you.'

'But what can we do? It's just our word against his, and I'll not have you blamed for that fire. I can't prove he was involved. He's forged my medical notes and convinced my friends I'm his delusional fiancée. I'd have to be delusional to be his fiancée.'

'He wouldn't have any claim over you if you were already married — to me.'

She pulled away and studied his face.

'Marriage is for life, not a quick fix.'

'I know. Sure, I know that, but it could be done at City Hall, and we'd stay as we are, so it could be annulled if you wanted. It'd be a way of getting you registered without anyone finding out who you are cos you'd have my name, and you'd be Sam's joint guardian. No matter what Allerton's connections are, he can't force anyone into bigamy. I'll look after you. I won't hurt you.'

She was still facing him, but it seemed more like she was looking right through him and far away out of this stinking city. The air here still stung the eyes and left a bad taste in the throat. Trust him to have messed up asking a girl to marry him. He'd planned it all out: he was going to ask her in Weston Snelding, by the old willow next to the stream. And he would've got her a nice ring. He'd already seen one he figured she might like. Now he'd loused it up, just like he loused everything up.

He turned away, but she took his hand and squeezed it.

'All right.'

Adam finished packing Sam's bags ready for the journey home. It was Friday morning, and the night had passed with just one interruption from Sam. With luck, the driving would be easier once they were away from Central City. Then tomorrow morning they could go to Weston Snelding for the second of Sam's baptism preparations, and after that they could stop by and get married in City Hall. Or should they get married first? That might be better, only they'd have to leave in plenty of time in case there was a long queue. He picked up a squeaky toy that had fallen on to the floor.

Jack's knock — two rapid taps, a pause, five more taps — sounded at the door.

'Don't bother packing,' Jack said as he came in, after Harry had opened the door. 'The Anti-Techs have set up road blocks. We're not going anywhere.'

'Not again,' Adam said. 'Can't we just smash our way through?'

'There's a limit to what I can get away with here, my boy. You may as well settle in and get comfortable.'

Jack left and Adam kicked one of the bed legs. Harry began to unpack Sam's bag.

'We ought to get more milk and nappies if we're going to be stuck here for a while,' she said.

Adam peered out of the window. The street outside was empty.

'Yeah. At least it looks like the rioters have learnt to keep clear of Jack's territory.'

Adam checked his pockets for his blackjack, and they set out with Sam in the harness on his back. The first pharmacy was shut and boarded up. So was the second and the third. They were now outside Jack's neighbourhood. Adam kept one hand in his coat pocket, grasping his blackjack. He eyed everyone they passed and checked round corners before turning into another street. At last they found a chemist open and bought some supplies. The pharmacist kept his hand under the counter, so Adam took care not to make any sudden move when he took out his wallet to pay for the goods. They left the shop but, as they were about to set off back to Betsy's, Adam saw a sign pointing to City Hall. It was only a quarter of a mile away and wasn't too much of a detour. He pointed it out to Harry.

'We may as well see if the registration desk is open,' he said. 'Have you got your birth certificate?'

'Of course –' she patted her jacket pocket '– but, well, shouldn't we get back?'

'It'll be safest if we get it done now — in case any of Allerton's friends are still around. Come on.'

He took her hand and hurried along the pavement. There were armed guards patrolling City Hall, but the place was open. Harry had to submit her shopping bag for inspection while Adam was patted down.

'I work for Jack Preston,' he said when they found his blackjack.

'Let's see your ID,' the guard said.

Adam took out his papers, and he was given a receipt for his blackjack and for the knife he kept strapped to his ankle.

'Perhaps we should come back some other time,' Harry said, edging away.

Another guard, the biggest of the lot, moved towards the door and leant against the frame with his arms folded.

'It's okay,' Adam said. 'Just put your stick in with my blackjack and knife. They ain't going to mess with any of Jack's people. That's right, ain't it?'

'Not if they behave themselves,' the guard in the doorway said.

Harry took out her stick and laid it on the desk next to Adam's blackjack.

'That's my dog's favourite fetching stick, so don't lose it,' she said. The man behind the desk reached forwards. 'Don't worry about any slimy bits, that'll just be doggy drool.' The man's hand paused over the stick. 'And you don't need to worry about that as the only dung he eats is rabbit droppings. I think.'

The man withdrew his hand. Adam led her down the corridors until they reached the registration hall. An armed guard stood in one corner. The queue wasn't as long as it had been for Sam's registration, and it was a lot quieter. Adam glanced round, half-expecting Allerton's friends to burst in. He kept slipping his hand into his pocket, only to remember that it was empty, but eventually they reached the counter.

Harry slid her birth certificate between the counter and the grille, and filled in a form labelled 'ADX26a' that had to be stamped and paid for. The clerk, a pasty faced middle-aged woman with a maroon tie, took out another form from a shelf behind her, wrote Adam and Harry's registration numbers in the provided spaces and handed it over for them to sign. This one was labelled 'ADX28'. Adam checked the numbers were correct before signing and paid the fee. The clerk stamped the form, handed over their new marriage certificate, then tapped away at the computer, made them sign a third form, 'ADY30', collected another lot of fees, updated Sam's adoption papers to include Harry's details and did some more stamping before handing their documents back.

'Next,' the clerk said.

Adam tucked his papers away in a pocket. Their weapons were just as they had left them on the lobby desk. They collected them and left the building.

'That seemed quick,' Harry said as they walked around an overturned dustbin. 'You have to give six months' notice to get married in a Catholic church.'

The spilt refuse stank of the rotting remains of takeaway leftovers.

'Six months?'

'Well, if you don't believe in divorce, it's a good idea not to marry in haste.'

'Marriage usually ain't a life or death issue,' Adam said. 'We ought to phone Father Bernard to tell him we can't make it tomorrow.'

'Can we find a church to go to in case we're still here on Sunday?'

'I'll be very surprised if we ain't. I think there's one nearby, but we can look it up when we get back to Betsy's.'

He stopped at a phone box, and Harry fished out last Sunday's church newsletter from her jacket pocket. She read out the number while he dialled.

'Hello, Father Bernard. It's Adam Trent. Me and my wife –' it was like saying 'my Phaeton' when he'd first shown it to Eric '– are stuck in Central City. We can't get out because of the blockades.'

'My heart alive, bor. We'd heard about the fire, but is that near you?'

'Sure, that's right. It was just at the bottom of the road where we're staying.'

'And is the baby safe?'

'Yeah, she's with us now. We've managed to get some more milk for her, which is something.'

'You must be hully frazzled, bor,' Father Bernard said. 'And thass puter weapons, they hev? The Major nearly choked hisself when he heard about that. We'll keep you in our prayers, tergether. You'll let us know how you're a-gorn on?'

'Sure, I'll keep you posted.'

'Where've you been?' Jack said as they entered Betsy's lobby.

Outside, the driveway was full of lorries — not just in the bays, but backed all the way up to the entrance. Inside, truckers were coming and going through the lobby, carrying bags, boxes and bundles. Jack had his tommy gun slung over one shoulder.

'We had to get some stuff for Sam,' Adam said.

'You should've left Sam and Harry behind,' Jack said, 'and gone with backup. How are you supposed to manage in a fight when you've got a baby with you?'

Jack moved to one side as Betsy walked past carrying a pile of blankets. There was the sound of hammering from the other end of the lobby.

'I'm sorry,' Adam said. 'What's going on? Where did the other trucks come from?'

'The protesters only went and blocked the outbound slip roads before they stopped the incoming ones. More people have arrived so we're all going to have to double up. Alf, help Betsy with those blankets. Hector, see if you can find more boards for the windows.'

Adam made his way around a trucker carrying an old cupboard door, stepped over a toolbox and headed upstairs with Harry behind him. There was a machine gun mounted by the window at one end of the corridor. Spud was kneeling by it, opening a case of drum magazines. Adam unlocked his door and let Harry in.

She had just eased Sam out of the harness on Adam's back when Eric arrived with some blankets. Jack followed on behind.

'We're in with you,' Eric said.

Adam looked around at Sam's things lying around on what little floor space they had.

'There ain't enough room.'

'We'll have to squeeze in,' Jack said. 'Even Betsy has to share. Tess and Hazel are both from out of town and can't get home. There's enough room on the floor between the window and that bed for Eric if we move the table outside and shift things over a bit.'

Eric dumped the blankets on the floor and took the top pillow from Adam's bed.

'What about you?' Adam said to Jack.

'I'll take the bed nearest Eric. You have the one by Sam.'

'But what about Harry?'

'She can share with you. She's slim enough to fit. That's everyone settled, so long as no one else turns up. Come on, Eric. Let's get our baggage.'

Adam sank down on the bed after Jack and Eric had left and rested his head in his hands.

'Mrs Burnley-Morris would have a thing or two to say about this if she found out,' Harry said. 'It's just as well we got married, otherwise I'd never have heard the end of it.'

'You ain't bothered about what she thinks, are you?'

'It would be most uncomfortable if she gave me funny looks across the dinner table.'

Adam was about to remark that it was highly unlikely that Harry and her godmother would ever meet across the dinner table again, but decided against it. He unfolded Sam's play mat on the bed and wound up the musical box in the centre of her mobile.

Jack and Eric soon returned. Adam and Eric shifted the furniture around under Jack's directions while Harry held Sam, and afterwards they all headed off to the dining room for lunch. It was packed, but the other truckers made space for them. Afterwards they returned to their room, and Jack produced his playing cards.

'If Harry's in, we're not playing for money,' he said. 'I'm not gaming with Miguel's protégé.'

'Jack, it's been quiet outside since Friday,' Adam said. 'Me and Harry would like to go out for a walk.'

It was Sunday morning. Harry was changing Sam in the bathroom. Jack was lounging on his bed, shuffling the cards. The previous day had been spent playing rummy, visiting the laundry room and listening to radio reports. Adam had been allowed to take Sam out in the pram, but only around the block and only with an armed escort.

Eric was sitting on one corner of the bed, trimming his toenails.

'Eric,' Jack said, 'see if you can round up some of the lads.'

'Actually, Jack,' Adam said, 'we'd sort of like to go on our own.'

'If you want a bit of privacy for a while, all you have to do is say. Eric and I can go for a walk with Sammy.'

'I didn't mean like that.'

Adam sat down on the bed and twisted a corner of the pillowcase. Jack put the cards down on the bedspread and leaned towards him.

'Was there somewhere in particular you'd like to go, my boy?'

'Well, sort of. If it ain't inconvenient.'

'It would be very inconvenient if you got yourself killed by rioters. You want to tell me where it is you want to go?'

The bathroom door clicked. Adam turned and looked at Harry.

'What's up?' she said.

'Adam was saying the two of you want to go out for a walk.'

'If that's okay with you,' Harry said.

'I don't know if it is.' Jack held Adam by the shoulder. 'Where is it you want to go, my lad?'

'I just want to go to church, that's all,' Harry said.

Eric took Sam from Harry and squeaked one of her toys. Jack relaxed his hold on Adam and leant back against the pillow.

'Why? What's made you go all suddenly religious?'

'I haven't suddenly gone religious. I always go to church on Sundays.'

Jack looked at her and then at Adam.

'That's right, Jack,' Adam said. 'That's where we go on Sunday mornings.'

'And there's me thinking you were just having a bit of fun in the back of your car.'

'Jack,' Harry said, 'it's important to me.'

'I don't give a damn what's important to you. The safety and welfare of my people is all that concerns me.'

Sam began to grizzle.

'Hey, Sammy,' Eric said, 'don't cry. Look, it's Mr Frog. Ribbet, ribbet.'

'Can't you give it a miss until we get home?' Jack said to Harry.

'There's one just a few streets away. It's not far.'

The cards slid off the bed, scattering on to the floor. Jack grabbed her wrist.

'You don't mean the Catholic one, do you? You've not been going to Stan's territory, have you?'

'No, we ain't,' Adam said. 'Honest we ain't. I've told Harry not to go anywhere near there. I take her to a little village. Stan don't go there.' He touched Jack's arm. 'I swear it, Jack. Harry ain't been nowhere near Stan's.'

Jack let go of her wrist.

'Harry, you're a damn powder keg. Of all the churches you could pick, you want to go to one of Stan's.'

'It's not one of Stan's,' Harry said. 'He's a hypocrite.'

'You do like your long words, don't you?'

'You know what I mean. He does the complete opposite of what he professes.'

'You won't live long if you say that to his face.'

'This is your neighbourhood here, isn't it?' Harry said and stepped closer to him. 'Please let me go, Jack.'

'Don't tread on my cards. Pick them up.'

Harry gathered them together, shuffled them and handed the pack back to Jack.

'All right,' he said. He swung his legs off the bed and picked up his fedora. 'I suppose it will break the monotony.'

'Are you coming too?'

'Of course I am. And so's Eric. My lad needs protection. We can hide my tommy gun in Sam's pram. There might be room for a couple of shotguns in there as well. I'll get Adam and Eric Berettas to go in their coat pockets.' He tilted his hat over his forehead. 'And you owe me one.'

— 19 —

INVESTIGATING DEL ROSARIO

Hadley sat at his desk looking through the morning's post. The first letter came from Central City and contained a brief note accompanied by a coroner's report. Another dead body. Another dead end. The door slammed open and Fenning came in looking like Black Shuck on a bad day.

'You know how Williams and Hale got our fraud case?' she said. 'Turns out thass the Colingham lot who dint want us or, at least, dint want me.'

'Where'd you hear that?'

'From Williams.' Fenning jerked her thumb in the direction of the neighbouring office. 'Colingham claimed we dint follow correct procedure on two occasions, but Williams say Jarrett hinted thass actually corse Colingham dunt like female detectives. That should be cops and robbers not cops and mawthers, that sorft bugger said.'

She kicked one of the desk legs and picked up Hadley's geode paperweight. He reached across and eased it out of her hands.

'You can kick my desk as much as you like, but don't harm my geode. What were the two occasions?'

'When we visited the bank and when we visited Miss Penderbury. They say we shoulda cleared it with them first, but dunt you tell me we wuz pulled off the case bein' as we dint cow-tow to 'em. I allus knew they were a duzzy lot over there. That Jarrett dint so much as look at me. He probably thought I ought to be at home bakin' cakes.'

Hadley leant back in his seat and fingered the rough crystals at the centre of the paperweight. One of Fenning's dark curls had fallen loose again.

'What about your theory that it was Allerton who sent Jarrett and Regan round to the coffee shop?' Hadley said. 'What's happened to all your excitement about the possibility of mob rivalry?' He rested the paperweight on the pile of post. 'Don't let Jarrett's comments sidetrack you. We're not welcome in Colingham because something rotten's going on there.' He handed her the coroner's report. 'Jane Lamm's dead. She was found drowned three weeks ago, but Central City have only just got around to replying to my request for information about her.'

'Rackon someone lured that poor mawther to the city and drowned her?' Fenning looked over the report. 'Thass the same coroner who said the Earl of Wynherne died of anaphylatic shock, hintut?'

'That's right.'

Hadley moved the paperweight aside and picked up the next envelope on the pile.

'And I spuz the coroner's also satisfied about the deaths of Dr Barnes and Mr Trescothic?' Fenning said. She perched on the edge of the desk and tugged on Hadley's lapel. 'Praps we should tell the historians where to find Allerton and see what do happen.'

'Fenning, that's most unprofessional.' Hadley turned the envelope round. There was no return address. 'Anyway, Molly says they've paid up and left.'

'I've heard they got stuck down Wash Lane outside Little Bartling,' Fenning said.

Hadley studied the postmark. It was smudged, but he could just make out the postal location.

'Where'd you hear that?' he said.

'My grandma heard that from the butcher. Apparently one of the farmers hatta pull their car outta the mud. D'you think they wuz lookin' for Belrosa? She seem like she's a-hidin' from someone.'

'Maybe.' Hadley tapped the envelope on the desk and handed it to her. 'You've got a letter from Norwich.'

'Me? Who's a-writing to me from Norwich?'

'You could always open it to find out.' Hadley handed her the knife Barney Coulgrane had given him. 'Maybe one of those historians took a fancy to you.'

Fenning slit open the envelope and removed the letter.

'Thass the Norfolk Constabulary logo,' she said. 'Why dint they have that on the envelope? Thass from a D.I. Cornell wanting our know about a certain Miguel Alberto del Rosario, suspect in a robbery five year ago in Norwich, believed to have moved to our area. Possibly near a hamlet called Little Bartling. Maybe thass what those historians wuz doin' there. They were askin' about del Rosario, but why do Cornell go a-writin' to me? Where do he get my name from? Thass a rum ole dew. That sound like Cornell dunt even know del Rosario's dead.' Fenning put down the knife and handed the letter over to Hadley. 'What d'you make of it?'

Hadley tucked the knife back into its leather sheath and slipped it into his pocket.

'I think,' he said, studying the letter, 'that since Williams and Hale have our fraud case, we ought to go back over del Rosario's murder for D.I. Cornell. See if you can get hold of the case notes from Williams and Hale's investigation. Maybe we should go back to Little Bartling and have another chat with Belrosa.'

Hadley rang the bell a second time and rapped on the round knocker. The oak door seemed to have more dents in it than he remembered. As though someone had given up on the bell and knocker and had hammered on the door with a heavy object about the size and shape of a sub-machine gun butt. A leaf fluttered past him and joined the moist brown carpet under his feet. Fenning squelched over to the window and looked in.

'Belrosa,' she said. 'Thass Sergeant Fenning here from Great Bartling with Inspector Hadley. You remember us, dunt yer?'

The door opened an inch, this time on a chain. Dark eyes peered through the gap.

'Why did you bring Quinn's men here?' Belrosa said.

'We dint,' Fenning said. 'We jist asked them for help, like you suggested.'

'I did not tell you to bring them here.'

'We dint ask them to come here. We thought they were a-gorta look for Lady Coulgrane in the city, like we asked them to.'

Hadley turned up his coat collar against the cold breeze.

'Did they bother you, Belrosa?' he said.

'Me? Why should they bother me? What have I done that the police should bother me?'

Hadley shifted his weight and moved his foot into the gap between the door and its frame.

'How did your door get so dented?' he said.

'It is an old cottage. Everything is dented.'

'They've orl gone back to the city now,' Fenning said. 'If you want to tell us anything in confidence, you kin.'

'What have I to say? I have nothing to say.'

Fenning put her head close to the gap. Dried rose petals fell from the bush next to her as a thorn snagged on her sleeve. Hadley unhooked it while she spoke.

'Do you know anything about a cuppla fellows posin' as historians who got stuck down Wash Lane?'

The door opened another inch.

'I heard something. What do you mean "posing"?'

'We think they're come from Norwich looking for a bloke called del Rosario.'

'One of them had light brown hair with a scar across his left jaw and a bent nose,' Hadley said. 'The other one was fair-haired with a canary tattoo on his right wrist. Does that mean anything to you?'

The door widened until the chain was taut, and Belrosa pressed her face against the gap.

'They are Ethan Hall's most trusted men,' she said.

'D'you mean the Norfolk Chief Constable?'

'Yes.' Belrosa's face crinkled as she smiled. 'Quinn will not like the Norwich police being here. They do not like each other.'

'Belrosa,' Fenning said. 'You mentioned suffin about a refuge. Is that a safe place to go?'

'Yes, of course. Jack Preston's men guard it.'

'Ent he a gangster?'

'So is your commissioner, but Jack he does not kill for fun, like some of them. He says to his men, "no frails".'
'Commissioner Quinn's a gangster?' Fenning said.
The chain slackened. Belrosa's face disappeared into the shadows. A dog barked in the lane behind the leylandii hedge.
'How do you know all this?' Hadley said.
The door pressed against his toes, but he kept his foot on the threshold.
'Everyone knows,' Belrosa said. 'They go to my nightclubs. Of course I talk to customers. Why should I not? They come to hear me sing. Why should I not drink with them afterwards?'
'What about Chief Constable Hall?' Fenning said. 'Is he a gangster as well?'
'He is the best friend of Jack Preston.'
'Are there any city police who ent gangsters?' Fenning said.
Belrosa laughed.
'You are like Lady Coulgrane. She asked me the same question.'
'When?' Hadley said. 'When did she ask?'
'I do not know.' Belrosa's forehead puckered. The smell of her perfume drifted though the doorway into the breeze that rattled the rose bush's dead leaves. The dog barked again and someone whistled. 'Yes, I remember now. She was wearing a black dress. She had been to her uncle's funeral. The day del Rosario was shot. She came here and walked up and down the room, asking questions about the police in Central City.'
'Did you tell her about the refuge?' Fenning said.
'No, I do not think so. She only asked about Quinn and his men.' The chain tautened again and Belrosa's dark eyes

studied Fenning through the gap. 'I do not know this man Allerton. I have not seen him, but I think that he is one of Quinn's special friends. Stay away from him. Do not tell him I spoke to you.'

Hadley and Fenning trudged down the muddy lane, returned to the squad Land Rover and set off for the cottage where del Rosario had once lived. The road passed the Bartling drainage mill. Its four wooden double-shuttered sails rotated in the wind. Marshland lay on the other side of the dyke. In the distance a small whirlwind spun like a bobbin, vibrating the radio mast that stood up tall on the horizon and then faded into nothing. The sky was overcast. Hadley turned up the vehicle's heater, but it couldn't compete against the icy draft that rattled the windows.

They followed the dyke for a while before turning down an unmade road. After a couple of miles, Hadley parked the car alongside a drainage ditch that lay between the lane and a tall hornbeam hedge whose coppery leaves danced in the breeze. A mossy thatch was just visible above the straggling topmost branches.

Pigs rooted in a nearby field. The landscape stretched on for miles, occasionally interrupted by a clump of trees or hedgerows or a wooden windmill. To the west was a dark line that Hadley guessed to be the boundary wall of the Wynherne Estate.

'Getting inta conversation with the neighbours might be tricky,' Fenning said. 'There's a ligger over there where we can cross.'

They headed over to the plank Fenning had pointed out and crossed the ditch over fast-flowing muddy water. Hadley took out his knife and cleared some of the bindweed that was tangled around the rotting wooden gate. After a bit of shoving he managed to open the gate halfway. He squeezed through the gap into an overgrown garden with Fenning following on behind. There was a peeling garden table and three chairs, one of which was lying on its side with a thistle growing up between its slats. A peacock perched on the roof of a tiled outhouse eyed Hadley as he walked past. The front door of the cottage was warped and damaged around the hinges. An empty spider's nest clung to a corner of one of the dark leaded windows. Fenning peered in through one of the panes.

'That certainly do need tricolatin',' she said. 'There's nowun here but the mice. Look at them ole curtains orl daggly and frazzled. I dunt spuz nowun want to live here arter what happened to del Rosario.'

Hadley removed a cobweb from her hat brim. The peacock flew down from the outhouse roof. Its large body and long tail feathers made it look top-heavy, but it landed lightly on the long grass and began pecking at the ground.

'What did Williams and Hale have to say about him?'

'He moved here four years ago,' she said, 'kept to hisself and hardly nowun saw him.' Fenning took a small torch out of her coat pocket and shone it through the window. 'Look, you kin still see the bullet holes.'

Hadley stood beside her on a patch of nettles and gazed through the glass, his hat brushing against hers. The wall opposite was a mass of deep holes. Bits of broken shelving dangled from twisted brackets. He could just make out the remains of a chalk outline, mostly scuffed away on the floor but still visible above the skirting board. In the middle of the room were dusty packing crates. Had del Rosario been preparing to leave when he was shot or had someone else started to clear up his effects afterwards but, for some reason, never finished? Why hadn't the place been tidied up and rented out again? Or was it as Fenning had suggested that no one would want to live here now? A bramble snagged against his trousers.

'How did the killer — or killers — manage to find him here?' Hadley said.

'As far as Williams and Hale could make out, Allerton happened to catch sight o' him last year and rackonised him from a wanted poster he'd seen when he was in Central City.'

'For the Norwich robbery?'

'I dunt know. That don't say in the report.' Fenning took out her notepad and consulted it. The peacock gave a hoarse wail and went back to pecking at the ground. 'Allerton claimed he mentioned it to Barney Coulgrane who went to the city to investigate, but he met with an accident on his way home from the train station. Allerton believed that someone who knew del Rosario had found out about Barney Coulgrane's enquiries and was able to trace del Rosario and dun him in time everyone was at the funeral.'

The peacock flew up on to the roof and perched on the thatch with its tail feathers dangling over the eaves. A ray of sunlight broke through the grey clouds and lit up the eye markings.

'Mrs Burnley-Morris told us Allerton sometime go to Central City,' Fenning said. 'Why do he do that if he's in fear of his life? If he go back there, why dunt he tell Quinn about del Rosario, instead of leaving it to his neighbour? Or why dunt he just phone Quinn if they're such good friends?'

Hadley unsheathed his knife and began to hack at the brambles growing up against the wall. Fenning flicked her fingernail against her notepad.

'What if that wuz del Rosario what rackonised Allerton,' she said, 'not the other way round?'

A prickly branch whipped back from Hadley's blade and scratched the back of his hand. The cold wind strengthened and whistled through the tiles on the outhouse. Water in the ditch on the other side of the hedge bubbled and churned. All the city police were gangsters. That's what Belrosa had implied. Had she laughed at Lady Coulgrane in the same way that she had laughed at Fenning? But Chief Constable Hall wasn't a gangster; he was just the best friend of a gangster. The nice gangster. The one who didn't kill for the fun of it. Killing was purely business not pleasure for Jack Preston.

'Someone reactivated that old trap,' Hadley said, 'knowing that Barney Coulgrane would go home that way from the station.'

'Lady Coulgrane musta suspected,' Fenning said. 'Thass why she asked Belrosa about the police in Central City. At least she know better than to go to Quinn for help.'

'Maybe she went to Norwich instead. One of those historians could've been Cornell. That's why he wrote to you.'

'Why me and not you?'

'Probably your lack of diplomacy when it came to not hiding your dislike of Quinn.'

Something rustled in the hedge. Hadley turned, but it was only a grey peahen. He cast his mind back to the day del Rosario had been shot. The day of Barney Coulgrane's funeral. At the wake Mrs Burnley-Morris, a governor of the local village school, had been telling people about Mr Allerton's impromptu donation for new playground equipment. Kind Mr Allerton. Such a gentleman. Just walked into the school, out of the blue, with a cheque. A week ago that day.

A week before the funeral Barney Coulgrane had been killed while Allerton was presenting the local school with a cheque. A nice little alibi. Amos had given Allerton such a filthy look at the wake that it had almost seemed as though they were heading for another funeral, but Hadley had assumed at the time that the old steward's anger was merely directed at an incomer's usurpation of the Coulgranes' status.

'I spuz there's no chance Allerton killed del Rosario?' Fenning said.

'No. I — and about eight hundred other people — can vouch for that.'

'Thass a sight o' people for a funeral, but he certainly dunt have an alibi for the sudden collapse of Lady Coulgrane's dad.'

A pheasant kok-kokked in a field on the other side of the lane. The peacock wailed in the melancholy tone that no other bird can match. Hadley shivered and put his gloves on. His coat flapped about his legs.

'I hope we find her before Quinn's men,' he said. 'If she's still alive.'

'There was that talk about her threatenin' Allerton with a shotgun. Maybe thass why Quinn's men came here with guns. Maybe they rackon the Wynherne army is a-hidin' her.'

'But they were disbanded after the anarchy.'

'You said yarself they wuz orl there at the funeral. Orl eight hundred onem.'

'They weren't all veterans.'

'Them and their children — more than half the congregation, praps?'

'Well, naturally. They make up most of the local inhabitants.'

The peahen scratched at the mud beneath the hedge.

'What next?' Fenning said.

'Grub. And I know just the place.'

Hadley parked the Land Rover in the car park by the Wynherne Arms. The other side of the lane abutted the boundary wall around the Wynherne Estate. Men were repointing it and replacing broken bricks. Further along, one of the watch towers was also being repaired.

'Reckon those shotguns are for clay pigeons?' Fenning said, pointing to the men on the watch tower.

'It's lucky Quinn's men have gone.'

'But they may come back.'

The pub was filled with locals but, as Hadley and Fenning walked in, the conversation stopped.

'Have you got a menu, Tom?' Hadley said to the landlord.

The landlord stared at him and jerked his thumb at the blackboard.

'How are you a-gornin' on, Mr Ludlow?' Fenning said.

Tom Ludlow picked up a beer glass and began wiping it. Hadley and Fenning placed their orders and took their frothy drinks to a table by a window that looked out on to a playground. The men in the pub mostly looked like farm labourers, and they were all staring at Hadley and Fenning.

'Thass a rum dew,' Fenning said quietly to Hadley. 'You ever had that reception here afore?'

'No. Tom was my best friend when we were kids. We used to spend hours on that tittermatorter.'

He pointed to the see-saw in the playground. A voice muttered behind him, but he didn't catch what was said. Fenning leant back in her seat.

'You were lucky,' she said in her normal volume. 'My brother and sister allus hogged it. Howsomever Grandma gan me more coshies so that dint signify.'

But the conversation still didn't return to the pub. The head on Hadley's half-pint of beer seemed to take up most of the glass. He could hear the faint clinking of trowels against brickwork outside. A whistling draught rattled the window. There was a fireplace at the other end of the room, but there were no vacant seats near it. An old mongrel lay on the floor in front of the hearth. Ash logs cracked and spat. Sullen faces stared at him. Faces he'd seen at Barney Coulgrane's funeral. He stood up, his chair scraping against the wooden floor, and went over to the bar. Fenning followed on behind him.

'What's going on, Tom?' Hadley said to the landlord. 'Why the cold shoulder? I'm not a stranger here.'

'Yit you a-go bringin' in nasty barrow-pig-arsed swoddies inta our homes.'

'Swoddies? I haven't brought any soldiers here.'

'They burst into our homes,' one man said.

'They turned everythin' anend,' another said.

'Give me a Swarston winder when I told them to clear off,' the first said, pointing to his black eye. 'And thumped the boy Dave in the throat.'

'Who did that?' Hadley asked. 'What soldiers are you talking about?'

'The city pleece, bor,' an old man said. 'Do you a-call them that.'

'They had a warrant,' the landlord said. 'You were in charge o' the case, Charlie.'

'But I didn't authorise that. I asked them to look for her in the city, but they came here and took over.'

'Why'd you get them involved?'

'Cos nowun told me Quinn's men were as bent as a springtooth harrow full of dokes,' Hadley said, slumping down on a bar stool.

'That explain why they dint allow any of us alonga them,' Fenning said.

An old farmer with grey hair and elijahs — strings tied just above the knees of his trousers — nudged her.

'One bloke even came snoutin' abowt under the gal's bed, and in her kelter anorl. She shruk and lammed him with the guzunder.'

'Was that empty?' Fenning asked.

The old man grinned at her. Hadley drummed his fingers on the bar top and stood up.

'I think we need to have a chat with Mr Allerton,' he said to Fenning.

The landlord eyed him and turned to his wife.

'Do you hurry along with Charlie and the lady's food, Marge. Two cheese sandwiches.'

The sandwiches were produced, and Hadley and Fenning ate while they listened to the locals.

'Engaged, my arse,' Tom said, refilling Hadley's glass. 'We orl know she hate him.'

'She rackon he had her uncle dun in,' another said, 'and we rackon she's right.'

'And she rackon he killed her dad.'

'How d'you know that given no one's seen her since her father's death?' Hadley asked.

Silence fell. People shifted in their seats, glanced at their neighbours and glared at him. The old farmer picked at the knot of his elijahs.

'Thass orl right,' Fenning said. 'We've been thinkin' that maybe she suspected foul play, and that maybe people round here helped her git away.'

'The trouble is,' Hadley said, 'we need more than suspicions. We need proof.'

'And what d'you rackon she's tryin' to do?' Tom said.

'You think she went to Norwich to find proof?' Everyone in the pub started to take an interest in the contents of their beer mugs. The dog sat up and scratched its throat. 'Tom,' Hadley said, 'Barney Coulgrane was just as much my hero as yours. Like you, I believe he was murdered, and I want to catch all the people involved in it because there's more than just one person we're up against.'

'She's as tough as he wuz,' Tom said, 'but thass a bad business woss a-gorn on in Central City. They caught her and lectrocuted her. Tried to drill a hole in her head.'

'What happened to her?'

'One onem Norwich gangsters rescued her jist in time.'

'Jack Preston?'

'No, his boy. Seem like he's taken a likin' to her.'

'Puter weapons,' the man with the elijahs said. 'Thass a bad business. And who were they a-gorta aim them at?'

Hadley and Fenning finished their meal, returned to the car and soon pulled into Allerton's drive. Hadley slowed down as he approached a speed bump. In front of him was 'Gentle Repose', which made it sound more like a retirement home or funeral parlour than a mansion house. The locals had another name for it. The blue building was roofed with smutts — matt black pantiles — and had crenellations above the bay windows. Over the centre of the house was a curving gable, and the wings on either side had step gables, but they lacked symmetry as only one was a crow-step gable. The end gables on either side of the house were straight with an end kick. There was also an adjoining thatched annexe that was painted half yellow and half pink, as though it was masquerading as a pair of semi-detached cottages.

Overall, the place looked as though it had been designed by someone who couldn't decided which of the traditional Norfolk styles to use, so had amalgamated all of them. The place was surrounded by sugar beet fields. Some of the beet had already been harvested and dumped in tumbling piles, covered with straw and earth to keep out the frost.

The Land Rover bounced over another speed bump and Hadley parked in a wide gravel area with small white statues dotted around its perimeter. As Hadley crunched over to the porch with Fenning, he heard a shot coming from the neighbouring Wynherne Estate.

'Jist someone arter some dinner,' Fenning said.

Another shot sounded.

'Yes,' Hadley said. 'Just someone after their dinner.'

He rang the bell. A blond-haired butler opened the door. He seemed young and handsome, not at all like Hadley's image of what a butler should look like, but there was an expression in the man's eyes that reminded Hadley of the first murder case he'd been assigned to as a detective sergeant. Hadley shivered as he walked into the black and white marble-tiled entrance hall. Ahead was a sweeping staircase, and to the side of it were closed doors, but dominating the entire area was a tank containing striped, spiny fish. A pump and water heater hummed in one corner of the tank.

'They look tropical,' Hadley said, after the butler had left them. 'He must have the generators running twenty-four hours a day.'

'I darst say that show he hold,' Fenning said as she bent down to look through the glass. 'But hent Mrs Burnley-Morris mobbed him about orl these pearks? Dunt this give har high-strikers?'

A fish peeped out from some weed and then darted behind a rock on the stoney floor of the tank. Hadley checked his voice recorder was charged, switched it on and tucked it into his coat pocket.

'And it's not even in the shed,' he said.

'I'm sorry to keep you waiting, Inspector.'

Allerton came down the stairs with a walking stick, one hand grasping the banister. He reached the bottom and took a deep breath.

'D'you have any news of Harriet?' he said. 'I had almost given up hope.'

'I'm sorry, sir, but we've had complaints about the door-to-door searches conducted by Commissioner Quinn's men.'

'She has to be found.'

Allerton limped towards them, his stick tapping against the chequered floor. His fingers brushed along the side of the fish tank. He was, as usual, wearing his large, green opal ring.

'You can't infringe on people's civil liberties like that,' Hadley said.

'Don't you understand, Inspector, that it's a matter of life and death? The specialist made it quite clear that without treatment she would die within three months. I'm sorry if their feelings were hurt, and I'll make sure reparations are made for any reasonable claims, but the life of my fiancée is at stake.'

He stood upright with one hand in the pocket of his purple smoking jacket.

'But why search the cottages?' Fenning said. 'None o' the locals would think o' harmin' har.'

'Maybe not intentionally, but she's in denial, and there's always the possibility that she's told them some story fed by her paranoid delusions. The people here are simple enough to believe her. They don't understand the intricacies of mental health problems.'

The pump continued to hum in the corner of the tank. Pity Allerton was spending all his money on keeping the fish warm instead of the hallway. Hadley wished he was wearing a thicker pair of socks.

'What's her financial situation?' Hadley said.

Allerton adjusted a fold in his cravat.

'Her father was badly in debt. I helped him out as much as I could, discreetly of course, but I'm afraid he left her with nothing.'

'So she dunt have noffin to return to even if she is found?' Fenning said.

Allerton waved his walking stick.

'Nothing? No, that's not true. I'll provide for her.'

'I've heard that one afore now. My sister-in-law's cousin's fiancé said the same thing, and the tewl died afore they were married, and she was left with noffin — well, almost noffin.'

'I'm sorry to hear that, but you're right.' He picked up a pot from a ledge below the tank and shook dried shrimps on to the water. A shoal of brown and white striped fish swam up to the surface, their large jaws wide open. Within seconds the shrimp had been sucked up into gaping mouths. 'I haven't made a will yet, but I can assure you I'll get one done, and I'll leave everything to her. I wouldn't have her left penniless. But the chances of her outliving me are very slim. I keep hoping, but it would be a miracle if she was still alive.'

'I'm sure she wouldn't want her tenants knocked about on her account,' Hadley said.

'*Her* tenants?' Allerton rested the shrimp pot back on the ledge. 'Is that how they think of themselves? Their loyalty would be more impressive if they showed more concern about her well-being. But I'm afraid I don't know what you mean by being knocked about. If there have been any incidents, you'll have to take that up with Commissioner Quinn.'

'Talkin' about the Commissioner,' Fenning said, 'how come you dint tell him when you rackonised del Rosario?'

Allerton tapped his stick on one of the marble tiles. The sound echoed around the hall.

'You know why I had to leave the city. Can you blame me for not wanting to draw attention to myself?'

'Mrs Burnley-Morris mentioned you've been trying to persuade the authorities to do something about the gangsters,' Hadley said. 'That's a very brave step to take for a man in your position.'

A door opened at one end of the room, and the side of a blond head poked round the jamb.

'I was impressed by Barney Coulgrane's bravery and determination,' Allerton said. 'He inspired me to take action. Gangsters rule the city. Jack Preston is the worst of them, and his girlfriend runs the red light district. If they've found poor Harriet, then I'm afraid there's no hope. He's not called Jack "Tommy Gun" Preston for nothing.'

'He has a Thompson sub-machine gun?' Hadley asked.

'He's responsible for their revival. Didn't you know that? I'm convinced he was the one who killed del Rosario.'

The head edged further into the doorway until the right eye was visible. The left side of the face was still behind the wooden frame. Hadley shivered.

'Whereabouts does Preston live?'

'He moves about a lot,' Allerton said, 'but he's often in Central City. I'm sure Commissioner Quinn can tell you everything you need to know about him.'

But perhaps not as much as Chief Constable Hall could. Allerton always seemed keen to look towards Colingham or Central City, but never the other way, towards Norwich. Fenning's suggestion of pointing the historians in Allerton's direction might not be such a bad idea. He had certainly recognised their photo.

'Do you often have fourses in Colingham with Miss Penderbury?' Hadley asked.

'Fourses? You mean tea? I'm on the medical board. She gives me regular updates on the hospital's efficiency.'

Very regular indeed no doubt — for someone who hadn't been working there long.

'Thank you for your time, Mr Allerton,' Hadley said and turned to go.

'Oh, Mr Allerton,' Fenning said, 'hev you considered the possibility that maybe Lady Coulgrane's changed her mind about bein' yar fiancée. After all, thass not like she can return a ring, seein' as how you dint give her one.'

'You're not still put out by that?' Allerton said. 'Don't independent women such as yourself consider that kind of thing outmoded?'

'Even independent mawthers like to know whether their bloke hev serious intentions.'

'I believe she knows exactly how serious I am.'

'And if she hev another fella, what then?'

'There is, of course, always the possibility that some fortune-hunter may try taking advantage of her state of health, but I hope to protect her from that.'

'Fortune-hunter?' Fenning said. 'I thought she dint hev no munny.'

'Some people seem convinced that a title equals wealth.'

Hadley stopped the car in front of the main gateway to Wynherne Hall. It was closed. There were two men on either side of it, and another one at the top of a nearby watchtower. Hadley wound down the window. Another gunshot sounded, louder than the others. One of the men on guard came over to Hadley.

'Is Amos in?' Hadley said, showing his ID.

The man stepped away from the car and spoke into a radio. Hadley glanced down the lane. The telegraph pole that had been damaged in the storm the night before Lady Coulgrane had disappeared was now mended. The two guards opened the gates, and Hadley was waved on. He drove over the cattle grid, past a thatched lodge and up the drive. In his rear-view mirror he caught sight of the gates closing just before he rounded a clump of trees. An archery range had been set up in a field to the right of the front lawn. Hadley parked in front of the old Gothic mansion and watched an archer drawing back a recurve bow.

'I was conceived here,' Fenning said.

The bowman released the string. The arrow sped across the field and thudded into the centre of a straw boss.

'Were you? You never said.'

'I dunt believe you've ever mentioned where you wuz conceived.'

'I can't say I can remember that far back. Were you born here?'

'No, the family had jist a-settled back home when I arrived. My sister was born here. Mum was pregnant with her when they come here. My brother was three. Dad was in the North-East regiment.'

Hadley rested his arms on the top of the steering wheel. He'd never thought to ask Fenning if her family had been here. Those who had been born after the anarchy didn't fit that era.

'Mine was in the South-West,' he said.

The bowman fitted the nock of another arrow into his string and drew it back to his face. Fenning touched Hadley's sleeve.

'I know,' she said. 'He dint make it, did he?'

'No.'

The arrow sped towards its fellow in the centre of the target.

'You coulda talked to me,' she said.

'You didn't live through it. I didn't think you'd understand.'

'I'd rather you talked: you can be quite unbearable when you're titchy.' She smiled and added, 'Sir.'

'I'm sorry, Sarah.'

'Thass orl right, Charlie.'

The oak front door of the mansion opened. A couple of Great Danes bounded out of the house and over to the car, barking. One of them put its front paws on Hadley's window. Large globules of saliva dangled from its mouth. Its breath condensed on the glass.

'Thass nice,' Fenning said. 'We've got a welcomin' committee.'

Hadley pulled the latch and tried to exert just enough pressure on the door to move the dog aside without harming it. A whistle sounded. The animal bounded away, and Hadley nearly tumbled out of the car. He regained his balance, got out and adjusted his hat. Amos stood by the front door, both dogs at his side, wagging their tails. The sound of metal being hammered started up behind a grove where Hadley remembered the forge to be.

He went over with Fenning to the foot of the steps leading up to the house. Amos looked down at them. The scars on his face stood out white against his weather-beaten skin.

'I remember playing just here with Tom Ludlow when Barney Coulgrane brought you in covered in blood,' Hadley said. 'He always looked so grand. We all wanted to be like him. He was our captain, our hero.' Another shot rang out, coming from the other side of the house. 'We want his murderer convicted, but shotguns and arrows are no match against machine guns.'

Amos patted one of the dogs.

'You a-gorta arrest Commissioner Quinn?' he said.

'We would if we could,' Hadley said. 'At least give us evidence against Allerton. I know you helped Lady Coulgrane run away. One word from you and this entire neighbourhood would've been out searching for her when she disappeared, but all you did was send Joe out to Great Bartling. Did he give her a lift on his way there? Her doctor is dead, the specialist is dead, his P.A. is dead. Tell us what really happened.'

'Do you come in.'

Amos turned and led them inside. The door to the study was open, and Hadley peeped inside. There was certainly no sense of a hushed abandonment in there that sometimes happens to rooms where there has been a death. The desk was strewn with documents, and a typewriter sat in the middle of it with a sheet of paper fed through it. The portrait of Lady Coulgrane was still hanging on the wall amongst her ancestors. She seemed to be smiling down at Hadley. He turned away and followed Amos into the sitting room.

Amos threw a log on to the fire and sat in an armchair opposite Hadley and Fenning. The dogs settled down by his feet, and he scratched his scarred chin.

'Barney Coulgrane allus rackoned there wuz a chance the anarchy might return. He larned her to fight. He hed her practisin' since she first larned to walk.'

'You think the anarchy's going to return?' Hadley said.

'Hent you heard the news, bor?'

'That's just in the city.'

'Thass allus where that start.'

The sitting room was at the back of the house. The sounds of shotgun fire were louder here.

'She's not sick, is she?' Hadley said.

'She had headaches every day for two months until she left here,' Amos said. 'Now she's farin' well. You a-gorta tell me thass the clean city air woss done that?'

'What happened the day she left?'

Amos tickled one of the dogs behind its ear and stroked its back.

'I told you me and the boy Joe were in the backus when we heard a-hallerin'. That was self-defence what she did to his leg. We wanted to hide her here, but she wunt. That bloke del Rosario rackonised Allerton, and she wanted proof. Allerton came back to snout around after you'd gone. Said he owned the place and told us to clear out.' Amos grinned and patted the other dog. 'We showed the tewl outta the grounds. That night Joe caught some bloke trying to climb up to her winder, but he slipped away. That was too dark to get a good view o' him, but he wunt himpin'. He could pample acrorst the flag as quick as a farrisee.'

'A young bloke, maybe?' Fenning said.

'Maybe. And maybe he have light hair or so that seemed to the boy Joe.'

'Can you show us her room?' Hadley said.

Amos led the way up the staircase. At the top, there was a wooden bench in a niche beneath a window. Next to it a door led into Lady Coulgrane's room. The walls were panelled with a dark stained wood. Hadley opened a few drawers. He closed the bedroom door so that he could investigate behind it, but there was nothing much there. Just three silver trophy cups on a shelf amongst some rosettes and a box of trinkets. Amos sank down on to the bed and buried his face in his hands.

Hadley opened the wardrobe. His brain seemed to be slowing down, as though a fog was spreading though it. What had the intruder been after? Allerton had certainly been quick to lay a claim on the property. Fenning went over to the bedside table and picked up a silver photo frame.

'Who's this?' she said.

'Thass har with Barney Coulgrane,' Amos said, looking up. 'A few weeks afore he died.'

'You mean thass Lady Coulgrane?'

'Thass right.'

'But she do look noffin like that picture downstairs.'

'Liquid skin. Mrs Burnley-Morris useter run on about how she should wear it when she was dressed up to cover her tan, but she can't stand the stuff. She said that itched. She last wore it on old year's night and scratched at it until that peeled and she looked like suffin undead, so Mrs Burnley-Morris gan up.'

'Is this how she normally look?' Fenning asked.

Amos slumped forward, his elbows against his knees.

'Most o' the time,' he said, looking at the ground. 'She only wear a dress when she hatta look smart, like when she go to church or parties.'

Hadley came over to look at the photo. There was Barney Coulgrane wearing a waxed jacket, flat cap and a shotgun tucked under his arm. A younger, slightly feminine version stood next to him.

Fenning swayed and sat down on the bed next to Amos. She put a hand on her forehead.

'I dunt fare so good.'

The fog in Hadley's brain seemed to be turning into a fist that was trying to punch its way out of his skull. He stared for a moment at Fenning and Amos. Then he dragged Fenning to her feet.

'Get out of here. Quick.'

He bundled the other two out of the room and opened the bedroom window. He then followed them and closed the door behind him.

'Did Lady Coulgrane usually have the window open or closed?' Hadley said as he helped Amos over to the bench at the top of the stairs.

'As far as I know, she like to keep it open. I shut it arter Joe saw the bloke snoutin' abowt.'

Hadley opened the window above the bench. The cold air made his eyes smart, but his head began to clear. He took a few deep breaths, then covered his face with a handkerchief and went back into the room. He looked around the walls and found a vent near the floor. It had been painted over a long time ago, but the paint was cracked around the screws. He unscrewed it with his penknife and peered inside. He started rummaging around in his pockets but swung round when he felt someone tapping his shoulder. Fenning was standing behind him, holding out a pair of gloves. He snapped them on, reached inside and pulled out a small canister. She held open an evidence bag and sealed it after Hadley dropped the canister into it. They left the room and returned to Amos.

'She went to Norwich, didn't she?' Hadley said. 'A couple of city detectives have been undercover in this area investigating del Rosario's death.'

Amos leant his head against the niche side wall.

'She's stuck in Central City by the blockades,' he said. 'She try to phone me when she can, but she dassent leave the building. She dunt want nowun to listen in so she dunt talk long, but she say she's a-married Jack Preston's boy.'

'That the one what rescued her?' Fenning said.

'You know about that?' Amos said. 'That wuz Allerton behind that. She saw him on a puter in Sector House, ordering them to cut outta piece of har brain.'

'My heart alive,' Fenning said. 'But she's orl right?'

'Amos,' Hadley said. 'Did she reinstate the Wynherne Army?'

'She dint want to. Thass why she went to the city to find proof. She dint want no killin'.'

'And now? Has she changed her mind?'

Amos picked at some dirt under his index fingernail. The breeze coming in through the window ruffled his greying hair.

'That med me raw when I heard what they tried to do to har. And I dunt like the sound o' har bein' married to a gangster. I said that was time to give the summons. She dint hev time to say yis or no. She had to hang up corse someone was a-comin'.'

The sound of arrows thudding against straw bosses came through the window, mingled with the blast of shotgun fire.

'Fenning,' Hadley said, 'see if you can send the canister to Cornell.'
'Dr Carmichael said he'd kept a spare blood sample from Lady Coulgrane's dad,' Fenning said. 'That would be great to have a second opinion.'
The bench creaked as Amos leant forwards.
'They dunt know who she is,' he said, 'except for har husband. He hent told Preston corse she asked him not to, but do Preston pressure him she think the boy might tell him all his know.'
'So why are the Norwich police interested in del Rosario?' Fenning asked.
'She mentioned him to Preston to see do he know about him.'
'What did she find out?'
'He dint seem to know del Rosario was dead. He seemed hully surprised by the news. She dint think he was fakin' it. He had no reason to bein' as he's friends with the Chief Constable.'
Hadley prodded a knothole in the bench. He'd looked out of that hole a long time ago while playing hide-and-seek with Tom Ludlow.
'Reply to Cornell's letter,' he said to Fenning, 'and then say we've got some things that need analysing, but we can't send them to the path. lab in Central City because of the blockades. Give them him as much information as you can without giving away where she is.'

— 20 —

Murder

The days passed: rummy, entertaining Sam, endless radio reports and speculation. It was not just the roads accessing Central City that had been blocked. Vehicles had been parked on a level crossing resulting in a derailment that had sent up clouds of steam and ash. The train had ploughed into a nearby electricity substation, cutting all power in the neighbourhood. Its carriages lay in a tumbled heap across the tracks. Engineers predicted it would take days to clear the wreckage.

The airport was now the only way in or out of the city, but most of the flights had been cancelled, and it was under heavy guard to keep out protesters. The shops were empty and food was being rationed. Jack's stash of canned food in Betsy's basement was constantly guarded by at least four of his men, all carrying tommy guns, and anyone in need had to apply to Jack in person.

It seemed to Adam that their room was getting smaller by the day. You couldn't move anywhere without tripping over someone. You couldn't find a place to sit where you wouldn't be in someone's way. The four of them — Adam,

Harry, Eric and Jack — sat on the two beds playing cards or passing Sam on to the next person when she became too heavy to hold. More and more Jack seemed to end up by Harry's side. Sometimes he'd lean close while he was talking to her, his eyes fixed on her face, but then he'd move away, and often he'd abruptly leave the room. Adam would see him through the window, smoking outside on his own. At night, Adam held Harry in his arms whilst she slept, her head resting on his chest, her hair tickling his throat.

He closed his eyes, willing himself to sleep, but the air seemed full of noise: Eric snoring at the far side of the room, Sam snuffling in her cot close to Adam, Harry's gentle breath that ruffled his pyjamas. He opened his eyes again. Faint patches of phosphorescence on Sam's mobile seemed to float in mid air like will-o'-the-wisps. He looked round and found Jack lying close by, watching Harry. Jack turned his back to them and lay motionless, apart from one hand that clutched the bedding.

Every morning, Jack would wind up his radio and they'd crowd round on the bed, listening for news. More disturbances, rioting, looting and shooting, but mostly outside of Jack's territory. Quinn could look after his own neighbourhood. Adam looked over at Harry: his wife, only they'd hardly had a minute alone since they'd got back from getting married. Harry rubbed her temples, got up and headed for the bathroom but stopped as another announcement came over the radio.

'News just in. A plane has landed at Central City airport with agents from sector one and a special squad of investigators.'

'Well isn't that great,' Jack said. 'More people to join the party. Where's the phone?'

Harry fetched it from under the bed and handed it over. Jack put the receiver to his ear.

'Sweet. We've got a line.' He started dialling. 'We're not quite in the stone age yet. Curly? Know anything about the new arrivals from sector one? Yeah? What kind of artillery have they brought along? All right. Keep me posted.' He handed the phone back to Harry, who tidied it away under the bed. He turned to Eric. 'Tell the lads to keep a low profile. If we don't get in their way they might not bother us.'

'Maybe they'll clear out once they've found out what happened at Sector House,' Eric said.

Adam felt his hand being squeezed. Harry had sat down next to him and had her hand in his. She was trembling.

'Yeah, and how long's that going to take?' Jack said.

The next morning Agent Rawls was on the radio informing everyone that he and Agent Kilic had made a promising start to their investigations into the unauthorised labs and the explosion at Sector House.

'The evidence clearly suggests that the explosion was caused by one of the illegal weapons,' Agent Rawls said on the radio. *'We are confident that all those involved in this subversive plot were killed in the accident.'*

'That sure was quick work,' Jack said. 'That's nice for them to have a convenient bunch of stiffs that can act as scapegoats.'

'But they were all responsible, weren't they?' Harry said.

She was sitting between Jack and Adam, holding Sam. Jack played with Harry's hair. It wasn't as ragged as it had been when she'd first arrived. Adam shifted his hand so that his arm was behind her back.

'I'm sure a lot of employees were killed,' Jack said. 'But who knows whether their bosses were there as well. I have a feeling that Agent Rawls is only interested in placating the protesters. Good luck to him.'

But the agents seemed all out of luck. The protesters showed no signs of abandoning the blockades. By Thursday evening Jack only had three cheroots left. He twirled one around his fingers and lounged against the pillows while Eric shuffled the cards, but his eyes were on Harry. At first his gaze was on her face but then it began to lower.

'It's funny to think I mistook you for a boy when we met,' he said. 'How long did you think you'd get away with it, Harry?'

'I don't know. To be honest, I wasn't expecting to share a room.'

'Didn't you have to share back home?'

Jack struck his thumbnail against a match but it didn't light.

'We had more than one room,' Harry said.

'More than one room? Sweet. But who wants to live in the country?'

'I do.'

Harry handed Sam over to Adam, then went into the bathroom and there was a sound of running water and soap lathering. She returned, picked up one of Sam's bottles and the tin of milk powder.

'I wish I could get your farm back for you,' Adam said to Harry, as he rocked Sam in his arms.

Jack made another attempt at striking the match.

'And what would you do then, my lad?'

'What d'you mean?' Adam said.

Harry's right hand shook as she tried to scoop out some of the powder. The spoon rattled against the side of the tin.

'What's up with you, Harry?' Jack said.

'Nothing. Why should anything be up with me?'

Jack jumped up and strode over to her. Adam shrank back, cradling Sam.

'Don't you snap at me, my girl. You've got the shakes.'

'I don't like being cooped up. That's all.'

He grabbed her right hand. She dropped the spoon in the tin.

'Little Miss Prim and Proper turns her nose up at the odd spliff, but she can't stand a few days without caffeine.'

Harry tried to pull her hand away.

'Jack, please,' Adam said.

He stood back up against the wall, clasping Sam to his chest. Jack swung round. He stared at Adam for a moment, then threw himself on to the bed, reached over the side, fetched the phone and dialled.

'Quinn?' he said. 'What are you doing about these protesters? Why haven't your men cleared the roads yet? Well, get them shifted. I don't give a damn about their rights. What about my right to eat? And to smoke? I'm down to three cheroots and, if those bastards aren't gone by the time I smoke the last one, I'll get the guns out and we'll blast our way out of this damn city. What do I care about public opinion? D'you think the people stuck here with no food are going to mind me clearing the blockades? They'll be grateful that someone's got off their arse to do something about the situation.'

With that, he slammed the phone down.

'Jack, you don't really mean that, do you?' Harry said.

'Sure I do.'

'But you can't shoot unarmed people.'

'Harry, my darling, hunger is a weapon, and that makes them a viable target. How much milk has Sam got left? Will you be able to sit around listening to her crying when you can't feed her? We're getting out of this place tomorrow — by any means necessary.'

The next morning Jack sat in an armchair in the lounge and smoked his last cheroot. He had sent Harry upstairs to pack Sam's things and ordered Adam and Eric to check that everyone had a full magazine in their tommy guns as well as spares. There was only one other person in the lounge, sitting in a corner reading an issue of *Generator Monthly*: Donnaghan. That was just like the lousy little bastard, trying to encroach on Adam's ground. It had better not be Adam's copy he was pawing. Jack exhaled some smoke.

'I see you're hard at work, Donnaghan,' he said.

'It's not my shift.'

Betsy hurried into the lounge.

'Jack, come and listen to the radio.'

He ran over to the lobby, and everyone crowded round.

'*Commissioner Quinn,*' the reporter said over the radio, '*I gather you personally went out to the blockades and persuaded the demonstrators to leave.*'

There were sounds of shouts and vehicles revving from the radio.

'*I knew that it was just a question of reasoning with them,*' Quinn said, his voice crackling above the racket.

'Oh, sure he did,' Jack said. 'Come on, let's go. Heads up. We may be about to drive into an ambush.' He looked around the crowd of truckers. 'Harry, you take Sam in your truck. I've got a shotgun you can take along. You weren't kidding about being able to handle one, were you?'

'No,' she said, 'but I don't shoot people.'

'It's a cinch after the first time.'

The truckers in the lobby were gathering their baggage, checking their guns and starting to move out. Harry made no attempt to join them. Jack rested a hand on her shoulder.

'What about all those stories about your Uncle Barney?' he said. 'You thought the world of him because he fought to protect people, not because he sat at home waiting to be killed.'

'That was different.'

'No, it wasn't. It was kill or starve. You want to stay here alone and unprotected?'

She stepped away, but just at that moment Donnaghan came out of the lounge and she nearly backed into him.

'Watch where you're going, you stupid arse,' Jack said to him. 'It's all right, you can come out now. The protesters have gone away.'

Harry glanced behind her, hurried over to Jack and held his sleeve.

'I'll take the gun,' she said. 'I'm tired of Central City.'

'Side-by-side or over-and-under?'

'Over-and-under.'

'I'll get you the twelve bore Winchester.'

Jack checked that Sam was securely fastened in Harry's truck. Sam stared at him with large, blue eyes and yawned.

'You'll be all right, kid,' he said.

He wrapped a bullet proof vest around her car seat. Harry was sitting in the driver's side, her hands gripping the steering wheel. The shotgun was by her side. Adam was standing by her truck, looking up at her.

'Come on, my lad,' Jack said. 'It's time to go.'

'See you later, Harry,' Adam said, but he stayed motionless until Jack patted him on the back.

Adam climbed into his own truck and Jack went over to the main gateway with Eric, Alf, Spike and Hector. Jack held his tommy gun ready and peered round the gatepost. At the end of the street, there were vehicles parked in the remains of Sector House's car park. Two men sat on a pile of rubble, smoking cigarettes.

Jack waved to the closest truck and it began to reverse out of Betsy's driveway. The smoking men stayed put. The truck backed out into the road and Jack signalled to the next one. As more manœuvred out, the first ones had to reverse up the street. A car tried to turn in at the junction but swung round and headed off in a different direction. Still no interest from the men at Sector House.

At last Jack ran over to his truck and drove out on to the road. He took the lead. With Eric, Alf, Hector and Spike after him in their trucks, they formed the vanguard of the convoy. Adam came next with Harry following and the remainder close behind her. The group was not to be broken up. No stopping at lights. No giving way to anyone.

Jack laid his tommy gun on his lap and drove along the streets, glancing at the pavements on either side, the entrances to dark alleys, piles of smashed up vehicles that might shelter hostile forces. A pale face peered out from behind a net curtain: not a sniper — they wouldn't give their position away like that. A shadow moved behind a bus shelter: just a kid hiding. He inched round each corner and checked his mirror to make sure the convoy was maintained.

He turned into the main route out of the city. It was lined with police cars. Quinn's men were clearing junk off the road. They moved aside when they saw Jack. A few smiled and nodded at him but most edged behind their vehicles, eyeing him. He picked up his handset.

'How's it going at the back, Lonny?'

The radio crackled with static for a few moments, then came the reply.

'No trouble yet.'

Jack turned on to the slip road. No blockages. The convoy followed him on to the dual carriageway and occupied both the near and offside lanes, but when they eventually crossed the border into Norfolk they spread out a little. They bypassed Colingham without incident. Jack radioed that the convoy no longer needed to be maintained, but he posted armed guards when they stopped for lunch at the lay-by.

It was evening when Jack pulled up into the depot with Eric behind him. Light streamed out from the windows in the main building. Adam soon followed in his truck and then Harry with Sam. Jack rubbed the back of his neck as he got out. He saw Harry park and then rest her head on the steering wheel. Sam was screaming. Adam jumped out of his vehicle and ran over to her.

'Hiya, Ned,' Jack called into the building. 'Make some room for Adam and Sammy. Harry, get her milk out.'

With that, Jack strode out of the premises and bought a packet of cheroots at the corner kiosk. When he returned, all was quiet. He found Adam in the reception room feeding Sam with Harry curled up in a tatty armchair next to him.

'You got that ready quick,' Jack said to her.

'Adam had her milk in the travel warmer.'

'Smart lad. Come on, Harry. I'll get you a coffee.'

Once Sam was settled in her pram, they set off back to the flat. They arrived to find the floor strewn with dirty magazines, empty cans, used tissues and other rubbish. Grant was sitting at the table, finishing off the last segment of a pizza.

'What's going on here?' Jack said. 'You are going to clean this mess up right now.'

'Harry's spuzzed to do that,' Grant replied.

Jack struck him. The boy staggered back and landed with a thump on the floor.

'She's not touching your filth.'

Grant dumped the rubbish sack in the bin and clumped off to the pub. Inside it was dim and the fire smoked and spat. Pool balls clicked in one corner of the room. A man was leaning over Rita's chair, talking to her. She didn't seem to be paying a lot of attention to him. Grant pulled up a seat next to her. She had one leg crossed over the other, her dress tight against her thighs.

'They've orl now a-come back,' Grant said to her. Rita sipped her drink. 'Jack lammed me, but that ent fair,' he said. 'Harry's spuzzed to do the tricolatin'. Thass why har rent's lower, but he raised mine.'

Rita lowered her glass and eyed him.

'She gets lower rent, does she?'

'I dunt see why I hatta do it. He's sorft on har. He lam everybody else, but he oont never lam har, even time she's puttin' on har parts wi' him.'

'Is that so?'

'Yeh, he's orl mure-hearted over har.'

Grant sidled his hand on to her leg. She slapped him. He slipped from his seat and bashed his knee against the table.

'Clear out of here,' she said.

Grant kicked a chair and stomped over to the inner porch door. He flung it open, but just as he went through, Masher slouched through the front door.

'Git outta the way,' Grant said.

Masher grabbed him, shoved him up against the peeling papered wall, but then let go and laughed.

'Keep your hair on,' Masher said. 'What's up with you?' He checked that the inner and outer porch doors were shut and tapped the side of his nose. 'I reckon I can cheer you up. I've got a nice little number, and I'll count you in, seeing as how I like you.'

'What is it?'

'Come with me, and I'll show you.' He peeked through the small window set in the inner porch door and pulled a jemmy out of a long pocket inside his coat. 'Here, you're going to need this.'

He shoved the steel crowbar down Grant's trousers.

'Blast, bor, thass cold.'

'Quit complaining,' Masher said. 'I can hardly hand it over when we get to where we're going.'

Grant followed Masher out of the pub, and walked with a stiff leg along the partially lit streets at the edge of Jack's neighbourhood and on into the Neutral Territory. Rain spat at his face. Masher nodded at a yellow mid-terrace house with a passageway between it and the house on the right. Honeysuckle grew up a trellis on the front wall from a cracked terracotta pot.

'Most of the houses here have got lodgers in their basement, but this little old widow is all on her own. She'll be a pushover.' Masher straightened his tie and hat. 'I'll go round the front and keep her occupied while you go round the back.'

Grant nipped into the passageway and stopped to adjust the jemmy that was slipping down his trouser leg. He heard the doorbell chime, then a few moments later the sound of a latch clicking back, followed by Masher's voice.

'Evening, ma'am. I've been commissioned by *The Morning Post* to do a survey regarding people's opinions of the recent events in Central City. I wonder if I could have a moment of your time to ask a few questions.'

'Archie? Is that you?' an old mawther's voice replied. 'It is you. I know my dear nephew anywhere.'

'Er — yeah sure, Auntie.'

'I knew you'd be along sooner or later. You must come to dear Albert's birthday party. All the others have said they'll come, and you're the only one left now.'

'I'd love to come, Auntie. When is it?'

'Tonight, dear. You must come in for a nice hot buttered crumpet and a cup of tea. You always liked buttered crumpets with your tea.'

'Yeah, sure I do, Auntie.'

'Come along in, Archie, and wipe your feet.'

Grant went down the dark, narrow passageway and tried the gate. It was bolted. He hauled, scrambled and heaved himself over the fence and eventually tumbled into the garden, landing on the jemmy. He stifled a yell and rolled around on a clump of rhubarb. He could smell a compost heap nearby. Next time he'd go round the front, and Masher could do the climbing.

He saw a light, limped over and peered into the kitchen. Masher was sitting at the table. A small, elderly woman placed a cup and saucer in front of him. She wore steel-rimmed glasses and a black dress edged with lace. Masher glanced up and frowned at Grant, so he ducked out of sight and found some steps leading down to the basement. At the bottom there was a pile of damp, dead leaves. He slipped, regained his footing and prized open a sash. He crawled in and took out his torch.

He was in what appeared to be a disused kitchen, covered in cobwebs and mildew. There was a sickly stench in the air. The old mawther must still be using a generator. The city generators smelt even worse than the ones back home. Something tugged at his hair. He swung the torch round. It was only a strip of flypaper dangling from the ceiling, speckled with dead flies.

He opened a door into a passageway and tried a room on his right. It had a bath lined with a thin, pungent film. There was a stained wheelchair next to it. Nothing worth stealing here, just a load of junk.

He tried another door off the passageway, which opened on to a larger room filled with oddments: a three-legged chair, packing crates, an old tin trunk, but a clear path stretched from the door to the foot of a staircase. Multiple sets of thin twin tracks, discolouring the threadbare maroon carpet, led up to a stair lift. He sat in it and fingered the chunky switches, wondering if he might be able to try it out without attracting attention. He wriggled in the seat and, as he did so, the torch light jumped around the room. It picked up the tracks in the carpet. Those must be from that datty old wheelchair going between the stair lift and the bathroom. A second set of tracks veered away from the main route. Grant followed it with his torch across the floor until the beam of light reached a carved wooden table leg, then upwards until it touched the table top and something sparkled back at him. A silver fork.

Grant stepped down off the chair lift and raised the torch higher. The pool of light moved across the table top until it reached a wine glass, more silver cutlery, then a jacket, a tie, a whiskered face lolling to one side, a pair of eyes staring back at him, unblinking. He panned around the table. Another face, another pair of lifeless eyes. And another, and another. Some male, some female. All but one of the chairs were occupied. In front of each seat a place was laid. Even the empty seat had a place laid out, complete with a fancy, flowery name label that read 'Archie'.

The torch slipped from Grant's hand and went out. He bent down and fumbled around for it. His fingers touched a cylindrical object. He grasped it and felt the surface. The switch had been knocked into the off position. He turned it back on, but the light was fading. He flipped out the crank handle and wound it up as he limped across the room. The mechanism whirred and clicked. He staggered back the way he had come, heaved himself out at the jemmied sash, skidded on the wet leaves, ran up the steps to the ground-floor kitchen window and peered round. Masher was slumped across the table.

Jack finished his meal and leant back in his chair. Tempers had been restored, and the four of them had been upbeat throughout supper. Sam had settled down to sleep in her cot. It was good to be back home. He probably ought to see Rita, but there was no hurry. He took out a cheroot but, before he could reach for a match, Grant stumbled into the room.

'She killed him. She's ony a squinny old mawther but she now dun him in.'

Jack turned to Harry.

'What's he saying?'

'A skinny old woman has just killed someone, but I don't know who.'

'Masher,' Grant said. 'The boy Masher.'

'His friend Masher.'

'You're kidding,' Jack said.

'I'm not makin' it up. She dun him in time he was yalmin' down his taay and she's now a-dossin' him in the claggy bath.'

'Well, that's a rum ole dew,' Harry said.

'What is?' Jack said.

'Apparently she killed him while he was having some tea and now she's giving him a bath — a moist bath.'

'Dunt be a duzzy tewl. That was orl claggy and reasty.'

'Sorry,' Harry said, 'it's a sticky, rancid bath. Where did the mawther kill him, bor?'

'In the Neutral Territory.'

'Oh brilliant,' Jack said. 'Bloody marvellous. As though we haven't got enough things to worry about right now. I'd better call Ethan.'

Ethan soon arrived with some coppers. With Harry's help, they finally managed to ease out what had happened from Grant, and he was taken away. It was getting late by that time. Jack sighed and decided that he may as well find Rita. He called Eric, and they set out to the pub. She was at their usual table. One of her pet bruisers was lounging against a pillar behind her, flipping a coin. Rita pursed her lips and folded her arms when she saw Jack.

'Where have you been?'

'What?' Jack said. 'Haven't you been following the news? I've been stuck in the middle of rioting and blockades for a week.'

'You were back hours ago.'

'Give me a break.' Jack sat down and Eric took the next seat. 'D'you have any idea what the traffic was like?'

'Yeah, and you really missed me, didn't you? Couldn't wait to rush over here to see me.'

'Sure, I couldn't wait to get my ear chewed off with your concern over my well-being.' Jack leant close to her. 'You want to know what's kept me busy this evening?'

The thug by the pillar stopped his coin-tossing and turned to look at Jack. Eric stretched out his hands, fingers interlocked, and cracked his knuckles.

'Oh, I know what's been keeping you busy,' Rita said. 'Harry's been serving you up a nice, tasty dish.'

'You got a problem with me having a cook and a cleaner?'

'Oh she cleans, does she? I thought you were getting the other kid to do it now. Can't have Harry spoil her immaculate farmer's fingers with dirty work, can we?'

'Says who?' Jack said, taking out his cigar case.

'Grant.'

Jack flicked the case open and selected a cheroot.

'You want to talk about Grant? Sure, let's do that. Let's talk about what he and your little precious Ralph have been up to this evening.'

Rita slammed her glass on the table.

'Why don't you lay off him for a change?'

'I wasn't the one laying into him.' Jack leant back in his seat. 'That was someone else.'

'What are you on about?'

'He's dead.'

Rita's fingernails clawed into her palms.

'You think you can kid me?' she said.

The bruiser walked over to her side, his hand in his pocket. Eric slid his fingers into his jacket.

'I'm not kidding you,' Jack said. 'Ralph, or Masher as he liked being called, has just been done in by a serial killer he was pulling a line on. Ethan's lads have gone round to investigate so maybe you can ask them about it when they get back. Or d'you want to view the body?'

Rita dragged her fingertips down her cheek, smudging her makeup. The bruiser came up and leant his hand on the back of her chair. Eric stretched out his legs. His seat scraped backwards on the wooden floor.

'You never liked him, did you?' Rita said to Jack. 'Maybe he'd still be alive if you'd taken more care of him, instead of always putting him down.'

'Oh, sure. If only I'd warned him about the perils of preying on little old ladies.' Jack tapped his cheroot against the case. 'He should never have targeted her. I've always said no frails, and if he'd listened he'd still be alive.'

'He had more guts than the losers you pick up.'

Jack stood up. His chair toppled over. Two more of Rita's men joined the bruiser behind her.

'All he had was a mean streak,' Jack said. 'If he'd had guts he would've picked on people bigger than him.'

'At least he wasn't a neurotic retard who's too emotionally stunted to grow up.'

There was no sound of conversation in the pub, no pool balls clicking against each other, just a log crackling on the fire. Rita's make-up was running below her eyes, revealing wrinkles. Jack put the cheroot back in the case and snapped the lid shut.

'And you say I was always putting your little git down,' Jack said. 'You've never given Adam a break.'

'You wasted a favour on him. You had a big fat favour that Stan owed you and you blew it on a nobody. But that's not enough for you, is it? Now you've picked up another nobody. And this one's got you twisted around her little finger.'

Jack tucked the case into his pocket and leant on the table, bending down close to her.

'No one's twisting me. You lay off Harry. She's Adam's girl.'

'Oh sure, she's Adam's girl. That the way you really want it? D'you think I don't know you?'

Jack slammed his fist on the table top.

'We are not having this conversation.'

He swung round. People moved aside as he strode out of the pub. Eric followed on close behind.

'I'm going to stop by to see Ethan,' Jack said to Eric as they turned a corner. 'You head off back home.'

'It's all right. I'll come with you.'

'Sure,' Jack said and smiled. 'I forgot Annie's on the front desk tonight.'

'Well, there is that but, you know, things have got a bit out of whack lately.'

'You think I need a bodyguard?'

'There's no harm in a bit of company.'

'Take a look at this letter Cornell got back from Fenning.'

Ethan handed an envelope over. Jack took it and settled down in the leather chair in Ethan's office. He had left Eric downstairs at the front desk with Annie. The windows looked out on to the dark night, only faintly illuminated by the lamp outside the police station. Jack slipped the letter out, unfolded it and began to read.

> Regarding your recent enquiries about Miguel Alberto del Rosario, I'm surprised Central City haven't informed you that he was wilfully murdered last year on the 28th of June by a person or

persons unknown with a Thompson sub-machine gun. Commissioner Quinn believes it to be the work of Jack Preston from Norwich, but he hasn't provided us with supporting evidence.

'Yeah, that was a real big surprise,' Jack said.

'Nice of her to point out there's no evidence. See the photo in the envelope?'

Jack looked inside it and shook out the photo. It was a snap of Cornell and van Loame in their car. He returned to the letter.

Interestingly, you're not the only person to make enquiries about the late del Rosario over the past few weeks. There have been a couple of armed men posing as historians staying at Great Bartling who have been asking about him. One of them has a canary tattooed on his right wrist. Enclosed a photograph of the two men.

'Nice undercover work from your boys,' Jack said.

'Yeah, well, it wasn't originally meant to be a stakeout, but there's more. Hadley and Fenning decided to check up on them at Colingham University. They drew a blank — unsurprisingly — but they met some fellow called Allerton who looked real rattled when he saw that photo, but denied knowing them.'

'Yeah?' Jack studied the snapshot. 'Do Cornell and van Loame know anything about him?'

'All they've heard is that there's a prominent beet farmer called Allerton who used to live in Central City, but they've not set eyes on him, but I'm wondering if that's why Quinn figured they were in Colingham.'

'Which means that Allerton's a buddy of Quinn's,' Jack said. 'And Harry's got a beef with some beet farmer who used to live in the city.'

'There's more.' Ethan went over to the door and glanced out of it. He then perched on the front of his desk near Jack. 'Miguel was living in a rented cottage owned by the Coulgrane family. He was shot while all the locals were at the funeral of the twelfth Earl of Wynherne, so there were no witnesses. According to Quinn's buddy Allerton, the earl went to Central City to investigate Miguel's background but met his death accidentally falling on a set of four-foot-long spikes.'

'Accidentally?'

'Guess who the coroner was. Perry, who would rule accidental death on a stiff found in a cement overcoat if it suited Quinn.' Ethan tapped the letter in Jack's hand. 'Reading between the lines, Hadley and Fenning think the earl was actually investigating Allerton because Miguel had recognised him.'

Jack sat up and stared at the letter.

'No way,' he said.

'No way? How d'you figure it?'

'No,' Jack said. 'I mean the earl. That's Harry's uncle. She said he was killed on account of something Miguel told him. You got a copy of that poster about Lady Coulgrane?'

'Yeah.' Ethan went over to one of the grey filing cabinets behind his desk and flicked through the folders. 'Here it is.'

He spread it out on the desk.

'Sure, that's Harry all right. How come I never saw that before? She's a pretty thing when she's dressed up, isn't she?'

'She must've been wearing liquid skin when it was taken,' Ethan said. 'Reckon Quinn knows?'

'I don't know. I can't see Quinn using up his resources in Great Bartling if he did, but someone spotted her in Central City. I'll have to make sure there's always someone watching over her while we're there. I can't leave it to Adam. He's got Sammy to look after.'

'Reckon he knows who she is?'

Jack thought for a few moments and remembered the expression on Adam's face when he had first seen the poster.

'Yeah, I've a feeling he does.'

Jack returned to the letter and skimmed through it to the final paragraph.

> I hope this satisfies your enquiries about Miguel Alberto del Rosario. I wonder if I could now ask you for assistance in return. Although we are no longer in the Norfolk Constabulary, the blockades around Central City are causing us an inconvenience. Would it be possible for one of your pathologists to examine a canister we found concealed in Lady Coulgrane's bedroom, which appears to cause dizziness and nausea? We also have a blood sample taken from the thirteenth Earl of Wynherne who died suddenly after convulsions. Central City have already examined another sample from him and found nothing, but it's always useful to have a second opinion.

Jack smiled. Hadley and Fenning were smart enough not to trust Quinn's people.

'Has Cornell answered Fenning?' Jack said.

'Not yet. I was thinking it might be an idea to send him and van Loame back out there and pick the stuff up in person, rather than trusting the usual channels. If we can pin accessory to murder on Quinn, we stand a fighting chance. By the way, what do you want done with Grant?'

'Whatever you like,' Jack said. 'He's a selfish, ungrateful, ill-mannered piece of work.'

'He's pretty shaken up, and he's just a kid. Everyone needs a second chance.'

'I'm not taking him back. He's filthy and he passes on everything to Rita.'

'I wasn't suggesting that.' Ethan put the poster back in the filing cabinet. 'Maybe social services can straighten him out.'

'He's a lost cause.' Jack folded the letter up and tucked it back into the envelope with the photo. 'It's your call, but just keep him out of my way.'

— 21 —

NIGHT TIME IN COLINGHAM

Colingham's electricity was generated at a nearby power plant fuelled by chicken droppings, so the town had street lights that were still lit at two o'clock in the morning. Hadley stopped at a junction and waited for the signal to change. Even the cinema still had lights on outside, illuminating the film posters, despite having closed for the night. Fenning, in the passenger seat next to him, twisted round and stared into the darkness. Hadley looked to see what had attracted her attention. There was movement in a dark alcove at the far end of the cinema. He gripped the steering wheel. A car turned into their street and the headlamps illuminated a young couple. Fenning sank back in her seat.

'They're a-gorta catch their death o' cold,' she said.

Hadley relaxed his grip. The traffic lights turned green, and he pulled on to the high street. The shops were all closed up for the night. The buildings were mostly brick and flint with pantiled roofs, but as Hadley drew closer to the private hospital, he passed newer houses with flat concrete tiles that fitted in as well as an urbanite in a troshin' barn. He turned into a side street round the back of the hospital. There were fewer street lights here than in the town centre. He parked in a dark spot beyond the reach of the two closest lamp posts.

Fenning reached behind her seat and grabbed a rucksack. Hadley checked there was no one in sight, and they set out on foot until they reached the rear of the private hospital. They were each wearing a dark hat and worsted suit with a black leather pair of gloves, which helped them to blend into the night. Fenning took out a coil of rope with a grappling hook and some rush matting from the bag.

The wall around the premises was ten feet high with cast iron spikes at intervals along the top. Hadley threw up the rope while Fenning kept watch. It missed and fell back down with a clatter. On the second attempt, the hook caught on a spike. Fenning rolled up the matting, tucked it through her braces and began to climb the wall. Once she reached the top, she hung on to the rope with one hand. With the other, she tugged the matting free and laid it on top of the spikes. She pulled herself up, balanced on the matting, checked all directions and gestured to Hadley. He slung the rucksack over his shoulders, climbed and turned the rope so that it hung down the other side of the wall. They lowered themselves into the hospital grounds, first Fenning then Hadley.

It was darker on that side of the wall. The occasional cloud drifted across the moon. The grounds mostly consisted of lawns and flower beds with a few trees. The main building lay up ahead, but only two windows showed any light. Hadley looked around, trying to fix the details in his mind to better locate the rope on their return. There was a tree nearby with a twisted branch — possibly a plum — and in front of it was the dark shape of a bench. The sound of a car engine grew loud. The top of the wall was illuminated, then returned to darkness. The noise of the vehicle faded into the distance.

Hadley crept along the grass bordering a gravel path with Fenning following on behind. To his left was a deep shrubbery around an old chestnut tree. There was a rustling sound amongst the plants followed by a high-pitched scream. He dropped down behind a statue and froze. He had lived long enough in the country to identify a fox shriek, but would the security guards recognise it as such? Fenning was by his side, so close that her breath warmed his cold cheek. They remained motionless for a few minutes, but there was no sign of alarm.

He looked around and made out the outline of the bird bath he'd seen from Miss Penderbury's window. He jumped over the gravel path, landed on the grass on the other side and ran over to the bird bath. He crouched low next to it, and Fenning dropped beside him.

They made a dash to the window straight ahead of them, and Hadley unslung the rucksack. He took out his knife, inserted it between the upper and lower sashes and slipped the catch. He eased up the lower sash. The pulley rumbled. The counterweight thudded inside the box frame. He sat on the sill. The room was dark and silent. He swung his legs round and ducked under the sashes. Fenning handed him a torch and a camera but remained outside to keep watch.

Hadley switched on the torch and panned round the room. A face stared back at him with glossy eyes. It was one of the posters he'd seen on his previous visit. A thin strip of light showed under the door. He padded over and checked that it was locked. He eased open the top drawer of the filing cabinet. Each folder had a name tag, and he soon found the one labelled 'Coulgrane, Harriet'. He lifted it out and noticed that the one behind it was labelled 'Coulgrane, Isabella'. On an impulse, he removed it too and laid them both on the floor.

He first looked through the daughter's thin file. It was just as he remembered: cover letter, sheet with the scan image and Mr Trescothic's report.

Hadley opened the second, much thicker, file. He lifted out the picture of the mother's brain scan and laid it next to the daughter's. Both had a shadow at the front of the left hemisphere, the same size and shape. One sheet had 'Isabella Coulgrane' written in the top right hand corner. The other had 'Harriet Catherine Isabella Coulgrane'.

Next, he compared the letters confirming the diagnosis. They were both photocopies of a typewritten document. They were identical, except for the final digit in the date. The first had the year ending with a 1. The other had the year ending with a 9. Hadley peered closely at it. The 9 was smudged, like you get when two typewriter keys are accidentally struck together. Both letters were addressed to 'Lady Coulgrane'. Eight years ago Bella Coulgrane's husband was only a lord. She hadn't lived long enough to see him elevated to an earl. Two Lady Coulgranes with identical scan images and identical diagnoses.

Hadley rested the torch and camera on the ground, undid his coat, took his arms out of the sleeves and pulled the coat over his head so that it formed a tent. He picked up the camera, pulled the lever to advance the film and photographed the documents. First individually, then with the matching sheets side-by-side. The flash illuminated the lining of his coat.

There was a distant murmur of voices and the sound of footsteps down the corridor outside. Hadley slipped his coat back on, tidied the documents away and returned the folders to the drawer. The name tag had come off Isabella Coulgrane's folder. Hadley swept the torch beam around the floor. The footsteps outside were approaching. He found the tag, fitted it back into place, eased the drawer shut and switched off the torch. A shadow broke the strip of light under the door, then disappeared as the footsteps continued down the corridor.

He returned to the window, climbed out and dropped down next to Fenning. He handed her the torch and camera and pulled the lower sash down. He slipped his knife between the sashes and jiggled the catch back into place.

They retraced their steps to the bird bath, over the gravel path and back to the tree with the twisted branch. The moon came out from behind a cloud and cast its pale light on a dark line on the wall. Hadley went over and grabbed it, but it was just a dead vine. He searched to the right of it and Fenning to the left. She gave a soft, 'Here', little more than a breath.

Hadley came over to her. She held the rope in her hand and gave it a tug. He pressed his ear against the wall. There was no sound. The moon went back behind a cloud. He nudged her and she began to climb. He heard her foot slip. He reached out to her, but she had regained her balance. She pulled herself up and crouched on the matting. Hadley heaved himself up. His arm and leg muscles were starting to ache. He scrambled up beside her and looked around. A cat yowled. The cloud was moving away from the moon. He turned the rope over the wall and gestured to Fenning. She clambered down.

Hadley picked up the matting, but one corner was caught on a spike. He tugged it until it came free, then tossed it to Fenning and eased the grappling hook down, so that the rope was looped around one of the iron spikes. He climbed down holding both ends of the rope. He pulled the hook end and the free end of the rope slid clear of the spike.

The sound of an engine approached. The end of the road was illuminated by a full-beam. Hadley stuffed the rope and matting into the rucksack, grabbed Fenning, pushed her against the wall and pressed himself close to her, his hat tilted across his face. She put her arms around him and buried her face in his neck. The vehicle turned into the road. The light grew brighter and then faded as the car drove past them. Once it had gone, Hadley let go of Fenning, picked up the rucksack and they headed back to the car.

Hadley drove back towards the town centre and stopped at a set of traffic lights. Another car pulled up alongside them. The interior light came on, and Hadley saw the heavy bulk of D.I. Jarrett in the passenger seat and the pock-marked face of D.S. Regan behind the wheel. Jarrett opened the window and indicated to Hadley to do the same.

'Lo, Hadley. Thought I recognised your car. What're you doing in Colingham at this time of night?'

'We went to see a fillum at the cinema,' Fenning said. 'Thass a rare treat for us Bartling lot.'

'Yeah, what did you see?'

'*The Killers.*'

Jarrett chewed on some gum and grinned.

'Shame on you, Hadley. What would the Chief Inspector say if he heard you'd been making out with your sergeant?'

The amber light came on. Hadley put the car into gear.

'Looks like you've lost the bet, Regan.' Jarrett turned back to Hadley and pointed his thumb at his sergeant. 'Regan reckoned you were too strait-laced to misbehave.'

The lights changed to green.

'No, you're the one who's lost,' Hadley said. 'Best not hold up the traffic. See you around.'

He drove off. The other car pulled in behind and followed them until they had left the town.

— 22 —

Unravelling

Jack was doing up his tie when the doorbell rang. Harry had just taken a pile of dirty breakfast crockery out of the room, Adam was trying to put a cardigan on Sam, and Eric had gone out to collect the post, so Jack went to the door and showed Doc Fisher in. The pathologist rested his briefcase on the dining-room table, polished his glasses with a piece of cloth and flipped the catches on his case. Jack leant against a chair, his arms resting on the back and one foot on a rung, and watched Adam stuffing some spare nappies into Sam's travel bag. Harry came in with a sponge and started to wipe the table.

'Harry,' Jack said. 'Sit down and roll up your sleeve.'

Harry looked from Jack to Fisher, who was pulling on a pair of gloves. The rubber snapped against his wrist. She backed away.

'Why?'

'You were injected with unknown dope,' Jack said.

Her cheeks flushed, but she continued wiping the table.

'That was nearly two weeks ago,' she said. 'I feel fine, and I've had quite enough of doctors trying to inject me.'

'He just wants a blood sample. If it makes you feel better, he's a forensic pathologist, not some quack.'

Harry tossed the sponge on the table. It landed with a splat.

'I'm not sure it does make me feel better.'

'Why do we have to argue over everything?' Jack said. 'Quit complaining and do as you're told for once.'

Adam looked up as he tucked a toy into Sam's bag.

'It's just a precaution,' Fisher said as he took a glass vacuum tube out of his case. 'You may feel fine now, but that doesn't mean there isn't something in your bloodstream that might have a long-term effect.'

'Adam can hold your hand if you're scared,' Jack said.

'I'm not scared.'

'Then button it –' Jack pushed her on to a chair '– and pull up your sleeve.'

Harry leant back in the seat and folded her arms. Adam zipped up Sam's bag and glanced at his watch.

'It's for the best, Harry,' he said. 'They might've used a dirty needle.'

'What?'

Harry unfolded her arms. Her hands thudded against the table top.

'You sure have a way with words, my boy,' Jack said. 'Come on, Harry. It won't take long.'

She rolled up her sleeve. Fisher swabbed an area of her skin with antiseptic. Eric came into the room with the morning paper.

'Here look,' he said, unfolding it. 'Ralph's made it on to the front page.'

Jack took the newspaper from him. Beneath the headline 'Tea and Crumpet Serial Killer' was a black and white photo of a stained bathtub and wheelchair.

'Would you look at that,' Jack said. 'Something's finally shut them up about Sector House, the riots and the Anti-Techs. Maybe we can all get back to normal again.'

'Ow!' Harry said.

Dark red blood began to flow into the glass tube. Jack glanced further down the page. Ethan's lads must've managed to prevent the press from taking photos. There was a pencil drawing of a table surrounded by corpses in various stages of decomposition. The newspaper's artist sure had a vivid imagination.

'Well that's real nice,' Jack said. 'The old dear was just trying to prepare a dinner party for her late husband.'

'What are itinerant dwilemongers?' Eric asked.

'Hucksters. This reporter must get paid per syllable.'

'Half the victims have already been identified as known cons,' Fisher said. 'Little old widows are magnets for that sort.' He withdrew the needle from Harry's arm. 'All done.'

'Give her a sweet and a sticker saying, "I was a brave girl",' Jack said.

'How'd she manage to lure them down into the cellar?' Harry asked as she adjusted her sleeve.

'She didn't. She killed them in the kitchen, just like she did with Ralph, and used the stair lift.' Jack turned the page. There was a diagram complete with arrows and stick figures, one of which had a pair of crosses for the eyes. 'Would you look at that. It says here it's highly likely she'll be sectioned.'

'No kidding.' Fisher closed his case. 'I'll have the sample sent to the lab. Then I'd better get back to the tea and crumpet stiffs. See you around, Jack.'

He picked up his hat, but Harry jumped up and stood by his side. She wasn't much shorter than the little pathologist.

'You don't think there is anything wrong with me, do you?' she said.

'Jack likes thoroughness, that's all.'

Fisher put his hat on and left. Eric patted Harry on the head. Jack gestured him to stop. Eric's reassurances were more likely to result in a headache than peace of mind.

'Quit worrying, Harry,' Jack said. 'And, Adam, don't be so paranoid.'

Jack turned to look at him. Adam was checking his watch, but he pulled his sleeve down over it. Harry took the newspaper from Jack. There was a slight tremor in her hands that made the sheets rustle.

'Poor old dear,' she said. 'I think it was very wrong of Grant and Ralph to prey on a defenceless widow.'

'Not so defenceless in this case,' Jack said. 'But, like Fisher said, frails are soft targets. Remember Wakeham the widow killer a few years ago?'

'No. It may seem like forever, but I've only been in the city for a couple of months.'

'It was in all the news.' Jack snatched the paper back from her. 'You do have a radio and newspapers in the country, don't you?'

'Of course we do, but there always seem to be murders going on in the city. Why should I remember any of them in particular?'

'He used to hang out with Blond Jim,' Eric said. 'He knocked off all them widows in Central City.'

'He was a right smarmy git,' Jack said. 'Used to wear a ring with a big gem that made him look like a —' Jack broke off as he saw Adam glancing at his watch again. 'Come on, out with it, my lad. What's eating you?'

'Is it okay if me and Harry go out this morning?'

'Where to?'

'Church.'

'It's Saturday.'

'Harry would like to get Sam christened so we want to sort it out.'

'All right,' Jack said. 'But give us plenty of notice.'

'What for?'

'The christening, of course. You were going to invite us, weren't you?'

'Yeah, sure, of course I was,' Adam said. 'Sure, I was. Only it's out in the country.'

'So? There's enough room for all of us in your car, isn't there? Eric can go in the front, and Harry and I can squeeze in the back with Sam.'

Adam and Harry left the flat shortly afterwards with Sam. Jack flicked open his cigar case but snapped it shut again.

'What's he thinking of, not wanting to invite me?'

'Maybe he's worried Stan might get to hear about it,' Eric said.

'Like I'm going to tell Stan. You know the way he goes on. He thinks he owns anyone who arrives from sector fifty-three, and it's likely he'll have the same attitude towards Catholics, just because his family go to church and he's got their cathedral in his neighbourhood. Harry's one of mine, and I won't have anyone filching any of my people. Adam should know better than that.'

※

'Slow down, Adam.'

'Yeah, it's all right. I've seen it.'

It wasn't like it was easy to miss. A tractor and its trailer were straddled across the lane by the turn into the village of Weston Snelding.

'Keep your hands in sight and don't look threatening,' Harry said.

'What? It's just a tractor stuck in the road.'

'No, it's not. I think they've reactivated the trap.'

A man in muddy oil-stained overalls lounged against the tractor cowling, his right hand hidden behind the radiator. Shadows moved behind the hedgerow. Another man with a lumpy weather-beaten face peered round from behind the trailer. His right hand was also out of sight. Adam knew that look. He glanced in the rear-view mirror. There was no one behind them, but the road was too narrow to turn in.

'What's going on? What trap?'

'That uneven section of road,' Harry said. 'It's like the ones we've got all around our farm back home. Haven't you noticed it clatter whenever we've driven over it? This is an ambush point. With luck they'll let us through, although we may need to wait for a runner to be sent to Father Bernard to confirm we have an appointment with him.'

'What?' The car was slowing. The revs dropped. The engine began to judder, sending vibrations up through his feet. 'I need to change gear or we'll stall.'

'Just don't look like you're reaching for a weapon.'

Adam depressed the clutch, moved his hand over to the gear stick and changed into first. He stopped the car a few yards from the tractor and rested his hands on the top of the steering wheel. On either side of the lane, the hedgerow reached up at least six feet in height. Sam gurgled from her seat in the back.

'How come you never told me about the trap before?'

'I assumed it was deactivated. I have a feeling they might have reactivated it when they heard about the rioting.'

The man with the lumpy face edged round from behind the trailer, still keeping his right hand out of view. What kind of weapon was he concealing? His shoulder was hanging low, as though he was holding something big. A shotgun? That would take a few seconds longer to draw than a pistol. But what help was that? The fellow's face looked like it had seen plenty of fights. Adam glanced out of his side window and saw the dark twin caverns of a double-barrelled muzzle peeking through the hedgerow, aimed straight at him.

Sam wriggled against her restraint, kicking her legs. The man by the tractor consulted a notepad, looked at Adam's car and gestured to his companions. The tractor's engine started up, and it was driven into the field, its chunky wheels throwing up clods on to the lane. The man waved Adam on.

'Reckon it's safe?' Adam said to Harry.

'Yes. I think someone from the church must've made a note of your numberplate.'

Adam nodded to the man and inched the car forwards in first gear. There was movement in the undergrowth on the verge. A pheasant tumbled out and dashed across the lane. Adam braked, then breathed out and put his foot back on the accelerator. In front was the metre-wide strip of road that was a shade darker than the surrounding tarmac. In his rear-view mirror he could see Sam's hand reaching out to her activity bar.

'What kind of a trap is it?'

'The ones back home opened on to a spiked pit. That's how my Uncle Barney was killed. Someone reactivated one of them.'

Oh great. He had to ask, didn't he? The palms of his hands were moist. He drove past the rear of the trailer and glimpsed into the field. There were two wooden contraptions like giant catapults. A man stood between them, staring back at Adam. The familiar clatter sounded under the Phaeton's wheels. The car passed the blockade point. In his mirror Adam saw the tractor reversing its trailer back on to the lane.

'I don't suppose there's another way out of the village,' Adam said.

'If there is, it won't be any different. We're better off going back out our usual route or it will look odd.'

'What are the things in the field?'

'Trebuchets. They're not very accurate, but if they fall short they'll block your progress and if they overshoot they'll block your retreat.'

How was he going to explain this to Jack? Oh, by the way, Jack. You know how we're all going to Sammy's christening? Well, we're going to have a load of guns and catapults pointing at us in a tight spot. You won't mind, will you? They won't harm us, honest.

'There you are, tergether,' Father Bernard said. 'I'm glad to see you. How are you farin'? Thass a rum ole dew, hintut? Do you come on trew. I'm now a-gorn to get the skep with the shruff for the fire from the yard. Are you hungry? There's some cake on the rally.'

Adam sat down with Harry and Sam in the sitting room. Through the window he could see the last bean pods of the season swaying in the breeze. The brass carriage clock ticked on the mantelpiece. The beard on the cricketing bloke in the old sepia print on the wall looked even bushier than Adam remembered. A figure wearing a wide-brimmed black hat passed the lattice of bean poles outside. Soon after Father Bernard came into the room with a basket of kindling. He removed his hat, stoked up the fire and fetched a plate with little cakes on it from a shelf built into the wall.

'Made by Mrs Harper,' Father Bernard said. 'My heart, she shruk when she heard you were stuck in Central City with orl that dewun. There was a scalder of them soon knockin' at the door skrowgin' round askin' how you wuz farin'.'

A gunshot sounded in the distance followed by a hubbub of rooks squawking and a multitude of wings flapping. Adam nearly dropped his cake. What was he doing jumping at gunfire? He was a gangster. Jack's lad. He could handle a tommy gun. The old spaniel wandered into the room and settled down on the hearthrug.

'I'm glad we were let into the village,' Adam said. 'We weren't expecting to find it blockaded.'

'Yis, bor. They orl git wound up and went for a meetin' in the plain. They put the block athwart the rud but the Major gan them yar licence number.'

The cake was starting to crumble in Adam's hands. He picked a raisin off the top. The dog looked up at him.

'We'd kinda like to invite a couple of our friends to Sam's christening. Would they be allowed in?'

'Do you jist give the Major thar names so he can add them to the list.'

A lump of Adam's cake fell on to the floor. The dog came over and wolfed it up. Oh great. Had anyone around here heard of Jack?

※

'We heard you were trapped inside the city by the riots,' Mrs Harper said. 'Was there really nuclear fallout and acid rain?'

It was Sunday morning and all the parishioners had gathered around Adam, Harry and Sam on the lawn outside the church after mass.

'My dear,' Mrs Widrow said, 'I've already told you, none of us would be alive now if a nuclear bomb had exploded.' She turned back to Adam and Harry. 'We all prayed for you. I'm so relieved to see you safe.'

Adam looked around the assembled people. The Major, leaning on a shooting stick, nodded at him. Had the priest mentioned to him about Adam bringing guests to Sammy's christening? How should he bring up the subject?

'We were all sure the anarchy would return.' Mrs Harper grabbed Harry's hand. 'You must leave the city. We can't bear to think of you living in that awful place.'

Two kids — what were their names? Billy and Irene? — were running around the lawn shooting each other with imaginary guns.

'It ain't that easy to leave,' Adam said.

'Do you mean you're not allowed to?' Mrs Harper said. 'Are you trapped there by some awful gangster boss?'

'No. I just mean we ain't got no jobs here or a place to stay. That's all.'

Okay, so he'd better not mention that Jack was his boss. He could just say how Jack had kind of adopted him. They'd go for that, wouldn't they?

'Oh, we can sort something out.' Mrs Harper turned to Major Widrow. 'You have an empty cottage to rent, don't you? And there's that place by the cricket pitch.' She turned back to Adam and tapped his arm. 'We'll keep you safe from those mobsters. They'll never find you here.'

'Quite right,' Major Widrow said. 'You're a mechanic, aren't you? I'll talk to Felton to see if he can take you on.'

'Mr Felton own the garage near the cricket pitch,' Father Bernard said. 'He's a masterous spin bowler.'

'He's with the Saint Peter's lot at the other end of the village. Decent folk. Their vicar's our prop forward.'

Adam looked at the people standing around him and then at Harry and Sam. The thatched cottage and the garage down the road stood clearly in his mind. He was strolling along the lane after spending all day working on engines and generators, going through the gate (the garden no longer overgrown but well-cared for) and into the house. There was Harry, smiling at him. Now he was sweeping her into his arms and kissing her.

Billy charged past with Irene in pursuit, the girl imitating the sound of a stuttering sub-machine gun. The boy ducked behind a tree and pretended to shoot back.

The image of the cottage dissolved and was replaced by a memory. Adam was sixteen, homeless and facing a murder rap. He'd finally escaped his mother, but then that man had tried to shove him around. Well, he wasn't going to put up with being the underdog any more. Now he was going to hit back, and he did, only he had his tools with him and he'd picked up his wrench. And he'd got nicked by a lousy, dirty, bent copper. But then Jack had come along. Maybe Jack had been impressed that Adam had managed to kill a man so much bigger than himself or perhaps it was a reward for getting rid of a man who was beginning to be a nuisance, but whatever the reason, Jack had sorted things and taken him in. For the first time in his life there was someone who cared about him, someone who was willing to protect him. Someone who called him 'good lad' or 'my dear boy'.

'Don't worry, my boy,' Major Widrow said. 'You'll be quite safe here. As soon as we heard about the riots, we re-enacted the village defence plan. No pressure. Think it over if you like.'

The traffic around Central City was better on Monday with only a few delays, and by the time Jack returned there on Thursday evening most of the streets had been cleared. He put his luggage in his room, checked up on Betsy and found the others in the dining room. He took the seat next to Adam. The room was full of truckers. Everything seemed back to normal. There had been no further protests, but Jack had kept men watching the boundaries of his territory. Reports had reached him that Quinn's people were closing ranks. Maybe Quinn was just mad at Jack for clearing the road blocks. Jack glanced at the window and saw Donnaghan's reflection approaching his back. He cut a piece of steak.

'You taken up residence here, Donnaghan?'

'There's a couple of coppers on their way to do an ID check.'

'What for? Aren't there any crimes to solve?'

Jack ate the piece of steak.

'Seems they think someone might have dodgy papers here. I was just wondering if I should take Harry round the back.'

'You ain't taking her nowhere,' Adam said, jumping to his feet.

Jack held Adam's arm.

'It's all right, my boy. I'll deal with this.'

Jack turned round and saw two coppers squeezing their way between rows of tables. Some of the truckers leant back in their seats or made a show of stretching their arms, causing obstructions to the policemen's route. What was Quinn trying to pull? Or maybe it wasn't Quinn behind this.

'I'm quite happy for them to look at my ID,' Harry said. 'I brought my birth certificate with me and got registered at City Hall.'

'Let me see,' Jack said. She handed over her papers. 'Mrs Trent? You're full of surprises.'

'We got married when we went out while we were stuck here,' Adam said.

'You're getting a bit secretive, my boy. Any particular reason why you didn't think to mention it?'

'Yeah,' Eric said. 'You could've invited us.'

'We stood in a queue at City Hall,' Adam said. 'Where's the fun in that?'

'We could've had a party.'

'How come you haven't got Harry a wedding ring?' Jack asked.

Adam shrugged.

'Ain't got round to it.'

'What kind of an excuse is that? Go round to Gordon's and tell him I sent you. It won't break the bank for a plain band of gold. And get yourself one at the same time.'

Jack turned his attention back to the approaching coppers and recognised them. They'd been in Ethan's constabulary until he'd taken their badges, but Rita had pulled a few strings for them and they'd got a transfer to Central City. The policemen were showing no interest in the ID of any of the truckers they passed, but they were looking straight at Harry. One of them tripped over Alf's chair legs. The other one managed to avoid the obstacle. They came over to Jack's table and stood next to Harry.

'ID check.'

Harry handed hers over. They took their time looking over it.

'Tell Rita that Harry had the sense to bring her birth certificate with her,' Jack said.

'It's just a random check.'

'Sure it is,' he said. 'It was real random the way you selected Harry. Beat it. And you can clear off as well, Donnaghan.'

'I was just trying to help,' Donnaghan said as the other coppers made their way back around the truckers.

'You saying I can't handle a couple of mugs like that?' Jack said.

Donnaghan picked at his stubbly moustache, looked at Harry and then walked away.

'Rita oughtn't to have gone behind your back like that,' Eric said.

'How d'you know it was Rita?' Harry said.

'Harry, my girl,' Jack said, leaning close to her. 'In case you hadn't noticed, you and Rita aren't exactly the best of friends. She must've thought she'd land you in hot water, thinking you had dodgy papers.'

'But I haven't seen her in ages. Why now?'

'She's lashing out on account of losing her little pet to a mad old biddy.' Jack patted Harry's hand. 'Don't worry, my girl. You're Adam's wife now and that gives you extra protection.'

Cornell reached up for the next rung. The wooden ladder creaked beneath him. The wind whipped his jacket about. If only it would blow in the other direction. At least then the wall in front of him would've given him some protection.

How old was this ladder? Had it been replaced since the anarchy? He glanced down. Fifteen feet below him stood van Loame with Hadley, Fenning and Amos. Fenning waved up at him.

If only she hadn't gone on about how she and Hadley had scaled that hospital wall in Colingham, then maybe Cornell would've kept his trap shut and he would've let van Loame volunteer to climb up the rickety, swaying ladder. He looked upwards and saw a young, weather-beaten face grinning back down at him.

'You orl right, bor?' Joe said.

'Sure, I am,' Cornell said. 'No sweat.'

Which wasn't exactly true. His shirt was sticking to his back. He grabbed another rung. The platform he was heading for was supported by a lattice of wooden props. The wind whistled through them. Lichen covered the post closest to Cornell. Whose crazy idea had it been for one of the Norwich cops to climb the tower on the off-chance they might be able to ID Quinn's buddy Allerton? Oh yeah, that would be Hadley.

Cornell pulled himself up on to this Fenland crow's nest, sat down on its floor and massaged his hands. It was around six feet square with four posts at each corner supporting a shallow roof. Three of the sides had five-foot-high partitions to afford the lookout some protection. The remaining side that faced the interior of the Wynherne Estate was open.

Joe unslung his binoculars and handed them to Cornell.

'The butler's in the garden, shootin'.'

'Shooting what?' Cornell said.

'Cans.'

Cornell staggered to his feet and grabbed a post in what he hoped would look a nonchalant manner. He trained the binoculars in the direction Joe indicated. On the lawn by the side of the painted mansion, he could see the back of a blond head.

'Where's the butler? All I can see is some blond kid.'

'Thass the butler,' Joe said.

Okay, so Fenning had said that Allerton's butler was a creepy fellow, but this wasn't quite the image that had come to Cornell's mind.

'I thought butlers were supposed to be all middle-aged and solemn.' He watched the young man on the lawn shoot the last can off a low wall and then walk over to the wall to replace the targets. The blond man turned and Cornell saw his face. 'That ain't no butler. That's Blond Jim.'

He turned the binoculars towards the house. There was a figure in one of the crenellation-topped bay windows looking out across the lawn. Cornell adjusted the focus. The wind was picking up, whistling through the gaps in the tower roof.

'Well? Did yer see him?' Fenning said.

'Let him get his breath back,' van Loame said.

'I've got my breath fine enough,' Cornell said, wiping his palms with his handkerchief. He turned to Hadley and Fenning. 'How come you don't recognise him?'

'You know Allerton?' Hadley said.

'That's Wakeham the widow killer.'

Van Loame whistled, but the sound was muffled by the wind shrieking through the tower struts.

'We've got Quinn by the short and curlies,' he said.

'I've never heard o' him,' Fenning said.

'You must've done. It was all over the radio.'

'When?'

'It must've been about seven or eight years ago.' Cornell turned to van Loame. 'You remember the date?'

'Eight years ago. Sometime in the summer.' Van Loame clamped his hand over his hat and moved closer to the wall, away from the wind. 'Yeah, it was July. A couple of months before Hammer Harmer bit the dust.'

'That musta been when the rogers hampered the radio mast,' Amos said.

'Who are the Rogers?' van Loame asked. 'They more of Quinn's buddies?'

'No, not Roger as in a person,' Hadley said. 'The rogers are the little whirlwinds we get across the marshes.'

'There wuz a great lot onem eight years ago,' Amos said. 'They caused a sight o' damage.'

'Must be why Wakeham picked this spot,' Cornell said. He turned to Hadley. 'Didn't you get the wanted bulletin in the post?'

'They usually get sent to Colingham, and they're supposed to forward copies throughout the district. Seems like it must've slipped their mind on that occasion.'

'So what happened about the widows, then?' Fenning asked as she turned up her coat collar.

'Wakeham liked high-society,' van Loame said, 'same as Quinn, and was quite a darling for a while until people began to notice he had a habit of inheriting money from rich widows, and they all happened to die exactly the same way. Quinn's buddy Perry wrote them all off as anaphylactic shock following a wasp sting.'

'That's how the thirteenth earl died,' Hadley said. 'So what happened to Wakeham?'

'People started riding Quinn about it. Quinn had to pull Wakeham in to save face, but I reckon Wakeham had something on Quinn. His men looked the other way while Wakeham escaped.'

'Wunt there an investigation?' Fenning said.

A loose curl flicked against her face. She turned her back to the wind.

'There was a lot of talk about one,' van Loame said, 'but then the whole business with Slim Hamilton distracted everyone.'

'Who's he?'

'A real nasty piece of work,' Cornell said, shading his eyes from the swirling dust and dead leaves. 'Six years ago we learnt that some missing folk in Central City were ending up on his dinner plate.'

'My heart,' Fenning said. 'He wuz a cannibal?'

'Some people turned to it during the anarchy,' van Loame said. 'Things got pretty wild back then. Jack Preston has a particular hatred of cannibals on account of them killing his family. He got tough and cleared Norwich of the bastards — that's how he got to be so prominent — but it seems some in Central City got the taste for it and didn't want to give up after law and order returned.'

'So you can imagine how Jack reacted when he found out about Slim,' Cornell said. 'He went completely nuts. He tried to get Quinn to help him bring down Slim, but Quinn just gave a wave of his hand and said that if Jack wanted to fight Slim, Quinn would look the other way, like it was just a little quarrel between Jack and Slim about nothing.'

'Even though Quinn knew what that stingy, push-arsed, reasty-stommicked dwainy-headed wagabond wuz a-dewun?' Fenning said.

'Slim had got too big. Jack lost a lot of men taking him out.' Cornell glanced up as the tower struts creaked. 'Once Slim was dead some of his men went over to Jack, but there were others Jack wouldn't take, even if they wanted to switch sides, so Jack left them to Quinn's men. And Quinn took the credit for the whole thing.'

'It got a lot of press coverage,' van Loame said, 'and the public forgot about Wakeham.'

'I wonder why Belrosa dint rackonise him,' Fenning said.

'Didn't she say she'd never met Allerton?' Hadley said.

Cornell looked from Fenning to Hadley.

'Belrosa? You don't mean the nightclub singer, do you?'

'Oh.' Fenning's cheeks reddened. 'Do you know har?'

'She never moved here, did she?' Cornell said. 'Who would've figured it?' He nudged van Loame. 'Next time someone skips town, we ought to have a look here.' Cornell tightened his trench coat belt and drew his lapels together. 'She walked out on her husband who was also her manager. She liberated him of some the wages she felt she was owed. He's in with Quinn. Don't worry. We ain't interested in her, we're just after Wakeham.'

'We kin arrest him if he's wanted,' Fenning said.

'Not without riot gear and a handful stutter guns. You're gonna need help on this one.'

Jack returned home to the flat on Friday evening with Adam, Eric, Harry and Sam, and after supper he went with Eric to the pub. Stan was there at the usual table. Droplets of sweat glistened on his temples. There was a new face amongst Stan's men: a red-headed lad who couldn't be more than eighteen. Jack sat on the bench along the wall by the window and stretched out his legs. Rita was at one end of the table in the seat next to Stan, but she gave no acknowledgement of Jack's arrival. The log fire spat and crackled nearby. Donnaghan was lurking around by the bar.

'How's things, Stan?' Jack said.

Stan drank his stout and placed his glass on the table.

'Not so bad.' He pointed to the redhead. 'You met me nephew Alroy?'

'Can't say that I have.'

'He's visiting from Central City.'

'You hit badly by the riots?' Jack said to the newcomer.

'Ma spent the whole time on her knees in the church.'

'You've met his ma, Jack,' Stan said, opening a packet of pork scratchings. 'She was at me niece's wedding.'

'Which one? You've got so many nieces, nephews and cousins that I lose track.'

'The one who married in May last year.'

'Yeah, sure I remember. So Alroy's her brother, is he?'

'No, he's her cousin.'

Alroy was staring at Jack like a witness at an identity parade. Jack waved to the barmaid.

'You're going to have to draw me a diagram one of these days, Stan.'

'And you, Jack, how did you cope with the rioting?'

'We missed the worst of it. We were trapped by the blockades, but I'm sure you don't want to hear about that all over again.'

The pub was getting to be like the side of a grave. Lots of people silently looking at the ground.

'Alroy tells me his ma saw you at mass, so I started wondering: what was me old friend Jack doing in church?'

Jack struck a match with his thumbnail, lit his cheroot and leant back.

'Harry's a Catholic. We had nothing better to do so we decided we may as well go along too.'

Alroy leant forward and helped himself to a pork scratching from the bag. A moist palm print marked the place where his hand had been resting on the table top.

'I've not seen her at mass,' Stan said. 'At least, I've not seen anyone matching her description. Rita tells me she's rather distinctive.'

'Maybe Jack can give you a better description,' Rita said and drained her glass. She put it down with a thud. It clinked against the other empties. 'A real thorough description.' The barmaid brought over Jack and Eric's drinks. 'Hey, you. Get me another one.'

'I gather Harry usually goes to church in the country,' Jack said to Stan. 'Adam drives her out there.'

'A real hard man, ain't he?' Rita said.

'Does Harry have something against our fine cathedral?' Stan said to Jack.

'Of course not, but I'm sure Adam wouldn't want to trespass on your territory without an invitation.'

'All he has to do is ask.'

The barmaid brought Rita another absinthe. Jack blew out a stream of smoke and took a sip of beer.

'Harry's from the country,' he said to Stan. 'Why the surprise that she feels more comfortable in a rural church? It's no slight against you or your people.'

'Yeah right,' Rita said. 'She never likes to slight people, does she?'

Stan turned and patted her hand.

'You're missing that poor boy, aren't you? He was a lively fellow. Shame you couldn't make his funeral, Jack.'

'We had to catch up on the week we'd lost from the blockades,' Jack said.

Rita threw back her drink.

'How come you never bring Harry here, Jack?' she said. 'She too grand for a pub? And now I see you're not even bringing Adam.'

'What's it to you if he wants to stay at home with his woman? I'm not one to begrudge him a bit of privacy.'

'There won't be much of that with a kid around.'

Alroy helped himself to another pork scratching.

'What's going to happen when the baby gets older?' Stan said. 'They can't take her around in a truck forever. Have you thought about that?'

'Sure I have. Adam can support the both of them. There are plenty of truckers with a wife and kids and they manage just fine.'

Jack leant back against the wall and took a drag on his cheroot. The landlord seemed to be devoting all his attention to wiping the bar counter. People glanced at Jack and Stan over the tops of their beer mugs. Stan's chair creaked beneath him. Alroy's teeth crunched on the pork scratchings.

'She should've had a proper church wedding,' Stan said. 'I'm surprised she considers queuing up in City Hall to be a valid marriage.'

'The important thing is that it's legitimate. The sleeping arrangements would've dictated a thing like that to a woman like our Harry. She's all very proper and upright.'

'Uptight, more like,' Rita said.

'Doesn't it bother you they didn't consult you first?' Stan said. 'Isn't Adam like a son to you? I wouldn't have allowed one of mine to go behind my back like that.'

No one seemed interested in playing darts or pool in the pub tonight. Everyone was keeping in tightly knit groups according to their territory. The smoke from Jack's cheroot mingled with smoke from a damp log on the fire. The air was hot and muggy.

'What makes you think he didn't talk to me first?'

'Word gets around.'

'Doesn't it just? Well I think he did the right thing by her. She's family now, and that's all that matters.'

'But she's not really though, is she?' Stan said. 'None of them are.'

Eric's chair scraped against the floor. It sounded unnaturally loud in the quiet pub.

'It's not blood that makes a family,' Jack said.

Stan swept his hands out, gesturing at his relatives gathered around him.

'Blood and marriage bind us,' he said. 'You gain loyalty through favours. I don't need to do that. Sure, I reward them when they do well — what parent wouldn't — but I already have their fealty running through their veins. But you, Jack, what ties d'you have?'

'You can't take loyalty for granted.'

'And you can't buy it. Poor Jack, you must get very lonely. No wonder you always surround yourself with people in your cosy little flat.'

A draft of cold air blew through the pub as the front door opened. Smoke billowed back into the fireplace. There was movement amongst the crowd by the entrance.

'Not at all,' Jack said. 'I happen to be very sociable. It's you I feel sorry for, Stan, not being able to get away from such a large, demanding family.'

'Why would I want to get away from me relatives? They know I'm head of the family, and they wouldn't make a big decision without consulting me.' Stan leant forwards. The folds of fat on his neck sagged over his collar. Perspiration glistened in the creases. 'D'you want to know what I think? I think that if Harry ever got her farm back, with all its generators, she'd be gone, and she'd likely take Adam with her.'

'Adam wouldn't walk out on me.'

'I think he would if she tempted him with a nice little family home.'

'You talking out of your arse again, Stan?' Ethan said, emerging from the crowd with Cornell and van Loame behind him. 'Adam owes Jack way too much to ever fool around but, more than that, Jack was the first person to show him any kindness. A lad in his position never forgets a thing like that.'

'I see you've got your faithful bloodhounds back,' Stan said. 'We were beginning to think Cornell and van Loame had got lost down some country lane on their touring holiday.'

'No, we had a great time,' van Loame said, pulling up a chair. 'Didn't we, Cornell?'

'Sure we did.'

— 23 —

Evidence

Cornell stood next to van Loame in the lift. With Ethan, Jack and Eric there as well, there wasn't a whole lot of room to move. Rita had sure looked a state in the pub, blubbing over that nasty little piece of work. Now, Fenning, she was good on the eyes. Pretty and smart — the best combination. So Rita had tried to get her boys in Central City to haul Harry in? That was a lousy thing to do.

'Wasn't it a bit dangerous for Harry to get registered with Quinn after her?' Ethan said to Jack while he recounted what had happened.

'You came in the pub too late to hear,' Jack said. 'Adam and Harry got married on the quiet in Central City during the blockades. Donnaghan earwigged on our conversation and reported back to Stan.'

The lift juddered to a halt, and Ethan pulled the grille doors open. The top floor was dim. Only two bulbs were lit in the corridor. Light seeped out from under the door to the gents, but the other rooms were dark. The lift began to clank as it responded to a summons from a lower floor. Ethan unlocked his office and flicked on the light switch, but

Cornell went on past to his and van Loame's office next door and fetched from his safe the file Hadley had given him. He brought it round and perched on the corner of Ethan's desk, pulling out some photos.

'First up, you'll be glad to hear Lady Coulgrane doesn't have a brain tumour,' Cornell said. 'Secondly, Allerton is Quinn's buddy, Wakeham the widow-killer.'

'Seriously?' Jack clicked open his cigar case. 'Talk about jackpot. Is there enough to hang them both?'

Cornell handed him the photos.

'Hadley took these pictures from the medical notes in Trescothic's office. That's Harry's brain specialist in Colingham. He was killed in a car crash the same day Harry's dad died. Trescothic's P.A., Miss Penderbury, had only recently started work for him and has since been seen cavorting with Wakeham. The old P.A. was a woman called Jane Lamm, who was offered a job in Central City but didn't live to tell the tale.'

'No wonder Quinn was so touchy about her,' Jack said. 'And there I was thinking it was on account of Donnaghan's bad habits.'

He attempted to strike a match but it broke in his hand.

'One of these days Donnaghan's going to take a one-way trip to the bottom of a peat bog,' Cornell said. 'Anyway, it seems Wakeham or Penderbury fiddled the notes. Harry's mother, who happened to be Lady Coulgrane at the time, was the one who had the brain tumour. Look, here's the mother's scan –' he placed it on the desk and pointed to the shadow on the left hemisphere '– and here's the daughter's scan.' He put that one alongside it and tapped the identical shadow. 'Take a look at the names.'

He indicated the right hand corners of the scans and the addressee on the letters from the specialist. In the distance the lift clanked and rattled.

'Here,' Eric said, 'how come both Harry and her mum are Lady Coulgrane? That don't make no sense to me.'

'Nix,' Cornell said. 'They didn't both have the title at the same time. A lord's wife is a lady. Harry's dad used to be a lord. Then he gets to be an earl, and an earl's daughter is a lady. Harry's mum would've become a countess, or something, only she was dead by then. That's what Hadley told us, anyway.'

'It sounds a bit nuts to me.'

'Anyhow,' van Loame said, 'Hadley and Fenning reckon that after Barney Coulgrane died, Wakeham decided to take advantage of the situation to muscle in on the Wynherne Estate. Only he didn't take Harry into consideration, so he had to find some way to put her out of the picture — with a bit of help from Quinn and his stooges in Colingham.'

'Quinn would back a louse like Wakeham,' Jack said. 'Just think how he was with Slim.'

He slammed a fist on to the desk. Cornell caught the picture of Ethan's wife and kids as it juddered across the surface of the desk. He put it back but glimpsed a shadow moving in the corner of the pebbled glass on the door.

'How d'you want to play it, Jack?' Ethan said.

'Harry usually goes shopping on Saturday mornings. I'll see if I can collar Adam while she's out. If I tell him what we know, he might loosen up and give us more info.'

Cornell eased himself over to the door, keeping watch for the shadow. He flung open the door, grabbed Donnaghan and hurled him into a chair.

'Eavesdropping again, Donnaghan?'

'No, I wasn't.' Donaghan shifted in the seat. 'Why would I want to eavesdrop?' He picked at his stubbly moustache. 'I wasn't listening in.' Eric and van Loame loomed over him. Donaghan twisted round. 'I came up to tell Jack it wasn't me who told Quinn about Adam and Harry getting married.'

'Yeah?' Cornell said. 'So how'd he find out?'

'It must've been Quinn's men who overhead.'

'Oh sure,' Jack said. 'They're well known for their ability to hear across a crowded room with at least fifteen different conversations going on. Clear out of here.'

Eric and van Loame hauled Donaghan to his feet, and Cornell grabbed him by the tie, shoved him out of the room and watched him walk down the corridor. A smaller figure was making his way in the other direction, towards Ethan's office. Light from one of the overhead bulbs glinted off a pair of round glasses.

'The sooner we get rid of Quinn, the sooner we can get rid of that scum,' Ethan said.

'Doc Fisher's here,' Cornell said. 'Come on in, doc.'

The pathologist hurried up the corridor.

'I'm glad you're all here,' Fisher said. 'Annie mentioned she'd seen you come in.'

'What have you come up with?' Jack said as he pulled up a chair for the doctor.

Fisher sat down, polished his lenses and took out a manilla folder from his case.

'The cannister has a motion sensor rigged to it that turns on a valve briefly. We found traces of carbon monoxide in it.'

'And that was in Harry's bedroom?' Jack said. 'No wonder she didn't look so good when she first came here.'

'The blood work I took from her last week showed up carbon monoxide in her red cells.'

'Will she be okay?'

'She should be, but I recommend high-pressure oxygen treatment, just to be on the safe side. I'll sort it out for you.'

'Thanks,' Jack said.

Cornell took the manilla folder from Fisher and opened it up.

'A motion sensor?' Cornell looked at the diagram in the pathologist's report. 'Oh great. Does that mean we're going to get more demonstrations?'

'Yeah,' Eric said. 'That sounds like the kind of thing going on in Sector House.'

'Let's just hope Quinn and Wakeham aren't connected with that lot,' Cornell said.

Eric's forehead creased, and he stroked his beard.

'What about Harry's father's blood sample?' Ethan asked Fisher.

'Knowing it was Wakeham we were up against, I had an idea what to look for,' Fisher said. 'I used to have a friend in the path. lab over in Central City. He's dead now, but he had a hunch about Wakeham's widows. They all had a puncture mark on the back of their neck. In most cases, there were convulsions and respiratory distress leading to cardiac arrest. Perry had put it down to anaphylactic shock following an insect bite or sting every time.'

'But your friend had another theory?'

'Yes. He discovered that Wakeham had a liking for tropical fish.'

'Sure, that's right,' Cornell said. 'I heard Hadley and Fenning talking about it in one of Hadley's voice recordings.'

'You saying Wakeham's knocking people off with tropical fish venom?' Jack said. 'He always was a bit theatrical.'

'I found scorpionfish venom in the blood sample Cornell and van Loame brought back,' Fisher said.

Eric tugged on his beard and his frown cleared.

'Wakeham has been to Sector House,' he said.

'What's that?' Jack said.

'Cornell was saying how he hoped Quinn and Wakeham weren't connected with that lot at Sector House, but it got me thinking cos it was at the back of my mind, so to speak.'

'How about you bring it to the front of your mind and share it with us?'

'It was about four years ago. We was looking for Miguel at the time. Remember how someone caught sight of him near Sector House and you sent us round to have a look? Didn't Spud say something about how Miguel had boasted how he was going to do the place over? Anyway, I was round that way with Spike and Hector, when I passed the gates to Sector House and saw Wakeham getting into a car in the driveway. I remember thinking how he must've had a lot of clout to get things cleared enough for him to show his face round town again. Spike gave a shout cos he thought he saw Miguel running down an alleyway, so I forgot all about Wakeham.'

'That could give us leverage against Quinn,' Ethan said. 'We bring up the whole business with Wakeham, and tie it all in with Sector House. Let's see Quinn wriggle his way out of this one.'

'Yeah, and have the Anti-Techs explode,' Jack said.

'How about we bring in the agents from sector one?' Cornell said. 'They're looking for a scapegoat right now, aren't they?'

— 24 —

KIDNAP

When Jack and Eric returned home to the flat, the others were already asleep. Eric was quick to follow suit, but Jack lay in bed thinking until he finally dozed off. He was woken up an hour later by Sam crying. The bunk above him creaked, and he heard Adam climbing down the ladder. The sound of Sam's cries moved across the dark room and out into the bathroom. Light seeped around the bedroom door, and Jack could hear the faint muttering of Adam and Harry's voices. The noise transferred to the kitchen. Jack put his head under his pillow, but the baby's wails continued.

'I'll take her out in the car,' Adam's voice said from just outside the bedroom door. 'Maybe it might settle her.'

Jack listened as the crying faded into the distance. He turned to the wall, but a few moments later tossed the other way again. He tried lying on his back, on one side and then the other, and even on his front, but sleep evaded him. He got up to fetch a glass of water but found Harry looking out of the kitchen window.

'What's up, Harry?' Jack said.

'He's been gone a long time.'

She was only wearing plaid cotton pyjamas — no dressing gown or slippers. She clutched her arms around her chest, shivering. There was a blue tinge to her feet.

'He'll be all right,' Jack said, but she didn't reply. He rested a hand on her shoulder. 'Get some sleep. There's no sense in the both of you staying awake.'

Harry nodded and left the kitchen. Jack glanced out of the window. The street was silent and empty. He poured some water into a glass and returned to his bunk. He was awakened an hour later by the sound of a key in the front door latch. A night light came on in the bedroom, and Jack could just make out Adam easing Sam out of her car seat. He laid her in the cot with the slow care of someone handling a live warhead. Adam then stumbled over to the night light to switch it off, but Jack called him softly.

Adam yawned and sat down on the edge of Jack's bunk. The room was quiet apart from the sounds of Sam snuffling, Eric snoring and Harry's slow measured breaths of deep slumber.

'Harry's going to have to quit trucking,' Jack said to Adam. 'You can't drive when you've been up half the night.'

'What if...?'

'What if what?'

Adam tugged Jack's sleeve.

'What if someone tries to hurt her, and I ain't there to stop them?'

Jack propped himself up on his elbow.

'You mean like in Central City?' he said. Adam nodded. He was barely visible in the dim light. 'I know a lot more about Harry than you think I do, my boy. Get some sleep. Ethan will call round later. We're going to sort things out for Her Ladyship.'

'I'm sorry, Jack. I did tell her to ask you for help, but you know how independent she is.'

'Harry and I have a mutual enemy. War's brewing, my boy. It's time we all started working together.'

Adam was asleep when Jack woke up, so he left him in peace. Eric soon joined Jack at the table. Harry was writing out a grocery list on a scrap of paper.

'Want anything from the shop?' she said.

'I could do with some more matches,' Jack said.

Harry jotted at the end of the list. A spot of ink stained the side of her index finger.

'We need more strawberry jam,' Eric said as he munched on a slice of toast.

Harry made another note, put the pen down and stood up.

'Don't go out of my territory,' Jack said.

'I'm just going to the little shops down the road.'

Harry lifted her waxed jacket off a peg. She was wearing a smart pair of grey trousers with burgundy braces. They didn't look like any of Adam's cast-offs. Her white shirt also seemed new, but the whole effect was marred by her stained, weather-beaten farm coat.

'Maybe Eric should go with you,' Jack said.

'I'm not in Central City now.' Harry unfolded the pram. 'I don't need a bodyguard in the heart of your territory.'

'All right, but don't be long.'

Harry picked Sam up. The baby's head turned unsteadily as she looked around the room. Her large, blue eyes fixed on Jack.

'Leave Sam with us,' he said. 'You'll be quicker without half the neighbourhood cooing over her.'

'It's okay, Sammy,' Harry said, settling Sam on to her activity mat. 'Uncle Eric and Uncle Jack will look after you.'

'Uncle Jack?'

Harry grinned.

'Would you rather be Gramps?'

'I ain't nobody's Gramps. All right, I'll be Uncle Jack. Go on, hop it. Don't forget my matches. I'm down to the last one, and I need a smoke.'

Harry picked up her hessian shopping bag. It had 'Titty-Totties' written on it in rainbow letters and a painted pair of smiling baby faces. She waved goodbye and left.

Eric knelt down next to Sam and jiggled her toys in front of her. Jack sat at the table and started to go through his accounts. The disturbances had caused a backlog, but there were fewer orders coming in and there'd been some cancellations. People were getting jittery with the agents from sector one around. He jotted down some notes and figures, then fetched his calculator from a drawer, put the stylus in a hole and slid it up and over. A number clicked round in the display area. He had just selected the hole for the next digit when there was a knock at the front door. Jack went over and let Ethan in.

'You had a word with Adam yet?' Ethan said as they went into the main room.

'Briefly. He's out for the count. He had to take Sam out for a ride during the night to quieten her.'

Jack looked over at Adam's bunk. There was movement under the bedding and the first mutterings of a sleeper beginning to stir. Outside in the street, a car engine started up. A radio came on in the next flat.

'That's hell, that stage.' Ethan tickled Sam under her chin. 'Cornell and van Loame will be round soon with a couple of cars. I reckon it's best if we go over to Great Bartling and pool our resources. You still want to talk to Adam while Harry's out?'

'No, let him sleep. We'll collar her when she comes in and head out once Adam's up.' Jack glanced at his watch. 'She should be back by now. Eric, go find out what's taking Harry so long.'

'Sure thing, Jack.'

Eric put his hat on and left. Adam's bunk creaked and the bedding was tossed aside. He pulled himself up by the side rail and rubbed his eyes.

'You okay?' Jack said.

'Yeah, I will be after I hit the shower.'

Adam hauled himself out of bed, climbed down the ladder and shambled out of the room. Jack returned to his seat at the table and Ethan pulled up a chair next to him.

'Reckon Quinn's on to Harry?' Ethan said. 'Those cops who checked her ID might've decided to do a bit of digging.'

The plumbing juddered, as it always did when the shower was in use.

'I'm certain that was just Rita trying to cause trouble,' Jack said. 'Quinn's got his hands too full with the fire and riots to worry about Rita's petty jealousies.'

Jack finished his calculation and entered another line in the ledger. He refilled his pen from an ink pot, sharpened his pencil and used it to randomly move the slots around on the calculator. The carbon tip snapped off, so he took out his knife and began to trim it again. The plumbing started knocking like a sham spirit at a seance. Sam began to grumble, so Ethan picked her up and jiggled her about. Jack shut the ledger and pushed it aside. The plumbing quietened down. Jack checked his watch.

'Why's she taking so long? It's not like she has far to go.'

'She might've got talking to someone. Maybe there's a queue at the till.'

Jack put the ledger away in the cupboard, went over to his bunk and dragged out the case from under it. He unlocked it, flipped the catches and took out his tommy gun. Adam returned from the bathroom, fastening his shirt buttons.

'What's up?' he said.

'We're going to head over to West Norfolk to sort things out,' Jack said. 'Harry's taking too long at the shops, so I've sent Eric out to find her.'

'Give me a gun, Jack.'

'Finish getting dressed and pack up Sam's things. We'll drop her off at Ethan's. Helen can look after her.'

'But what about Harry?'

'I said I sent Eric out. Do as you're told.'

Adam laced his shoes, and Ethan helped gather together Sam's things. Jack put on his trench coat and checked the pocket for his Beretta. The front door slammed open. Heavy footsteps thudded in the hall. Eric ran into the room. His hat was awry. He was out of breath. His face was red. In his hand, he held a hessian bag. Egg yolk and strawberry jam had seeped out though the fibres and trickled down a painted cherubic face.

'I can't find her anywhere,' he said, 'but I found this lying on the pavement.'

Jack, sitting in the back of Cornell's car, removed the clip from his Beretta, pulled back the slide and checked there was a round chambered. His tommy gun lay by his feet. Adam was next to him, opening up a drum magazine to see how many rounds of ammunition were left in it. Ethan was in the front passenger seat beside Cornell. They raced along the dual carriageway following van Loame's car. Their flashing blue lights reflected off a Morgan roadster as they roared past it. A low-lying mist covered the fields on either side of the road.

'How do we know where they've taken her?' Adam said. 'She may have been taken to Stan's territory. Or they might be taking her to Central City.'

'We don't have enough resources to raid both Quinn and Stan's territories,' Jack said. He slapped the clip back into the Beretta. 'Wakeham will know where she is, and he'll tell us with the right amount of persuasion. We'll pick up some of Harry's people, then we'll have enough men to deal with Wakeham and Blond Jim and anyone else who gets in our way.'

Cornell followed van Loame on to the slip road that led off the dual carriageway. Eric's large head was visible in the rear window of van Loame's car. Cornell had filled Adam in about the events in West Norfolk, and Adam had told them what had happened in Sector House. Jack put the Beretta back in his pocket and picked up his tommy gun. So there really had been high-tech weapons there, but at least it sounded like they weren't fully operational. Was that the only stash they had or were there others in the sector? If Harry and Adam had come clean about it sooner, she wouldn't need rescuing again. But she had to have it her own independent way, didn't she?

The mist thickened and thinned as they wound their way along narrow country lanes. They passed a sign pointing in the opposite direction to Great Bartling.

'Ain't we gonna get the Great Bartling police to help?' Adam said.

The car skidded round a corner. Mud and loose stones thudded against the running board.

'They can come and play if they want,' Jack said, 'but we're heading straight to the Wynherne Estate.'

'Watch out for the traps.'

'What traps?' Ethan said.

'Ambush points on the roads with big spiked pits,' Adam said. 'They were the first line of defence during the anarchy. That's how Harry's Uncle Barney was killed.'

'Yeah, that was in Hadley's report,' Cornell said as he turned into a narrow lane, 'but Perry ordered them all to be filled in at the inquest last year.' The rear lights of the car in front turned off the lane. 'What's van Loame doing? That's Wakeham's driveway.'

Ethan picked up the radio handset.

'Hey, van Loame. What gives? I thought we were going next door.'

'Blue lights ahead, boss.' Van Loame's voice crackled over the receiver. *'Someone's beaten us to it.'*

They turned a corner past a clump of trees. The mist glowed blue and faded, then glowed again. Cornell swerved to one side as an ambulance emerged from the fog and raced by them in the opposite direction. There were still flashing blue lights ahead, and not just from van Loame's car. Cornell pulled back on to the driveway. There was a crowd of people gathered around something. Jack slung his tommy gun strap over his shoulder, opened the door and stood on the running board. Then he jumped from the car as it slowed to a stop.

'Harry!' he called, as he pushed his way through the mass of country folk. 'Harry?'

He could hear Adam's voice calling her elsewhere in the fog. Weather-beaten faces studied him, but he was let through.

The mist began to thin, and he saw a blond-haired body in grey trousers lying face down on the ground. The once white shirt was stained red.

'Harry?' Adam's voice called from further away.

'Over here,' came her reply.

Jack swung round and ran towards the sound of her voice. The autumn sunlight filtered through the fading mist, and he soon saw her sitting on a pile of sugar beet. Her hair was tousled, her lip was split and she had a bruise forming on her temple, but other than that she looked fine. Jack made to embrace her, but noticed Adam by her side, so instead he nudged her chin with his knuckles.

'Lo, trouble,' he said. 'You okay?'

'A bit bruised, but I got rescued in the nick of time again. I haven't done very well in the whole defending myself business, have I?'

Jack ruffled her hair.

'We all need backup.'

He looked around. Wakeham's body was sprawled over a low wall. One arm was flung back behind it. A blob of blood dangled on the tip of the index finger at the end of a trail down the sleeve from a stained rent in his shirt. Jack studied the wound. It wasn't from a gunshot — more like a flat blade that had pierced the chest between the ribs.

A breeze picked up, dispersing the damp filaments of mist. They were at the end of the driveway in front of a large house. There was a van parked crookedly by the porch and two police Land Rovers with blue lights flashing. A man and woman in tweed suits approached Jack.

'I take it you're Jack Preston,' the man said.

'Sure, that's right. And I reckon you're probably Hadley and Fenning. What happened?'

'I was ambushed,' Harry said. 'They threw a sack over me, bundled me into a van and brought me here.'

'Amos had men on the watch towers along the border of the Wynherne Estate and Allerton's property,' Hadley said. 'They saw the van pull in, but we only got here a few minutes before you. Amos was about to tell us the rest of it.'

Hadley indicated to a gnarled man with a scarred face.

'The van come down the loke west o' the wall,' Amos said. 'The boy Joe was on one o' the towers, and he was sure that was m'lady hallerin' in the sack. He radioed for help, and he and th'others on the tower orl ran down, and I joined up wi' them. Allerton come lollopin' along and then realised he'd been copped. The duzzy lummox tried to bop behind the wall, but the path was on the huh, and he blundered. Then he pulled hisself back up and showed a gun, saying he'd kill har. Well, we were orl suffin savage afore, but that made us raw.' Amos kicked one of Wakeham's dead ankles. 'I lumped inta him wi' a stick.'

'A very sharp stick,' Hadley said.

Jack studied the crowd. For an angry mob, there sure seemed an absence of weapons. They must've hidden them before the police turned up, but Hadley wasn't showing any signs of looking for them. Jack headed over to the blond corpse.

'Who was in the ambulance?' Ethan said.

'The two who kidnapped Lady Coulgrane, or Lady Trent I should say.'

'What's with the Lady Trent stuff?' Eric said. 'I thought Harry was just Mrs Trent now.'

'Technically I'm Lady Trent,' Harry said, 'but I didn't think it would be a good idea to use my title when I registered.'

'Does that mean Adam's a lord?'

'No, I'm afraid not.'

'I still reckon the whole thing's nuts.'

Jack rolled the body over with his foot. It was Blond Jim. His chest was peppered with holes.

'No one's going to be crying over you, pretty boy,' he said. 'That's sure like Quinn to have all his rotten eggs in the same basket.'

There was a torn fletch on the ground. Jack pressed it into the mud with his shoe until it was hidden. He would never have figured Blond Jim being knocked off by arrows. He turned round and saw Cornell tugging at Wakeham's unbloodied hand.

'What're you doing, Cornell?'

Cornell twisted and wrenched Wakeham's opal ring off a dead finger.

'Take a look at this.' Cornell pulled it free. 'I think the catch must've been knocked when he fell.'

'What catch?'

'Put on some gloves,' Cornell said.

Jack took out a leather pair from his coat pocket and put them on. Cornell handed over the ring. The gem wasn't real. It was hollow and on a hinge. He opened it. There was a spike underneath that looked like the tip of a hypodermic needle. Jack turned to Hadley.

'Reckon that would match the puncture mark you found on Harry's dad?'

'I'm certain of it,' Hadley said. 'Judging from the position of the earl's body, my guess is that he was sitting at his desk and Wakeham was standing behind him. There was a chequebook on the desk. I suspect the earl was attempting to pay off his debt. Wakeham jabbed him in the back of the neck and he fell off the chair.'

'Good work, Cornell,' Ethan said. 'Get Fisher to check it for toxin when we're back.' He turned to Jack. 'So what next?'

'I have an idea,' Harry said.

'Today, on In Focus, *we will be speaking to Mr Fulton Robbins, President of the Anti-Technology League –'* the female voice crackled and faded over the radio on Hadley's desk; Fenning adjusted the tuning dial *'– and Agent Rawls, one of the investigating officers from sector one.'*

'I hope thass pre-recorded,' Fenning said. 'That bloke's spuzzed to be on his way here.'

Harry looked out of the window at the statue of her Great-Grandpa Reggie lancing a raider. There weren't as many people in the town square as was usual for a Saturday afternoon, and those who were out weren't stopping for a chat with their neighbours.

The radio fizzed and then cleared as the voice of Kirsty Gosling, presenter of *In Focus,* continued:

'Mr Robbins, you've been quite outspoken over the whole Sector House business.'

The radio faded out again. Hadley twitched the aerial. Harry resumed her surveillance out of Hadley and Fenning's window, but there was still no sign of the agents from sector one. Jack, Adam and the others were next door in Williams and Hale's office. It had been Harry's idea that they stay out of sight while she found out which side the agents were on.

' — have been here for nearly two weeks,' a young man's voice phased back in over the radio in strident tones. *'But what progress have they made? None.'*

'*It takes time to piece evidence together,*' a gravelly voice said. '*But we have already identified some of the officials responsible.*'

Harry tried to visualise the speaker. The newspaper had only shown distant blurred photos of the investigating agents. Agent Rawls had a deeper and far more pronounced drawl than Jack and Ethan's hybrid accents, which made her imagine a much larger man than either of them.

'*So the only people you've been able to identify are all dead?*' said the energetic voice of Fulton Robbins. '*Don't you think that's a bit odd?*'

'*Not when you consider that the people closest to the explosion were those closest involved,*' the gravelly voice said.

'*And dead men don't talk.*' The radio began to crackle again. '*Who authorised it? Who paid for it?*'

'A serial killer,' Harry said.

Fenning nudged the tuning dial. Music from another station cut across the current affairs programme. Harry watched one of the police Land Rovers pull into the town square. There was still no sign of the agents. Had they decided not to come? The radio signal cleared.

'*We're working closely with the police,*' the gravelly voice said. '*In fact, their computers are providing an invaluable means for following the paper trail.*'

'*Oh sure,*' the energetic voice said. '*And no one's ever been able to forge computer records. How do we know the police aren't involved? How do we know you're not developing new technology to destroy us all?*'

The radio crackled and fizzed again. A female torcher's lament throbbed and faded. Hadley tapped the wood and chrome housing while Fenning wiggled the aerial. Harry picked up a newspaper from Hadley's desk. It had a picture of Fulton Robbins on the front page looking as though he was declaiming to the masses. He seemed a handsome man in his twenties, slightly dishevelled, but in an appealing manner that seemed to suggest that while he wasn't a stuffy official, he wasn't an unkempt rogue.

The singer's voice faded and the static cleared.

'Excessive technology nearly annihilated us,' the young man's voice said.

'Safeguards have been employed to prevent that situation,' the gravelly voice said.

Harry tossed the newspaper back on to Hadley's desk, yawned and wondered if the programme's presenter had gone off for a tea break.

'But they clearly don't seem to be working.'

'Thass a lively lad, that fella,' Fenning said. 'Maybe Agent Rawls will be glad to have new information.'

'He might not be so keen on it when he finds out it involves Quinn.' Harry stared out of the window again and saw an unmarked car pull up outside the police station. 'Look. I think that's them.'

Fenning came over to her side.

'They musta bin in a hurry to git here,' she said. 'Look at them ony half-dressed. No hats and their jackets undone. And what're they doing wearin' sunglasses on a day like this? Have they got suffin wrong with thar eyes?'

'It's a bit of an old-fashioned look, isn't it?' Harry said.

'Ah well, thass furrin parts for you.'

Brenda, one of the police secretaries, showed the two agents in. As Fenning had observed, their jackets were undone, but that was presumably to give easy access to the shoulder holsters Harry glimpsed when they moved their arms to shake hands, with a hard but perfunctory jerk. They wore belts instead of braces and had no waistcoats. The only difference in their appearance was that Rawls was black and Kilic was white. They even had the same bland expressions.

'Thank you for coming,' Hadley said.

'Make it quick,' Rawls said. 'We're not here to see the sights.'

Agent Rawls, with his deep gravelly voice, turned out to be no bigger than Ethan. He sat down on the other side of the desk, opposite Hadley, Fenning and Harry. Kilic sat further off, the wrong way round on his seat. His left arm leant on the chair back. His right hand was out of sight. If he was planning on using his gun, he had both the door and desk covered.

Hadley related his and Fenning's findings. He already had his case notes laid out on his desk. Rawls leant back in his seat with his arms folded. His dark glasses were like the unlit windows of an empty house.

'Did you have a warrant to search Miss Penderbury's office?' he said.

'Are you saying we should've applied to Commissioner Quinn for a warrant to investigate him?' Hadley said.

'As I understand it, you were investigating this Allerton guy.'

'And Quinn vouched for him. Allerton was Wakeham the serial killer.'

'Can you prove it?'

'Wakeham's case is in the police files. Look.' Hadley handed over a manilla folder. 'All the details are there. Quinn was covering for him.'

Agent Rawls flicked through the contents of the folder and tossed it back on the desk.

'This has the Norfolk Constabulary logo on it. You're in Central Constabulary.'

'What difference do that make?' Fenning said.

Agent Kilic took a stick of gum out of his pocket and unpeeled the wrapper. He put the grey slab in his mouth, scrunched up the foil and tossed it on to the floor. He chewed for a moment, then a bulge appeared in his cheek.

'Police regulations are there to protect the innocent,' he said. 'Lone wolves put that in jeopardy.'

Harry thumped her fist on the desk. The now silent radio rattled against the wooden surface close to the edge.

'And pedantries can protect the guilty,' she said. 'So you're making a thorough investigation, are you?'

'He sound a caution, that Fulton Robbins,' Fenning said.

Hadley sat between the two women, turning his paperweight over in his hands. Harry wondered how much damage the stone would do if thrown and how good his aim might be.

'Mr Robbins asked some interesting questions, didn't he?' Harry said. She rummaged in her jacket pocket and fished out an Anti-Tech leaflet. 'I think he might like to hear what happened to me in Sector House.'

'We'd like to hear from you how the fire started,' Agent Rawls said.

'Inspector Hadley has my statement right here.' Harry tapped one of the documents on the desk. 'Would you like to read it, or does it have the wrong logo on it?'

'Why didn't you report it to the Central City police after the incident?'

'Because they're a bunch of crooks.'

Agent Kilic leant further forwards across the back of his chair. His jaws chomped up and down as he chewed on his gum.

'Do you deny you're part of a criminal organisation who was trying to destroy a government building?' he said.

'Don't you try making me a scapegoat.' Harry picked up the newspaper and leant back. 'Did you find a scapegoat for the riots in sector fifty-nine?'

Rawls looked at the newspaper in her hands and pushed the bridge of his sunglasses with his forefinger.

'You're mistaken,' he said. 'There's been no mention of any riots in the news.'

Harry tossed the newspaper back down. It slid across the desktop. Rawls moved as though to grab it, then pulled his hand away.

'That doesn't mean there hasn't been any,' Harry said. 'It was le Movement Contra la Technologie that started it. Just like it was the Anti-Technology League who blockaded Central City. And who started the coup in sector seventy?'

Kilic stopped chewing on his gum. Rawls glanced at his partner.

'You've been misinformed,' Kilic said.

'Are you saying a refinery didn't get destroyed over there? Fifty-foot-high flames, armoured cars, mortars going off, shell craters everywhere.'

'Where'd you hear that?'

'Word gets around. Telling everyone that the whole world is united in peace and prosperity isn't going to make it happen. Next thing you know, there'll be riots spreading across all sectors.'

'It stops here,' Agent Rawls said, 'by whatever means serves the good of the people.'

Kilic resumed his gum chewing.

'You're a gangster's moll,' he said, 'married to the mob, and your boss has a girlfriend who runs the red light district.'

Harry leapt to her feet and one hand reached to the back of her jacket. The westering sun shone through the window and glinted off Kilic's dark glasses. The chair he was sitting on had a solid back, and his reverse position shielded all but his legs and head. Harry moved her hand so that it was in view again.

'I'm not a moll,' she said. 'And Jack doesn't have anything to do with Rita's business.'

'Says you.'

Harry sat down and leant on Hadley's desk. The photo on the front page of the newspaper stared up at her.

'How are you going to silence Fulton Robbins?' she said. 'He'll listen to me.'

'You going to tell him you were part of a gang prepared to shoot your way through his blockade?' Rawls said. 'How d'you think public opinion will feel about you driving with a shotgun on one side and a baby on the other?'

'A stolen baby, at that,' Agent Kilic said.

'She's not stolen.' Harry slammed her fist on the desk. The radio toppled over the edge and crashed to the floor. 'She's registered and legally adopted.'

'She's stolen. You precious husband kidnapped her and forced his mother into signing adoption papers. That's the kinda guy you married.'

Hadley and Fenning turned to look at Harry.

'Get your facts right before you try going public with that one, Agent Kilic,' Harry said. 'I was the one who found Sammy. I was the one who saved her life. So you've got the Neutral Territory backing you, as well? That's not going to be enough. My influence isn't limited to West Norfolk. There are people living in villages around Norwich who'll listen to me, and you'll never shift their opinion of Adam's mother. And if you're thinking that farmers don't matter, just remember where food and beet comes from. You want to keep a lid on it, do you? You're not going to find it so easy if you go against me.'

'Farmers won't risk bankrupting themselves,' Rawls said.

Harry lowered her voice so that it wouldn't carry to the next office.

'D'you really think Allerton risked conning my father for a pittance? Only thing is, what Allerton didn't realise was that all my father inherited was a title. Barring a few legacies, my uncle left everything to me. I went to the city to prove Allerton was a murderer, not because I was penniless. And now I know people who can point me to the best city lawyers who will deal with my mother-in-law and the rest of the Neutral Territory. They're not fighters. They'll switch sides for the right amount of cash.'

— 25 —

Escalation

'Electric handcuffs?' Mrs Widrow said. 'Whatever do you mean?'

Harry had gone to Weston Snelding with Adam and Sam as usual, and they were now standing on the grass outside the little wooden chapel. Sunday mass had finished. Mist lingered around the gravestones on the slope beyond the far side of the lawn. Parishioners — with coats fastened, necks wrapped in scarves and gloves covering their hands — had shown every sign of hurrying home, but they had stopped and turned as Mrs Widrow's voice had carried through the cold autumn air. It had been easy enough to get on to the topic of electric handcuffs. Harry had simply made sure that she was within Mrs Widrow's hearing when she complained to Adam about how sore and itchy the electrical burns on her wrists were.

Mrs Harper hurried over to Mrs Widrow's side as Harry pulled back her sleeves and displayed her wrists. It was not long before there was a crowd craning their necks to see. Only the boy Billy and his friend Irene continued running around on the lawn.

'Luckily Adam saw them snatch me,' Harry said.

'Snatch you?' Mrs Widrow said. 'Whatever happened? I knew we should never have let you leave the village.'

'Was it the mobsters?' Mrs Harper said.

'No, it was the people in Sector House,' Harry replied.

'You mean where they had all those laser weapons?'

'They didn't just have lasers.' Harry shuddered. 'Adam saved my life.'

Everyone turned to Adam. Billy and Irene stopped chasing each other round the lawn and pushed their way through the crowd.

'Did you see any onem lasers?' Billy asked Adam.

'Sure, I did. I found the lab where they were made.'

Adam related how he had rescued Harry and what he had witnessed. There followed an assortment of exclamations ranging from 'my heart alive' to 'good man — excellent work' accompanied by a slap on the back from the Major. No one seemed at all bothered that Adam happened to have the necessary equipment for breaking and entering.

One of the younger women stifled a shriek when he came to the fireball and dragging Harry out.

'How romantic,' Mrs Harper said.

'I always knew they were up to no good in the city,' Mrs Widrow said. 'Didn't that Mr Robbins guess something was going on?'

'A government building with a secret armoury can only mean one thing,' Major Widrow said. He grabbed Adam's hand and shook it. 'If it hadn't been for you, Mr Trent, those weapons might be pointing at us right now.'

'You may not be getting lasers aimed at you,' Adam said, 'but you might be getting bullets coming this way. There's going to be fighting soon enough. Those agents from sector one want to make Harry a scapegoat, but I ain't gonna let that happen.'

'Certainly not. Neither will we. I'll get on to East Belingford. They'll want to be in on the action.'

'I've got a cousin over in Mundleton,' Carrie Bramley said. 'I know they'll all want to help. I'll head over there right now.'

'We hed a rugger match aginst Rotham Mardlegate yisty,' Mr Simmons said. 'They wuz sayin' they've also brought back their village defence plan.'

Other villages were mentioned with volunteers to spread the news. Mrs Widrow took a notepad out of her handbag and began to write up a list of supplies likely to be needed by field hospitals. Mrs Harper looked over Mrs Widrow's shoulder and made various suggestions.

Harry stood in the little hallway of Jack's flat and put on her jacket. She could hear the men in the main room, making preparations. Ethan had come round with Cornell and van Loame, and not long after Spike, Hector and Alf had turned up. Harry unfastened her stick and held it loosely by her side, in a fold of her coat. No one was going to put a sack over her head this time.

She left the flat, glanced over the banister into the empty stairwell and listened for movement. All was quiet, apart from the faint murmur of a radio in a neighbouring flat. She made her way down the steps and checked the front door of the building before going out. Jack could make all the battle plans, but Harry wasn't going to be stuck in a siege again without supplies. And it wasn't as though it was far to the shop. The street was empty. She walked down the lane and turned into an alleyway that cut across to the next road. Her rubber soles barely made a sound on the pavement, but someone else's boots clomped behind her. Harry swung round. Donnaghan's bulk blocked the view out of the passageway. One hand was in his trouser pocket. His face was red. His breath wheezed and formed a mist in the cold air. Harry edged backwards. He was out of uniform. His shirt was partially tucked in, but a frayed corner dangled out below his stained jacket.

'I've got a message for Jack,' he said. 'There's been a new development.'

'You've taken a wrong turn if you were looking for Jack,' Harry said. 'His flat's the other way, and Ethan's there as well. Sounds like you should give your message to him. He's your boss, isn't he?'

'Not for much longer.' Donnaghan pulled a derringer out of his pocket. 'I tried to be nice to you, but you snubbed me.'

Harry eyed the small double-barrelled pistol: two shots only, but at this distance one was enough to kill her. The alleyway was bordered by high walls. There was nothing to duck behind for cover.

'You're all alone in Jack's neighbourhood,' Harry said. Her fingers felt along the control panel of her concealed stick. 'Run back to Stan while you can.'

'Things have changed. The balance of power is shifting, and Jack's falling behind.' Donnaghan stepped closer with an unsteady gait. His misty breath reeked of alcohol. Thin blood vessels threaded about his nose like a red and purple mesh. 'D'you know how he helped Adam out? Adam could be looking at life imprisonment if certain evidence came to light. Then what will happen to the little girl and to yourself?' He moved forward again and leered, displaying fragments of food stuck between his yellow teeth. 'Of course, the evidence could remain buried if you persuaded me nicely.'

'What kind of sap d'you think I am? Is that your usual line? You're right about the balance of power shifting, but not in your favour.'

'Oh sure, you think you've got friends in high places. The little lady they all want to please.' His gun hand began to shake. 'Why should Adam get you? Jack gives him everything. What about me? Why should I be put behind some kid from the gutter?' His finger trembled on the pistol trigger. 'But don't be too sure of your friends any more because things are changing, and if you don't do as I say Adam will end up in a deep dark cell where he will never ever —'

Donnaghan swept his arms in an emphatic gesture. Harry swung her stick up and pressed the button. The ends shot outwards. The fore end smacked into his chest, and he was hurled backwards. His gun jerked out of his hand, struck the alley wall and clattered on to the pavement, but before he, too, hit the ground, Harry wheeled the stick round, briefly retracting it to clear the wall, and whacked his head. The impact sent a tremor up her arm and wrenched her shoulder. He was flung sideways into the other wall, blood and spittle flying from his mouth. His skull slammed against the bricks, and he collapsed into a heap on the floor.

Harry stood and stared at the crumpled body. Blood trickled down his pudgy nose, merged with a trail of mucus oozing from a nostril and splashed on to the pavement. She turned and ran back, her boots pounding against the ground.

'So it all hinges on which way Rawls and Kilic swing,' Jack said, tapping his pen on the table. He looked round. 'Where's Harry got to?'

'She said something about lunch,' Adam said.

'As much as I like her cooking, I don't want to fight on a full stomach. Tell her to just make sandwiches.'

'I can't smell nothing cooking,' Eric said.

Ethan opened the living room door and called to Harry, but Jack looked up at the pegs and realised that her jacket was missing. He snatched up his tommy gun and flung open the front door. Footsteps echoed up the stairwell. He ran over to the banister and saw Harry.

'Where've you been?' he said. 'What the hell d'you think you're doing sneaking out like that?'

'I've killed him, Jack. I think I've killed him.'

She reached the top of the stairs, clasped her stomach and tried to catch her breath.

'Harry!' Adam hurried over to her, brushing past Jack. 'What happened?'

'I went to get some groceries. I thought we ought to stock up.'

'You idiot,' Jack said. She swayed. He grabbed her by the front of her jacket and hauled her away from the stairwell. 'Don't you think I had that in hand?'

'Leave her alone,' Adam said. He seized Jack's arm. Jack looked down at him. Adam let go. 'I'm sorry, Jack. She's in shock.'

'I know,' Jack said, still staring at Adam. He then looked over to the doorway and saw Eric standing there. 'Eric, go clean up the stick. Come inside, Harry.'

He led Harry into the living room, and Adam followed. Jack steered her into a seat and leant over her.

'Now, what happened, and where'd you get the stick?'

'I went out to the shops.'

'Sure, just like yesterday. And just like yesterday you thought you were perfectly safe, despite the fact that war is about to break out.'

Adam pulled up a chair next to Harry and held her hand, but he didn't look at Jack.

'Was it another one of Wakeham's buddies who attacked you?' Adam said.

'It was Donnaghan.'

Adam leapt to his feet.

'I'll kill him. Jack, give me a gun. I'm gonna waste him.'

Jack grabbed him.

'Harry says he's already dead.' He pushed Adam back down on to the seat and turned to Harry. 'Where's the body?'

'In the alley that goes to the shops.'

'Cornell, van Loame,' Jack said. 'Go check it out.'

Eric returned with the now clean stick.

'Where'd you get this?' he said as he gave it back to her. 'I ain't never seen it before.'

Harry pressed the middle of the stick and the ends retracted.

'I found it in Miguel's cottage.'

'I picked up another one just like it in Sector House,' Adam said. 'That must've been where he got it.'

'I don't think they suspected Miguel had broken into Sector House,' Harry said. 'It didn't look like anyone had searched the place after he was shot. He must've got in the same way as Adam. I think they just killed him because he'd recognised Allerton — Wakeham — not because he'd been in Sector House.' She laid the stick on the table and began to shake. Adam put his arm around her. A tear trickled down her cheek. 'I never wanted to kill anyone.'

'I'd've done it for you, if I'd been there,' Adam said, 'but don't cry about wasting a bastard like that.'

'Quit trying to be so independent, Harry,' Jack said. He rested a hand on her shoulder. 'You're one of us, so don't go wandering off on your own any more.'

Cornell bent over Donnaghan and felt for a pulse.

'He's still alive.'

'I suppose we ought to call an ambulance,' van Loame said.

'Yeah, I suppose so.'

Cornell radioed and left van Loame to watch over Donnaghan while he went to wait for the paramedics at the far end of the alleyway where the thoroughfare was wider. There was a policeman walking the beat past the little row of shops on the other side of the street. The copper ambled over the road. His gut sagged over the top of his trousers and a blackjack hung on his hip.

'Lo, Bryson,' Cornell said. 'I thought you had the day off today.'

'I did a swap with Donnaghan.'

'I didn't realise you were his buddy.'

'I'm not.' Bryson blew his nose on a brown-stained handkerchief. 'I was just doing him a favour, that's all.'

Cornell fingered the gun in his pocket and checked the street. An elderly woman came out of one of the shops with a string bag. Two men came out of the neighbouring off-licence, leant against a wall and flipped their bottle lids, but one of them noticed Cornell, nudged his companion and they sloped away. A siren wailed in the distance. Cornell turned back to Bryson.

'Why do someone like Donnaghan a favour?'

'It means he owes me one, don't it?' Bryson stuffed the handkerchief away and rubbed his nose with the back of his hand. 'Those sirens coming this way?'

'Yeah. Your pal Donnaghan's met with a nasty accident.'

'I told you. He's not my pal. I was just doing him a favour. He did my Saturday morning beat, and I'm doing his Sunday afternoon, so he can spend time with his family.'

'Yeah? What family?' An ambulance turned into the street, its blue lights flashing. Cornell flagged it. He directed the paramedics up the alleyway and turned back to Bryson. 'So when'd he ask you for this favour?'

'I don't know. What's it matter?'

'If I'm asking, it matters.'

The blue lights from the ambulance reflected off the shop windows. Two days in a row Harry had been intercepted on a trip here. What had Wakeham's associates been doing here, in the heart of Jack's territory, yesterday morning?

The paramedics came back out of the alleyway with a gurney. Donnaghan was laid out on it, his head bound up with bandages and gauze. A patch of hairy belly showed below his shirt and wobbled like a mouldy blancmange as the stretcher bumped down the kerb. Van Loame followed on behind and then came over to Cornell.

'That's some accident,' Bryson said. 'Who did it?'

'He tripped over his laces,' van Loame said as the paramedics lifted the stretcher into the ambulance. He turned to Cornell. 'Let's head back before Stan hears the news. We'll need to move fast.'

'Was it Adam Trent?' Bryson said. 'He's got one hell of a grudge against Donnaghan. I always figured it was a matter of time before he wasted him.'

'Nix,' van Loame said. 'Don't overtax your brain. Get back to your beat.'

'Hold on,' Cornell said. 'You never answered my question, Bryson.'

The ambulance pulled away and switched its siren back on. Cornell glanced around. For the moment the street was empty. Bryson was staring after the retreating vehicle. Cornell nodded to van Loame. They shifted round so that they flanked Bryson, and then both leant against him so that he was trapped between them. Cornell was a good five inches taller than Bryson, and van Loame had another inch on that. Bryson tried to move his arms. His breath whistled through his nose.

'When did Donnaghan ask you to be a good pal and do him a favour?' Cornell said.

'I don't know.' Bryson's cheeks were red and puffy. His cap stank of sweat. 'Friday, I suppose.'

'You suppose?' Cornell said. 'What a bright-eyed copper you are. When on Friday d'you suppose that might've been?'

Bryson scuffed his shoe on the pavement and flexed his hands. Cornell checked the street. It was still empty. He leant harder against Bryson.

'You know,' van Loame said, 'I figure when a copper gets too forgetful, it may be time he starts thinking about retirement. You getting forgetful, Bryson?'

'Friday evening,' Bryson said. 'Sure I remember. It was Friday evening.'

'When exactly on Friday evening?' Cornell said.

'I don't know. I don't keep looking at my watch.'

A figure turned into the street, but it was too distant to recognise. Cornell eased away from Bryson and looked at him. Bryson's eyes darted from one side to another.

'You still owe Jack money?' Cornell said.

'What's that got to do with anything?'

'He might decide he wants it back — right now. Maybe he might send Adam and Eric round to collect.' Cornell glanced over his shoulder at the approaching pedestrian, then stared back at Bryson. 'You were right about Adam having a grudge against Donnaghan. Now he's got another one on account of Donnaghan trying to mess with his wife. She's got a neat line in self-defence, but Adam's still pretty mad. You want him to think you're pally with Donnaghan?'

Bryson stepped back, and his eyes widened, rearranging the creases in his puffy face.

'It was at The Blue Diamond, Friday night, maybe a bit before midnight,' he said. 'I didn't have nothing to do with it.'

The figure coming down the street was clearer now. An unshaven fellow with his jacket undone. One of Rita's people.

'Get back to your beat, Bryson,' Cornell said in a low voice. 'Stay sharp and button it.'

'Keep watch,' Cornell said to van Loame after he checked the locker room was empty.

'What're you hoping to find?' van Loame said as he leant against the door frame and glanced out.

'Donnaghan fingered Harry. He got Bryson out of the way after he earwigged on us.'

Cornell walked down the aisle looking at the name tags on the police lockers. They were back at headquarters, and Cornell was playing a hunch. Donnaghan was a hoarder and had enough protection — or so he'd think — not to worry about disposing of evidence. The room smelt of cigarette butts, stale sweat and boot polish. Some of the lockers had pictures stuck to them: a cartoon character; a humorous clipping; a woman wearing a come-and-get-me smile and very little else. Fenning wouldn't like that. What was he doing thinking about Fenning? What did it matter what she thought? The locker tops were covered with dust, old newspapers and magazines. There was a poster on a wall of a smug politician. His face was speckled with dried-up chewing gum.

'What does it matter now?' van Loame said. 'Donnaghan ain't going to harm her no more, and Stan'll side with Quinn regardless.'

The sounds of chanting and marching footsteps came in through the window from the street outside. Cornell glanced out at the crowd, all wrapped up in thick scarves and gloves, holding the usual placards. The Anti-Techs were back on their Sunday afternoon circuit.

'It might help shift Rawls and Kilic off the fence.'

He turned his attention back to the lockers and saw one that had been badly keyed. The door had Donnaghan's name on it. The neighbouring lockers were unscratched. Cornell pulled out a knife from his pocket and fitted the blade in the gap between the door and its frame.

'Can't you just pick the lock?' van Loame said.

'There ain't no time for niceties. Just keep an eye on the corridor.'

Cornell wiggled the blade and forced up the lever. The door flung open. A rolled-up poster slid out. Cornell caught it, straightened it out and saw a face like a china doll with golden ringlets — the missing Lady Coulgrane. There were other duplicate posters in the locker. He moved them aside and opened a small cardboard box. It was filled with trinkets: a brooch with a bent pin, an ear-ring missing its butterfly, a broken bracelet. Cornell closed the box and pulled out a magazine from under it.

It was a well-thumbed copy of *Generator Monthly*. A torn strip of paper with a phone number on it served as a bookmark. He turned to the marked page and an image of Harry smiled back at him. She still had the golden ringlets but not the china-doll face. Cornell flipped back to the front cover and checked the publication date. He took the magazine over to van Loame and showed it to him.

'He's known who she was all this time,' Cornell said. 'It wasn't Jack he was tailing in Central City; it was Harry.'

'But he kept it from Quinn.' Van Loame picked up the scrap of paper and looked at the phone number. 'That's the Wynherne area code, same as Great Bartling. He wanted the reward all to himself, I guess. It's a safe bet that's Wakeham's number, but Hadley'll be able to confirm it. Quinn's going to be as sore as a drilled tooth when he finds out he's wasted time poking an ants' nest in West Norfolk.'

'He'll be even sorer when the ants turn up to bite him,' Cornell said.

Footsteps sounded in the corridor outside. Van Loame peered round the door jamb.

'It's Sullivan,' he said.

Cornell ran back to Donnaghan's locker and stuffed the magazine and posters back into it. He leant against the locker door and tried to push the lever back in place with his knife. The footsteps grew louder. The blade got stuck in the gap. Cornell tugged at it and pulled it free. He grabbed someone's discarded copy of *The Police Gazette*, lounged next to van Loame and slipped his knife back into his pocket.

Sullivan came into the room. He had dark wavy hair and a physique that boasted of frequent trips to the gym. He turned his brown and green flecked eyes on Cornell and van Loame.

'Hard at work, you two?' he said. 'Or are you still recovering from your holiday?'

'A copper's work isn't all chasing after criminals. We've got to brush up with the latest news.' Cornell turned a page of the police magazine. 'Look at that: improvements in DNA analysis. That'll be useful.'

'I heard you called in an ambulance over near Jack's,' Sullivan said.

Cornell turned to van Loame.

'First he complains we're not working,' he said, 'then he complains we have been. How d'you figure that?'

'There's just no pleasing some people,' van Loame said.

'You want to say who the ambulance was for?' Sullivan said.

Cornell turned to the next page of the magazine.

'What's got you so interested?'

Sullivan leant his hand against the locker next to Cornell. His jacket seams were taut over his biceps.

'Stan's got a niece over at A&E,' he said. 'Seems it was Donnaghan who was brought in. Seems someone smashed his head in with a blunt instrument.'

'Is that so?' Cornell said.

'Stan's not very happy about it. Especially with it happening so close to Jack's. Stan's wondering if it might be someone who's been known to make those kind of threats against Donnaghan.'

'Well, you can put Stan's mind at rest. It wasn't Adam, if that's what you're suggesting.'

'And I suppose he's got a rock solid alibi, has he?' Sullivan said.

'Sure he has.' Cornell turned to van Loame. 'How many were there of us who were with Adam when it happened?'

'Let's see –' van Loame began counting off on his fingers '– there was you, me and the boss, Jack, Eric, Spike, Hector and Alf. I make that eight.'

'Stan's been having a word with Quinn,' Sullivan said, 'and Quinn doesn't like to hear about coppers getting their heads bashed in. He's put me in charge of the investigation, so I thought I'd come along and have a quiet word with you, seeing as how you got to the scene so quick.'

'Did you think we'd moved our office to the locker room?' Cornell said. 'Or did you want to pick up something to assist with the conversation?' Cornell rolled up the police magazine and slapped it against his palm. 'Maybe DNA analysis will show that Donnaghan's just a lousy lummox.'

'A lousy lummox? You're a fake, Cornell. Just like your boss and his friend. This isn't a school boy game.'

'A fake?' Cornell said. 'Sure, we're all fakes. You, me, even Stan O'Brien. He's never set foot in sector fifty-three. Nor had his parents or his grandparents. We're all play-acting. Even Agents Rawls and Kilic are just playing at being men in black. Go and report back to Stan and Quinn that Donnaghan tried to assault Adam's wife but, being a Coulgrane, she defended herself.'

'We need to move fast.' Jack put another drum magazine into his bag. The sound of high heels echoed up the stairwell outside. 'Great, that's all I need. Eric, check the bottom shelf of the cupboard. There should be some more clips in there.'

The footsteps approached. The front door slammed. Rita strode into the room. She looked around. Hector and Alf were leaning over a map laid out on the table, Spike was loading cartridges into the partitions of a drum magazine,

Ethan was rocking Sam, and Harry was sitting with Adam, her head resting against his shoulder.

'What the hell is going on here, Jack?' Rita said as she walked over to him with a hand on her hip.

'Just a quiet Sunday afternoon.' Jack slung the strap of his tommy gun over his shoulder. 'Isn't that right, Ethan?'

'Sure it is.'

Rita pointed at Harry.

'D'you know what she's done? She's attacked one of Stan's people.'

'No, one of Stan's people tried to attack one of mine. What Harry did was self-defence.'

'It was GBH.' Rita swung round and prodded Jack in the chest. 'You know what this means? Stan will retaliate.'

'Is that so?' Jack said. 'And there I was thinking we were going to have a nice quiet evening.'

'She's started a war.'

'She didn't start it. Quinn and his buddy Wakeham did that.'

Rita's make-up cracked and flaked around her eyes as she frowned.

'What?'

Jack wiped off a spot of oil from his gun barrel with a rag.

'The twelfth Earl of Wynherne discovered that his neighbour was Wakeham the widow-killer, courtesy of Miguel del Rosario. Quinn had Miguel knocked off and fingered me for it.' Jack tossed the rag on to the table. 'The earl was also knocked off, so I've sided with the Coulgranes. Savvy?'

'You're going to war over a thing like that?' The wrinkles in her neck were getting harder to cover up. Time was one thing Rita couldn't defeat. 'And you didn't even think to consult me?'

'Well, you and Harry weren't exactly getting along.'
Rita swung round to look at her.
'What's she got to do with anything?'
'She happens to be Lady Harriet Coulgrane,' Jack said. 'You up to speed now?'
Rita turned back to Jack. Her mouth puckered. Her nostrils flared.
'You two-faced bastard.' She prodded him in the chest, but his waistcoat absorbed the impact. 'Don't forget, Jack. I've got friends.'
'Then quit prodding me, and go play with them.'
She slapped him. His cheek stung beneath the blow.
'We're through, Jack.'
'No kidding.' Once Rita had stormed out of the flat, Jack turned to Eric. 'Go bolt the front door, Eric my lad.'

— 26 —

SETTLING UP

'All right,' Jack said as he stood in front of the depot. 'Alf, Hector and Spike, you take your load to Central City. Give a case to Cornell and van Loame. They're going to rendezvous with the West Norfolk lot and show them the way. They'll pick up the extra guns when they get to Central City, but Harry's lads'll need a bit of training before they head out.'

'I hope they learn fast,' Hector said.

A police van pulled into the depot, swung round and stopped in front of Jack. Van Loame got out and helped Alf put a case in the back. Cornell came over to Jack's side as he unfolded a map.

'The Weston Snelding lot have put up road blocks all around Norwich in case Stan or the Neutral Territory call in reinforcements from Colingham,' Jack said. 'I've marked your route out. Show them your badge and they'll let you through. You got enough vests?'

'Yeah,' Cornell said. 'We caught Sullivan trying to make off with them, but he didn't get far.'

Van Loame shut the rear doors, and soon he and Cornell pulled out of the depot, with three trucks following on behind.

Gun fire sounded in the distance. The usually packed streets outside were empty.

Adam laid Sam in her cot and put a blanket over her. He wound up the mobile and turned to Harry, who was breaking open a shotgun.

'Eric will bring round more cartridges,' he said as he tightened the straps on her bullet proof vest. 'Don't stand directly in front of any of the windows.'

They cleared away Jack's carved holly box of playing cards, an ash tray, newspaper and sundry other objects from the table and heaved it over on to its side. They half-carried, half-dragged it towards the cot, then stripped the beds and stuffed the pillows, blankets and mattresses between the table and the cot. Sam lay asleep behind this makeshift shield, her tiny nose snuffling. Her pulse showed in the soft spot on the top of her head. Adam piled the chairs in front of the table, but that just made Sam's protection look even more inadequate. He leant over the cot and stroked her sparse hair.

'Bye, Sammy.' He picked up his tommy gun. 'I'd better head off.'

He turned to go, but Harry grabbed him, pulled him back and kissed him. He dropped the gun and took her in his arms. Her lips were soft. Her breath brushed his cheek. The side of her nose pressed against his. She smelt faintly of baby oil, but the thick padding of the bullet proof vest kept them apart.

'Marry me properly,' he said. 'In church and everything.'

'I'd like that.'

'I wanted to ask you all romantic like by the old willow next to the stream in Weston Snelding.'

'Come back alive and you still can.'

Jack ducked aside as fragments of flint and mortar sprayed his face. Then he aimed his tommy gun through the ancient bars and raked the cars on the far side of the street. Jack and Ethan's group had managed to take the Chapelfield stretch of the old city wall. It had been easier than they'd expected. Stan's men who had been on lookout in one of the ruined towers had surrendered without a fight. Even Ciaran, one of Stan's supposed stalwarts, had climbed down without a second thought and, like Harry, had vented his opinion that Stan was a hypocrite, although he had phrased it in far coarser terms than she had, and he had added a few choice words about Donnaghan as well.

So much for fealty running through their veins. Jack fired again through the barred opening. Unfortunately, Stan still had men beyond the wall who weren't being so accommodating. They had taken up positions behind the vehicles on the other side of the street. Bodies lay here and there in the road. A Molotov cocktail came hurtling upwards from behind the remains of a van. Jack fired at it as it tumbled through the air, then ducked aside as it exploded. Glass shards and burning alcohol struck against the old flint and newer brickwork.

Jack knocked debris off his hat and returned fire through the opening. Flame burst from the gun muzzle. Brass cartridge cases spat from the breech, showering the pavement by his feet, until the magazine was empty. Ethan was further down the wall, shooting through one of the arrow loops, but he stopped and held his radio to his ear. Another flaming bottle hurtled across the road, but it failed to clear the wall. Jack pulled out his gun's third hand, removed the drum, clicked a new one in place, and tucked the third hand away. Ethan was heading down the wall towards him. Another explosion blasted the wall, sending down chunks of flint.

'The Neutral Territory has ditched Stan,' Ethan said as he dropped down by Jack's side. 'They've arrested Adam's mother and Bartrum — that dodgy politician. They tried to arrest Rita as well.'

'She must've nagged them. They're obviously not as tolerant as me.'

'No, it was Harry.'

A barrage of bullets thudded into the wall near the grilled opening. Jack shot back and ducked next to Ethan.

'What was Harry?' Jack said.

'She paid off the Neutral Territory.'

'With what?'

Ethan fired a round through the opening.

'Her dad wasn't the one with the money,' he said over the return volley. 'She got a packet from her uncle.'

'Well, that sure was nice of her to say.' Jack raked the vehicles again and hit a man who was just about to launch another incendiary from behind a car. The bottle smashed on to the cowling. Jack and Ethan took cover. 'I'll kill her bloody independence. She's supposed to be home looking after Sammy.'

'Nix. She got your solicitors to do it on her behalf.'

There was an explosion and a blast of hot air. Smoke streamed in through the grill accompanied by the stench of burning biofuel.

'So what happened to Rita?' Jack said.

'She didn't take kindly to being arrested. One of the guards at City Hall shot her when she went for her pistol.'

'So you've switched sides?' Hadley said.

'It was never a case of sides,' Agent Kilic said. 'We merely reviewed the evidence.'

'Thass allus nice when the law review the evidence,' Fenning said.

They were in Central City in a road that led up to the police headquarters. A couple of trucks were blocking off the end of the street, and traffic was being redirected. The buildings here were tall and flush with the pavement. Hadley couldn't decide whether they were domestic or business properties. Most of them had a small brass plaque on the front door, but there was no telling if the names engraved on them were advertising a professional or just belonged to the owner. The windows had drawn venetian blinds. Maybe there were only frightened residents hiding behind them, or maybe there were killers with unseen carbines aimed through the slats.

Hadley and Fenning had tommy guns. Kilic had some kind of machine pistol, but it wasn't a model that Hadley recognised. Rawls and the specials who had come over from sector one with the agents were similarly armed. They stood further up the road away from Jack's men who were gathered around the trucks. Spud strode over to Hadley.

'The perimeter's secured. Looks like all civilians have cleared the area.' Spud turned to Kilic. 'You ain't gonna be fighting in those shades are you?'

'What of it?'

'Suit yourself. On your eyes be it if the lenses shatter.'

Hadley went over to the trucks and banged on their sides. D.I. Williams, D.S. Hale and most of the Great Bartling police force jumped down from one. Out of the other truck came Amos, Joe, Tom Ludlow, Fenning's brother and brother-in-law and others who were either Wynherne veterans or their descendants. They ran along the street, hugging the walls until they reached the corner. Spud used a mirror to check round it. He gestured to move onwards. The truckers ran out first. Hadley followed on with Fenning by his side. They dropped down behind a brick bus shelter. Others fanned out and took up positions behind vehicles and a retaining wall around the car park in front of the police headquarters. Another group from West Norfolk led by Alf and Hector approached from the other direction and took cover further up the street.

Hadley peered round the shelter. The reaction of the city coppers who were caught outside the building was swift. They dived behind their vehicles or dashed inside through the front door. There was the sound of multiple guns cocking and muzzles appeared over the tops of the police cars. Then there was silence as both sides eyed up each other. Hadley unhitched a small megaphone from his belt and raised it to his mouth.

'Quinn, you are under arrest for conspiracy to murder, helping a known murderer escape justice, and aiding and abetting the murder of the twelfth and thirteenth Earls of Wynherne. Come on out with your hands up.'

For a moment nothing happened. Then a window opened on the second storey.

'Who the hell are you?'

'Detective Inspector Hadley from West Norfolk. Come on out.'

A pudgy face peered out of the window.

'I'll have your badge for inciting a civil disturbance.'

'Can't you see we have Agents Kilic and Rawls backing us?'

Fenning snatched the megaphone.

'Quinn, we're in Norfolk, so we ought to be in the blooda Norfolk Constabulary not blooda Central Constabulary. You should never have poked yar snout inta our affairs.'

She handed the megaphone back to Hadley.

'The building is surrounded,' he said. 'Come out with your hands up.'

The face moved out of sight and was replaced by a gun barrel. Windows all across the front of the building slid open. Hadley caught sight of Amos crouched behind a nearby van and nodded to him. The old steward put a bugle to his lips and rang out the Wynherne call to arms. The last notes were still echoing off the tall buildings when Quinn's men started firing.

Hadley gripped the front compensator with his left hand and squeezed the tommy gun trigger with his right. The recoil slammed the butt into his bullet-proof vest, but he kept a tight hold. His shots sprayed the wall around Quinn's window. The returning fire smashed off fragments of brick from the bus shelter. Something stung his temple. A broken tile tumbled from the roof and missed his face by a few inches. His muscles ached from the strain of keeping the thrashing gun in his grasp. His left palm was moist. He felt the compensator slip from him as the gun jerked upwards, but at that moment it stopped firing. The magazine was empty.

He removed the third hand, fumbled and dropped it. The small device bounced on the ground away from the shelter. Bullets were still thundering past him. He reached out with the gun barrel and used it to drag the rectangular piece of metal towards him through the pile of spent cartridge cases. He picked it up, inserted it into the magazine chute and locked the bolt back. Another tile smashed next to him as he slid the magazine out. He had just finished inserting a new drum when the shooting stopped. Hadley peered round the shelter. A white rag waved out of a shattered window.

'They're not givin' up already, are they?' Fenning said.

'Fenning, that's most inappropriate,' Hadley said.

He wiped his left palm against his trouser leg. Something wet was trickling down the side of his face. Amos was still a few yards away behind the van — although it was now only fit for the scrap yard.

'City folk hent got no stayin' power,' he said to Hadley and Fenning.

The splintered double front doors of the police headquarters swung open, dislodging a shard of glass. Quinn stumbled out as though he'd been shoved from behind.

'You're under arrest for the wilful murder of Barnabas Coulgrane,' Hadley said, removing a pair of handcuffs from his belt.

'I heard you the first time, but I didn't murder him. D'you think I know how to work your traps? That needs local knowledge.'

'There ain't none o' us that'd harm a Coulgrane,' Amos said.

'People in Colingham know about your traps,' Quinn said, 'but the anarchy is history to them. Your stories bore them.'

'Who reactivated that trap?' Hadley said.

'What's in it for me if I tell you?'

Amos prodded his gun at Quinn's stomach.

'That pod o' yars oont need a fy-out.'

Quinn looked down at the gun and then up at the old man's scarred face. A bead of sweat appeared on Quinn's forehead.

'It was Jarrett and Regan.'

Jack walked up the stairs to the flat with Eric and Adam. Eric's arm was bandaged and in a sling. As Jack reached the landing he saw Harry standing in the open doorway. He hitched up his tommy gun.

'What're you doing making a target of yourself like that?' he said to her.

'I saw you out the window.'

'So you were making a target of yourself in the window as well, were you?'

'No, I wasn't. I rigged up a periscope.'

She turned away and walked over to the kitchen. The men went into the living room. Adam checked Sam while Eric — using only his uninjured hand — righted a chair from the barricade in front of the cot and sat down. Harry returned with three bottles of beer.

'I hear you paid off the Neutral Territory,' Jack said as he took one from her.

'I thought it would help.'

'You didn't, perhaps, think it worth mentioning beforehand?'

Jack took out his penknife and flipped the bottle top. Harry glanced at Adam and moved closer to Jack.

'I thought it might put Adam off from asking me to marry him if he knew I had lots of money,' she said.

Adam looked up, then turned away and leant over Sam's cot. He adjusted her blanket and moved her toy frog a fraction.

'Aren't you already married?' Jack said.

'Not properly in a church, but we are going to be now.'

There came the sound of cheering and shouts from the street outside. A car horn tooted.

'Are you telling me that we had to wait for a tongue-tied boy to pluck up the nerve to tell his girl how he felt before we could get the Neutral Territory off our backs and the sector one agents on our side?' Jack put his penknife away. 'Do we get glasses to go with this, or are you expecting us to drink from the bottle?'

'I've only got one pair of hands.' Harry perched the other two beers on the edge of the bookcase. 'I was just going to get them.'

She righted another one of the chairs, put it next to Jack and left the room. Jack leant against one of the bed posts and eyed Adam.

'Don't be mad at Harry,' Adam said. 'She wouldn't have left us in the lurch.'

'And what if you hadn't asked her?'

Adam righted the remaining chairs.

'Well, she did kind of take the initiative,' he said.

'You're the one who ought to be taking the initiative.'

Jack went over to the table and pulled on it with one hand. Adam grabbed the other end, and they lifted it back into position. Jack put his bottle on the table and fetched his card box and ash tray. Adam tugged on his sleeve.

'You'll be my best man, won't you, Jack?'

Jack moved a couple of the chairs to their place by the table. Sam began to grizzle.

'Sure I will, my boy.'

Harry came back with the beer mugs and set them on the table. Jack looked around the cramped room. The bunks were still stripped, their metal springs exposed. The thin mattresses lay in a heap on the floor amid the pillows and sheets. Sam kicked her legs against the cot.

'I suppose you'll be wanting to go back to your farm, Harry,' Jack said.

Adam lifted Sam up and hugged her. Harry opened a bottle, poured the beer into a mug and handed it to Eric.

'You told me I couldn't carry on trucking with Sammy to look after.' She put the newspaper and a box of matches on to the table in front of Jack who stood with one hand resting on the back of a chair. 'So I thought maybe I could take her to my farm Monday to Fridays while you three are away and come back here at weekends. Would that be okay?'

Jack poured beer into his glass and set the bottle down.

'Sure, that'll be fine.' A blob of froth trickled down the side of the bottle. 'No, sweetheart.' He kissed her on the top of her head. 'You take Adam home with you.'

'You serious, Jack?' Adam said.

'Sure I am.'

'You'll come and visit?'

'If I'm invited.'

'Of course you are,' Harry said. 'In fact, I'll be very much offended if you don't.'

Hadley sat in his car in the street behind Colingham Private Hospital with Fenning by his side. The waning crescent moon was out, but there were no stars visible. This time they were parked directly under one of the lamp posts. No need for any wall climbing tonight—thankfully. His muscles still ached from the fight that afternoon, and the fast drive back from Central City hadn't helped.

Fenning yawned and stretched.

'Are you sure this'll work?' she said.

'I think they've been on the lookout for us in Colingham ever since we interviewed Miss Penderbury.' Hadley rubbed his neck. 'Remember how they found us last time we were here? The car that passed us after we cleared the wall might've been on the prowl and noticed my licence plate.'

'Or maybe that was jist chance.'

Hadley drew his coat closer. Their breath misted up the windscreen.

'Maybe you're right,' he said. 'But Williams and Hale are watching the Colingham police station, and there are others staking out Jarrett and Regan's apartments, so hopefully they'll be spotted soon. It's not like we can put out a bulletin on them.'

Hadley drummed his fingers on the steering wheel. Had news reached Colingham of the events in the city? Had they been tipped off?

Fenning touched the surgical tape on Hadley's temple.

'You shoulda had stitches in that,' she said.

'There wasn't time.'

'I spect the scar'll look rugged on you.'

Hadley turned to her, but a bright light reflected off his rear-view mirror. He shielded his eyes from the glare and flipped up the mirror. A car pulled up behind them, its full beams still on. The doors opened. Two figures silhouetted against the headlamps walked over.

'I wunt doubt yar plans agin,' Fenning said.

A heavy-built figure clad in a trench coat blocked the view from Hadley's window, and thick calloused knuckles rapped on the glass. Hadley wound it down.

'Back in town again, Hadley? Did you want a quiet little street to make out with your sergeant?'

'We're on official business, Jarrett. We're about to make an arrest.'

'Is that so? Regan, you heard anything about a Bartling cop being given permission to make an arrest in Colingham?'

'Nope.' Regan leant against the cowling. 'Maybe we missed a memo.'

'Perhaps we'd better get out,' Hadley said.

'Yeah, I reckon you'd better.' Jarrett yanked open the door. 'I think you need to come along to the station with us so we can get this cleared up.'

Hadley stepped out of the car, and Fenning got out the other side.

'Jarrett and Regan –' Hadley unclipped the truncheon from his belt '– you're charged with the wilful murder of Barnabas Coulgrane, twelfth Earl of Wynherne. Anything you say may be taken down in evidence and used against you in a court of law.'

'Who the hell d'you think you are?'

'I'm the police officer who arrested the former Commissioner Quinn this afternoon — with the full backing of Agents Kilic and Rawls.'

A blur moved across Hadley's peripheral vision. Pain stabbed the back of his skull. The truncheon flew from his grasp as he lost balance. His leg smacked against the running board. He rolled to one side, fumbling in his pocket. Jarrett came at him with a blackjack raised. Hadley staggered to his feet, pulled out his knife and whipped off its leather sheath. The blackjack whacked across his hand, and the knife clattered to the ground. Hadley kicked Jarrett's kneecap with a jar that vibrated back up his leg. Jarrett gave a roar and dropped the blackjack. He dragged Hadley to his feet, smacked him against the car and clutched his neck.

Hadley tried to pull Jarrett's fingers away as they dug into his throat, but his right hand was shot with pain and had no strength. His back was bent over the car's cowling. He gasped for air. For a moment he thought he heard a loud crack behind him, then all he could hear was the blood pounding in his ears. His nostrils were filled with Jarrett's foul breath.

Just then, Jarrett cried out, let go and slumped to the ground. Fenning stood over him with Hadley's bloodstained knife. Hadley gasped, trying to suck air into his swollen windpipe. For a moment it felt like he'd never be able to breathe again. Fenning undid his tie and top button. He coughed and spluttered and slid down the side of his car on to the running board, rubbing his throat with his uninjured hand, but he signalled to her that he was all right.

Fenning knelt down and peered under the car.

'That blooda Regan kicked my truncheon outta reach.'

Hadley looked round and saw Regan lying unconscious at the foot of the hospital wall with a thick bloody nose. He remembered the crack he had heard.

'How'd you knock him out?' he said, his voice croaking like an old dying man.

'I head-butted him, and the wall did the rest.'

She stood up, dusted her knees and brushed her hair away from her eyes. A purple bruise was beginning to show on her forehead. She got out a first aid kit from the car, disinfected her hands with the alcohol spray and began bandaging Hadley's hand. Jarrett was lying on the ground, clasping his side. Blood seeped through his coat.

'You'd best radio an ambulance for them,' Hadley said. 'Perhaps I should've asked Williams and Hale to provide backup.'

'What for? We dint need 'em.' Fenning leant over the fallen man. 'That'll larn you to ignore me.'

— 27 —

The Wynherne Estate

Jack looked up at the tall brick wall passing by on his left. An empty tower came into view. He was sitting in the passenger seat next to Adam as they drove down a lane, following Harry's Land Rover. Eric was in the back of the Phaeton with Sam, squeaking her toy frog and attempting to croon a lullaby in his deep rumbling voice. His arm was still in a sling, despite his claim that the injury was just a scratch.

All of Adam's possessions, including his motorbike, had been packed into the back of Harry's vehicle. She was taking him and Sam home. Jack and Eric were only going to stay long enough to see Adam settled and then they'd head back. There was too much to be done in the city to be gone for more than a few days.

Harry's Land Rover slowed and turned left, so Adam did likewise, and they passed over a cattle grid that lay between open wrought iron gates. To their right was a small thatched lodge. Beyond that was a field with straw bosses set up for archery practice that reminded Jack of his old school so much that he half-expected to see the ancient school groundsman picking up fallen fletches and complaining about broken nocks ruining the lawnmower. On the other side of the driveway there was a stretch of heathland with a line of smashed-up scarecrows that looked as though they'd been used for machine gun practice. Most of them were lolling against the ground, their posts snapped, but there was one left standing. It was missing an arm and half its pumpkin head had been blown off but it grinned back with a partial mouth and one black painted eye.

They came to the end of the driveway and parked in front of the Gothic mansion. Two stories high, and above that dormer windows set in the roof, it towered over them in grey stone and leaded windows. Gargoyles leered from the guttering, pipe ends visible in their open mouths.

Adam switched off the engine and stared out of the car window.

'You've got to be kidding me,' he said.

'Welcome to your new home, my boy,' Jack said, with one foot already out on the running board.

Harry walked over from her vehicle, her boots crunching over the gravel drive.

'What d'you think?' she said.

'So much for your little farm.' Jack stepped down and closed the car door behind him. 'I reckon Adam's in shock. He probably figured your gatehouse was your cottage.'

'Didn't Cornell or van Loame describe the place?'

'I think they must've left that out of their report,' Jack said.

'Well, I thought you might've guessed I didn't live in a cottage after you found out who I was.' Harry helped Jack fetch the cases from the boot while Adam unbuckled Sam's seat. 'The housekeeper has sorted out some rooms –' Harry opened the oak front door and led them inside '– but she's not here at the moment so I'll show you the way.' She turned up a wide staircase with carved wooden eagles at the ends of the bannisters. 'Adam, Sam and I will be sleeping on the first floor. Jack and Eric, you've got the attic.'

'Don't mess around, Harry,' Eric said. 'I ain't falling for that.'

'For what?'

'Sleeping in an attic. With the water tank and spiders and stuff.'

'There's no avoiding spiders in the house.' Harry put Sam's bags down on a wooden bench set into a window alcove and put her own and Adam's bags on the floor next to it. 'All my grandparents slept there. You've got the newest beds in the house. Not that that's saying much: the four-poster on this floor is three hundred years old, I think.' She led them down a corridor lined with oil paintings depicting people, dogs, horses and battle scenes. Scuffed wooden floorboards creaked beneath their feet. 'There's another staircase by the kitchen, but it's much narrower. Joe used it to fetch my stuff after I stabbed Allerton.'

'Any secret passages?' Jack said.

'I'll show you them later, and I expect Amos will give you a guided tour of the armoury.'

'Sweet.'

Harry drew aside a long, dark green velvet curtain that concealed an opening in the passage wall. The rings scraped against the brass rod. Behind was a staircase leading up into the shadow.

'Mind your heads,' she said.

'It ain't haunted, is it?' Eric said.

'Not that I've heard.' Harry climbed to the top and turned on to a short panelled corridor with three doors. 'That one's your room, Eric, and this one's yours, Jack. That's the bathroom over there.'

'I knew you were kidding about the attic,' Eric said.

'I wasn't kidding,' Harry said. 'If you really want to know, that section of panelling slides open and leads to the storage area. You're welcome to explore it, but it's not very interesting.'

Jack pressed down the thumb latch and opened the door to his room. It was clean and tidy and smelt of old wood. The ceiling sloped down with a break in it around the dormer window. Jack looked out on to the back of the estate. Close by the house, there was a kitchen garden and next to that a sunken lawn with a sundial in the middle of it. In one corner there was an ancient oak with a tree house in its leafless branches. Beyond that was an orchard, a paddock with some horses in it, a fenced-off chicken run and a field of pigs with their half-cylindrical shelters. There was a footpath between the chickens and pigs with a brick shed at one end. Stretching off into the distance were vast flat tracts of stubble criss-crossed with dykes. The boundary wall dwindled off into a faint blur on the horizon.

Once they had deposited all their baggage in their rooms, Harry showed them around the farm. The tour included a trip to the shed Jack had seen from his window. Inside it, the Type 1 prototype was still operational. Jack left Adam listening to Amos recounting the life and times of Edward Bostock and went outside to light a cheroot. Eric held Sam with his good arm and was showing her the chickens. Jack leant against the shed wall and exhaled a cloud of smoke into the cold air. Harry came out of the shed and headed over to him. She was once more wearing her hobnailed boots, weather-beaten wax jacket and flat cap, looking much the same as when they had first met.

'D'you forgive me for holding out on you?' she said.

Jack tapped ash off his cheroot.

'D'you forgive me for being a mean old gangster?'

'You're not so mean really.'

'You're going to kill my reputation, but let's call it quits,' he said. 'I've got something for you.' He pulled a crumpled brown envelope out from an inside pocket of his trench coat. 'A bit of kindling for your fire.'

Harry took it and turned it over in her hands, but made no attempt to open it.

'What is it?'

'A statement made by a copper eight years ago witnessing that a sixteen year old beat a man to death with a wrench. It was self-defence, but you wouldn't guess that from the way it was told. The witness was later persuaded that his memory wasn't so good, and his statement disappeared for a while.'

Harry held the envelope with just the tips of her forefingers against opposing corners, as though she was holding something contaminated.

'What happened to the witness?' she said.

'He suffered a severe injury so his memory's likely to be a bit hazy,' Jack said. 'Oh now, don't look at me like that. You were the one who beat him up.'

'You mean Donnaghan?'

'Sure I mean Donnaghan.' Jack flicked at the end of his cheroot. 'The yellow bastard was quite happy to turn his back when a great brute of a man picked a fight with a kid, but he was quick to step in all official-like when the lad defended himself. Just a single lucky blow, but you'd think it was full scale battery from Donnaghan's account.' Across the path, on the other side of the fence, a chicken pecked at a rotten log. It turned one of its eyes on Jack, ruffled its feathers and continued its search for grubs. 'An armed copper who won't stop a kid from being beaten up is lower than any crook, but that wasn't the story Donnaghan told in his statement. He made himself out a hero for arresting a violent thug.'

There was a strong sickly smell coming from the shed. Above the hum of the generator, Jack could hear the muffled voices of Adam and Amos.

'Ethan took one look at the supposed thug that Donnaghan had arrested and smelt a rat,' Jack continued. 'Then he found out the so-called victim was none other than Hammer Harmer.'

'I've never heard of him.'

'Let's just say no one wept over his death. Anyway, Ethan told me about it, so I went along to see the kid. His story was way more believable. The year before, Ethan had taken Donnaghan's badge and thrown him in the clink, but Stan had got Quinn to intervene who had him reinstated, so Ethan didn't have a hope of straightening things out for a homeless boy without connections.'

'But you managed it,' Harry said.

'Stan happened to owe me a favour at the time, so I got him to persuade Donnaghan to forget the incident.'

'You did that for a boy you didn't know?'

Jack rolled the cheroot between his thumb and forefinger.

'I'm no angel, Harry. It's true I felt sorry for the kid and I couldn't stand Donnaghan, but even more I hated the way it was affecting Ethan. He couldn't fix things, so I did. Anyway, Donnaghan's statement went for a hike, and I took Adam in, but it turned out to be the best return of a favour I ever got from Stan. Not that Rita ever saw it that way.'

Eric had turned away from the chickens and was now showing Sam the pigs. Further down the path between the hedge that bordered the pig field and the wire fence around the chicken run, two Great Danes played together. Their jaws were open, displaying sharp teeth and drool, as they jumped against each other, but it was just for show in a rough and tumble game. Harry tapped the envelope.

'The statement got mis-filed?'

'It disappeared, but it looks like Donnaghan gave it to Stan. Ethan found it yesterday when he and his lads went over Stan's place. We reckon Stan was going to use it against Adam when the Neutral Territory decided to join the party, but you took care of that, and we took care of Stan.' The dogs bounded down the path, their tails wagging. 'It means a lot to me that you didn't walk out on Adam or persuade him to do a bunk when you had the chance to go home.'

Harry took a couple of biscuits from her jacket pocket and tossed them to the dogs.

'I wouldn't have done that,' she said.

'I know.' Jack smiled. 'Look after him.' He stubbed out his cheroot and ducked into the doorway. 'Adam, you've got the rest of your life to gaze at the generators.'

'But, Jack, I want to see all of them this morning.'

'That'd take orl week,' Amos said.

'Adam, darling,' Harry said, 'I'm afraid I might've underestimated the number when you asked me how many I had.'

'My dear boy,' Jack said, 'it wouldn't surprise me if Harry owned every generator in West Norfolk.'

After lunch, Jack and Eric played billiards while Adam took Sam outside to look at the tractors before her afternoon nap. Eric managed remarkably well given that he was restricted to using only one hand and a cue rest, but Jack was still first to reach one hundred. They had just finished the game when Jack was summoned to the study by the housekeeper.

'You know,' Jack said when he found Harry seated behind a solid oak desk, 'I never reckoned that I'd one day be told that her ladyship wished to see me in the study.' The room was like his headmaster's office only that had had pictures of muddy rugger teams holding trophies on the walls instead of family portraits. 'There's a mug shot I recognise.'

Harry looked up at the picture of herself.

'I'm going to have that moved. I've had quite enough of seeing it staring at me from noticeboards.'

'I don't know about that,' Jack said. 'It's kind of cute. So what did milady want to see me about?'

'I wanted to ask you a favour.'

'Okay, you've been rumbled,' Jack said as he perched on the edge of the desk. 'What've you done with the real Harry? She never asks anyone for a favour.'

Harry leant back in her leather-padded seat. A ray of sunlight shone through the casement window, on to the cluttered desk. Dust motes drifted and sparkled in the beam.

'We could call it a job offer, if you prefer,' Harry said.

'A job? You mean you be my boss?'

'I'd rather be your friend.'

'So would I.' Jack picked up a framed photo from the desk of Harry and a blond-haired man who bore a striking resemblance to her. 'But Norwich and Central City have both been shaken up like a cocktail and I need to make sure no one tries to take advantage of the chaos.' He put the photo back on the desk. 'You've got plenty of people working for you. What d'you need me for?'

'I wasn't going to ask you to work on my farm.' Harry got up, went over to a cabinet and brought out two glass tumblers. 'Allerton died intestate, and it just so happens that Inspector Hadley and Sergeant Fenning witnessed him saying that he intended to leave me everything.' She fetched a bottle of single malt whisky from the cabinet and poured a shot into one of the glasses and gave it to Jack. 'Hadley has a voice recorder that he uses in interviews so Allerton's comments are down on tape.'

'I'll have to remember that if he ever interviews me,' Jack said. Harry replaced the whisky bottle and brought out a blue sherry bottle. 'I thought you were an abstainer.'

'Only when I'm on the alert.'

'You mean when you don't trust your company?' Jack moved from his perch on the edge of the desk to a chair. 'So you can claim Wakeham's estate?'

'The ruling's already been made in my favour,' Harry said as she dragged her chair round the desk, so that she was next to him.

'Anyone likely to contest it?'

'Miss Penderbury. She says Allerton promised to marry her.'

'She was a mug if she believed that.' Jack leant back in his seat, crossed his right leg over his left and sipped his whisky. 'Penderbury?' He cast his mind back to Cornell's report. 'She the one Hadley and Fenning burgled?'

'I don't think they'd like you phrasing it in that way but, yes, that's the one. Hadley and Fenning have done some more digging and it turns out that one of her neighbours saw someone matching Trescothic's description visit her the evening he died, and they both went out in his car.'

'And he just happened to get drunk and wrap his car round a tree? That sure was careless of him. What about your G.P.'s accident?'

'There was a fund-raising party for the local school that evening. Most of the neighbourhood had turned out to support it, including me, Dr Barnes and Allerton. I happened to overhear Allerton telling Dr Barnes that he was very concerned about my health and all those headaches I was having.'

'Yeah, I bet he was real concerned.' Jack found a gap on the desk surface amidst a mass of paperwork and put his glass down. The disturbance set the dust motes dancing in the beam of sunlight. 'Did you get on your high horse and tell him to mind his own business?'

'I did get a bit miffed, although at the time I couldn't understand how he knew about the headaches. I didn't want my dad worrying, so I hadn't told anyone except Amos and Dr Barnes.' Harry topped up Jack's glass. 'I certainly didn't want Allerton spreading rumours, so I told him I'd had a scan and the results were negative.'

'And you told him to button it in your own charming little way?'

'I did indicate that I'd be pretty annoyed if he told my father about it,' Harry said.

The shaft of sunlight disappeared. Jack looked up and saw a couple of farmhands passing the window. They were hauling a large wheelbarrow that contained the remains of the scarecrows that had been used as target practice. The ray of light returned and the dust motes were visible again.

'Did you tell him that Amos knew?' Jack said.

'No. That was none of Allerton's business.' Harry put her empty glass on the desk and leant back in her chair. 'Anyway, Dr Barnes said that he was arranging some blood tests to find out the cause of my headaches, and that was the end of the conversation, but that night Dr Barnes died. The blood tests never happened.'

'And your medical notes got switched.' Jack swirled the whisky around in his glass. Harry's prompt reaction to a sudden bout of headaches must've thrown Wakeham. She was business-like even in matters of her health. Wakeham must've panicked. 'So why didn't Amos tell Hadley he'd seen the results when you disappeared?'

'Because I told him not to.' Harry turned the framed picture on her desk so that it was facing her. 'I met Amos after I legged it. I had a job persuading him not to dash off and kill Allerton there and then. He's had a grudge against him ever since Uncle Barney died, but I told him not to say anything because I didn't know how extensive Allerton's connections were. I didn't want Amos to be next.'

'He looks like he can watch his own back.'

Harry stared down at the floor beside the desk. She looked paler than usual. Her hair had grown since they'd first met and small curls were beginning to form ringlets at the side of her face. She continued talking with her gaze on the ground and a distant voice that Jack had never heard her use before.

'With so many people dying I didn't want to risk losing Amos as well. It would've just been his word against Allerton's and I needed someone I could trust to look after my farm. When I saw that the results from my scan had been switched, I knew I was in danger and I knew Dad had been murdered. I was certain that Uncle Barney had been killed because Miguel had told him something about Allerton, but I had to prove it. Amos didn't want me to go to the city, but I thought I'd have more chance of finding the evidence there than here.'

'But you never figured the first person you'd meet would be able to tell you everything you needed to know about Wakeham. All you had to do was ask.'

Harry looked up at him. Her solemn expression was banished by a smile that creased the corners of her eyes.

'But then I wouldn't have met Adam and Sam, and we wouldn't have had such good times.'

'Like Sector House blowing up and being trapped by riots and demonstrations?'

'Exactly.' Harry picked up a headed letter from the pile of papers on the desk. 'Now that my ageing family solicitor has realised that I'm neither a child nor a raving lunatic, he's had a look at the contract Allerton made my father sign and has declared it invalid as it doesn't state the amount borrowed, so my father's debt to Allerton is cancelled.'

Jack glanced over the solicitor's letter. Wakeham had been a fool to pull such a stunt, but Harry and her father must've looked a soft touch once her uncle was out of the picture. Jack handed the letter back.

'I don't suppose it makes a difference now,' Jack said. 'You've got all Wakeham's estate, so it comes back to you either way.'

'Actually it does make a difference.' Harry returned the bottles to the drinks cabinet, perched on the edge of the desk and pushed a thick, white envelope across the surface. The ray of sunlight had moved but the dust motes still drifted about in it. 'My father was a funny old boy. I never thought he'd have anything to do with solicitors, but it turns out he wrote a will before he died. He left everything he had to the oncology department at the Colingham National Health Hospital.'

'Didn't your mother get treated at the private hospital?'

'Yes, and my brother. Uncle Barney and Grandpa Eddie shared the costs.' Harry stared at the floor beside the desk, then turned away. 'I have a feeling Dad was more with it that I'd ever given him credit. I think Allerton must've tried to sneak round to see Dad while I was out again, after Dr Barnes died. Maybe something aroused Dad's suspicions.' Harry straightened some of the papers on her desk. 'I'll never know for certain, but it accounts for the will and perhaps his death as well.'

She picked up the empty glasses and placed them on a small side table, her back to Jack.

'So what's the job you wanted me to do?' he said.

She turned and sat back down beside him.

'Get me all the information you can about those widows Wakeham killed. How much he obtained from them, and if they have any family who ought to have the money.'

'He wouldn't have gone after anyone if he thought there were relatives who'd kick up.'

'I didn't think so, but I want to make sure. I know you can tell the difference between a genuine claimant and someone trying to chance their luck.'

'Maybe I can,' Jack said, 'but I've already got widows to look after. Some of my lads didn't make it.'

'Some of mine didn't either. Neither you nor I will abandon those who depend on us, but there's more that I'd like done. I'm going to sell Allerton's estate and all his possessions. His house is an ugly pile of bricks, but I know a beet farmer who's interested in the land. I'm going to create a trust with the proceeds to extend the work of the refuge you set up. Or, rather, I'd like you to do it — if you're willing. I was fortunate when I left home. Others aren't so lucky. You can be managing director.'

'Managing director? Do I get an office?'

'Naturally. And you get to hire staff — so you'll still be the boss.'

'Sweet. All right, Harry. You've got yourself a deal.'

Adam and Harry sat along the bank of a stream beneath the bare arms of an old oak tree. The water trickled over the stoney bed. Further downstream it disappeared into a thicket of birch and alder. The low autumn sun glinted through the treetops.

'I rather miss Weston Snelding,' Harry said.

'That was just a daydream. This is yours.'

'No. This is ours.'

Adam put his hand in his pocket.

'I've got something for you.' He pulled out a small, blue box and gave it to her. She opened the hinged lid. Inside, a ring was held in place in a white satin-covered mount. The thin, gold band was topped by a little sapphire and diamond. 'I know it ain't quite the right order. In fact, I seem to have done everything in the wrong order.'

Harry lifted the ring from its mount, slipped it on to her finger and kissed him.

'Why didn't you ask me to marry you properly in the first place?' she said.

'I was afraid you'd say no. You weren't exactly forward.'

'You wouldn't have liked me if I'd been forward.'

'A little bit of encouragement would've helped.'

'I was sure I was giving you some encouragement.'

He smiled and kissed her.

'You've got a funny idea of encouragement.'

'Anyway, everything's worked out. You kept me sane in that place. I don't like to think of what would've happened if I hadn't met you.'

'Then don't think about it.'

He put his arm around her, and she rested her head on his shoulder. A breeze rattled the branches of the oak behind them. The stream continued eddying around its stoney bed and through the tree roots that reached down the bank and into the water. A tractor trundled along a distant field. If he remained still, he could just make out the faint hum of a generator.

Acknowledgements

Many thanks to my writing tutor Dr Ian Nettleton for providing such thorough and valuable critiquing. Thank you also to Keith Skipper for advice about the Broad Norfolk dialect, and thank you to the Friends of Norfolk Dialect (FOND) for their excellent resources. Thank you to my great friend Magdalene Pritchett for the paintings incorporated into the jacket.

Thank you to all my writing buddies from various courses for their helpful input and particularly to my friend Rebecca Barrow who encouraged me to go on the diploma course. Thank you also to all my family and friends for their support, encouragement and comments, especially to my husband, Gavin Cawley, who not only managed to read the entire first draft but was also brave enough to give an honest opinion!

Norfolk Dialect

In general I'm quite particular about putting apostrophes in their correct place. However an abundance of them in dialect can make the page look as though it's suffering from an insect infestation and can be hard to read. Therefore, most of the dialect words here don't have them, with a few exceptions to avoid ambiguity. Consider them words in their own right rather than abridged forms of words found in a standard English dictionary.

'That' is used instead of 'it' when it's the subject of the sentence (for example, 'that look like rain') but not when it's the object (for example, 'I like it').

acrorst across.
afore before.
agin again.
allus always.
anend on end.
anorl and all.
arter after.
athwart across.

atwin between.

backus out-house.
bein' as because of.
beck small stream.
bewful beautiful.
Black Shuck the phantom hell-hound said to roam East

Anglia, also called Old Shuck.
blar cry or weep.
blunder fall over.
bop duck down.
bor Norfolk way to address males.
botty fussy.

caution surprising news.
chimley chimney.
claggy moist or sticky.
coont couldn't.
corfee coffee.
coshies sweets.
cuckoo cocoa.
cuppla couple of.

daggly (1) damp; (2) ragged.
darst dare.
dassent dare not.
datty dirty or grubby.
dewun doing.
ding sharp blow.
dint did not.
directly immediately.
do in addition to the standard sense and in place of 'does', 'do' can also mean 'if' ('do you go to the shop, buy me a paper') or 'do' can be used to indicate the imperative (for example, when Admiral Nelson said 'do you weigh anchor', it was an order not a question).
doke a dent.
doss to toss.
dunt don't.
duzzy silly or stupid.
dwainy sickly.
dwile floor-cloth.

elijahs string or straps worn just above the knees over trousers.
ent am not.

fare (1) feel; (2) seem.
fare ye well, tergether goodbye.
farrisee a fairy.
fillum film/movie.
fourses tea break.
frazzled (1) anxious; (2) frayed.
furriner foreigner.
fy-out to clean out (ditches).

gan gave.
git get.
gorta going to.
granfar grandfather.
guzunder chamber pot.

haller to shout loudly.
hamper to damage.
har her.
hatta had to, have to.
hent haven't.
high sprites ghosts.
high-strikers hysterics.
himp to limp.
hin chicken.
hintut isn't it.
hold to have money.
hoss (1) horse; (2) be boisterous.
howsomever however.
huh, on the not level.
hully used for emphasis.
hutch a chest or cupboard.

jam (1) to stamp on; (2) to walk heavily.
jip (1) aggravation; (2) pain.
jollifircearshuns fun and games.

kelter condition.

lam to beat, thump or strike.
larn to teach.
ligger (1) plank bridge over a ditch; (2) float, made of reeds, for pike-fishing.
loke blind alley or short lane.

lollop to walk slowly or ungainly.
lummox clumsy person.

mardle (1) chat or gossip; (2) pond.
masterous expression of admiration.
mawkin scarecrow.
mawther girl or woman.
midnight woman midwife.
mob to scold.
mow in to help out or join in.
munny money.
mure-hearted tender-hearted.
my heart alive expression of surprise.

nijjert to assist in childbirth.
noffin nothing.
now just (as in 'he's now a-comin').
nowun no one.

old year's night new year's eve.
on of.
onem of them.
oont won't.
orl all.

pample tread lightly or quickly.
pearks gadgets.
pensy fretful.
pishamire ant.
plain a town square or open space.
pleece police.
pod belly or gut.
pollywiggle tadpole.
praps perhaps.
primmicky affected.
puckaterry (1) in a temper; (2) in a muddle.
push a boil or large spot.
puter computer.
putting on his/her parts misbehaving.

queer ill (to feel).

rafty damp weather.
rally a shelf built into a wall.
rare unusual or used for emphasis.
raw angry.
reasty rancid.
roger a miniature whirlwind that sweeps across the marshes (named after Roger Bigod).
rud road.

rum ole dew a very strange business.

sadly unwell.
sar sir.
scalder a crowd.
screws rheumatic aches and pains.
shanny scatter-brain.
shink I should think so.
shoulda should've.
shruff bits of sticks or twigs for firing.
shruk shrieked.
sight (1) great number; (2) small number.
skep big wicker basket used on a farm or in a garden.
skrowge crowd together, squeeze or push.
slusspot one who drinks too much.
snout nose.
sorft soft.
spar a rafter.
spect expect.
spuffle (1) to speak pompously; (2) to waffle.
spuz suppose.
squinny lank or thin.
squit nonsense.

stingy (1) cold; (2) cruel or mean.
stommick stomach.
suffin something.
Swarston winder black eye (Swardeston window).
swimmers Norfolk dumplings.
swoddy a soldier.

taay tea.
tempest thunderstorm.
terday today.
tergether (1) together; (2) form of address, used in the singular as well as plural.
tewl fool.
thack to thrash or thump.
tidy (1) fair; (2) good.
time while.
titchy irritable or touchy.
tittermatorter see-saw.
titty-totty very small.
trew through.
tricolate repair or spruce up.
trosh to thresh.
troshel doorstep or threshold.

wagabond vagabond.
winder window.
wittles food.
woulda would've.
wunt wasn't.

yalm eat hungrily.
yar your.
yard a cottage garden.
yars yours.
yis yes.
yit yet or nor.

Further information about the Norfolk dialect can be found on the Friends of Norfolk Dialect (FOND) website www.norfolkdialect.com

About the Author

Dr Nicola Talbot was born and grew up on the South coast of England in Seaford, East Sussex. She graduated with a first class honours degree in mathematics in 1991 and post-graduated with a PhD in Electronics Systems Engineering in 1996, both at the University of Essex. She moved to Norfolk in the mid-1990s, first living in Norwich and now in Saxlingham Nethergate.

As a chartered mathematician (member of the Institute of Mathematics and its Applications) and a computer programmer, her research work has included a Bayesian approach to analysing the risk associated with foodborne botulism at the Institute of Food Research, Norwich, and machine learning statistical pattern recognition techniques with the University of East Anglia. She was awarded a diploma in creative writing at the University of East Anglia in 2011 and is now an independent writer, publisher and book production editor.

OTHER WORKS BY THIS AUTHOR

Crime Fiction

'I've Heard the Mermaid Sing.' (Short story ebook.)
ISBN 978-1-909440-04-3

Illustrated Children's Fiction

'The Foolish Hedgehog.' ISBN 978-1-909440-01-2

'Quack, Quack, Quack. Give My Hat Back!'
ISBN 978-1-909440-03-6

Text Books

'LaTeX for Complete Novices.'
ISBN 978-1-909440-00-5

'Using LaTeX to Write a PhD Thesis.'
ISBN 978-1-909440-02-9

Lightning Source UK Ltd.
Milton Keynes UK
UKOW02f0246030914

237944UK00001BA/7/P

9 781909 440050